The Message

The Message

✦

God's Revelation to Humanity

"This is the Scripture in which there is no doubt, a guide for the righteous."
(The Message 2:2)

ProgressiveMuslims.Org

iUniverse, Inc.
New York Lincoln Shanghai

The Message
God's Revelation to Humanity

iUniverse books may be ordered through booksellers or by contacting:

iUniverse
2021 Pine Lake Road, Suite 100
Lincoln, NE 68512
www.iuniverse.com
1-800-Authors (1-800-288-4677)

ISBN-13: 978-0-595-29035-2 (pbk)
ISBN-13: 978-0-595-75355-0 (cloth)
ISBN-13: 978-0-595-78112-6 (ebk)
ISBN-10: 0-595-29035-3 (pbk)
ISBN-10: 0-595-75355-8 (cloth)
ISBN-10: 0-595-78112-8 (ebk)

Printed in the United States of America

Disclaimer

This work represents a translation of the divine words as revealed by the Almighty over 1,400 years ago and in no way is the translation itself divine or perfect. Any shortcomings are purely due to human error and the reader is always advised to independently **verify** what he/she reads.

"And do not uphold what you have no knowledge of. For the hearing, eyesight, and mind, all these you are responsible for." (The Message 17:36)

To God. This work is a very small way of saying 'Thank You' for all Your blessings and mercy upon us, beyond measure, and beyond limits. May You overlook our constant shortcomings, and never abandon us to our destructive tendencies and desires.

Contents

Preface

"A.L.R, a Scripture which We have sent down to you so that you may take the people out of the darkness and into the light." (The Message 14:1)

During the seventh century A.D. a man by the name of Mohammed, who was from the lineage of Abraham, was given the overwhelming task of being God's messenger to deliver the words of the Almighty to humankind.

The message that was given to this prophet represented a culmination of all previous teachings/laws, as well as a recording of the most accurate human history in relation to God.

> "And We have sent down to you the Scripture with truth, authenticating what is present of the Scripture and superseding it. So judge between them by what God has sent down, and do not follow their desires from what has come to you of the truth. For each of you We have made laws, and a structure; and had God willed, He would have made you all one nation, but He tests you with what He has given you; so strive to do good. To God you will return all of you, and He will inform you regarding that in which you dispute." (The Message 5:48)

The inspiration and guidance that was achieved in the early days of the message was enough to create an empire whose legacy in science, mathematics, and medicine are still with us today. An empire who understood that the message had contained within its pages the blueprint for the most adaptive social, economic, scientific, and legal systems as designed by the Almighty for the benefit and advancement of humankind.

However, with the progression of time, and even though its words were continually recited, the essence of the message became lost to the people until the point where the spark and meanings that had once been an inspiration to generations simply became empty words…

This tragedy has been carried with us all the way into the 21st century whereby the bulk of 1.2 billion people who claim to be the inheritors of God's words are struggling with poverties, wars, economic set-backs, and social injustices…A legacy that has been prophesized in the Scripture whereby the messenger's complaint against his followers is that they will abandon the very message he struggled to deliver:

> "And the messenger said: 'My Lord, my people have deserted this Quran.'" (The Message 25:30)

Perhaps it is now time for humankind to once again walk in the footsteps of our great patriarch Abraham and those prophets who came after him…Perhaps it is now time for us to once again study and contemplate the words of the Almighty as they deserve to be studied and contemplated.

Welcome to the path of God Alone.

Welcome to **The Message**.

Methodology For This Translation

This work is the culmination of years of group research and study into the Scripture and its nature, and is an attempt to reintroduce people to God's words with authenticity and objectivity.

The most significant points that the reader needs to be aware of with regards to this translation are as follows:

1. Chapter Headings

In reviewing the oldest written records of the Scripture, it was found that no actual chapter names as used in current printed editions ever existed (e.g. 'the cow, the family of Imran, the women, etc.') and that they were later insertions to ease reference.

Image from chapter 10 of 'Sanaa Quran' dated around 800 A.D.[1] which shows no chapter name/heading

While this translation does use numeric chapter headings to ease reader reference, the removal of the 'names' has been done to maintain authenticity of the revealed text.

2. The 'Basmallah'

Current printed editions of the Scripture record the 'Basmallah' (the title which reads: 'In the name of God, the Almighty, the Merciful') as a stand-alone state-

---

1.   Scan made available by UNESCO (http://www.unesco.org/).

ment which, although included in all printed editions, is not counted as a verse except in the 1:1.

To clarify the issue of whether the remaining Basmallah's are indeed part of the revealed Scripture or not, a study of older copies of the Scripture has been conducted and this showed that all the Basmallah's are indeed part of the revealed text and were previously separated by a '*' or an '/' as were all the other verses.

Image from chapter 3 of 'Gold Quran' dated around 800 A.D.[2] which shows a verse stop after the 'Basmallah'

This translation has included the Basmallah's in nearly all chapters while following the common convention of not numbering them with the exception of 1:1.

3. Different Versions/Meanings

One of the least known facts regarding the Scripture is the existence of slight textual variations between existing printed versions (up to 10 nearly similar variations are accepted, with the two most prominent being known under the names of 'Hafs' and 'Warsh')[3].

While there is no variation with regards to the bulk text of the Scripture (i.e. nearly the same number of words, and sequence of words, in all versions), there is a slight difference in some of the meanings, pronunciations, and spelling of certain words.

---

2.   Scan made available by John Hopkins University (http://goldkoran.mse.jhu.edu/).

3.   Al-Qiraat Al-Ashr Al-Mutawatira, by Allawi Mohammed Balfaqeeh (Published by Dar Al-Mahajir)

وَٱتَّخِذُواْ   وَٱتَّخَذُواْ

Verse 2:125 meaning 'You shall take' (Hafs) and 'They have taken/made' (Warsh)

The approach taken in this translations has been to compare all variations and follow the 'best' meaning in light of the overall spirit of the Scripture and our knowledge regarding the essence of God being 'goodness'.

4. Hafs/Warsh Verse Numbering

In addition to the textual variation between the existing printed versions, there is also the issue of the location of verse 'stops' which significantly differ from one version to the other.

Although the 'Warsh' style of separating the verses is found to be more in-line with the older surviving texts, the approach of this translation has been to remain with the common 'Hafs' numbering of verses as being the most prevalent amongst Muslims (Warsh being limited mainly to parts of North Africa).

5. The Missing 'Basmallah'

One of the strangest aspects of the printed Scripture is the lack of a 'Basmallah' at the beginning of chapter 9. Information written regarding this subject indicates that there is confusion as to whether the Scripture is comprised of 114 chapters, or whether it is comprised of 113 chapters (some scholars have argued that a merger of chapters 8 & 9 is possible due to the lack of the Basmallah).

In reviewing the older written texts, it was found that the ability to realize the separation between chapters 8 & 9, without a Basmallah, was nearly impossible without referring to the man-made injection of the chapter name to highlight the beginning of a new chapter.

Image from chapter 9 of 'Gold Quran' showing inserted chapter name to mark separation

Although this translation retains the structure of having 114 chapters, it is being pointed out for the sake of transparency that the beginning of chapter 9 is only possible to be maintained with manual effort without the presence of a Basmallah.

The Scripture & Quran

One of the most glaring observations that will be made by any reader of the Scripture (either as a translation or in original Arabic form), is a unique feature which is the presence of 'initials' marking 29 out of the 114 chapters:

No.	Chapter No.	Quranic Initials
1	2	A.L.M.
2	3	A.L.M.
3	7	A.L.M.S'.
4	10	A.L.R.
5	11	A.L.R.
6	12	A.L.R.
7	13	A.L.M.R.
8	14	A.L.R.
9	15	A.L.R.
10	19	K.H'.Y.A'.S'.
11	20	T'.H'.
12	26	T'.S.M.
13	27	T'.S.
14	28	T'.S.M.
15	29	A.L.M.
16	30	A.L.M.
17	31	A.L.M.
18	32	A.L.M.
19	36	Y.S.
20	38	S'.
21	40	H.M.
22	41	H.M.
23	42	H.M, A'.S.Q.

No.	Chapter No.	Quranic Initials
24	43	H.M.
25	44	H.M.
26	45	H.M.
27	46	H.M.
28	50	Q.
29	68	N.

This phenomenon has been interpreted by most scholars with the common answer of: 'God and His messenger know best'. However, an examination of the Scripture reveals that there is a unique distinction that is made between different sections of God's Book.

The most obvious example of this distinction is the existence of both a 'warning' to people from attempting to invent the Scripture, as well as a 'challenge' to people to try and replicate even one chapter like it!

> "So <u>woe to those who write the Scripture</u> with their hands then Say: 'This is from God,' so that they can seek a cheap gain! Woe to them for what their hands have written and woe to them for what they gained." (The Message 2:79)

> "And if you are in doubt as to what We have sent down to Our servant, then <u>bring a chapter like this</u>, and call upon your witnesses other than God if you are truthful. And if you cannot do this; and you will not be able to do this; then beware the Fire whose fuel is people and stones, it has been prepared for the rejecters." (The Message 2:23-24)

This difference has been found to be caused by the existence of two separate books within the Scripture. One of these books is identified as '**Quran**' while the other is simply '**Kitaab**' (Scripture/Book).

Some of the features of the 'Quran' have been recorded as follows:

• Quran can humble a mountain (59:21).

• Quran was sent down in one night (44:3, 97:1).

- Quran cannot be replicated by men and Jinn (17:88).

- Quran contains a healing for the hearts (17:82).

- Quran is what the prophet's followers have abandoned (25:30).

- Quran is to be paid attention to when related (7:204).

- Quran disturbs the disbelievers with its words (10:15).

- Quran gives detail to the Scripture (10:37).

- Quran is related to the 7 pairs (15:87).

- Quran contains a barrier from understanding by disbelievers (17:45).

- Quran alone makes the disbelievers run away in aversion (17:46).

- Quran being recited at dawn is witnessed (17:78).

- Quran is full of examples cited for mankind (17:90).

- Quran contains the 'Zikr'/Reminder (38:1).

- Quran disturbs the rejecters, they seek to speak over it (41:26).

- Quran is to be used to warn all mankind with (6:19).

- Quran has been made easy to learn (54:17).

- Quran is preserved in a tablet (85:21-22).

In identifying which part is which, a further study of the Scripture reveals that the part called 'Quran' has indeed been clearly distinguished/marked by God Himself:

> "The Almighty. He has **marked**[4] the Quran." (The Message 55:1-2)

Therefore, in returning to the subject of the initialled chapters, we can see that the markings put in-place by the Almighty are none other than the initials them-

---

4.   Although the Arabic word 'alama' has been mostly translated as 'taught/teach', one of its meanings is to 'mark/differentiate'.

selves which differentiate that which is **Quran** from the remainder of the Scripture:

29 'marked' chapters = Quran/Scripture
85 'unmarked' chapters = Scripture Only

The knowledge of this distinction within the Scripture will serve not only to enlighten the reader as to the relation of various chapters/verses, but also serves to emphasize the importance that is to be placed by the reader on every word and letter used by God as it is meant for a purpose (some of which you will discover, while others may remain hidden until God decides otherwise).

"And if it is recited to them, they Say: 'We believe in it. It is the truth from our Lord. Indeed, we had submitted before it.'" (The Message 28:53)

How To Study The Scripture

If you are one of those who wish to seek knowledge and improve on your understanding of the Scripture, then we have identified seven key study points which may be put to use by both novices and experts. These points will appear to be quite obvious once you read them, but sometimes to be reminded benefits us all.

1. Language Is Not A Barrier

The first point of contention in the study of the Scripture typically is language. Many of the 1 billion people who want to uphold the Scripture have been informed that God's book can only be recited or studied in Arabic and that any translation will not give the proper meaning. The flip-side is that these same appointed scholars will then tell the Arabic speakers that the Scripture is 'too difficult' for them to understand and that they should leave its understanding to the experts!

Of course, the Scripture itself says that language is **not** a barrier to its understanding as God is the One who is making it understood to people who open their hearts to Him.

> "And had We made it a non-Arabic compilation, they would have said: "If only its verses were made clear!" Non-Arabic and Arabic, Say: "For those who believe, it is a guide and healing. As for those who disbelieve, there is a deafness in their ears, and they are blind to it. These will be called from a place far away." (The Message 41:44)

God's Book is unlike any other book on Earth as it is subject to His system and laws, which state that only the sincere/pure will be allowed understanding (not the language or qualifications or expertise of the reader).

> "It is an honourable Quran. In a protected record. None can grasp it except those pure. A revelation from the Lord of the worlds." (The Message 56:77-80)

2. Look At The Full Verse

Quoting the Scripture out of context is by far the single biggest mistake that even seasoned students continue to fall into. This method of quoting can be used to justify any desire or any view no matter how un-Godlike it may appear.

For example, a favorite quote which is repeated by many unknowledgeable groups is that the Scripture promotes killing and violence as evidenced by the verse: "And kill them wherever you find them" (2:191).

However, once we use the method of **full context**, then a totally different picture appears regarding the same issue:

> "And kill them wherever you find them, and expel them from where they expelled you, and know that persecution is worse than being killed. And do not fight them at the Restricted Temple unless they fight you in it; if they fight you then kill them, thus is the reward of the disbelievers." (The Message 2:191)

Here we have a case of warfare being engaged in, and the people who were driven out being allowed to fight and reclaim their land/territory...A far cry from the sporadic killing that is implied when quoting out of context.

3. Look To The Surrounding Verses

Another crucial point to studying the Scripture properly is to always look at the verses preceding and following a specific verse/subject. An example of how the wrong understanding can be derived if this is not done can be seen in the following:

> "And Moses said to his people: 'O my people, you have wronged your souls by taking the calf, so repent to your Maker, and kill yourselves. That is better for you with your Maker, so He would forgive you. He is the Forgiving, the Merciful.'" (The Message 2:54)

This verse on its own creates an enigma as Moses is asking his people to commit suicide while suicide is punishable with being cast in Hell (4:29-30). However, when we look at the 'wider' picture that occurs in the verses before and after then the story takes on a completely different light:

> "And We appointed a meeting time for Moses of forty nights, but then you took the calf after him while you were wicked. Then We forgave you after that, perhaps you would be thankful. And We gave Moses the Scripture and the criterion, perhaps you would be guided. And Moses said to his people: 'O my people, you have wronged your souls by taking

the calf, so repent to your Maker, and kill yourselves. That is better for you with your Maker, so He would forgive you. He is the Forgiving, the Merciful.' And you said: 'O Moses, we will not believe you until we see God openly!' So the lightning bolt took you while you were still staring. Then We resurrected you after your death that you may be appreciative. And We shaded you with clouds, and sent down to you manna and quails: 'Eat from the goodness of the provisions We have provided you.' They did not wrong Us, but it was their souls that they wronged." (The Message 2:51-57)

It was the design of the Almighty to resurrect this particular group from the Children of Israel to manifest His signs. Thus, once they refused to kill themselves, God made them die anyway and then resurrected them to make His will done…Thus the paradox is removed since God is the only One who may take life as it is His gift to begin with.

4. Be Aware Of Multiple Meaning Words

Some Arabic words, like in English, may have more than one related meaning. Thus ascribing the 'wrong' meaning may sometimes create contradictions between verses in the Scripture or give a strange understanding to the topic the verse is addressing.

In such cases, the advice from the Scripture itself is to follow the **best** meaning derived…

"The ones who listen to what is being said, and then follow the best of it. These are the ones whom God has guided, and these are the ones who possess intelligence." (The Message 39:18)

A clear example of a multi-meaning word and how its incorrect application can cause serious problems is the word 'Daraba' which occurs in 4:34 and is primarily used to mean 'beat/strike'.

"The men are to support the women by what God has gifted them over one another and for what they spend of their money. The upright women who are attentive, and keep private the personal matters for what God keeps watch over. As for those women from whom you fear a desertion, then you shall advise them, and abandon them in the bed-chamber, and '**Idriboohun**'; if they obey you, then do not seek a way over them; God is High, Great." (The Message 4:34)

The choice of 'beat/strike' in this example creates a bizarre meaning as the verse is dealing with the issue of resolving a husband/wife dispute, and that if the final step were to 'beat' ones wife then that is a sure guarantee for ending the marriage rather than fixing it!

The word 'Daraba' has at least 6 meanings in Arabic and are all used within the Quran:

- "O you who believe, if you **attack** (Darabtum) in the cause of God then make a clear declaration, and do not say to those who greet you with peace: 'You are not a believer!' You are seeking the vanity of this world; but with God are many riches. That is how you were before, but God favoured you, so make a clear declaration. God is expert over what you do." (The Message 4:94)

- "So how will it be when the Angels put them to death, **striking** (Yadriboona) their faces and their backs?" (The Message 47:27)

- "So We **sealed** (Darabna) upon their ears in the cave for a number of years." (The Message 18:11)

- "Shall We **take-away** (Na'drib) the reminder from you, because you are a transgressing people?" (The Message 43:5)

- "Have you not seen how God **cites** (Daraba) the example of a good word is like a good tree, whose root is firm and its branches in the sky." (The Message 14:24)

- "As for the poor who face hardship in the cause of God, and they cannot **leave** (Darban) the land; the ignorant ones think they are rich from their modesty; you know them by their features, they do not ask the people repeatedly. And what you spend out of goodness, God is fully aware of it." (The Message 2:273)

As such, the best understanding which can be used and which will then give a logical and consistent meaning to the issue of working towards the resolve of matrimonial strife is that the husband yields by 'leaving/separating' rather than letting the wife carry out her wish to leave:

"The men are to support the women by what God has endowed them over one another and for what they spend of their money. The upright women who are attentive, and keep private the personal matters for what God keeps watch over. As for those women from whom you fear a desertion, then you shall advise them, and abandon them in the bedchamber, and separate from them; if they obey you, then do not seek a way over them; God is High, Great." (The Message 4:34)

5. Arrange Similar Topic Verses Together

The study point which has been lacking from Muslims for many centuries is the ability to arrange the verses of the Scripture by order of subject/topic to seek its meaning.

Looking to the example of 'divorce,' we find that the subject is scattered in three different chapters (chapter 2, chapter 33, and chapter 65) which, when placed together, provide a more extensive picture of the proceedings and laws regarding divorce...

"For those who are discontent with their wives, let them wait for four months. If they reconcile, then God is Forgiving, Merciful." (The Message 2:226)

"And if they insist on the divorce, then God is Hearer, Knowledgeable." (The Message 2:227)

"And the divorced women shall wait for three menstruation periods; and it is not lawful for them to conceal what God has created in their wombs, if they believe in God and the Last Day. And their husbands would then have just cause to return together, if they both wish to reconcile. And for what obligations the women are owed, so similarly must they fulfil their obligations. But the men will have a greater responsibility over them in this. And God is Noble, Wise." (The Message 2:228)

"The divorce is allowed twice. So, either they remain together equitably, or they part ways with kindness. And it is not lawful for you to take back anything you have given the women unless you fear that they will not uphold God's limits. So if you fear that they will not uphold God's limits, then there is no sin upon them for what is given back. These are God's limits so do not transgress them. And whoever shall transgress God's limits, then these are the wicked." (The Message 2:229)

"So if he divorces her again, then she will not be lawful for him until she has married another husband. If the other husband divorces her, then there is no sin that they come back together if they think they will uphold God's limits. These are God's limits, He clarifies them for a people that know." (The Message 2:230)

"And if you have divorced the women, and they have reached their required interim period, then either you remain together equitably, or part ways equitably. And do not reconcile with them so you can harm them out of animosity; whoever does so is doing wickedness to his soul; and do not take God's revelations lightly. And remember God's blessings towards you, and what was sent down to you of the Scripture and the wisdom, He warns you with it. And be aware of God and know that God is Knowledgeable in all things." (The Message 2:231)

"And if you divorce the women, and they have reached their required interim period, then do not prevent them from remarrying their husbands if they amicably agree amongst themselves out of what is best. This is to remind any of you who believe in God and the Last Day, this is better for you and purer; and God knows while you do not know." (The Message 2:232)

"O you who believe, if you marry the believing women, then divorced them before having intercourse with them, then there is no interim required of them. You shall compensate them, and let them go in an amicable manner." (The Message 33:49)

"O you prophet, if any of you have divorced the women, then they should be divorced while ensuring that their required interim is fulfilled, and keep count of the interim. You shall reverence God your Lord, and do not evict the women from their homes, nor should they leave, unless they have committed a proven adultery. And these are

God's limits. And anyone who transgresses God's limits has wronged his soul. You never know; perhaps God will make something come out of this." (The Message 65:1)

"Then, once the interim is fulfilled, either you remain together equitably, or part ways equitably and have it witnessed by two just people from among you; and give the testimony for God. This is to enlighten those who believe in God and the Last Day. And whosoever reverences God, He will create a solution for him." (The Message 65:2)

"And He will provide for him whence he never expected. Anyone who puts his trust in God, then He suffices him. God's commands will be done. God has decreed for everything its fate." (The Message 65:3)

"As for the women who have reached menopause, if you have any doubts, their interim shall be three months. And as for those whose menstruation has ceased, and those who are already pregnant, their interim is until they give birth. And anyone who reverences God, He makes his matters easy for him." (The Message 65:4)

"This is God's command that He sends down to you. And anyone who is aware of God, He remits his sins, and will improve his reward." (The Message 65:5)

"You shall let them reside in the home you were in when you were together, and do not coerce them to make them leave. And if they are pregnant, you shall spend on them until they give birth. Then, if they nurse the infant, you shall pay them their due for such. And you shall maintain the amicable relations between you. If you disagree, then another woman may nurse the child." (The Message 65:6)

Here is a summary of the rules for divorce as obtained when arranging all similar verses:

- A 'cooling-off' period of four months is required before commencing a divorce. (2:226)

- If they still insist on divorce, then the wife and husband must remain together in the same home during the 'interim-period.' (65:1)

- If the couple reconcile, then divorce may be retracted and cancelled at any point during the interim period. (2:229)

- The divorce is automatically retracted if sexual intercourse takes place between the husband and wife during the interim period. (65:1)

- The interim period required is three menstruation periods. The interim for women who no longer menstruate is three months. The interim for pregnant women is until they deliver (2:228, 65:4)

- There is no interim period required if the divorce takes place while no sexual intercourse has ever taken place between the couple. (33:49)

- If the couple still wishes to follow through with the divorce after the end of the interim period, then two witnesses are required to complete the process. (65:2)

- If this is the 3rd divorce, then the couple may not remarry each other unless the woman marries another man and then divorces from him. (2:230)

As shown in the example above, the simple step of examination of all related verses gives a very detailed conclusion that can be applied in any modern and civil society.

6. Look To Examples In The Scripture/Quran

Once a meaning is derived, the final accuracy test is to compare such a meaning to the stories related in the Scripture/Quran if such a story can be found. The reason being that the stories related in the Scripture are 'live' examples for us to learn from and compare situations. These stories have not been placed there without purpose or simply for our entertainment.

> "We relate to you the best stories through what We have inspired to you in this Quran; and before it you were of those who were unaware." (The Message 12:3)

One of the clearest examples for using this method is to deal with the issue of 'theft'. There is one verse that gives the law for theft and its interpretation can vary widely depending on which meaning is ascribed to the Arabic words:

"The male thief, and the female thief, you shall 'Iqta' (cut/cut-off/sever/ separate) 'Aydiyahum' (their hands/resources/belongings/possessions) as a punishment for their crime, and to serve as a deterrent from God. God is Almighty, Wise." (5:38)

The scholars of today and the past have all gone for the 'cut-off the hand' understanding and thus we witness scenes of amputations being carried out in countries which claim to uphold the Scripture:

[Yusufali Translation]: As to the thief, Male or female, cut off his or her hands: a punishment by way of example, from Allah, for their crime: and Allah is Exalted in power. (5:38)

However, had they gone through the extra step of looking to the 'examples' within the Scripture for application, they would have come to a far different conclusion. The story of Joseph with his brothers provides the clearest and simplest example for how to deal with the subject of theft...

"They said: 'By God, you know we did not come to cause corruption in the land, and we are no thieves!' He said: 'What shall be the punishment, if you are not truthful?' They said: 'The punishment is that whomever it is found in his bags, then to compensate is his punishment. It is such that we punish the wicked.'" (The Message 12:73-75)

Thus, the proper meaning/translation of the verse becomes:

"The male thief, and the female thief, you shall cut from (Iqtau) their resources (Aydiyahum) as a punishment for their crime, and to serve as a deterrent from God. God is Almighty, Wise." (The Message 5:38)

Such a meaning also conforms to the overall laws of God's justice: that the punishment should never exceed the crime 16:126.

7. Be Patient And Seek God's Help

Even with all the skill and knowledge we may possess, the study of the Scripture will always be lacking if God is not sought for help and assistance. After all, He is the ultimate teacher of mankind in all things, especially the Scripture.

"When you read the Quran, you shall seek refuge with God from Satan the outcast. He has no authority over those who believe, and who put their trust in their Lord. His authority is over those who follow him, and set him up as a partner." (The Message 16:98-100)

Also, do not be scared or confused if your findings or understanding does not conform to what others have said or taught for years or centuries…Truth does not need to conform to the majority to be truth.

"And if you obey the majority of those on Earth they will lead you astray; that is because they follow conjecture, and that is because they only guess." (The Message 6:116)

Finally, remember we are here on this planet to serve God and walk in His path, and not to serve our own agendas and our own egos:

"You alone we serve, and You alone we seek for help." (The Message 1:5)

Conclusion

You now should have the necessary tools to educate yourself to the Scripture's system and method for deriving meanings and laws…Try to make it a habit of seeking the answers for yourself through the guidance of God…Do not be quick to ask 'others' what God says regarding this or that matter, but try to establish the bond with God directly yourself…It is only through this self-awareness that people can have a defense mechanism against the misinformation and ignorance that has been taught for many generations.

Learn to let God be the focus of your actions and your life, and let His words be your guide to success in this life and the next…What will count is not how much wealth we accumulate or how powerful we become, but how we use that wealth to help others and how we use our power and position to help mankind towards betterment.

> "O you who believe, do not be distracted by your money and your children from the remembrance of God. And those who do this, then they are the losers. And give from that which We have provided to you, before death comes to one of you, then he says: "My Lord, if only You could delay this for a short while, I would then be charitable and join the righteous!" And God will not delay any soul if its time has come. And God is Expert to all that you do." (The Message 63:9-11)

We are certain that upon reading and studying the Scripture you will find more than what you expected. For, although it is 'finite' in its words and pages, it is 'infinite' in its knowledge and lessons.

ProgressiveMuslims

www.ProgressiveMuslims.Org

.

Chapter 1

بسم الله الرحمن الرحيم

---

1. In the name of God, the Almighty, the Merciful.
2. Praise be to God, the Lord of the worlds.
3. The Almighty, the Merciful.
4. King of the Day of Judgment.
5. You alone we serve, and You alone we seek for help.
6. Guide us to the straight path.
7. The path of those whom You have blessed, not those who have incurred the wrath, nor the misguided.

Chapter 2

بسم الله الرحمن الرحيم

In the name of God, the Almighty, the Merciful.

1. A.L.M.
2. This is the Scripture in which there is no doubt, a guide for the righteous.
3. Those who believe in the unseen, and honour the oath of allegiance, and from Our provisions to them they spend.
4. And those who believe in what was sent down to you, and what was sent down before you, and regarding the Hereafter they are certain.
5. These are the ones guided by their Lord, and these are the winners.
6. As for those who reject, whether you warn them or do not warn them, they will not believe.
7. God has sealed upon their hearts and upon their ears, and over their eyes are covers. They will incur a great retribution.
8. And from the people are those who Say: "We believe in God and in the Last Day," but they are not believers.
9. They seek to deceive God and those who believe, but they only deceive themselves without noticing.
10. In their hearts is a disease, so God increases their disease, and they will have a painful retribution for what they have denied.
11. And if they are told: "Do not make evil in the land," they Say: "But we are the reformers!"
12. No, they are the evildoers, but they do not perceive.
13. And if they are told: "Believe, as the people have believed," they Say: "Shall we believe as the fools have believed?" No, they are the fools but they do not know.

14. And if they come across those who have believed, they Say: "We believe," and when they are alone with their devils they Say: "We are with you, we were only mocking."
15. God mocks them, and leaves them prolonged in their transgression.
16. These are the ones who have purchased straying for guidance; their trade did not profit them, nor were they guided.
17. Their example is like one who lights a fire, so when it illuminates what is around him, God takes away his light and leaves him in the darkness not seeing.
18. Deaf, dumb, and blind, they will not revert.
19. Or like a cloud from the sky, in it is darkness and thunder and lightning. They place their fingers in their ears from the lightning strikes out of fear of death; and God is aware of the rejecters.
20. The lightning nearly snatches away their sight, whenever it lights the path they walk in it, and when it becomes dark for them they stand. Had God willed, He would have taken away their hearing and their sight; God is capable of all things.
21. O mankind, serve your Lord who has created you and those before you that you may be righteous.
22. The One who made the land a habitat, and the sky a structure, and He sent down from the sky water with which He brought out fruit as a gift to you. So do not make any equals with God while you now know.
23. And if you are in doubt as to what We have sent down to Our servant, then bring a chapter like this, and call upon your witnesses other than God if you are truthful.
24. And if you cannot do this; and you will not be able to do this; then beware the Fire whose fuel is people and stones, it has been prepared for the rejecters.
25. And give good news to those who believe and do good works, that they will have estates with rivers flowing beneath. Every time they receive of its fruit, they Say: "This is what we have been provisioned before," and they are given its likeness. And there they will have pure spouses, and in it they will abide.
26. God does not shy away from citing the example of a mosquito, or anything above it. As for those who believe, they know that it is the truth from their Lord. As for the rejecters, they Say: "What does God want with this example?" He lets many stray by it, and He guides many, but He only lets stray the evildoers.

27. The ones who break their pledge to God after making its covenant, and they sever what God had ordered to be delivered. And they make corruption on Earth; these are the losers.

28. How can you reject God when you were dead and He brought you to life? Then He makes you die, then He brings you to life, then to Him you return.

29. He is the One who created for you all that is on Earth, then He attend to the universe and made it seven universes, and He is aware of all things.

30. And your Lord said to the Angels: "I am placing a successor on Earth." They said: "Would You place in it he who would corrupt in it, and spill blood, while we sing Your glory, and praise You?" He said: "I know what you do not know."

31. And He taught Adam the description of all things, then He displayed them to the Angels and said: "Inform Me the descriptions of these things if you are truthful."

32. They said: "Glory be to You, we have no knowledge except that which You have taught us, You are the Knowledgeable, the Wise."

33. He said: "O Adam, inform them of the description of these," so when he informed them of their descriptions, He said: "Did I not tell you that I know the unseen of heavens and Earth, and that I know what you reveal and what you were hiding?"

34. And We said to the Angels: "Yield to Adam," so they yielded except for Satan, he refused and became arrogant, and became of the rejecters.

35. And We said: "O Adam, reside you and your mate in the paradise, and eat from it bountifully as you both wish, and do not approach this tree, else you will be of those who did wrong."

36. So, the devil tricked them from it, and he brought them out from what they were in, and We said: "Descend; for you are enemies to one another; and on Earth you will have residence and provisions until the appointed time."

37. Adam then received words from His Lord, so He forgave him; He is the Forgiver, the Merciful.

38. We said: "Descend from it all of you, so when the guidance comes from Me, then whoever follows My guidance, they will have nothing to fear, nor will they grieve."

39. And those who disbelieve and deny Our revelations, they are the dwellers of Hell, in it they will abide.

40. O Children of Israel, remember My blessings that I had blessed you with, and fulfill your pledge to Me that I may fulfill My pledge to you, and revere Me alone.

41. And believe in what I have sent down, authenticating what is already with you, and do not be the first to disbelieve in it! And do not purchase with My verses a cheap gain, and of Me you shall be aware.

42. And do not confound the truth with falsehood, nor keep the truth secret while you know.

43. And honour the oath of allegiance, and contribute towards betterment, and kneel with those who kneel.

44. Do you order the people to do good, but forget yourselves, while you are reciting the Scripture? Do you not understand?

45. And seek help through patience, and through the oath of allegiance. It is a difficult thing, but not so for the humble.

46. The ones who conceive that they will meet their Lord and that to Him they will return.

47. O Children of Israel, remember My blessings that I had blessed you with, and that I had preferred you to all the worlds!

48. And beware of a Day where no soul can avail another soul, nor will any intercession be accepted from it, nor will any ransom be taken, nor will they have supporters.

49. And We saved you from the people of Pharaoh; they were punishing you with severe retribution, killing your children, and raping your women. In that was a great trial from your Lord.

50. And We parted the sea for you, thus We saved you and drowned the people of Pharaoh while you were watching.

51. And We appointed a meeting time for Moses of forty nights, but then you took the calf after him while you were wicked.

52. Then We forgave you after that, perhaps you would be thankful.

53. And We gave Moses the Scripture and the criterion, perhaps you would be guided.

54. And Moses said to his people: "O my people, you have wronged your souls by taking the calf, so repent to your Maker, and kill yourselves. That is better for you with your Maker, so He would forgive you. He is the Forgiving, the Merciful."

55. And you said: "O Moses, we will not believe you until we see God openly!" So the lightning bolt took you while you were still staring.

56. Then We resurrected you after your death that you may be appreciative.

57. And We shaded you with clouds, and sent down to you manna and quails: "Eat from the goodness of the provisions We have provided you." They did not wrong Us, but it was their souls that they wronged.

58. And We said: "Enter this town, and eat from it as plentifully as you wish. And enter the passageway by crouching, and Say: "Our load is removed," so that your errors will be forgiven, and We will increase for the good doers."

59. But the wicked altered what was said to them to a different saying, thus We sent down upon the wicked an affliction from the heaven for what they had transgressed.

60. And Moses was seeking water for his people, so We said: "Strike the rock with your staff." Thus twelve springs burst out of it; each tribe then knew from where to drink. "Eat and drink from God's provisions, and do not roam the Earth as corruptors."

61. And you said: "O Moses, we will not be patient to one type of food, so call for us your Lord that He may bring forth what the Earth grows of its beans, cucumbers, garlic, lentils, and onions." He said: "Would you trade that which is lowly with that which is good?" Descend to Egypt, you will have in it what you have asked for. They were thus stricken with humiliation and disgrace, and they remained under God's wrath for they were disbelieving in God's signs, and killing the prophets with no justification; this is for what they have disobeyed and transgressed.

62. Surely those who believe; and those who are Jewish, and the Nazarenes, and the Sabiens, whomever of them believes in God and the Last Day and does good work; they will have their reward with their Lord, with no fear over them, nor will they grieve.

63. And We took your covenant, and raised the mount to be above you: "Take what We have given you with strength, and remember what is in it that you may be righteous."

64. Then you turned away after this. And had it not been for God's favour upon you and His mercy, you would have been of the losers.

65. You have come to know who it was amongst you that transgressed the Sabbath, We said to them: "Be despicable apes!"

66. And We did this as a punishment for what they had done in it and also afterwards, and a reminder to the righteous.

67. And Moses said to his people: "God orders you to slaughter a heifer." They said: "Do you mock us?" He said: "I seek refuge with God that I not be of the ignorant ones."

68. They said: "Call upon your Lord for us that He may clarify which it is." He said: "He says it is a heifer neither too old nor too young, an age between that. So now do as you are commanded."

69. They said: "Call upon your Lord for us that He may clarify what color it is." He said: "He says it is a yellow heifer with a strong color, pleasing to those who see it."
70. They said: "Call upon your Lord for us that He may clarify which one it is, for the heifers all look alike to us and we will, God willing, be guided."
71. He said: "He says it is a heifer which was never subjugated to plough the land, or water the crops, free from any blemish." They said: "Now you have come with the truth." And they slaughtered it, though they had nearly not done so.
72. And you had murdered a person, then disputed in the matter; God was to bring out what you were keeping secret.
73. We said: "Strike him with parts from it." It is thus that God brings the dead to life, and He shows you His signs that you may comprehend.
74. Then your hearts became hardened after that, they became like stone or even harder; but even from the stones there are rivers that burst forth, or from them are those that crack so that the water comes forth, or from them are what fall from the fear of God; God is not unaware of what you do.
75. Did you expect that they would believe with you, when a group of them had heard God's words then altered them knowingly after having understood?
76. And when they come across those who believe, they Say: "We believe!", and when they are alone with each other they Say: "Why do you inform them about what God has said to us? Then they would use it in argument against us at your Lord. Do you not understand?"
77. Do they not know that God knows what they conceal and what they declare?
78. And amongst them are Gentiles who do not know the Scripture except by hearsay, and they only conjecture.
79. So woe to those who write the Scripture with their hands then Say: "This is from God," so that they can seek a cheap gain! Woe to them for what their hands have written and woe to them for what they gained.
80. And they said: "The Fire will not touch us except for a few number of days." Say: "Have you taken a pledge with God? If so, then God will not break His pledge. Or do you say about God what you do not know?"
81. Indeed, whoever gains a sin, and is surrounded by his mistakes; those are the people of the Fire, in it they abide eternally.
82. And those who believe and do good work, they are the people of Paradise, in it they abide eternally.
83. And We took the covenant of the Children of Israel: "You shall not serve except God, and regard your parents, and regard the relatives, and orphans,

and needy, and say kind things to the people, and honour the oath of allegiance, and contribute towards betterment." But then you turned away, except a few of you; you were objecting.

84. And We have taken a covenant with you: "You shall not spill each other's blood, nor drive each other out from your homes." And you agreed to this while bearing witness.

85. But then here you are killing each other and driving out a group of you from their homes; you act towards them with evil and animosity. And if they come to you as prisoners, you ransom them while it was forbidden for you to drive them out! Do you believe in some of the Scripture and disbelieve in some? The punishment for those amongst you who do so is humiliation in this worldly life, and on the Day of Resurrection they will be returned to the most severe retribution. God is not unaware of what you all do.

86. These are the ones who have purchased this worldly life instead of the Hereafter. The retribution will not be reduced for them, nor will they be supported.

87. And We gave Moses the Scripture, and after him We sent the messengers. And We gave Jesus son of Mary the clear proofs, and We supported Him with the Holy Spirit. Is it that every time a messenger comes to you with what your souls do not desire, you become arrogant? A group of them you deny, and a group of them you kill!

88. And they said: "Our hearts are sealed!" No, it is God who has cursed them for their rejection, for very little do they believe.

89. And when a Scripture came to them from God, authenticating what is with them; while before that they were mocking those who rejected; so when what they knew came to them, they rejected it! God's curse be upon the rejecters.

90. Miserable indeed is what they purchase with their souls, that they disbelieve in what God has sent down as a resentment that God would send down from His grace to whom He pleases of His servants; thus they have incurred wrath upon wrath. And the rejecters will have a humiliating retribution.

91. And if it is said to them: "Believe in what God has sent down;" they Say: "We believe only in what was sent down to us," and they reject what came after it, while it is the truth authenticating what is with them. Say: "Why then did you kill God's prophets if you were believers?"

92. And Moses had come to you with clear proofs, then you took the calf after him; you were wicked!

93. And We took your covenant, and raised the mount to be above you: "Take what We have given you with strength, and listen." They said: "We hear and disobey!", and they had consumed the calf inside their hearts by their disbelief. Say: "Miserable indeed is what your belief orders of you if you are believers!"
94. Say: "If the abode of the Hereafter has been set exclusively for you with God, to the exception of all other people, then you should wish for death if you are truthful!"
95. They will never wish for it because of what their hands have done; and God is aware of the wicked.
96. And you will find them the most obsessive people regarding long life; as well as those who have set up partners; each one of them wishes that he could live a thousand years. It will not change for him the retribution even if he lived so long, God is watchful over what you do.
97. Say: "Whoever is an enemy to Gabriel, then know that he has sent it down into your heart by God's permission, authenticating what is already present, and a guide and good news for the believers."
98. "Whoever was an enemy to God and His Angels, and His messengers, and Gabriel, and Michael, then so God is the enemy to the disbelievers."
99. We have sent down to you clear verses; only the evil ones would disbelieve in them.
100. Is it that each time they make a pledge, a group of them breaks it? Alas, most of them do not believe.
101. And when a messenger came to them from God, authenticating what was with them, a group of those who had already received the scripture placed God's scripture behind their backs as if they did not know.
102. And they followed what the devils recited regarding Solomon's kingship. Solomon did not reject, but it was the devils that rejected by teaching people magic, and teaching them what was sent down on the two Angels in Babylon, Haroot and Maroot. They did not teach anyone until they would Say: "We are a test, so do not lose faith!" Thus they teach what can separate between a person and his mate; but they cannot harm anyone except by God's permission. And they learn what harms them and does not benefit them, and they have known that he who purchases such has no place in the Hereafter. Miserable indeed is what they purchased with their souls if only they knew!
103. And had they believed and been righteous, it would have brought them a reward with God which is far better if they knew!

104. O you who believe, do not Say: "Shepherd us," but Say: "Be patient with us," and listen. For the rejecters is a painful retribution.

105. Neither do those who have rejected from among the people of the Scripture, nor from among those who have set up partners, wish that any good comes down to you from your Lord. But God chooses with His mercy whom He wishes; and from God is the greatest favour.

106. We do not duplicate a sign, or make it forgotten, unless We bring one which is like it or even greater. Did you not know that God is capable of all things?

107. Did you not know that to God is the kingship of the heavens and Earth, and that you do not have besides God any guardian or supporter?

108. Or do you want to ask your messenger as Moses was asked before? Whoever replaces belief with rejection, he has indeed strayed from the right path.

109. Many of the people of the Scripture have wished that they could return you to being rejecters after your believing, out of envy from their souls after the truth was made clear to them. You shall forgive them and overlook until God brings His will. God is capable of all things.

110. And honour the oath of allegiance, and contribute towards betterment; and what you bring forth of good for your souls you will find it with God. God is watching what you do.

111. And they said: "None shall enter Paradise except those who are Jewish or Nazarenes;" this is what they wish! Say: "Bring forth your proof if you are truthful."

112. No; whosoever submits himself to God, while doing good, he will have his reward with his Lord. There will be no fear over them, nor will they grieve.

113. And the Jews said: "The Nazarenes have no basis," and the Nazarenes said: "The Jews have no basis," while they are both reciting the Scripture! Similarly, those who do not know have said the same thing. God will judge between them on the Day of Resurrection in what they disputed.

114. And who are more wicked than those who boycott God's temples; so that His name not be mentioned in them; and they seek their destruction? They will not be able to enter them except in fear; they will have humiliation in this world and in the Hereafter a painful retribution.

115. And to God belongs the east and the west, so wherever you turn, there is God's presence. God is Encompassing, Knowledgeable.

116. And they said: "God has taken a son!" Be He glorified. To Him is all that is in the heavens and in the Earth, all are humbled to Him.

117. Initiator of heavens and Earth, when He decrees a command, He merely says to it: "Be" and it is.

118. And those who do not know said: "If only God would speak to us, or a sign would come to us." It is the same thing that the people before them have said, their hearts are so similar! We have clarified the signs for a people who comprehend.

119. We have sent you with the truth as a bearer of good news and warner. You will not be questioned about the people of Hell.

120. Neither the Jews nor the Nazarenes will be pleased with you until you follow their creed. Say: "The guidance is God's guidance." And if you follow their wishes after the knowledge that has come to you, then there is none who can help or protect you against God.

121. Those to whom We have given the Scripture and they recite it as it truthfully deserves to be recited; they believe in it. As for those who disbelieve in it, they are the losers.

122. O Children of Israel, remember My blessings that I have bestowed upon you, and that I have preferred you over all the worlds.

123. And beware of a Day when no soul can avail another soul, nor will any amendment be accepted from it, nor will any intercession help it; they will not be supported.

124. And Abraham was tested by commands from His Lord, which he completed. He said: "I will make you a leader for the people." He said: "And also from my progeny?" He said: "My pledge will not encompass the wicked."

125. And We have made the Sanctuary to be a model for the people and a security. And they took the model of Abraham to make the oath of allegiance. And We had entrusted to Abraham and Ishmael: "You shall purify My Sanctuary for those who visit, those who are devoted, and for those who kneel and prostrate."

126. And Abraham said: "My Lord, make this town secure, and provide for its inhabitants of the fruits for whoever believes in God and the Last Day." He said: "As for he who rejects, I will let him enjoy for a while, then I will force him to the retribution of the Fire, what a miserable destiny!"

127. And as Abraham raised the foundations for the Sanctuary with Ishmael: "Our Lord accept this from us, You are the Hearer, the Knowledgeable."

128. "Our Lord, and let us submit to You and from our progeny a nation submitting to You, and show us our rites and forgive us; You are the Forgiving, the Merciful."

129. "Our Lord, and send amongst them a messenger from among themselves, that he may recite to them Your revelations and teach them the Scripture and the wisdom, and purify them. You are the Noble, the Wise."

130.And who would abandon the creed of Abraham except one who fools himself? We have selected him in this world, and in the Hereafter he is of the righteous.

131.When his Lord said to him: "Submit," he said: "I submit to the Lord of the worlds."

132.And Abraham enjoined his sons and Jacob: "O my sons, God has selected the system for you, so do not die except as ones who have submitted."

133.Or were you present when death came to Jacob and he told his sons: "Who shall you serve after I am gone?", they said: "Your god, and the god of your fathers Abraham, and Ishmael, and Isaac; One god and to Him we submit."

134.That was a nation that has passed away; to them is what they have earned, and to you is what you have earned; and you will not be asked regarding what they did.

135.And they said: "Be Jews or Nazarenes so that you may be guided!" Say: "No, rather the creed of Abraham, monotheism; for he was not of those who set up partners."

136.Say: "We believe in God and in what was sent down to us and what was sent down to Abraham, and Ishmael, and Isaac, and Jacob, and the Patriarchs, and what was given to Moses and Jesus, and what was given to the prophets from their Lord; we do not make a distinction between any of them and to Him we submit."

137.So, if they believe exactly as you have believed, then they are guided; but if they turn away, then they are in opposition and God will suffice you against them, and He is the Hearer, the Knower.

138.Such is God's coloring, and who better than God in coloring. And to Him we are in service.

139.Say: "Do you debate with us regarding God? He is our Lord and your Lord, and we have our work and you have your work, and to Him we are believers."

140."Or do you say that Abraham and Ishmael and Isaac and Jacob and the Patriarchs were all Jewish or Nazarene?" Say: "Are you more knowledgeable or is God?" Who is more wicked than one who conceals a testimony with him from God? God is not unaware of what you do.

141.That was a nation that passed away, to them is what they earned and to you is what you have earned; you will not be asked about what they did.

142.The foolish from amongst the people will Say: "What has turned them away from the focal point that they were on?" Say: "To God is the east and the west, He guides whomsoever He wishes to a straight path."

143. And as such, We have made you a balanced nation so that you may be witness over the people, and that the messenger may be witness over you. And We did not make the focal point that you became on except to distinguish who follows the messenger from those who will turn on their heels. It was a great thing indeed except for those whom God had guided; God was not to waste your belief. God is Merciful and Compassionate over the people.

144. We see the shifting of your face towards the sky; We will thus set for you a focal point that will be pleasing to you: "You shall set yourself towards the Restricted Temple; and wherever you may be, you shall all set yourselves towards it." Those who have been given the Scripture know it is the truth from their Lord. And God is not unaware of what you do.

145. And if you come to those who have been given the Scripture with every sign they will not follow your focal point, nor will you follow their focal point, nor will some of them even follow each others focal point. And if you were to follow their desires after the knowledge that has come to you, then you would be one of the wicked.

146. Those to whom We have given the Scripture know it as they know their own children; and a group of them hides the truth while they know.

147. The truth is from your Lord, so do not be one of those who doubt.

148. And to each is a direction that he will take, so you shall race towards good deeds. Wherever you may be, God will bring you all together. God is capable of all things.

149. And from wherever you go out, you shall set yourself towards the Restricted Temple; it is the truth from your Lord; and God is not unaware of what you do.

150. And wherever you go out, you shall set yourself towards the Restricted Temple. And wherever you may be you shall set yourselves towards it; that the people will have no room for debate with you, except those of them who are wicked. You shall not fear them, but fear Me; so that I may complete My blessings upon you and that you may be guided.

151. As We have sent a messenger to you from amongst yourselves to recite Our revelations to you, and purify you, and teach you the Scripture and the wisdom, and teach you what you did not know.

152. So remember Me that I may remember you, and be thankful to Me and do not disbelieve.

153. O you who believe, seek help through patience and through the oath of allegiance, God is with the patient ones.

154. And do not say of those who are killed in the sake of God that they are dead; no, they are alive but you do not perceive.

155. And We will test you with some fear and hunger, and a shortage in money and lives and fruits. And give good news to those who are patient.

156. The ones who, when afflicted with adversity, they Say: "We are to God and to Him we will return."

157. For those there will be allegiances from their Lord and a mercy, they are the guided ones.

158. The Safa and Marwah are amongst God's symbols. So whosoever makes Pilgrimage to the Sanctuary, or is merely passing through, commits no error that he should traverse within them. And whoever donates for goodness, then God is Appreciative, Knowledgeable.

159. Surely those who conceal what We have sent down to them of the clarity and the guidance, after We Had made it clear for the people in the Scripture; these will be cursed by God and be cursed by those who curse.

160. Except those who repent and amend and make clear; for those I will accept their repentance, for I am the One who accepts repentance, the Merciful.

161. Surely, those who have disbelieved and then died as disbelievers; they will be cursed by God, and the Angels, and all the people.

162. They will abide therein, where the retribution will not be lightened for them, nor will they be reprieved.

163. And your god is but One god, there is no god but He; the Almighty, the Merciful.

164. Surely, in the creation of heavens and Earth, and the differences between night and day, and the ships that sail in the sea for the benefit of the people, and what God has sent down of water from the sky so He brings the Earth back to life after it had died, and He sent forth from it every creature, and the movement of the winds and the clouds that have been designated between the Earth and the sky are signs for a people that understand.

165. And from among the people are some who take other than God as equals to Him, they love them as they love God; but those who believe love God more strongly; and when those who were wicked see the retribution, they will see that all power belongs to God, and that God is severe in retribution.

166. When those who were followed will disown those who followed them, and they will see the retribution, and all excuses have abandoned them.

167. And those who followed them said: "If we only could have a chance to disown them as they have disowned us." It is such that God will show them their works which will be regretted by them; they will not leave the Fire.

168.O mankind, eat of what is in the Earth as good and lawful, and do not follow the steps of the devil, he is to you a clear enemy.

169.He only orders you to evil and sin, and that you may say about God what you do not know.

170.And if they are told: "Follow what God has sent down," they Say: "No, we will follow what we found our fathers doing!" What if their fathers did not understand anything and were not guided?

171.And the example of those who disbelieve is like one who repeats what he has heard of calls and shouts; deaf, dumb, and blind, they do not understand.

172.O you who believe, eat of the good things We have provided for you, and be thankful to God; if it is Him you serve.

173.He has only forbidden for you what is already dead, and the blood, and the meat of pig, and what was dedicated to other than God. Whoever finds himself forced out of need and without disobedience or animosity, then there is no sin upon him. God is Forgiving, Merciful.

174.Surely, those who conceal what God has sent down of the Scripture, and they purchase with it a cheap price; they will not eat in their stomachs except the Fire, and God will not speak to them on the Day of Resurrection, nor will He purify them, and they will have a painful retribution.

175.These are the ones who have purchased straying for guidance, and retribution for forgiveness; they have no patience towards the Fire.

176.This is because God has sent down the Scripture with truth; and those who have disputed in the Scripture are in far opposition.

177.Piety is not to turn your faces towards the east and the west, but piety is one who believes in God and the Last Day, and the Angels, and the Scripture, and the prophets, and he gives money out of love to the relatives, and the orphans, and the needy and the wayfarer, and those who ask, and to free the slaves; and he honours the oath of allegiance, and he contributes towards betterment; as well as those who keep their pledges when they make a pledge, and those who are patient in the face of good and bad and when in despair. These are the ones who have been truthful, and they are the righteous.

178.O you who believe, equivalent execution in warfare has been decreed for you in the case of mass killings; the free for the free, and the slave for the slave, and the female for the female. Whoever is forgiven anything by his brother, then it is to be followed with good deeds and kindness towards him; that is an alleviation from your Lord, and a mercy. Whoever transgresses after that, he will have a painful retribution.

179. And through equivalent execution in warfare, you will be protecting life, O people of understanding, that you may be righteous.

180. It is decreed for you that if death should come to any of you, that it is best if he leaves a will for his family and relatives out of goodness; this is a truth for the righteous.

181. Whoever alters it after having heard, then the sin will be upon those who alter it. God is Hearer, Knowing.

182. If anyone fears harm or sin from his beneficiary, then reconcile what is between them. God is Forgiving, Merciful.

183. O you who believe, fasting has been decreed for you as it was decreed for those before you, perhaps you may be righteous.

184. A few number of days; however, if an of you is ill or traveling, then the same number from different days; and as for those who can do so but with difficulty, they may redeem by feeding the needy. And whoever does good voluntarily, then it is better for him. And if you fast it is better for you if you knew.

185. Ramadhan is the month in which the Quran was revealed as a guide to the people and a clarification of the guidance and the criterion. Therefore, whoever of you witnesses the month, then let him fast therein. And whoever is ill or traveling, then the same number from different days. God wants to bring you ease and not to bring you hardship; and so that you may complete the count, and glorify God for what He has guided you, that you may be thankful.

186. And if My servants ask you about Me, I am near answering the calls of those who call to Me. So let them respond to Me and believe in Me that they may be guided.

187. It has been made lawful for you during the night of fasting to approach your women sexually. They are a garment for you and you are a garment for them. God knows that you used to betray your souls so He has accepted your repentance, and forgiven you; now you may approach them and seek what God has written for you. And you may eat and drink until the white thread is distinct from the black thread of dawn; then you shall complete the fast until night; and do not approach them while you are devoted in the temples. These are God's boundaries, so do not transgress them. It is thus that God makes His revelations clear to the people that they may be righteous.

188. And do not consume your money between you unjustly by bribing the decision makers so that you may consume a part of the other people's money sinfully while you know!

189. They ask you regarding the crescent moons, Say: "They are a timing mechanism for the people as well as for the Pilgrimage." And piety is not that you would enter a home from its back, but piety is whomever is righteous and come to the homes from their main doors. And be aware of God that you may succeed.

190. And fight in the cause of God against those who fight you, but do not transgress, God does not like the aggressors.

191. And kill them wherever you find them, and expel them from where they expelled you, and know that persecution is worse than being killed. And do not fight them at the Restricted Temple unless they fight you in it; if they fight you then kill them, thus is the reward of the disbelievers.

192. And if they cease, then God is Forgiving, Merciful.

193. And fight them so there is no more persecution, and so that the system is God's. If they cease, then there will be no aggression except against the wicked.

194. What is done in the restricted month may be retaliated in the same month, and murder shall be punishable by execution. Whoever attacks you, then you shall attack him the same as he attacked you; and be aware of God, and know that God is with the righteous.

195. And spend in the cause of God, but do not throw your resources to disaster. And do kindness, for God loves those who do kindness.

196. And complete the Pilgrimage and the visit for God. But, if you are prevented, then make what is affordable of donation, and do not shave your heads until the donation reaches its destination; but whoever of you is ill or has an affliction to his head, then he may redeem by fasting or giving a charity or a sacrifice. But if you are able, then whoever continues the visit until the Pilgrimage, then he shall provide what is affordable of donation; but for he who cannot find anything, then he must fast for three days during the Pilgrimage and seven when he returns; this will make a complete ten; this is for those whose family is not present at the Restricted Temple. And be aware of God, and know that God is severe in retribution.

197. The Pilgrimage is towards the months which have been appointed. So whosoever decides to perform the Pilgrimage therein, then there shall be no sexual approach, nor vileness, nor baseless argument in the Pilgrimage. And any good that you do, God is aware of it; and bring provisions for yourselves, though the best provision is righteousness; and be aware of Me O people of understanding.

198. There is no sin upon you to seek goodness from your Lord. So when you disperse from Arafaat, then remember God towards the decree which is restricted, and remember Him as He has guided you, for you were before that straying.

199. Then you shall disperse from where the people dispersed, and seek God's forgiveness; God is surely Forgiving, Merciful.

200. When you have completed your rites, then remember God as you remember your fathers or even greater. From among the people are those who Say: "Our Lord, give us from this world!", but in the Hereafter he has no part.

201. And some of them Say: "Our Lord, give us good in this world, and good in the Hereafter, and spare us from the retribution of the Fire."

202. These will have a benefit for what they have gained; and God is quick in judgment.

203. And remember God during a few number of days. Whoever hurries to two days, there is no sin upon him; and whoever delays, there is no sin upon him if he is being righteous. And be aware of God, and know that it is to Him that you will be gathered.

204. And from among the people are those whose words you admire in this worldly life, but God is witness as to what is in his heart, for he is the worst in opposition.

205. And if he gains power, he seeks to corrupt the Earth and destroy its crops, and people's lineage. God does not like corruption.

206. And if he is told: "Be aware of God," his pride leads to more sin. Hell shall be sufficient for him; what a miserable abode!

207. And from among the people is he who develops his soul by seeking God's favour; God is kind to His servants.

208. O you who believe, join in peace, all of you, and do not follow the footsteps of the devil. He is to you a clear enemy.

209. But if you slip after the clarity has come to you, then know that God is Noble, Wise.

210. Are they waiting for God to come to them shadowed in clouds with the Angels? The matter would then be finished! And to God all matters will return.

211. Ask the Children of Israel how many clear signs did We give them? And whoever changes God's favour after it has come to him, then God is Mighty in retribution.

212. This worldly life has been made pleasing to the disbelievers, and they mock those who believe. And those who are righteous will be above them on the Day of Resurrection; God provides for whoever He wishes without a price.

213. The people used to be one nation, then God sent the prophets as bearers of good news and warners, and He sent down with them the Scripture with the facts so that they may judge between the people in what they were disputing. But after receiving the clarity, the people disputed in it due to animosity between them. And God guided those who believed with His permission regarding what they disputed in of the truth. And God guides whoever He wishes to a straight path.

214. Or did you expect that you would enter Paradise, while the example of those who were before you came to you; they were stricken with adversity and hardship, and they were shaken until the messenger and those who believed with him said: "When is God's victory?" Yes indeed, God's victory is near.

215. They ask you what they should spend, Say: "What you spend out of goodness should go to your family and the relatives and the orphans, and the needy, and the wayfarer. And any good you do, God is fully aware of it."

216. Warfare has been decreed for you while you hate it; and perhaps you may hate something while it is good for you, and perhaps you may love something while it is bad for you; God knows while you do not know.

217. They ask you about the restricted month: "Is there fighting in it?" Say: "Much fighting is in it, and to repel from the path of God and to disbelieve in Him, and at the Restricted Temple, to drive its inhabitants out is far greater with God, and persecution is worse than being killed." And they still will fight you until they turn you back from your system if they are able. And whoever of you turns back from his system, and he dies while disbelieving, then these have nullified their work in this life and the next; these are the people of the Fire, in it they will abide eternally!

218. Those who believe, and those who have immigrated and strived in the cause of God; these are seeking God's mercy, and God is Forgiving, Merciful.

219. They ask you about intoxicants and gambling. Say: "In them is great harm, and a benefit for the people; but their harm is greater than their benefit." And they ask you how much are they to give, Say: "The excess." It is thus that God clarifies for you the revelations that you may think.

220. In this world and the next; and they ask you regarding the orphans, Say: "To fix their situation is best, and if you are to care for them, then they are your brothers." And God knows the corrupt from the good, and had God wished He could have made things difficult. God is Noble, Wise.

221. And do not marry the females who set up partners until they believe. For a believing servant is better than one who sets up partners even if she attracts you. And do not marry the males who set up partners until they believe. For a believing servant is better than one who sets up partners even if he attracts you. Those invite to the Fire, while God is inviting to Paradise and forgiveness by His leave. He clarifies His revelations for the people that they may remember.

222. And they ask you about menstruation? Say: "It is harmful, so retire yourselves sexually from the women during the menstruation, and do not approach them until they are cleansed. When they are cleansed, then you may approach them as God has commanded you." God loves the repenters and He loves the cleansed.

223. Your women are a cultivation for you. So approach your cultivation as you wish towards goodness. And be aware of God and know that you will meet Him, and give good news to the believers.

224. And do not make God the subject of your casual oaths. Be pious and righteous and reconcile among the people; and God is Listener, Knower.

225. God will not call you to account for your casual oaths, but He will call you to account for what has entered your hearts. God is Forgiving, Compassionate.

226. For those who are discontent with their wives, let them wait for four months. If they reconcile, then God is Forgiving, Merciful.

227. And if they insist on the divorce, then God is Hearer, Knowledgeable.

228. And the divorced women shall wait for three menstruation periods; and it is not lawful for them to conceal what God has created in their wombs, if they believe in God and the Last Day. And their husbands would then have just cause to return together, if they both wish to reconcile. And for what obligations the women are owed, so similarly must they fulfil their obligations. But the men will have a greater responsibility over them in this. And God is Noble, Wise.

229. The divorce is allowed twice. So, either they remain together equitably, or they part ways with kindness. And it is not lawful for you to take back anything you have given the women unless you fear that they will not uphold God's limits. So if you fear that they will not uphold God's limits, then there is no sin upon them for what is given back. These are God's limits so do not transgress them. And whoever shall transgress God's limits, then these are the wicked.

230.So if he divorces her again, then she will not be lawful for him until she has married another husband. If the other husband divorces her, then there is no sin that they come back together if they think they will uphold God's limits. These are God's limits, He clarifies them for a people that know.

231.And if you have divorced the women, and they have reached their required interim period, then either you remain together equitably, or part ways equitably. And do not reconcile with them so you can harm them out of animosity; whoever does so is doing wickedness to his soul; and do not take God's revelations lightly. And remember God's blessings towards you, and what was sent down to you of the Scripture and the wisdom, He warns you with it. And be aware of God and know that God is Knowledgeable in all things.

232.And if you divorce the women, and they have reached their required interim period, then do not prevent them from remarrying their husbands if they amicably agree amongst themselves out of what is best. This is to remind any of you who believe in God and the Last Day, this is better for you and purer; and God knows while you do not know.

233.And the divorced mothers are allowed to suckle their children two full years, if they wish to complete the suckling. And the man for whom the child is born is responsible for both their provisions and clothing equitably. We do not burden a soul beyond its means. No mother shall be harmed because of her child, nor shall a father be harmed because of his child. And for the guardian is the same requirement. So if they wish to separate out of mutual agreement and council, then there is no sin upon them. And if you want to hire nursing mothers, then there is no sin upon you if you return what you have been given equitably. And be aware of God, and know that God is watching over what you do.

234.And for those of you who pass away and leave widows behind, then their widows will have a required interim period of four months and ten days. So when they reach their required interim, then there is no sin upon you for what they do to themselves equitably. And God is Expert to what you do.

235.And there is no sin upon you if you openly propose marriage to these women, or you keep it between yourselves. God knows that you will be thinking of them, but do not meet them secretly, unless you have something righteous to say. And do not consummate the marriage until the required interim is reached in the Scripture. And know that God knows what is in your souls, so be aware of Him, and know that God is Forgiving, Compassionate.

236. There is no sin upon you if you divorce the women before having sexual intercourse with them, or before committing to what was agreed for them. Let them have recompense, the rich according to his means, and the poor according to his means. Recompense which is in goodness, a responsibility for those in kindness.

237. And if you divorce them before having sexual intercourse with them, but you have already agreed to the dowry; then you must give half of what you have agreed, unless they forgive or the guardian over the marriage contract forgives. And if you forgive, it is closer to righteousness. And do not forget the favour between you; God is Seer over what you do.

238. Maintain the oaths of allegiance, and especially the middle oath of allegiance; and stand devoutly for God.

239. But if you are in a state of worry, then you may do so while walking or riding. If you become secure, then remember God as He has taught you what you did not know.

240. And those of you who pass away and leave widows behind; a testimony to them that they may enjoy for one year without being made to vacate. If they leave then there is no sin upon you for what they do to themselves in goodness; and God is Noble, Wise.

241. And for the divorced women to have recompense is an obligation upon the righteous.

242. It is such that God clarifies to you His revelations that you may comprehend.

243. Did you not see those who left their homes in groups, all the while they were weary of death; so God said to them: "Die," then He resurrected them. God has great favour over the people, but most people are not thankful.

244. And fight in the cause of God and know that God is the Hearer, the Knowledgeable.

245. Who will lend God a loan of goodness that He may multiply it for him many times over? God collects and He distributes, and to Him you will return.

246. Did you not note the leaders of the Children of Israel after Moses, they said to their prophet: "Send us a king that we may fight in the cause of God;" he said: "Are you not concerned that if fighting is decreed upon you, you will then not fight?" They said: "And why should we not fight in the cause of God when we have been driven out from our homes with our children." So it was, that when fighting was decreed for them they turned away, except for a few of them! God is fully aware of the wicked.

247. And their prophet said to them: "God has sent Saul to you as a king." They said: "How can he have the kingship when we are more deserving than him, and he has not been given an abundance of wealth?" He said: "God has chosen him over you and increased him in knowledge and stature." God grants His sovereignty to whom He chooses; and God is Encompassing, Knowledgeable.

248. And their prophet said to them: "The sign of his kingship shall be that he brings to you the ark in which there is tranquility from your Lord and the legacy of what was left behind by the descendants of Moses and the descendants of Aaron being carried by the Angels. In this is a sign for you if you are believers."

249. So when Saul set out with the soldiers, he said: "God will test you with a river, whoever drinks from it is not with me, and whoever does not taste from it except one scoop with his hand is with me." They all drank from it, except a few of them. So when he and those who believed with him crossed it, they said: "We have no power today against Goliath and his soldiers!" But the ones who understood that they would meet God said: "How many a time has a small group beaten a large group by God's leave, and God is with the patient ones!"

250. And when they came forth to Goliath and his soldiers, they said: "Our Lord grant us patience, and make firm our foothold, and grant us victory over the disbelieving people."

251. So they defeated them by God's leave, and David killed Goliath, and God gave him the kingship and the wisdom and taught him what He wished. And if it were not for God defending the people against themselves, then the Earth would have long been corrupted. But God has done favour over the worlds.

252. These are God's revelations, We recite them to you with truth, and you are of the messengers.

253. Such messengers, We have preferred some over others; some of them talked to God, and He raised some of them in rank, and We gave Jesus son of Mary the proofs and We supported him with the holy spirit. And had God wished, the people after them would not have fought after the proofs had come to them, but they disputed, some of them believed and some of them disbelieved. Had God wished they would not have fought, but God does whatever He wishes.

254. O you who believe, spend from what We have provided for you before a Day will come when there is no trade, nor friendship, nor intercession; and the disbelievers are the wicked.

255. God, there is no god but He, the Living, the Sustainer. No slumber or sleep overtakes Him; to Him belongs all that is in heavens and in the Earth. Who will intercede with Him except by His leave? He knows their present and their future, and they do not have any of His knowledge except for what He wishes. His throne encompasses all of the heavens and the Earth and it is easy for Him to preserve them. He is the Most High, the Great.

256. There is no compulsion in the system; the proper way has been made clear from the wrong way. Whoever rejects evil, and believes in God, then he has grasped the most solid branch that will never break. God is Hearer, Knower.

257. God is the ally of those who believe, He brings them out of the darkness and into the light. As for those who reject, their allies are the evil ones, they bring them out of the light and into the darkness; these are the people of the Fire, in it they will abide eternally.

258. Did the news come to you of the person who debated with Abraham regarding his Lord, while God had given him a kingship? Abraham said: "My Lord is the One who gives life and death," he said: "I bring life and death." Abraham said: "God brings the sun from the east, so you bring it from the west." The one who disbelieved was confounded! And God does not guide the wicked people.

259. Or the one who passed through a town, where all its inhabitants had passed away. He said: "How can God possibly resurrect this after its death?" So God put him to death for one hundred years, then He resurrected him. He said: "How long have you stayed here?" He said: "I have stayed here a day or part of a day." He said: "No, you have stayed here for one hundred years! Look at your food and drink, they have not changed, but look at your donkey! And We will make you a sign for the people; and look at the bones how We grow them, then We cover them with flesh." So when it was clear to him what happened, he said: "I now know that God is capable of all things!"

260. And Abraham said: "My Lord, show me how you resurrect the dead." He said: "Do you not already believe?" He said: "I do, but it is so my heart can be relieved." He said: "Choose four birds, then cut them, then place parts of the birds on each mountain, then call them to you; they will come racing towards you. And know that God is Noble, Wise."

261. The example of those who spend their money in the cause of God is like a seed that sprouts forth seven pods, in each pod there is one hundred seeds;

and God multiplies for whoever He chooses, and God is Encompassing, Knowledgeable.

262. Those who spend their money in the cause of God, then they do not follow what they have spent with either insult or harm; they will have their reward with their Lord, there is no fear over them nor will they grieve.

263. Kind words and forgiveness is far better than a charity that is followed by harm. God is Rich, Compassionate.

264. O you who believe, do not nullify your charities with insult and harm; like the one who spends his money in vanity to show the people, and he does not believe in God and the Last Day. His example is like a stone on which there is dust, then it is subjected to heavy rain which leaves it bare. They cannot do anything with what they earned; and God does not guide the rejecting people.

265. And the example of those who spend their money seeking God's grace, and to save their souls, is like the example of a garden that is on a high ground and is subjected to a heavy rain, and because of that it produces double its crop. And if no heavy rain comes, then light rain is enough. And God is Seer over all you do.

266. Does anyone of you desire that he have an estate with palm trees and grapevines, and rivers flowing beneath it, and in it for him are all kinds of fruits, then he is afflicted with old age and his progeny is weak, and a whirlwind with fire strikes it and it all burns? It is thus that God makes clear for you the signs that you may reflect.

267. O you who believe, spend from the good things that you have earned, and from what We have brought forth from the Earth. And do not select the rotten out of it to give, while you would not take it yourselves unless you close your eyes regarding it. And know that God is Rich, Praiseworthy.

268. The devil promises you poverty and orders you to evil, while God promises forgiveness from Him and favour. God is Encompassing, Knowledgeable.

269. He grants wisdom to whom He chooses, and whoever is granted wisdom, has been given much good. Only those with understanding will remember.

270. And whatever you spend out of your monies, or whatever you pledge as a promise, then God knows it. The wicked have no supporters.

271. If you openly give charity, then it is acceptable; but if you conceal it and give it to the poor, then that is better for you. And He cancels some of your sins; and God is Expert to all that you do.

272. You are not responsible for their guidance, but it is God who will guide whoever He wishes. And whatever you spend out of goodness is for your own

souls. And anything you spend should be in seeking God's presence. And whatever you spend out of goodness will be retuned to you, and you will not be wronged.

273. As for the poor who face hardship in the cause of God, and they cannot leave the land; the ignorant ones think they are rich from their modesty; you know them by their features, they do not ask the people repeatedly. And what you spend out of goodness, God is fully aware of it.

274. Those who spend their money in the night and in the day, secretly and openly, they will have their reward with their Lord, there is no fear over them nor will they grieve.

275. Those who consume financial interest, they do not rise except as the one who is being beaten by the devil out of direct touch. That is because they have said: "Trade is like financial interest." While God has made trade lawful, and He has forbidden financial interest. Whoever has received understanding from His Lord and ceases, then he will be forgiven for what was before this and his case will be with God. But whoever returns, then they are the people of the Fire, in it they will abide eternally.

276. God wipes out the financial interest and He grants growth to the charities. And God does not like any wicked sinner.

277. Those who believe and do good works, and honour the oath of allegiance, and contribute towards betterment; they will have their rewards with their Lord and there is no fear over them nor will they grieve.

278. O you who believe, be aware of God and give up what is left of the financial interest if you are truly believers.

279. And if you will not do this, then take notice of a war from God and His messenger; but if you repent, then you will have back your principal money, you will not be wronged nor will you wrong.

280. If the person is facing insolvency, then you shall wait until he becomes able. And if you relinquish it as a charity it is better for you if you knew.

281. And be aware of a Day when you will be returned to God then every soul will be paid what it has earned, they will not be wronged.

282. O you who believe, if you borrow debt for a future period, then you shall record it. And let a scribe of justice record it for you; and let not the scribe refuse to record as God has taught him. Let him record and let the person who is borrowing dictate to him, and let him be aware of God, and let him not reduce from it anything. If the one who is borrowing is immature or weak or he cannot dictate himself, then let his guardian dictate with justice; and bring two witnesses from amongst your men; if they are not two men,

then a man and two women from whom you will accept their testimony, so that if one of them becomes occupied, then the one can recall the other. And let the witnesses not refuse to come if they are called. And do not fail to record it no matter how small or large until its maturity. That is more just with God and better for the testimony, and better that you do not have doubts; except if it is a trade to be done on the spot between you, then there is no sin upon you if you do not record it. And have evidence if you trade. No scribe shall be harmed nor any witness; for if you do so then it is vileness on your part, and be aware of God and God teaches you and God is aware of all things.

283. And if you are traveling or do not find a scribe, then a pledge of collateral. So, if you have entrusted each other in this manner, then let the one who was entrusted deliver his trust, and let him be aware of God his Lord. And do not hold back the testimony. And whoever holds it back, then he has sinned in his heart, and God is aware of what you do.

284. To God is what is in the heavens and in Earth, and if you declare what is in your souls or hide it, God will call you to account for it. He will forgive whom He wishes, and punish whom He wishes, and God is capable of all things.

285. The messenger believes in what was sent down to him from his Lord. And the believers, all who believe in God, and His angels, and His Scriptures, and His messengers: "We do not differentiate between any of His messengers;" and they said: "We hear and obey, forgive us O Lord, and to you is our destiny."

286. God does not burden a soul beyond its means. For it is what it earns, and against it is what it earns. "Our Lord, do not mind us if we forget or make mistakes; our Lord, do not place a burden upon us as You have placed upon those before us; our Lord, do not place upon us what we cannot bare; pardon us, and forgive us, and have mercy on us; You are our patron, so grant us victory over the disbelieving people."

Chapter 3

بسم الله الرحمن الرحيم

In the name of God, the Almighty, the Merciful.

1. A.L.M.

2. God, there is no god but He, the Living, the Sustainer.

3. He sent down to you the Scripture with truth, authenticating what is present with it; and He sent down the Torah and the Injeel.

4. From before as a guidance for the people, and He sent down the Criterion. Those who rejected God's revelations, they will have a painful retribution, and God is Noble, extracting in Revenge.

5. For God nothing is hidden in the Earth or in the heavens.

6. He is the One who pictures you in the wombs as He pleases. There is no god but Him, the Noble, the Wise.

7. He is the One who sent down to you the Scripture, from which there are governing verses; they are the essence of the Scripture; and others which are similar. As for those who have disease in their hearts, they will follow what is similar from it seeking to confuse, and seeking to derive an interpretation. But none know its interpretation except God and those who are well founded in knowledge, they Say: "We believe in it, all is from our Lord." And none will remember except the people of understanding.

8. "Our Lord, do not make our hearts deviate after You have guided us, and grant us from You a mercy; You are the Grantor."

9. "Our Lord, You will gather the people for a Day in which there is no doubt; God does not break His appointment."

10. As for those who rejected, neither their money nor their children will avail them anything from God. They are the fuel for the Fire.

11. Like the behaviour of the people of Pharaoh and those before them. They rejected Our signs so God took them for their sins. God is awesome in retribution.

12. Say to those who have rejected: "You will be defeated and gathered towards Hell, what a miserable abode!"

13. There was a sign for you in the two groups that met. One was fighting in the cause of God, and the other was rejecting. They thus saw them as twice their number with their eyes. And God supports with His victory whom He wills. In this is a lesson for those with vision.

14. It has been adorned for people to love the desire of the most modern things, and buildings, and ornaments made from gold and silver, and trained horses, and the livestock, and fields. These are the enjoyment of the world, and with God are the best goods.

15. Say: "Shall I inform you of what is greater than all this? For those who believe in their Lord will be estates with rivers flowing beneath, in them they abide eternally, and with pure mates, and an acceptance from God. And God is watcher over the servants."

16. The ones who Say: "Our Lord, we believe, so forgive us our sins, and spare us the retribution of the Fire."

17. The patient, and the truthful, and the devout, and the givers, and the seekers of forgiveness in the late hours of the night.

18. God bears witness that there is no god but He, as do the Angels, and those with knowledge, He is standing with justice. There is no god but Him, the Noble, the Wise.

19. The system with God is submission, and those who received the Scripture did not dispute except after the knowledge came to them out of jealousy between them. And whoever rejects God's signs, then God is swift in judgment.

20. If they debate with you, then Say: "I have submitted myself to God, as well as those who follow me." And say to those who have received the Scripture and the Gentiles: "Have you submitted?" If they have submitted then they are guided, and if they turn away, then you are only to deliver, and God is watcher over the servants.

21. Those who reject God's revelations and kill the prophets unjustly, and kill those who order justice from amongst the people; inform them of a painful retribution.

22. These are the ones whose works will be lost in this world, and in the Hereafter they will have no supporters.

23. Did you not see those who were given a portion of the Scripture being invited to God's Scripture to judge between them, then a group of them turns away while they are adverse?

24. That is because they said: "The Fire will not touch us except a few number of days," and they were arrogant by what they invented in their system.

25. How shall it be when We gather them on the Day in which there is no doubt; and every soul shall receive what it has earned, and they will not be wronged.

26. Say: "Our god, Possessor of kingship; you grant kingship to whom You please, and revoke kingship from whom You please, and honour whom You please, and humiliate whom You please; in Your hand is goodness. You are capable of all things."

27. "You blend the night into the day, and blend the day into the night; and you bring the living out of the dead, and bring the dead out of the living; and You provide for whom You please with no reckoning."

28. Let not the believers take the rejecters as allies instead of the believers. And whoever does so will have nothing with God; for you are to be cautious of them as they deserve. And God warns you of Himself, and to God is the destiny.

29. Say: "If you hide what is in your chests or you reveal it, God will know." And He knows what is in the heavens and what is in the Earth; and God is capable of all things.

30. The Day every soul will find what good it had done present, and what bad it had done; it wishes that between them was a great distance. And God warns you of Himself, and God is Compassionate towards the servants.

31. Say: "If you love God then follow me so God will love you and forgive your sins." God is Forgiver, Merciful.

32. Say: "Obey God and the messenger." But if they turn away, then God does not like the rejecters.

33. God has selected Adam, and Noah, and the family of Abraham, and the family of Imran over the worlds.

34. A progeny each from the other, and God is Hearer, Knower.

35. When the wife of Imran said: "My Lord, I have vowed to You what is in my womb, dedicated, so accept from me, You are the Hearer, the Knower."

36. So when she delivered she said: "My Lord, I have delivered a female," and God is fully aware of what she delivered, "And the male is not like the female, and I have named her Mary, and I seek refuge for her and her progeny with You from the outcast devil."

37. So her Lord accepted her a good acceptance, and made her grow into a good growth, and charged Zachariah with her. Every time Zachariah entered upon her in the temple enclosure, he found provisions with her. He said: "O Mary, from where did you get this?" She said: "It is from God, God provides for whom He wishes without reckoning."

38. It was then that Zachariah called on his Lord, he said: "My Lord, grant me from You a good progeny, You are hearer of the prayers."

39. The Angels called to him whilst he was standing making the oath of allegiance in the temple enclosure: "God gives you good tidings of John, authenticating the word from God, and a master, and steadfast, and a prophet from the upright."

40. He said: "My Lord, how can I have a son when old age has reached me and my wife is sterile?" He said: "It is as such that God does what He pleases."

41. He said: "My Lord, make for me a sign" He said: "Your sign is not to speak to the people for three days except by symbol, and remember your Lord greatly, and glorify at dusk and dawn."

42. And the Angels said: "O Mary, God has selected you and cleansed you, and He has selected you over the women of the worlds."

43. "O Mary, be devoted to your Lord and prostrate and kneel with those who kneel."

44. This is from the news of the unseen that We inspire to you. You were not with them when they drew straws as to which one of them will be charged with Mary; you were not with them when they disputed.

45. And the Angels said: "O Mary, God gives good news of a word from Him. His name is the Messiah, Jesus the son of Mary. Honourable in this world and in the Hereafter, and from among those who are made close."

46. "And he speaks to the people from the cradle, and in old age, and is from among the upright."

47. She said: "My Lord, how can I have a son when no human has touched me?" He said: "It is thus that God creates what He wills, when He decrees a command, He merely says to it "Be," and it is."

48. And He teaches him the Scripture and the Wisdom and the Torah and the Injeel.

49. And as a messenger to the Children of Israel: "I have come to you with a sign from your Lord; that I create for you from clay the form of a bird, then I blow into it and it becomes a bird by God's leave, and I heal the blind and the leapers, and give life to the dead by God's leave, and I prophesize for you

what you shall eat and what to store in your homes. In that is a sign for you if you are believers."

50. "And authenticating what is present with me of the Torah, and to make lawful some of that which was forbidden to you; and I have come to you with a sign from your Lord, so be aware of God and obey me."

51. "God is my Lord and your Lord, so serve Him, this is a Straight Path."

52. So when Jesus felt their rejection, he said: "Who are my supporters to God?" The disciples said: "We are God's supporters, we believe in God and we bear witness that we have submitted."

53. "Our Lord, we believe in what You have sent down, and followed the messenger, so record us with those who bear witness."

54. And they schemed and God schemed, but God is the best schemer.

55. God said: "O Jesus, I will seize you, and raise you to Me, and cleanse you of those who have rejected, and make those who have followed you above those who rejected until the Day of Resurrection; then to Me is your return so I will judge between all of you in what it was that you disputed."

56. "As for those who have rejected, I will punish them severely in this world and in the Hereafter, they will have no supporters."

57. "And as for those who believed and did good works, We will pay them their reward; God does not like the wicked."

58. This We recite to you from the revelations and the wise reminder.

59. The example of Jesus with God is similar to that of Adam; He created him from dust, then He said to him "Be" and he was.

60. The truth is from your Lord, so do not be of those who doubt.

61. Whoever debates with you in this after the knowledge has come to you, then Say: "Let us call our children and your children, our women and your women, ourselves and yourselves, then, let us call out, and we shall make God's curse upon the liars."

62. This is the narration of truth, there is no god but God; and God is the Noble, the Wise.

63. And if they turn away, then God is aware of the corruptors.

64. Say: "O people of the Scripture, let us come to a common understanding between us and between you; that we do not serve except God, and do not set up anything at all with Him, and that none of us takes each other as patrons beside God." If they turn away, then Say: "Bear witness that we have submitted."

65. "O people of the Scripture, why do you debate us regarding Abraham when the Torah and the Injeel were not sent down except after him? Do you not understand?"

66. Here you have debated in what you knew; so why then do you debate in what you do not know? God knows while you do not know.

67. Abraham was neither a Jew nor a Nazarene, but he was a monotheist who submitted; he was not of those who set up partners.

68. The most legitimate people to Abraham are those who followed him; and this prophet, and those who believed; and God is the supporter of the believers.

69. A group from the people of the Scripture wished that they could misguide you, but they only misguide themselves and they do not notice.

70. "O people of the Scripture, why do you reject God's signs while you are bearing witness?"

71. "O people of the Scripture, why do you dress the truth with falsehood and conceal the truth while you know?"

72. And a group from among the people of the Scripture said: "Believe in what was revealed to those who believed during the beginning of the day, and reject it by the end of it, perhaps they will return."

73. "And do not believe except to those who follow your system." Say: "The guidance is God's guidance." "That anyone should be given similar to what you have been given, or that they debate with you at your Lord." Say: "The bounty is in God's hand, He gives it to whom He chooses, and God is Encompassing, Knowledgeable."

74. He specifies with His mercy whom He chooses, and God is with Great Bounty.

75. And from among the people of the Scripture are those whom if you entrust him with a large amount he gives it back to you, and there are those whom if you entrust with one gold coin he will not return it to you unless you are standing over him. That is because they said: "We have no obligation towards the Gentiles." They say about God lies while knowing.

76. Indeed, anyone who fulfils his pledge and is righteous, then God loves the righteous.

77. The ones that purchase with God's pledge and their oaths a small price, those will have no portion in the Hereafter, and God will not speak to them nor look at them on the Day of Resurrection nor purify them, and they will have a painful retribution.

78. And from amongst them is a group that twist their tongues with the Scripture so that you may think it is from the Scripture, while it is not from the Scripture, and they say it is from God while it is not from God, and they say about God lies while they know.

79. It is not for a human that God would give him the Scripture and the authority and the prophethood, then he would say to the people: "Be servants to me rather than God!", rather: "Be devotees for what you have been taught of the Scripture, and for what you studied."

80. Nor does He order you that you take the Angels and the prophets as patrons. Would He order you to rejection after this, while you have submitted?

81. And God took a covenant from the prophets: "For what I have given you of the Scripture and wisdom, then a messenger will come to you authenticating what is with you. You will believe in him and support him." He said: "Do you testify, and agree to this burden?", they said: "We testify." He said: "Then bear witness, and I am with you bearing witness."

82. Whoever turns away after that, then they are the wicked ones.

83. Is it other than God's system that they desire, when those in the heavens and the Earth have submitted to Him voluntarily or by force? And to Him they will be returned.

84. Say: "We believe in God and what was sent down to us and what was sent down to Abraham and Ishmael and Isaac and Jacob and the Patriarchs, and what was given to Moses and Jesus and the prophets from their Lord. We do not make any distinction between them, and to Him we submit."

85. And whoever follows other than submission as a system, it will not be accepted from him, and in the Hereafter he is of the losers.

86. How can God guide a people who have rejected after believing, and they witnessed that the messenger is true, and the clarity had come to them? God does not guide the wicked people.

87. To these the punishment will be that God's curse will be upon them as well as that of the Angels and the people all together!

88. Eternally they will abide in it, the retribution will not be lightened for them, nor will they be reprieved.

89. Except those who repent after this and make amends, then God is Forgiver, Merciful.

90. Those who have rejected after their belief then increased in rejection, their repentance will not be accepted, they are the strayers.

91. Those who have rejected and died while they are rejecters, if the Earth full of gold were to be ransomed with it would not be accepted from any of them. For these there will be a painful retribution and they will have no supporters.

92. You will not reach piety until you spend from what you love; and whatever you spend, God is aware of it.

93. All the food was made lawful to the Children of Israel except what Israel forbade for himself before the Torah was sent down. Say: "Bring the Torah and recite it if you are truthful."

94. Whoever invents lies about God after this, these are the wicked.

95. Say: "God bears truth. Follow the creed of Abraham, monotheism, and he was not of those who set up partners."

96. The first Sanctuary established for the people is the one in Bakk'a, blessed, and a guidance for the worlds.

97. In it are clear signs: the place of Abraham. And whoever enters it will be secure. And God is owed from the people to make Pilgrimage to the Sanctuary, whoever can make a path to it. And whoever rejects, then God has no need of the worlds.

98. Say: "O people of the Scripture, why do you reject God's signs, while God is witness over what you do?"

99. Say: "O people of the Scripture, why do you repel from the path of God those who believe? You wish to twist it while you were witness. And God is not unaware of what you do."

100. O you who believe, if you obey a group of those who received the Scripture they will turn you after your belief into rejecters!

101. And how can you reject when God's revelations are being recited to you and with you is His messenger? And whoever holds firmly to God has been guided to the straight path.

102. O you who believe, revere God as He deserves to be revered, and do not die except as ones who have submitted.

103. And hold firmly to the rope of God, all of you, and do not be separated. And remember God's blessing upon you when you were enemies and He united your hearts, then you became with His blessing as brothers; and you were on the verge of a pit of fire and He saved you from it; it is thus that God clarifies for you His signs that you may be guided.

104. And let there be a nation from amongst you which calls towards goodness, and orders kindness, and deters from evil. And these are the successful ones.

105. And do not be like those who separated and differed after the clarity had come to them. And for them is a painful retribution.

106. The Day on which faces will be whitened and faces will be blackened; as for those whose faces will be blackened: "Did you reject after believing? Taste the retribution for what you rejected."

107. As for those whose faces are whitened, they are in God's mercy, in it they abide eternally.

108. These are God's revelations, We recite them to you with truth. God does not want wickedness for the worlds.

109. And to God is all that is in heavens and in the Earth; and to God the events will be returned.

110. You were the best nation that emerged for the people, you ordered towards kindness and deterred from evil, and believed in God. If the people of the Scripture believed it would have been better for them; from amongst them are believers, but most remain wicked.

111. They will not harm you except in being an annoyance, and if they fight you they will turn and flee, then they will not be supported.

112. They are stricken with humiliation wherever they are found, except through a rope from God and a rope from the people. And they stayed in God's wrath and were stricken with humiliation; that is because they were disbelieving in God's signs and killing the prophets without just cause; that is for what they disobeyed and were transgressing.

113. They are not all the same, from the people of the Scripture are a nation that is upright; they recite God's revelations during the night and they prostrate.

114. They believe in God and the Last Day and order kindness and deter from evil, and they hasten in goodness; these are of the righteous ones.

115. And what they do of good will not be turned back, and God is aware of the righteous.

116. As for those who rejected, neither their money nor their children will avail them anything from God. These are the people of the Fire, in it they abide eternally.

117. The example of what they spend in this world is like a wind in which there is a frost; it afflicts the field of the people who wronged themselves, and thus destroys it. God did not wrong them, but it was their souls that they wronged.

118. O you who believe do not take protection from any besides yourselves; they will only disrupt you greatly. They wish that you suffer; the hatred appears from their mouths and what their chests hide is greater! We have made clear for you the signs if you comprehend.

119. Here you love them while they do not love you, and you believe in the whole Scripture. And if they meet you they Say: "We believe," and if they are alone they bite their fingers out of frustration at you. Say: "Die in your frustration, God is aware of what is in the chests."

120. If any good befalls you it disturbs them, and if any bad befalls you they rejoice with it. And if you are patient and righteous their planning will not harm you at all. God is Encompassing all they do.

121. Recall when you departed from your family to prepare for the believers their stations for battle, and God is Hearer, Knowledgeable.

122. When the two parties from among you were concerned that they should fail; while God was their supporter. In God the believers should trust.

123. God had granted you victory at Badr, while you had been the lesser, so revere God that you may be thankful.

124. When you said to the believers: "Is it not enough for you that your Lord would supply you with three thousand of the Angels sent down?"

125. Indeed, if you are patient and are righteous and they come and attack you, He will supply you with five thousand of the Angels battle trained.

126. And God did not give this except as good news to you, and so that your hearts may be assured with it. Victory is only from God, the Noble, the Wise.

127. Thus He would sever a group of those who reject, or disgrace them; then they will turn back frustrated.

128. You will have no say in the matter, for He may pardon them, or punish them; for they are wicked.

129. And to God is what is in the heavens and the Earth, He forgives whom He pleases, and He punishes whom He pleases; and God is Forgiving, Merciful.

130. O you who believe, do not consume financial interest multiplying over, and revere God that you may succeed.

131. And be aware of the Fire that has been prepared for the rejecters.

132. And obey God and the messenger so that you may obtain mercy.

133. And race towards forgiveness from your Lord and a Paradise whose width encompasses the width of the heavens and the Earth; it has been prepared for the righteous.

134. The ones who spend in prosperity and adversity, and who repress anger, and who pardon the people; God loves the good doers.

135. And those who, if they commit any evil, or wrong themselves, they remember God and seek forgiveness for their sins. And who can forgive the sins

except God? And they do not persist in what they have done while they know.

136.To these the reward will be forgiveness from their Lord and estates with rivers flowing underneath, eternally abiding in it. Excellent is the reward of the workers.

137.Many nations have come before you, so roam the Earth and see how the punishment for the liars was.

138.This is a clarification for the people and a reminder for the righteous.

139.Do not be weak, and do not grieve, for you will have the upper hand, if you are believers.

140.If you are wounded, then know that the other group is also wounded. And such are the days, We alternate them between the people, so that God will know those who believe, and so He may make witnesses from among you; and God does not like the wicked.

141.And God will test those who believe and He will destroy the rejecters.

142.Or did you think that you would enter Paradise without God distinguishing those who would strive amongst you and knowing those who are patient?

143.And you used to long for death before you came upon it; so now you see it right in-front of you!

144.And Mohammed is but a messenger, like many messengers that have passed before him. If he dies or is killed will you turn back on your heels? And whoever turns back on his heels, he will not harm God in the least. And God will reward the thankful.

145.It is not permitted for a soul to die except by God's leave in an appointed record. And whoever wants the rewards of this world We give him of it, and whoever wants the reward of the Hereafter, We give him of it. And We will reward the thankful.

146.And many a prophet had a large number of devotees fighting with him. They did not waver by what afflicted them in the cause of God, nor did they become weak, nor did they become discouraged; and God loves the patient ones.

147.And they did not say except: "Our Lord, forgive us our sins and our shortcomings in our responsibility, and make firm our foothold, and grant us victory over the rejecting people."

148.So God gave them the reward of this world and the best reward of the Hereafter; and God loves the good doers.

149.O you who believe, if you obey those who have rejected, then they will turn you back on your heels and you will turn back as losers.

150. It is God who is your Patron, and He is the best victor.

151. We will cast terror in the hearts of those who rejected, because of what they have set up besides God while He never sent down any authority to do so, and their destiny is the Fire. Miserable is the abode of the wicked.

152. And God has fulfilled His promise to you, that you would overwhelm them by His leave; but then you failed and disputed in the matter and disobeyed after He showed you what you had sought. Some of you want this world, and some of you want the Hereafter. Then He let you retreat from them that He may test you; and He has pardoned you. God is with great favour over the believers.

153. For you were climbing to the high ground and would not even glance towards anyone, and the messenger was calling to you from behind. Therefore He gave you worry to replace your worry, so that you would not have sadness by what has passed you, or for what afflicted you, and God is Expert over what you do.

154. Then He sent down to you after the worry sanctity in sleepiness, it overtook a group of you; and another group was worried about themselves, they were thinking about God other than the truth, the thoughts of the days of ignorance. They Say: "Why are we involved in this affair?" Say: "The entire affair is for God." They hide in their souls what they do not show to you, they Say: "If we had a say in this affair then none of us would have been killed here." Say: "If you were inside your own homes, then the ones who have been marked for death would have gone forth to their resting place." God will test what is in your chests and bring out what is in your hearts. God is Knowledgeable as to what is in the chests.

155. Those of you who turned away on the day that the two hosts met, it was the devil who caused them to deviate because of some of what they had gained. And God has pardoned them, for God is Forgiver, Compassionate.

156. O you who believe do not be like those who rejected and said to their brothers when they were marching in the land or on the offensive: "If they were here with us they would not have died nor been killed." God will make this a source of grief in their hearts, and God grants life and death, and God is watching over what you do.

157. And if you are killed in the cause of God or die, then forgiveness from God and mercy is far greater than all they can put together.

158. And if you die or are killed, then to God you will be gathered.

159. It was a mercy from God that you were soft towards them; had you been harsh and mean hearted, they would have dispersed from you; so pardon

them and ask forgiveness for them, and consult them in the matter; but when you are convinced, then put your trust in God; God loves those who trust.

160. If God grants you victory then none can defeat you, and if He abandons you then who can grant you victory after Him? And towards God the believers should put their trust.

161. It was not for any prophet that he should embezzle, and he who embezzles will be brought with what he has embezzled on the Day of Resurrection, then every soul will be given what it has earned without being wronged.

162. Is one who follows the pleasure of God, as one who draws the wrath of God and whose abode is Hell? What a miserable destiny!

163. They are grades with God, and God is seer of what they do.

164. God has bestowed favour upon the believers by sending them a messenger from amongst themselves reciting His revelations and bettering them and teaching them the Scripture and the wisdom, and they were before in manifest darkness.

165. And so it was when you suffered setback; even though you afflicted them with twice as much setback; you said: "Where is this coming from?" Say: "It is from yourselves." God is capable of all things.

166. And what you suffered on the day the two hosts met was by God's leave, and to let the believers know.

167. And to let those who are hypocrites know, that they were told: "Come fight in the cause of God or defend," they said: "If we knew how to fight we would have followed you." They are closer to disbelief then they are to belief. They say with their mouths what is not in their hearts, and God is aware of what they conceal.

168. Those who remained and said to their brothers: "If they obeyed us they would not have been killed." Say: "Then avert death away from yourselves if you are truthful!"

169. And do not think that those who are killed in the sake of God are dead. No, they are alive at their Lord receiving a bounty.

170. Happy with what God has granted them from His favour, and they rejoice for those who have yet to follow after them. There is no fear over them nor do they grieve.

171. They rejoice with God's bounty and favour; God will not waste the reward of the believers.

172.Those who have answered God and the messenger after they were afflicted with wounds. For those of them who did good and were righteous is a great reward.

173.The ones who the people said to them: "The people have gathered against you, so be fearful of them," but it only increased their faith and they said: "God is enough for us, and He is the best to put our trust in."

174.So they came back with a reward from God and a bounty, no harm would touch them. And they had followed the pleasure of God, and God is the One with great pleasure.

175.It is only the devil trying to create fear for his allies, so do not fear them, but fear Me if you are believers.

176.And do not be saddened by those who rush into disbelief. They will not harm God in the least. God does not wish to make for them any share in the Hereafter, and they will have a painful retribution.

177.Those who have purchased rejection with belief will not harm God in the least, and they will have a painful retribution.

178.And let not those who reject think that We are providing for them out of the goodness of themselves. We are only providing for them so that they may increase in transgression, and they will have a humiliating retribution.

179.God was not to leave the believers as they were without distinguishing the rotten from the good. And God was not to let you know the future, but God chooses from His messengers whom He wishes; so believe in God and His messengers. And if you believe and are righteous, then you will have a great reward.

180.And let not those who are stingy with what God has given them of His bounty think that it is good for them, no, it is evil for them. They will be surrounded by what they were stingy with on the Day of Resurrection. And to God will be the inheritance of the heavens and the Earth; and God is Expert over what you do.

181.God has heard the words of those who said: "God is poor and we are rich!" We will record what they have said and their killing of the prophets without just cause; and We will Say: "Taste the retribution of the Fire!"

182.This is for what their hands have brought forth, and God does not wrong the servants.

183.Those who said: "God has pledged to us that we should not believe in a messenger unless he brings us an offering which the fire will not devour." Say: "Messengers have come to you before me with clarity and with what you have said, so why did you kill them if you were truthful?"

184. If they reject you, then messengers before you were also rejected; they came with clarity and the Psalms, and the Scripture of enlightenment.

185. Every soul will taste death, and you will be recompensed your dues on the Day of Resurrection. Whoever is swayed from the Fire and entered into Paradise, he has indeed won. This worldly life is nothing more than the enjoyment of vanity.

186. We will test you in your wealth and in yourselves, and you will hear from those who have been given the Scripture from before you and from those who set up partners much annoyance.

187. And God took the covenant of those who were given the Scripture: "You will make it clear to the people and not conceal it." But they threw it behind their backs and purchased with it a cheap price. Miserable indeed is what they have purchased.

188. Do not think that those who are happy with what they have been given, and they love to be praised for what they did not do; do not think they are saved from the punishment. For them is a painful retribution.

189. And to God is the sovereignty of heavens and Earth, and God is capable of all things.

190. In the creation of heavens and Earth, and the difference between night and day, are signs for those with understanding.

191. Those who remember God while standing, and sitting, and on their sides, and they ponder in the creation of the heavens and the Earth: "Our Lord you did not create this without purpose, be You glorified, spare us the retribution of the Fire!"

192. "Our Lord, whoever You admit to the Fire has been disgraced. The wicked will have no supporters."

193. "Our Lord, we have heard a caller inviting to the faith: "Believe in your Lord," so we have believed. Our Lord forgive us our evil deeds and remit our sins, and take us with the obedient ones."

194. "Our Lord, and grant us what You have promised through Your messengers, and do not embarrass us on the Day of Resurrection. You do not break the promise."

195. Their Lord answered them: "I do not waste the work of any worker from among you, be you male or female, you are all as each other. For those who emigrated and were driven-out from their homes and were harmed in My cause, and they fought and were killed, I will remit for them their sins and admit them to paradises with rivers flowing beneath; a reward from God; and God has the best reward."

196. Do not be deceived by the success of those who disbelieved throughout the land.

197. A brief enjoyment, then their abode is Hell. What a miserable abode!

198. As for those who revere their Lord, they will have paradises with rivers flowing beneath; eternally they reside in it as a dwelling from God. What is with God is better for the obedient.

199. And from the people of the Scripture are those who believe in God and what was sent down to you and what was sent down to them; fearful to God, they do not purchase with God's revelations a cheap price. These will have their reward with their Lord. God is quick in reckoning.

200. O you who believe, be patient and call for patience, and bond together and revere God that you may succeed.

Chapter 4

بسم الله الرحمن الرحيم

In the name of God, the Almighty, the Merciful.

1. O mankind, be aware of your Lord who has created you from one soul and He created from it its mate and sent forth from it many men and women; and be aware of God whom you ask about, and the relatives. God is watcher over you.

2. And give the orphans their money, and do not replace the good with the bad, and do not consume their money to your money; for truly it is a great sin!

3. And if you fear that you cannot be just to the orphans, then marry those whom you see fit from their mothers, two, and three, and four. But if you fear you will not be fair, then only one, or whom you are already betrothed to. This is best that you do not face financial hardship.

4. And give the women their property willingly, and if they remit any of it to you of their own will, then you may take it with good feelings.

5. And do not give the immature ones their money that God has entrusted to you, and spend on them from it and clothe them, and speak to them in goodness.

6. And test the orphans until they reach the age of marriage, then if you determine in them sound judgment, then give them their wealth, and do not deliberately consume it wastefully or quickly before they grow up. And whoever is rich, then let him not claim anything, and if he is poor then let him consume only in goodness. If you give to them their wealth, then make a witness for them, and God is enough for Reckoning.

7. For the men is a portion from what the parents and the relatives left behind, and for the women is a portion from what the parents and relatives left behind, be it little or much; a forced portion.

8. And if the distribution is attended by the relatives and the orphans and the needy, then you shall give them part of it and say to them a kind saying.

9. And what if it was them who had left behind them a weak progeny, would they not be concerned for them? Let them revere God and let them say what is appropriate.

10. Those who consume the money of the orphans illicitly, in fact they are consuming fire in their bellies, and they will endure the Blaze.

11. God directs you regarding the inheritance of your children: "To the male shall be as that given to two females. If they are only females and more than two, then they will have two thirds of what is inherited. And if there is only one female, then she will have one half, and to his parents each one of them one sixth of what is inherited if he has children. If he has no children and his parents are the heirs, then to his mother is one third; if he has siblings then to his mother is one sixth. All after a will is carried through or a debt. Your parents and your children, you do not know which is closer to you in benefit, a directive from God, God is Knowledgeable, Wise."

12. And for you is half of what your wives leave behind if they have no children; but if they have a child then to you is one quarter of what they leave behind. All after a will is carried through or a debt. And to them is one quarter of what you leave behind if you have no child; but if you have a child then to them is one eighth of what you leave behind. All after a will is carried through or a debt. And if a man or a woman has no one, but has a brother or sister, then to each one of them is one sixth, but if they are more than this then they are to share in one third. All after a will is carried through or a debt, which does not cause harm. A directive from God, and God is Knowledgeable, Compassionate.

13. These are God's limits, and whoever obeys God and His messenger, He will admit him to estates with rivers flowing beneath, eternally abiding therein. This is the greatest victory.

14. And whoever disobeys God and His messenger, and transgresses His limits, He will admit him to a Fire in which he abides eternally, and he will have a humiliating retribution.

15. And those women who commit lewdness, you shall bring four witnesses over them from amongst you; if they bear witness, then you shall restrict them in the homes until death takes them, or God makes for them a way out.

16. And the two men who commit it from amongst you, then you shall punish them. If they repent and amend, then leave them alone. God is Redeemer, Merciful.

17. Repentance is only for those who commit sin out of ignorance and then repent soon after; these will be forgiven by God, God is Knowledgeable, Wise.

18. And there will be no repentance for those who commit sin until death comes upon one of them, then he says: "I repent now!", nor for those who die while they are disbelievers. To those We have prepared a painful retribution.

19. O you who believe, it is not lawful for you to inherit the women by force, nor that you become harsh with them to take away some of what you have given them, unless they commit a clear lewdness. And live with them in kindness. If you dislike them, then perhaps you may dislike something and God makes in it much good.

20. And if you wish to replace one wife instead of another, and you have given one of them a large amount, then do not take anything from it. Would you take it by falsehood while it is clearly a sin?

21. And how can you take it when you have become intimate with each other, and the women have taken from you a strong covenant.

22. And do not marry what your fathers had married from the women, except what has already been done. It is a lewdness, and an abhorrence, and a bad path.

23. Forbidden for you are your mothers, and your daughters, and your sisters, and your fathers' sisters, and your mothers' sisters, and the daughters of your brother, and the daughters of your sister, and your foster mothers who suckled you, and your sisters from suckling, and the mothers of your wives, and your step-daughters residing in your homes from your wives which you have already consummated the marriage with; if you have not consummated the marriage then there is no sin upon you; and the wives of your sons that are from your seed, and that you join between two sisters except what has already been done. God is Forgiving, Merciful.

24. And the already married from the women, except those who become widowed; God's scripture is over you; and permitted for you is what is beyond this, if you are seeking with your money to be protected and not for illicit sex. As for those whom you have already had joy with them, then you shall give them their wage as an obligation. There is no sin upon you for what you agree to after the obligation. God is Knowledgeable, Wise.

25. And whoever of you cannot afford to marry the believing independent women, then from the still dependant believing young women. God is more aware of your faith, some of you to each other. You shall marry them with the permission of their parents and give them their wage in kindness; to be protected, not for illicit sex or taking lovers. If they become protected, then any of them who comes with lewdness shall have half the punishment of what is for the independent women of the retribution. This is for those who fear hardship from among you. But if you are patient it is better for you, and God is Forgiver, Merciful.

26. God wants to make clear for you and guide you to the ways of those before you, and pardon you, and God is Knowledgeable, Wise.

27. And God wants to pardon you, but those who follow their lusts want that you would be diverted into a great diversion.

28. God wants to make easy for you; and mankind was created weak.

29. O you who believe, do not consume your money between you unjustly, except through a trade which is mutually agreed by you. And do not kill yourselves; God is Merciful towards you.

30. And whoever does so out of animosity and transgression, We will cast him to a Fire; and this for God is very easy.

31. If you avoid the major sins that you are forbidden against, then We will cancel your existing sins and admit you to a generous entrance.

32. And do not envy what God has favoured some of you over others. For the men is a portion of what they gained, and for the women is a portion of what they gained. And ask God from His favour, God is knowledgeable over all things.

33. And for each We have made inheritors for what was left behind by the parents and the relatives. And those whom are dependant on you, you shall give them their portion. God is witness over all things.

34. The men are to support the women by what God has gifted them over one another and for what they spend of their money. The upright women who are attentive, and keep private the personal matters for what God keeps watch over. As for those women from whom you fear a desertion, then you shall advise them, and abandon them in the bedchamber, and separate from them; if they obey you, then do not seek a way over them; God is High, Great.

35. And if you fear a split between them, then send a judge from his family and a judge from hers. If they want to reconcile, then God will bring them together. God is Knowledgeable, Expert.

36. And serve God and do not set up anything with Him, and be kind to the parents, and the relatives, and the needy, and the neighbour who is of kin, and the neighbour next door, and the friend far away, and the traveller, and those who are still dependent. God does not like the arrogant, the boastful.

37. Those who are stingy and order the people to stinginess, and they conceal what God has given them from His bounty. We have prepared for these disbelievers a painful retribution.

38. And those who spend their money to show-off to the people, and they do not believe in God or the Last Day. And whoever has the devil as his companion, then what a miserable companion!

39. What would bother them if they believed in God and the Last Day and spent from God's provisions? God is aware of them.

40. Indeed, God does not wrong an atom's weight; and if it is good He will double it. And He grants from Himself a great reward.

41. How is it then when We bring forth from every nation a witness, and bring you as a witness over these?

42. On that Day those who rejected and disobeyed the messenger will wish that the Earth would swallow them; but they cannot hide anything said from God.

43. O you who believe, do not approach the oath of allegiance while you are intoxicated, until you know what you are saying. Nor if you have had intercourse, unless travelling, until you bathe. And if you are ill, or traveling, or one of you has excreted feces, or you had sexual contact with the women, and could not find water, then you shall select from the clean soil; you shall wipe your faces and hands. God is Pardoning, Forgiving.

44. Did you not see those who have been given a portion of the Scripture? They purchased straying, and they want you to stray from the path.

45. And God is fully aware of your enemies; and God is enough as a supporter, and God is enough as a victor.

46. From amongst the Jews there are those who take the words out of context, and they Say: "We hear and disobey, and listen but let not any listen, and shepherd us," in a twisting of their tongues and as a mockery of the system! And had they said: "We hear and obey, and listen, and watch over us," it would have been better for them and more upright; but God has cursed them for their disbelief, they do not believe except very little.

47. O you who have received the Scripture, believe in what We have sent down authenticating what is with you, before We cast down faces and turn them

on their backs or curse them as the people of the Sabbath were cursed. And God's will is always done.

48. God does not forgive that partners be set up with Him, and He forgives what is beside that for whom He wills. Whoever sets-up partners with God has indeed invented a great sin.

49. Did you not see those who boast about themselves? No, it is God who promotes whom He wills, and they will not be wronged in the least.

50. See how they invent upon God the lies; is that not enough as a clear sin?

51. Did you not see those who were given a portion of the Scripture, they believe in witchcraft and evil, and they say to those who disbelieved: "You are better guided than those who believed the path."

52. These are the ones whom God has cursed, and whoever God curses, you will not find for him a victor.

53. Or would they have a portion of the sovereignty? If so, then they would not give the people a speck.

54. Or do they envy the people for what God has given them of His bounty? We have given the descendants of Abraham the Scripture and the wisdom; We have given them a great kingship.

55. Some of them believed in it, and some of them turned from it. In Hell will be enough flames.

56. Those who have rejected Our signs, We will admit them to a Fire. Every time their skins are cooked, We replace them with other skin that they may taste the retribution. God is Noble, Wise.

57. And those who believe and do good, We will admit them to estates with rivers flowing beneath, eternally they abide therein, in it they will have pure spouses, and We will admit them to a vast shade.

58. God orders you to deliver anything you have been entrusted with to its owners. And if you judge between the people, then you shall judge with justice. It is always the best that God prescribes for you. God is Hearer, Seer.

59. O you who believe, obey God and obey the messenger and those entrusted amongst you. But if you dispute in any matter, then you shall refer it to God and His messenger if you believe in God and the Last Day. That is better and more suitable for knowing.

60. Did you not see those who claimed they believed in what was sent down to you and what was sent before you? They wanted to seek judgment using evil, while they were ordered to reject it. It is the devil who wants to lead them far astray.

61. And if they are told: "Come to what God has sent down and to the messenger," you see the hypocrites turning away from you strongly.

62. Why then, when a tragedy befalls them for what their hands have brought forth do they come to you swearing by God that they only wanted to do good and reconcile?

63. These are a people whom God knows what is in their hearts, so turn away from them and advise them, and speak to their souls with a clear saying.

64. We do not send a messenger except to be obeyed by God's leave. And had they come to you when they had wronged themselves and sought God's forgiveness, and the messenger sought forgiveness for them, they would have then found God to be Pardoning, Merciful.

65. No, by your Lord, they will not believe until they make you judge in what they dispute with each other, then they will not find in their souls any animosity for what you have decided, and they will yield completely.

66. And had We decreed for them: "Kill yourselves," or "Leave your land," they would not have done so except for a few of them. And if they had done what they were advised with, it would have been better for them and helped to strengthen them.

67. Then We would have given them from Us a great reward.

68. And We would have guided them to a Straight Path.

69. And whoever obeys God and the messenger will be among those whom God has blessed from the prophets and the truthful and the martyrs and the upright. What an excellent companionship!

70. That is the bounty from God; and God knows what is best.

71. O you who believe, take your precaution by going out in clusters, or going out all together.

72. And from among you will be those that would lag behind, so that if disaster afflicts you he would Say: "God has blessed me that I was not a martyr with them!"

73. And if favour from God benefits you, he will speak as if there had been affection between you and him: "Oh, I wish I had been with them so I would win a great prize."

74. Let those who seek to purchase the Hereafter rather than this world fight in the cause of God. And whoever fights in the cause of God and is killed or attains victory, then We will grant him a great reward.

75. And why do you not fight in the cause of God, when the weak amongst the men and women and children Say: "Our Lord, bring us out of this town

whose people are wicked, and grant us from Yourself a Supporter, and grant us from Yourself a Victor!"

76. Those who believe fight in the cause of God, while those who reject fight in the cause of evil; so fight the supporters of the devil, for the planning of the devil is weak.

77. Did you not see those who were told: "Restrain yourselves, and honour the oath of allegiance, and contribute towards betterment." But when fighting was decreed for them, a group of them feared the people as much as they feared God or even more so. And they said: "Our Lord, why did You decree fighting for us? If only You would delay for us till another time." Say: "The enjoyment of this world is little, and the Hereafter is far better for those who are aware; you will not be wronged in the least."

78. Wherever you may be, death will find you, even if you are in fortified towers. If any good befalls them, they Say: "This is from God," and if any bad befalls them, they Say: "This is from you!" Say: "All is from God;" what is wrong with these people, they barely understand anything said!

79. Any good that befalls you is from God, and any bad that befalls you is from yourself. We have sent you as a messenger to the people and God is enough as a witness.

80. Whoever obeys the messenger has obeyed God; and whoever turns away, We have not sent you as a guardian over them.

81. And they Say: "Obedience," but when they emerge from you a group of them prepares for other that what you have said, and God records what they planned. So turn away from them and put your trust in God. God is enough for your trust.

82. Do they not reflect on the Quran? If it was from any other than God they would have found it very different.

83. And if any matter regarding security, or fear, comes to them they make it publicly known, but if they had referred it to the messenger and to those entrusted from them then it would have been known by those who studied it from them. And had it not been for God's grace upon you and His mercy, you would have followed the devil, except for a few.

84. So fight in the cause of God; you are not responsible except for yourself. And enjoin the believers: "Perhaps God will put a stop to the might of those who disbelieved." And God is far Mightier and far more Punishing.

85. Whoever intercedes a good intercession, he will have a reward of it; and whoever intercedes an evil intercession, he will receive a share of it. And God has control over all things.

86. And if you are greeted with a greeting, then return an even better greeting or return the same. God is Reckoning over all things.

87. God, there is no god but He. He will gather you for the Day of Resurrection in which there is no doubt. Who is more truthful in saying than God?

88. What is the matter with you that you are divided into two groups over the hypocrites, while God has regressed them for what they have earned? Do you want to guide those whom God misguides? Whoever God causes to be misguided, you will never find for him a way.

89. They hope that you would reject as they rejected, then you would be the same. Do not take any of them as allies until they emigrate in the cause of God. If they turn away, then take them and kill them where you find them; and do not take from them any ally or supporter.

90. Except for those who reach a people between whom you have a covenant, or if they come to you with a reluctance in their chests to fight you or to fight their own people. Had God willed He would have given them strength and they would have fought you. But if they retire from you, and did not fight you, and they offer you peace; then God does not make for you a way against them.

91. You will find others who want to be safe amongst you and safe amongst their own people. Every time they are returned to the test, they fall back in it. If they do not withdraw from you, and offer you peace, and restrain their hands, then you shall take them and kill them where you find them. For these We have given you a clear authority.

92. And it is not for a believer to kill another believer except by accident. And whoever kills a believer by accident, then he shall set free a believing slave, and give compensation to the family; except if they remit it. If he was from a people who are enemies to you, and he was a believer, then you shall set free a believing slave. And if he was from a people between whom you had a covenant, then a compensation to his family, and set free a believing slave. Whoever does not find, then the fasting of two months sequentially as a repentance from God; God is Knowledgeable, Wise.

93. And whoever kills a believer intentionally, then his reward shall be Hell, eternally abiding therein, and God will be angry with him, and curse him, and for him is prepared a great retribution.

94. O you who believe, if you attack in the cause of God then make a clear declaration, and do not say to those who greet you with peace: "You are not a believer!" You are seeking the vanity of this world; but with God are many

riches. That is how you were before, but God favoured you, so make a clear declaration. God is expert over what you do.

95. Not equal are those who stayed behind from the believers; except those disabled; with those who strived in the cause of God with their money and lives. God has preferred those who strive with their money and lives over those who stayed behind by a grade; and to both God has promised goodness; and God has preferred the strivers over those who stay by a great reward.

96. Grades from Him and forgiveness and a mercy. God is Forgiving, Merciful.

97. Those whom the Angels seize, while they had wronged their souls; they said: "What situation were you in?", they said: "We were oppressed on Earth." They said: "Was God's Earth not wide enough that you could emigrate in it?" To these their abode will be Hell; what a miserable destiny!

98. Except for those who were oppressed from the men, women, and children who could not devise a plan nor could be guided to a way.

99. For these, perhaps God will pardon them. God is Pardoner, Forgiving.

100. Whoever emigrates in the cause of God will find in the land many spoils and a bounty. And whoever leaves his home emigrating to God and His messenger, then is overcome by death; his reward has fallen to God, and God is Forgiving, Merciful.

101. And if you are on the offensive in the land, then there is no harm that you shorten from the oath of allegiance, if you fear that the disbelievers will try you. The disbelievers are to you a clear enemy.

102. And if you are with them and you perform the oath of allegiance for them, then let a group from amongst them stand with you and let them bring their weapons; and when they have prostrated then let them stand guard from behind; and let a group who has not yet made the oath of allegiance come and make the oath of allegiance with you, and let them be wary and let them bring their weapons with them. The rejecters hope that you would neglect your weapons and goods so they can come upon you in one blow. There is no sin upon you if you are impeded by rainfall, or if you are ill, that you place down your weapons. And be wary. God has prepared for the rejecters a humiliating retribution.

103. So when you are done making the oath of allegiance, then remember God while standing, or sitting, or on your sides; then, when you are relieved, you shall honour the oath of allegiance. Indeed, the oath of allegiance for the believers is a timed decree.

104. And do not falter in the pursuit of the remaining group. If you are feeling pain, then they are also feeling pain as you are; and you seek from God what they do not seek. God is Knowledgeable, Wise.
105. We have revealed to you the Scripture with truth that you may judge between the people by that which God has shown you, and do not be an advocate for the treacherous.
106. And seek forgiveness from God; God is Forgiver, Merciful.
107. And do not argue on behalf of those who betray themselves. God does not like those who are betrayers, sinners.
108. They may conceal this from the people, but they do not conceal it from God, and He was with them when they schemed what He does not approve of to be said. God is Encompassing what they do.
109. Here you are arguing on their behalf in this world, but who will argue on their behalf with God on the Day of Resurrection? or who will be their sponsor?
110. And whoever does any evil, or wrongs himself, then seeks God's forgiveness; he will find God Forgiving, Merciful.
111. And whoever earns any sin, then he has brought it on himself. And God is Knowledgeable, Wise.
112. And whoever does a mistake or wrongdoing, then blames it on an innocent person; he has incurred falsehood and a clear sin.
113. And had it not been for God's favour upon you and His mercy, when a group of them were insistent on misguiding you; they would not have misguided except themselves, nor would they harm you in anything. And God has sent down to you the Scripture and the wisdom, and He has taught you that which you did not know. God's grace upon you is great.
114. There is no good in most of what they desire, except whoever orders a charity or kindness or reconciliation between the people. And whoever does this seeking God's favour, We will give him a great reward.
115. And whoever is hostile to the messenger after the guidance has been made clear to him, and he follows other than the path of the believers; We will grant him what he has sought and deliver him to Hell; what a miserable destination.
116. God does not forgive to have partners set up with Him, but He forgives other than that for whom He pleases. Whoever sets-up partners with God has indeed strayed a far straying.
117. They are only calling on females beside God. Indeed, they are only calling on a persistent devil.

118. God has cursed him; and he had said: "I will take from Your servants a size-able portion."

119. "And I will misguide them and make them desire, and I will command them, so that they will mark the ears of the livestock, and I will command them so they will make change to God's creation." Whoever takes the devil as a supporter other than God, then he has indeed lost a great loss.

120. He promises them and makes them desire, but what the devil promises them is only vanity.

121. For these, their abode shall be Hell, they will find no escape from it.

122. As for those who believe and do good work, We will admit them to estates with rivers flowing beneath, eternally they will abide therein. God's promise is truth; and who is more truthful in saying than God?

123. It will not be by what you desire, nor by what the people of the Scripture desire. Whoever works evil, he will be paid by it; and he will not find for himself besides than God any supporter or victor.

124. And whoever works good be he male or female, and he is a believer, then these will be admitted to Paradise, and they will not be wronged in the least.

125. And who is better in the system than one who submits himself to God, and is a good doer, and he followed the creed of Abraham in monotheism? And God has taken Abraham as a friend.

126. And to God is what is in heavens and in the Earth; God is Encompassing over all things.

127. And they seek a ruling regarding the women, Say: "God will give you a ruling regarding them and what is being recited to you in the Scripture regarding the orphan's mothers whom you wish to marry, but have not given them what was decreed for them; as well as the weak from the children: That you stand for the orphans in equality." Whatever good you do, then God is aware of it.

128. And if a woman fears from her husband desertion, or ill-treatment, then there is no sin for them to reconcile between themselves; and reconciliation is good. And the souls are brought by need. And if you are kind and do right, then God is expert over what you do.

129. And you will not be able to be fair regarding the women even if you make every effort; so do not sway too greatly and leave her as one hanging in a void. And if you reconcile and do right, then God is Forgiving, Merciful.

130. And if they separate, then God will provide for each of them from His bounty. God is Vast, Wise.

131. And to God is what is in the heavens and the Earth; and We have recommended to those who were given the Scripture before you, and you, to be aware of God. And if you reject, then to God is all that is in heavens and in Earth; God is Rich, Praiseworthy.

132. And to God is all that is in the heavens and all that is in the Earth; and God is enough as a Caretaker.

133. O you people, if He wills, He could make all of you cease to exist; then He would bring others in your place. God is most capable to do this.

134. Whoever seeks the reward of this world, then with God is the reward of this world and the Hereafter. God is Hearing, Watchful.

135. O you who believe, stand with justice as witnesses to God, even if against yourselves, or the parents or the relatives. Even if he be rich or poor, God is more worthy of them, so do not follow your desires from being just. And if you twist or turn away, then God is Expert over what you do.

136. O you who believe; believe in God and His messenger, and the Scripture which was sent down to His messenger, and the Scripture that was sent before. And whoever rejects God, and His Angels, and His Scriptures, and His messengers, and the Last Day; then he has strayed a far straying.

137. Those who believe, then reject, then believe, then reject, then they increase in rejection; God was neither to forgive them nor to guide them to the path.

138. Give news to the hypocrites that they will have a painful retribution.

139. Those who take the rejecters as allies instead of the believers: "Do they seek glory with them?" All glory belongs to God.

140. And it has been sent down to you in the Scripture, that if you hear God's revelations being rejected and ridiculed in, then do not sit with them until they move on to a different subject; if not, then you are like them. God will gather the hypocrites and the disbelievers in Hell all together.

141. Those who linger and observe you, if you have a victory from God they Say: "Were we not with you?" And if the rejecters have success, they Say: "Did we not side with you and deter the believers from you?" God will judge between you on the Day of Resurrection, and God will not grant the rejecters any success over the believers.

142. The hypocrites seek to deceive God, while He is deceiving them; and if they stand to make the oath of allegiance, they do so lazily, only to show the people; they do not remember God except very little.

143. They are swaying in-between, neither belonging to this group nor to that group. Whoever God will misguide, you will not find for him a way.

144. O you who believe, do not take the rejecters as allies instead of the believers. Do you want God to have a reason against you?

145. The hypocrites will be in the lowest level of the Fire; and you will not find for them a victor.

146. Except those who repent, and amend, and hold fast to God, and purify their system to God; then these will be with the believers. And God will grant the believers a great reward.

147. What would God want with your punishment if you were only thankful and believed? God is Appreciative, Knowledgeable.

148. God does not like that any negative sayings be publicized, except if one is wronged. God is Hearer, Knowledgeable.

149. If you reveal what is good or hide it, or forgive what is bad, then God is Pardoner, Capable.

150. Those who rejected God and His messengers, and they want to make a distinction between God and His messengers, and they Say: "We believe in some and reject some!", and they desire to take a path in-between.

151. These are the true rejecters; and We have prepared for the rejecters a humiliating retribution.

152. And those who believe in God and His messengers and do not make a distinction between any of them, We will give them their rewards. And God is Forgiving, Merciful.

153. The people of the Scripture ask you to bring down to them a scripture from the heavens. They had asked Moses for even more than that, for they said: "Let us see God plainly!", so the lightning bolt took them for their wickedness. Then they took the calf after the clarity had come to them, and We pardoned them for this; We gave Moses a clear authority.

154. And We raised the mount to be above because of the covenant they took, and We said to them: "Enter the passageway by crouching." And We said to them: "Do not transgress the Sabbath;" and We took from them a solemn covenant.

155. So, for the breaking of their covenant, and their rejection of God's signs, and their killing of the prophets without justice, and their saying: "Our hearts are layered over." Indeed, God has stamped upon their hearts because of their rejection; they do not believe, except for a few.

156. And for their rejection and them saying about Mary a great falsehood.

157. And their saying: "We have killed the Messiah Jesus the son of Mary, the messenger of God!" They did not kill him, nor did they crucify him, but it appeared to them as if they had. Those who dispute are in doubt of him,

they have no knowledge except to follow conjecture; they did not kill him for a certainty.

158. For God raised him to Himself; and God is Noble, Wise.

159. And from the people of the Scripture are few who would have believed in him before his death, and on the Day of Resurrection he will be witness against them.

160. Because of the wickedness from those who are Jews, We made forbidden to them the good things that were lawful to them; and for their deterring many from the path of God.

161. And for them taking financial interest when they were told not to, and for them consuming peoples money unjustly. We have prepared for the disbelievers amongst them a painful retribution.

162. But those of them who are firm in knowledge, as well as the believers, they believe in what was sent down to you and what was sent down before you; and those who honour the oath of allegiance, and those who contribute towards betterment, and those who believe in God and the Last Day; to these We will give them their reward greatly.

163. We have inspired you as We have inspired Noah and the prophets after him. And We inspired Abraham, and Ishmael, and Isaac, and Jacob, and the Patriarchs, and Jesus, and Job, and Jonah, and Aaron, and Solomon; and We have given David the Psalms.

164. And messengers of whom We have narrated to you from before, and messengers We have not narrated to you; and God spoke to Moses directly.

165. Messengers who were bearers of good news and warners, so that there will be no excuse for the people with God after the messengers. God is Noble, Wise.

166. But God bears witness for what He has sent down to you with His knowledge, and the Angels bear witness; and God is enough as a witness.

167. Those who have rejected and turned away from the path of God, they have strayed a far straying.

168. Those who have rejected and did wrong, God was not to forgive them, nor guide them to a path.

169. Except to the path of Hell, in it they will abide eternally. For God this is very easy.

170. O mankind, a messenger has come to you with truth from your Lord, so believe; that is better for you. And if you disbelieve, then to God is what is in heavens and Earth. And God is Knowledgeable, Wise.

171. O people of the Scripture, do not overstep in your system, nor say about God except the truth. Jesus the son of Mary was no more than God's mes-

senger and the fulfillment of His word to Mary, and a spirit from Him. So believe in God and His messengers, and do not Say: "Trinity." Cease, for it is better for you. God is only One god, be He glorified that He should have a son! To Him is all that is in the heavens and what is in the Earth. God is enough as a caretaker.

172. The Messiah is not too proud to be a servant to God, nor are the Angels who are close to Him. Whoever is too proud from His service, and is arrogant, then He will gather them all towards Him together.

173. As for those who believe and do good works, He will give them their rewards and increase for them from His bounty. And as for those who are too proud and arrogant, He will punish them a painful retribution, and they will not find besides God any supporter or victor.

174. O mankind, a proof has come to you from your Lord, and We have sent down to you a guiding light.

175. As for those who believe in God and hold fast to Him, He will admit them in a mercy from Him and a bounty, and He will guide them to Himself, a Straight Path.

176. They seek a ruling from you, Say: "God gives you the ruling for those who have no descendants. If a person passes away and has no children but has a sister, then she shall receive half of what he leaves behind. And he will inherit her fully if she has no child. However, if he has two sisters, then they will receive two thirds of what he left behind; and if he has siblings, male and female, then the male shall receive twice what the female receives." God makes clear to you that you do not stray; God is aware of all things.

Chapter 5

بسم الله الرحمن الرحيم

In the name of God, the Almighty, the Merciful.

1. O you who believe, honour your contracts. Made lawful for you are all the animals of the livestock, except that which is being recited to you, and what you are not allowed to hunt of the game while you are under restriction. God decrees as He pleases.

2. O you who believe, do not violate God's decrees, nor the restricted month, nor the donations, nor what is regulated, nor the safety made by the Restricted Sanctuary; for they are seeking a bounty from their Lord and a blessing. And when it is permitted for you, then you may hunt. And let not the hatred of another people; because they had barred you from the Restricted Temple; make you aggress. And bond together in piety and righteousness, and do not bind together in sin and aggression. And be aware of God, for God's retribution is severe.

3. Forbidden to you is that which is already dead, and the blood, and the meat of pig, and what was sacrificed to other than God, and that which has been strangled, and that which has been beaten to death, and that which has fallen from a height, and that which has been gored, and that which the wild animals have eaten from except what you managed to rescue, and what has been slaughtered on alters, and what you divide by the arrows of chance. This is all vile. Today the rejecters have given up from your system, so do not fear them, but fear Me. Today I have perfected your system for you, and completed My blessings upon you, and I have accepted submission as the system for you. So, whoever is forced by severe hunger and not seeking sin, then God is Forgiving, Merciful.

4. They ask you what was made lawful to them, Say: "All the good things have been made lawful for you, and what the trained dogs and birds catch, you teach them from what God teaches you." So eat from what they have captured for you and mention God's name upon it, and be aware of God. God is quick in reckoning.

5. Today, the good things have been made lawful to you, and the food of those who have been given the Scripture is lawful for you, and your food is lawful for them; and the independent from the believing women, and the independent from the people of the Scripture before you, if you have given them their dowries, protected, chaste, and not seeking to take lovers. And whoever rejects belief, then his work has fallen, and in the Hereafter he is of the losers.

6. O you who believe, if you rise to perform the oath of allegiance, then wash your faces and your hands up to the elbows, and wipe your heads and your feet to the ankles; and if you have had intercourse, then you shall bathe. And if you are ill, or traveling, or you have excreted feces, or you have had sexual contact with the women, and you could not find water, then you shall select from the clean soil; you shall wipe your faces and your hands with it. God does not want to make any hardship over you, but He wants to cleanse you and to complete His blessings upon you that you may be appreciative.

7. And recall God's blessings over you and His covenant that He has bound you with, for which you have said: "We hear and obey," and be aware of God; for God knows what is inside the chests.

8. O you who believe, stand for God and be witnesses for justice, and let not the hatred towards a people make you avoid being just. Be just, for it is closer to righteousness, and be aware of God. God is expert over what you do.

9. God has promised those who believe and do right that they will have forgiveness and a great reward.

10. And those who reject and deny Our revelations, they are the dwellers of Hell.

11. O you who believe, recall God's blessings upon you when a group desired to aggress against you, and He restrained their hands from you. And reverence God. And in God the believers should put their trust.

12. God has taken the covenant of the Children of Israel and sent from them twelve representatives, and God said: "I am with you if you honour the oath of allegiance, and contribute towards betterment, and believe in My messengers, and support them, and give God a loan of righteousness; then I will cancel your sins and admit you into estates with rivers flowing beneath." Whoever rejects after this from you, then he has strayed from the path.

13. But because of them breaking their covenant, We have cursed them, and made their hearts become hardened; they take the words out of context; and they forgot much of what they were reminded of. And you will still discover betrayal in them except for a few; so pardon them and overlook; God loves the good doers.

14. And from those who have said: "We are Nazarenes," We have taken their covenant and they have forgotten much of what they were reminded of; so We planted between them animosity and hatred till the Day of Resurrection; and God will inform them of what they had done.

15. O people of the Scripture, Our messenger has come to you to clarify for you much of what you were hiding from the Scripture, and to pardon over much. A light has come to you from God and a clarifying Scripture.

16. God guides with it whoever follows His acceptance, to the ways of peace; and He brings them out of the darkness and into the light by His leave; and He guides them to a Straight Path.

17. Rejecters indeed are those who have said: "God is the Messiah the son of Mary." Say: "Who has any power against God if He had wanted to destroy the Messiah son of Mary, and his mother, and all who are on Earth!" And to God is the sovereignty of heavens and Earth and all that is in-between; He creates what He pleases. God is capable of all things.

18. And the Jews and the Nazarenes said: "We are God's children, and His loved ones." Say: "Then why does He punish you for your sins?" No, you are merely humans from what He has created. He forgives whom He pleases, and He punishes whom He pleases. And to God is the sovereignty of heavens and Earth and all that is in-between, and to Him is the destiny.

19. O people of the Scripture, Our messenger has come to clarify for you after a lack of messengers; so that you cannot Say: "No bearer of good news or warner has come to us;" for a bearer of good news and a warner has come to you; and God is capable of all things.

20. And Moses said to his people: "My people, remember God's favour upon you that he made amongst you prophets, and made you kings, and he gave you what He had not given any from the worlds."

21. "O my people, enter the holy land that God Has decreed for you, and do not turn your backs, or you will become losers."

22. They said: "O Moses, in it are a mighty people, and we will not enter it until they leave. So when they leave, then we will enter it."

23. Two men who were from among those that were aware; and God had bestowed upon both of them; said: "Enter upon them through the gate, if

you enter it then you will be the victors; and put your trust in God if you are believers."

24. They said: "O Moses, we will never enter it as long as they are in it, so go you and your Lord and fight, we will stay right here!"

25. He said: "My Lord, I do not posses except myself and my brother, so separate between us and between the wicked people."

26. He said: "Then it has become forbidden for them for forty years, and they will be lost in the land." Do not be sorrowful over the wicked people.

27. And recite for them the news of Adam's two sons in truth. They had both made an offering, and it was accepted from one of them, and not accepted from the other. He said: "I will kill you!"; he said: "God only accepts from the righteous."

28. "If you stretch your hand to kill me, I will not stretch my hand to kill you, for I fear God, the Lord of the worlds."

29. "I want you to have both my sin as well as your own sin, and you will then be among the dwellers of the Fire. Such is the reward of the wicked."

30. So he found it in himself to kill his brother; so he killed him. He thus became one of the losers.

31. So God sent forth a raven to scratch the land and show him how to deal with the sin inflicted upon his brother. He said: "O my, am I not able to be like this raven and deal with the sin inflicted upon my brother!" So he became of those who regretted.

32. It is because of this that We have decreed for the Children of Israel: "Anyone who kills a person who has not committed murder, or who has not committed corruption in the land; then it is as if he has killed all the people! And whoever spares a life, then it is as if he has given life to all the people." Our messengers had come to them with clarification, but many of them are, after this, still corrupting on the Earth.

33. The recompense of those who fight God and His messenger, and seek to make corruption in the land, is that they will be killed or crucified or that their hands and feet be cut off on alternate sides or that they be banished from the land; that is a disgrace for them in this world and in the Hereafter they will have a great retribution.

34. Except for those who repent before you overpower them, then know that God is Forgiving, Merciful.

35. O you who believe, be aware of God and seek a way to Him, and strive in His cause; that you may succeed.

36. Those who have rejected, if they had all that is on Earth and the same again with it to ransom against the retribution of the Day of Resurrection, it will not be accepted from them; and they will have a painful retribution.

37. They want to get out of the Fire, but they can never leave it; and they will have a permanent retribution.

38. The male thief, and the female thief, you shall cut from their resources as a punishment for their crime, and to serve as a deterrent from God. God is Noble, Wise.

39. Whoever repents after his wrongdoing and makes reparations, then God will accept his repentance. God is Forgiving, Merciful.

40. Did you not know that God possesses the sovereignty of heavens and Earth. He punishes whom He wills and He forgives whom He wills; and God is capable of all things.

41. O messenger, do not be saddened by those who increase in disbelief from among those who said: "We believe" with their mouths while their hearts did not believe. And from among the Jews, there are those who listened to lies; they listened to people who never came to you; they distort the words from their context, and they Say: "If you are given this, then take it, but if you are given anything different, then beware!" And whoever God wants to test, then you will not posses anything for him against God. These are the ones whose hearts God did not want to cleanse; in this world they will have humiliation, and in the Hereafter they will have a great retribution.

42. They listen to lies, and consume money illicitly. If they come to you, then you may judge between them or turn away from them; and if you turn away from them then they cannot harm you in the least; and if you judge then judge between them with justice. God loves those who are just.

43. And how can they make you their judge when they have the Torah, in which is God's judgment; then they turn away after that. Those are not believers.

44. We have sent down the Torah, in it is guidance and a light; the prophets who have submitted judged with it for those who are Jews, as well as the Rabbis, and the Priests, for what they were entrusted of God's Scripture, and they were witness over. So do not fear the people but fear Me; and do not purchase with My revelations a cheap price. And whoever does not judge with what God has sent down, then these are the rejecters.

45. And We have decreed for them in it that a life for a life, and an eye for an eye, and a nose for a nose, and an ear for an ear, and a tooth for a tooth, and wounds to be similar; and whoever remits anything of it, then it will cancel

sins for him. And whoever does not judge with what God has sent down, then these are the wicked.

46. And We sent in their footsteps Jesus the son of Mary, authenticating what was present with him of the Torah. And We gave him the Injeel, in it is guidance and light, and to authenticate what is present with him of the Torah, and a guidance and lesson for the righteous.

47. And let the people of the Injeel judge with what God has sent down in it. And whoever does not judge with what God has sent down, then these are the vile ones.

48. And We have sent down to you the Scripture with truth, authenticating what is present of the Scripture and superseding it. So judge between them by what God has sent down, and do not follow their desires from what has come to you of the truth. For each of you We have made laws, and a structure; and had God willed, He would have made you all one nation, but He tests you with what He has given you; so strive to do good. To God you will return all of you, and He will inform you regarding that in which you dispute.

49. And judge between them by what God has sent down, and do not follow their wishes, and beware lest they divert you away from some of what God has sent down to you. If they turn away, then know that God wants to inflict them with some of their sins; and most of the people are corrupt.

50. Is it the judgment of the days of ignorance that they seek? Who is better than God as a judge for a people that comprehend?

51. O you who believe, do not take the Jews and the Nazarenes as allies, for they are allies to one another; and whoever takes them as such from amongst you is one of them. God does not guide the wicked people.

52. You will see those who have a disease in their hearts hurrying to them, saying: "We fear that a disaster will befall us!" Perhaps God will bring a victory or a decree from Himself, then they will become regretful over what they had kept hidden within themselves.

53. And those who believe said: "Were these the ones who swore oaths by God that they are with you?" Their works have collapsed, and they have become losers.

54. O you who believe, whoever from among you turns away from His system, then God will bring a people whom He loves and they love Him; humble towards the believers, proud towards the rejecters; they strive in the cause of God and do not fear to be blamed by those who blame. This is God's grace, He bestows it upon whom He wills; God is Encompassing, Knowledgeable.

55. For your supporter is God and His messenger and those who believe; they honour the oath of allegiance, and contribute towards betterment while yielding.

56. And whoever allies God and His messenger and those who believe; then the party of God are the ones who will be victorious.

57. O you who believe, do not take as allies those who have taken your system as fun and games from among those who have been given the Scripture before you and the rejecters. And be aware of God if you are believers.

58. And if you call to the oath of allegiance, they take it as fun and games. That is because they are a people who do not understand.

59. Say: "O people of the Scripture, do you hate us simply because we believe in God and in what was sent down to us and what was sent down before?" Alas, most of them are vile.

60. Say: "Shall I inform you of worse than this as a punishment from God? Those whom God cursed and became angry at them, and He made from them apes and pigs and servants of evil. Those have a worst place and are more astray from the right path."

61. And if they come to you they Say: "We believe," while they had entered in with rejection and went out with the same. God is aware of what they were hiding.

62. And you see many of them hasten to sin and transgression and consuming money illicitly. Miserable indeed is what they were doing.

63. Did not the Rabbis and Priests deter them for speaking evil and consuming money illicitly? Miserable indeed is what they had done.

64. And the Jews said: "The hand of God is tied-down!" Their hands will be tied-down, and they will be cursed for what they have said. No, His hands are wide open spending as He wills. And for many of them, what has been sent down to you will increase them in rebellion and rejection; and We have cast between them animosity and hatred until the Day of Resurrection. Every time they ignite the fire of war, God puts it out; and they seek to make corruption in the land; and God does not like the corrupters.

65. And if the people of the Scripture only would have believed and been aware, We would have cancelled for them their sins and admitted them to estates of Paradise.

66. And if they had honoured the Torah and the Injeel, and what was sent down to them from their Lord, they would have been rewarded from above them and below their feet. From among them is a pious nation, but most of them only do evil.

67. O messenger, deliver what was sent down to you from your Lord, and if you do not then you have not delivered His message; and God will protect you from the people. God does not guide the disbelieving people.

68. Say: "O people of the Scripture, you are not upon anything until you honour the Torah and the Injeel and what was sent down to you from your Lord." And for many of them, what was sent down to you from your Lord will only increase them in transgression and rejection. So do not feel sorry for the rejecting people.

69. Surely those who believe; and those who are Jewish, and the Sabiens, and the Nazarenes, whomever of them believes in God and the Last Day and does good work; then they will have nothing to fear nor will they grieve.

70. We have taken the covenant of the Children of Israel and We sent to them Our messengers. Every time a messenger came to them with what their souls did not desire, a group of them they would reject, and a group of them they would kill.

71. And they did not consider it might be a test, so they were blind and deaf. But God would have accepted the repentance from them; but many of them were still blind and deaf. God is watcher over what they do.

72. Rejecters indeed are those who have said: "God is the Messiah son of Mary!" And the Messiah said: "O Children of Israel, serve God, my Lord and your Lord. Whoever sets-up partners with God, then God will forbid Paradise for him, and his destiny will be the Fire; and the wicked will have no supporters."

73. Rejecters indeed are those who have said: "God is a trinity!" There is no god but One god. If they do not cease from what they are saying, then those who reject from among them will be afflicted with a painful retribution.

74. Would they not repent to God and seek His forgiveness? God is Forgiving, Merciful.

75. The Messiah son of Mary, is no more than a messenger; like whom messengers have passed away; and his mother was trustworthy, they used to eat the food. See how We clarify the signs for them, then see how they deviate.

76. Say: "Do you serve other than God what cannot harm you or benefit you?" God is the Hearer, the Knower.

77. Say: "O followers of the Scripture, do not overstep in your system other than the truth, and do not follow the desires of a people who have been misguided before, and they misguide many; and they strayed from the right path."

78. Cursed are those who have rejected from among the Children of Israel by the tongue of David and Jesus son of Mary. That is for what they have disobeyed, and for what they transgressed.

79. They would not stop each other from doing sin. Wickedness is what they used to do.

80. You see many of them allying the rejecters. Wicked is what their souls have provided for them, for God's wrath is upon them, and in the retribution they will abide.

81. And if they had only believed in God and the prophet, and what was sent down to him, then they would not have taken them as allies; but many of them are corrupt.

82. You will find the people with the greatest animosity towards those who believe are the Jews and those who have set up partners; and you will find the closest in affection to those who believe are those who said: "We are Nazarenes;" that is because amongst them are Priests and Monks, and they are not arrogant.

83. And if they hear what was sent down to the messenger you see their eyes flooding with tears, for what they have known as the truth, they Say: "Our Lord, we believe, so record us with the witnesses."

84. "And why shouldn't we believe in God and what has come to us of the truth? And we yearn that our Lord admits us with the righteous people."

85. So God rewarded them for what they have said with paradises that have rivers flowing beneath them, in them they shall abide; such is the reward of the good doers.

86. And those who rejected and denied Our revelations; they are the dwellers of Hell.

87. O you who believe, do not forbid the good things that God has made lawful to you, and do not aggress; God does not like the aggressors.

88. And eat from what God has provided for you, good and lawful; and be aware of God in whom you believe.

89. God will not hold you for your unintentional oaths, but He will hold you for what oaths you have made binding; its cancellation shall be the feeding of ten poor from the average of what you feed your family, or that you clothe them, or that you free a slave; whoever cannot find shall fast for three days; this is a cancellation for making your oaths when you swear. And be careful from making oaths. It is such that God clarifies for you His revelations that you may be thankful.

90. O you who believe, intoxicants, and gambling, and altars, and arrows of chance are tools of affliction used by the devil. You shall avoid him so that you may be successful.

91. The devil only wants to cause strife between you through intoxicants and gambling, and to repel you away from remembering God and from the oath of allegiance. Will you be deterred?

92. And obey God and obey the messenger, and be aware. If you turn away then know that it is the duty of the messenger to deliver the clarity.

93. There is no sin upon those who believe and do good works for what they eat if they are aware and believe and do good work, then they are aware and believe, then they are aware and do good; God loves the good doers.

94. O you who believe, God will test you with some of the game for hunting coming within reach of your hands and your spears, so that God will know who reveres Him when unseen. Whoever aggresses after this, then he will have a painful retribution.

95. O you who believe, do not kill any game while you are restricted; and whosoever of you kills it deliberately, then the recompense is to value what was killed against the livestock, which shall be judged by two equitable persons from you, and to make such as a donation to reach the Kaaba. Or, its expiation shall be in using it to feed the needy ones, while he abstains from it; that is to suffer the results of his deed; God forgives what has past. And whosoever returns, then God will seek vengeance from him. God is Noble, capable of vengeance.

96. Lawful for you is the catch of the sea, to eat it as enjoyment for you and for those who travel; and forbidden for you is the catch of the land as long as you are under restriction; and be aware of God to whom you will be gathered.

97. God has made the Kaaba to be the Restricted Sanctuary, to enforce for the people, and for the restricted month, and for the donations, and for regulation; that is so you know that God knows what is in heavens and what is in Earth, and that God is aware of all things.

98. Know that God is powerful in retribution, and that God is Forgiving, Merciful.

99. The messenger is only to deliver. And God knows what you reveal and what you conceal.

100. Say: "The bad and the good are not equal, even if the abundance of the bad pleases you." So be aware of God, O you who have understanding, that you may succeed.

101.O you who believe, do not ask about things which, if revealed to you, would harm you; and if you ask about them after the Quran has been sent down, then they will become clear to you. God pardons for them, and God is Forgiving, Compassionate.

102.A people before you had asked the same, then they became rejecters in it.

103.God did not institute any combination of livestock, nor livestock liberated for oaths, nor ones that give twin births, nor a stallion freed from work; but the people who rejected invented lies to God, and most of them do not understand.

104.And if they are told: "Come to what God has sent down, and to the messenger;" they Say: "We are content with what we found our fathers doing." What if their fathers did not know anything nor were guided?

105.O you who believe, you are responsible for yourselves; none who are misguided can harm you if you are guided. To God is your return, all of you, and then He will inform you of what you have done.

106.O you who believe, witnessing a will if death is approaching to one of you shall be done by two who are just amongst you. Or, if you have ventured out in the land, then two others may suffice if death is approaching you; you will hold them after making the oath of allegiance, and they will swear by God if you have doubt: "We will not purchase with it any price, even if he was a near relative, and we will not conceal the testimony of God, or else we are then of the sinners."

107.If it is then found out that they had lied, then two others will take their place from those who were present, and they will swear by God: "Our testimony is more truthful than their testimony, and if we aggress, then we are of the wicked."

108.This is best so that they would bring the testimony on its face value, for fear that their oaths would be discarded after being made. And be aware of God, and listen; God does not guide the wicked people.

109.The Day God will gather the messengers and He will Say: "What was the response you received?"; they said: "We have no knowledge, you are the Knower of all the unseen."

110.God said: "O Jesus son of Mary, recall My blessings upon you and your mother that I supported you with the Holy Spirit; you spoke to the people in the cradle and in old age; and I taught you the Scripture and the wisdom, and the Torah, and the Injeel; and you would create from clay the shape of a bird, then blow into it and it becomes a bird by My leave; and you heal the blind and the leaper by My leave; and you brought out the dead by My leave.

And I have restrained the Children of Israel from you, that you came to them with proofs; but those who rejected amongst them said: "This is clearly magic!""

111. "And I inspired the disciples that you shall believe in Me and My messenger; they said: "We believe, and bear witness that we have submitted.""

112. And the disciples said: "O Jesus son of Mary, can your Lord send down for us a feast from heaven?" He said: "Be aware of God if you are believers."

113. They said: "We want to eat from it and so our hearts become relieved, and so we know that you are truthful, and so that we can become a witness over it."

114. Jesus son of Mary, said: "Our Lord and god, send down to us a feast from heaven, that it becomes a joy to us from the first to the last, and a sign from You, and provide for us, you are the best provider."

115. God said: "I will send it down to you, but whoever rejects after this from amongst you, I will punish him a punishment like no one else from the worlds will be punished!"

116. And God will Say: "O Jesus son of Mary, did you tell the people to take you and your mother as gods instead of God?" He said: "Be you glorified, I cannot say what I have no right of. If I had said it then You know it, You know what is in my soul while I do not know what is in Your soul. You are the Knower of the unseen."

117. "I only said to them what You commanded me to say, that you shall serve God my Lord and your Lord; and I was witness over them as long as I was with them, but when You seized me, You were watcher over them. You are witness over all things."

118. "If You punish them, then they are Your servants, and if You forgive them, then You are the Noble, Wise."

119. God will Say: "This is a Day when the truth will benefit the truthful; they will have estates with rivers flowing beneath, eternally they will abide therein; God has become pleased with them and they are pleased with Him. Such is the greatest victory."

120. To God is the sovereignty of heavens and Earth and all that is in them; and He is capable of all things.

Chapter 6

بسم الله الرحمن الرحيم

In the name of God, the Almighty, the Merciful.

1. Praise be to God who created the heavens and the Earth, and Who made darkness and light; yet those who have rejected their Lord continue to deviate.

2. He is the One who created you from clay, then decreed a fixed time period for you; a time only known by Him. Yet you still deny.

3. And He is God in the heavens and the Earth. He knows your secrets and what you reveal; and He knows what you earn.

4. And every sign that came to them from their Lord, they turned away from it.

5. They have denied the truth when it came to them. The news will ultimately come to them of what they were mocking.

6. Did they not see how many generations We have destroyed before them? We granted them dominance over the land more than what We granted you, and We sent the clouds to them abundantly, and We made rivers flow beneath them; then We destroyed them for their sins, and established after them a new generation.

7. And if We had sent down to you a scripture already written on paper, and they touched it with their own hands, then those who have rejected would Say: "This is but clear magic!"

8. And they said: "If only an Angel were sent down to us?" But if We had sent down an Angel, then the matter would be over, and they would not be reprieved.

9. And if We had chosen an Angel, We would have made him appear as a man, and We would have confused them in what they already are confused.

10. Messengers before you were ridiculed; but those who mocked them suffered the consequences of what they ridiculed.

11. Say: "Roam the Earth, then see what the punishment of the rejecters was!"

12. Say: "To whom is all that is in heavens and Earth?" Say: "To God." He has decreed mercy on Himself, that He will gather you to the Day of Resurrection in which there is no doubt. Those who have lost their souls, they do not believe.

13. And for Him is what resides in the night and in the day; and He is the Hearer, the Knower.

14. Say: "Shall I take other than God as an ally; the initiator of heavens and Earth; while He feeds and is not fed!" Say: "I have been commanded to be the first who submits." And do not be of those who set up partners.

15. Say: "I fear if I disobey my Lord, the retribution of a great Day!"

16. Whoever He spares from it, then He has had mercy on him; and that is the clearest success.

17. And if God were to inflict you with harm, then none can remove it except Him; and if He were to bless you with good, then He is capable of all things.

18. And He is the Supreme over His servants; and He is the Wise, the Expert.

19. Say: "Which is the greatest testimony?" Say: "God is witness between me and you, and He has inspired to me this Quran that I may warn you with it and whomever it reaches, that you bear witness that along with God are other gods!" Say: "I do not bear witness!" Say: "He is only One god, and I am innocent of what you set up!"

20. Those to whom We have given the Scripture know it as they know their children. Those who lost their souls, they do not believe.

21. And who is more wicked than one who invents lies about God, or denies His revelations! The wicked will never succeed.

22. And the Day We gather them all, then We say to those who set up partners: "Where are your partners whom you used to claim?"

23. Then, their only excuse was to Say: "By God, our Lord, we did not set up partners!"

24. See how they lied to themselves; and that which they invented deserted them.

25. And from them are those who listen to you; and We have made covers over their hearts to prevent them from understanding it, and a deafness in their ears; and if they see every sign they will not believe; even when they come to you they argue, those who reject Say: "This is nothing but the tales from the past!"

26. And they are deterring others from it, and keeping away themselves; but they will only destroy themselves, yet they do not notice.

27. And if you could see when they are standing over the Fire, they Say: "If only we could be sent back, we would not deny the revelations of our Lord, and we would be believers!"

28. No, it is merely what they have been concealing that has now become evident to them; and if they were sent back they would return to what they were deterred from doing, they are but liars!

29. And they had said: "There is only this worldly life, and we will not be resurrected!"

30. And if you could see them when they are standing at their Lord; He said: "Is this not the truth?", they said: "Yes, by our Lord," He said: "Then taste the retribution for what you have rejected."

31. Losers are those who have denied their meeting with God; until the Hour comes to them suddenly, then they Say: "We deeply regret that which we have wasted in it," and they will carry their burdens on their backs; miserable indeed is their burden.

32. This worldly life is nothing more than games and a diversion, and the abode of the Hereafter is far better for those who are righteous. Do you not understand?

33. We know that you are saddened by what they say; they are not rejecting you, but it is God's revelations which the wicked disregard.

34. Messengers before you were denied, but they were patient for what they were denied, and they were harmed until Our victory came to them; there is no changing the words of God. News of the messengers has come to you.

35. And if their aversion has become too much for you, then perhaps you could make a tunnel in the Earth, or a ladder to the heavens, and bring them a sign. Had God willed, He would have gathered them to the guidance; so do not be of the ignorant ones.

36. Only those who listen will respond. As for the dead, God will resurrect them, then to Him they will return.

37. And they said: "If only a sign was sent to him from his Lord!" Say: "God is able to send a sign, but most of them would not know."

38. And there is not a creature in the Earth, or a bird that fly's with its wings, but are nations like you. We did not leave anything out of the record; then to their Lord they will be gathered.

39. And those who deny Our signs, they are deaf and dumb, in darkness. Whoever God wishes He misguides, and whoever He wishes He makes him on a straight path.
40. Say: "We will see when God's retribution comes to you, or the Hour comes to you, if you will still call on any other than God. If you are being truthful."
41. "No, it is Him alone you will call on; and He will remove that which you called Him for, if He wills; and you will forget what you set up."
42. And We have sent others to nations before you. We then took them with adversity and hardship, perhaps they would implore.
43. If only they had implored when Our punishment came to them; but their hearts hardened, and the devil adorned for them what they used to do.
44. So when they forgot what they had been reminded of, We opened for them the gates of all opportunities; and when they were happy with what they were given, We took them suddenly! They were confounded.
45. It was thus that the remainder of the wicked people were wiped out; and praise be to God, the Lord of the worlds.
46. Say: "Do you see that if God were to take away your hearing and your eyesight, and He seals your hearts; which god besides God can bring it to you?" Look how We cite the revelations, but then they turn away.
47. Say: "Do you see if God's retribution comes to you suddenly, or gradually, will anyone be destroyed except the wicked people?"
48. And We do not send the messengers except as bearers of good news and warners; whoever believes, and does good, then there is no fear for them nor will they grieve.
49. And those who deny Our revelations, the retribution will inflict them for their vileness.
50. Say: "I do not say to you that I posses God's treasures, nor do I know the future, nor do I say to you that I am an Angel. I merely follow what is inspired to me." Say: "Are the blind and the seer the same? Do you not think?"
51. And warn with it those who realize that they will be gathered to their Lord; they do not have besides Him any protector nor intercessor; so that they may be righteous.
52. And do not turn away those who call on their Lord at dawn and dusk seeking His presence; you are not responsible for their judgment, nor are they responsible for your judgment; if you turn them away, then you will be of the wicked.

53. And it is such that We test them with one another, so that they may Say: "Are these the ones whom God has blessed from amongst us?" Is God not aware of the thankful?

54. And if those who believe in Our revelations come to you, then Say: "Peace be upon you, our Lord has decreed mercy upon Himself, that any of you who commits sin out of ignorance and then repents afterwards and amends, then He is Forgiving, Merciful."

55. And it is such that We explain the revelations, and make clear the way of the criminals.

56. Say: "I am warned not to serve those you call upon other than God" Say: "I will not follow your desires, otherwise I would go astray and I would not be of those guided."

57. Say: "I am on a clarity from my Lord and you have denied it. I do not have what you hasten towards; the judgment is with God only; He carves out the truth, and He is the best decider."

58. Say: "If I had what you were hastening towards, then the matter between us would have been resolved. And God is fully aware of the wicked."

59. And with Him are the keys to the unseen, none know them except He. And He knows what is in the land and in the sea; and not a leaf falls except with His knowledge; nor a seed in the darkness of the Earth; nor anything moist or anything dry; all is in a clear record.

60. And He is the One who seizes you at night, and He knows what you have done during the day, then He sends you back to it until a fixed span; then to Him is your return and He will inform you of what you used to do.

61. And He is the Supreme over His servants, and He sends over you guardians. So that when the time of death comes to one of you, Our messengers seize him, and they do not neglect any.

62. Then they are returned to God, their true Patron; to Him is the judgment and He is the swiftest in reckoning.

63. Say: "Who rescues you from the darkness of the land and the sea?" you call on Him openly and secretly: "If You save us from this, we will be of the thankful!"

64. Say: "God will save you from it and from all distresses, yet you still set up partners!"

65. Say: "He is able to send retribution from above you or from below your feet, or He will make you belong to opposing factions, then He will let you taste the might of each other." See how We cite the revelations, perhaps they may comprehend.

66. And your people denied it, while it is the truth. Say: "I am not a guardian over you!"
67. "For every news there is a time, and you will come to know."
68. And if you encounter those who make fun of Our revelations, then turn away from them until they move on to a different topic; and if the devil lets you forget, then do not sit after remembering with the wicked people.
69. And the righteous are not required to take responsibility for them, but a reminder so perhaps they will be aware.
70. Leave alone those who have taken their system as fun and games, and this worldly life has tempted them. And remind with it that a soul will suffer for what it has earned, it will not have besides God any supporter nor intercessor; and even if it brings all justice, none will be accepted from it. These are the ones who have suffered with what they have earned; for them will be a boiling drink, and a painful retribution for what they had rejected.
71. Say: "Shall we call upon other than God what cannot benefit us or harm us, and we turn back on our heels after God has guided us?" This is like the one whom the devils have managed to mislead on Earth, he is confused, having friends who call him to the guidance: "Come to us!" Say: "The guidance is God's guidance, and we have been ordered to submit to the Lord of the worlds."
72. And you shall honour the oath of allegiance, and be aware; and to Him you will be gathered.
73. And He is the One who created the heavens and the Earth with truth, and the day He says: "Be," then it is! His saying is truth; and to Him is the sovereignty, the Day the trumpet is blown. Knower of the unseen and the seen; He is the Wise, the Expert.
74. And Abraham said to his father, Azar: "Will you take idols as gods? I see you and your people clearly misguided."
75. And it is such that We showed Abraham the kingdom of heavens and Earth, so that he will be of those who have certainty.
76. When the night covered him, he saw a planet, and he said: "This is my Lord." But when it disappeared he said: "I do not like those that disappear."
77. So when he saw the moon rising, he said: "This is my Lord." But when it disappeared he said: "If my Lord will not guide me, then I will be amongst the wicked people!"
78. So when he saw the sun rising, he said: "This is my Lord, this is bigger." But when it disappeared he said: "My people, I am innocent of that which you have set up."

79. "I shall turn my face to the One who initiated the heavens and the Earth, in monotheism, and I am not of those who set up partners."

80. And his people debated with him. He said: "Do you debate with me regarding God, when He has guided me? I do not fear that which you have set up except if my Lord wishes it so; my Lord encompasses all things with knowledge; will you not remember?"

81. "And how can I possibly fear what you have set up; yet you do not fear that you have set up partners with God, for which He has not sent down to you any authority! So which of our two groups is more worthy of security if you know?"

82. Those who believe and do not dress their belief with wrongdoing; they will have security, and they are guided.

83. And such was Our argument that We gave Abraham over his people; We raise the degree of whom We please. Your Lord is Wise, Knowledgeable.

84. And We granted him Isaac and Jacob, both of whom We guided; and Noah We guided from before; and from his progeny is David, and Solomon, and Job, and Joseph, and Moses, and Aaron. It is such that We reward the good doers.

85. And Zachariah and John, and Jesus, and Elias; all were from the upright.

86. And Ishmael and Elisha and Jonah and Lot; and each We have preferred over the worlds.

87. And from their fathers and their progeny and their brothers We have also chosen; and We guided them to a straight path.

88. Such is the guidance of God, He guides with it whom He pleases of His servants. And if they set up partners, then all that they had worked would fall away from them.

89. Those to whom We have given the Scripture, and the law, and the prophethood, if they reject it, then We will entrust it to a people who will not reject it.

90. These are the ones guided by God; so let their guidance be an example. Say: "I do not ask you for a wage; this is but a reminder for the worlds."

91. And they did not appreciate God as He deserves to be appreciated, for they said: "God has never sent down anything to any human being." Say: "Who then has sent down the Scripture which Moses had come with, a light and a guidance for the people? You treat it just as paper, you show some of it and conceal much, and you were taught what neither you nor your fathers knew." Say: "God has." Then leave them playing in their folly.

92. And this is a Scripture which We have sent down, blessed, authenticating what is present with him, and that you may warn the capital of the towns and those around it. And those who believe in the Hereafter believe in it, and they are dedicated to their oath.

93. And who is more wicked than one who invents lies about God, or says: "It has been inspired to me," when We did not inspire anything to him; or who says: "I will bring down the same as what God has sent down." And if you could only see the wicked at the moments of death when the Angels have their arms opened: "Bring yourselves out, today you will be given the severest punishment for what you used to say about God without truth, and you used to be arrogant towards His revelations."

94. "And you have come to Us individually, just as We had created you the first time; and you have left behind you all that We have provided for you; and We do not see your intercessors with you that you used to claim were with you in partnership; all is severed between you, and what you have claimed has abandoned you."

95. God is the splitter of the seeds and the grains; He brings the living out from the dead and He brings the dead out from the living. Such is God; so why are you deluded?

96. Initiator of morning and Maker of the night to reside in; and the sun and the moon for counting. Such is the measure of the Noble, the Knowledgeable.

97. And He is the One who made for you the stars, to guide you by them in the darkness of the land and the sea. We have explained the signs to a people who know.

98. And He is the One who initiated you from one person; with a place for stability and development. We have explained the signs to a people who comprehend.

99. And He is the One who sent down water from the sky, and We brought out with it plants of every kind. We brought out from it the green, from which We bring out multiple seeds; and what is from the palm trees, from its sheaths hanging low and near; and gardens of grapes and olives and pomegranates, similar and not similar. Look at its fruit when it blossoms and its ripeness. In this are signs for a people that believe.

100. And they made partners with God from among the Jinn, while He had created them. And they invented for Him sons and daughters without them having any knowledge! Be He glorified and far above what they describe.

101. Originator of the heavens and the Earth, how can He have a son when He did not take a wife? And He created all things and He is knowledgeable over all things.
102. Such is God, your Lord, there is no god but He; creator of all things, so serve Him. And He is caretaker over all things.
103. The eyesight cannot reach Him, yet He can reach all eyesight; and He is the Subtle, the Expert.
104. "Visible proofs have come to you from your Lord; so whoever can see, does so for himself, and whoever is blinded, does the same. I am not a watcher over you."
105. It is thus that We cite the revelations and that they may Say: "You have studied," and We will make it clear for a people who know.
106. Follow what is inspired to you from your Lord; there is no god but He, and turn away from those who have set up partners.
107. And if God had willed, they would not have set up partners. And We did not place you over them as a guardian, nor are you over them as a sponsor.
108. And do not insult those who call on other than God, lest they insult God without knowledge. And We have similarly adorned for every nation their works; then to their Lord is their return and He will inform them of what they had done.
109. And they swore by God using their strongest oaths; that if a sign came to them they would believe in it. Say: "The signs are from God; and how do you know that once it comes, that they would not disbelieve?"
110. And We divert their hearts and eyesight, as they did not believe in it the first time; and We leave them wandering in their transgression.
111. And if We had sent down to them the Angels, and the dead spoke to them, and We had gathered before them everything, they still would not believe except if God wills. Alas, most of them are ignorant.
112. And as such, We have permitted the enemies of every prophet, human and Jinn devils, to inspire in each other with fancy words in order to deceive. Had your Lord willed, they would not have done it. You shall disregard them and their fabrications.
113. That is so the hearts of those who do not believe in the Hereafter will listen to it, and they will accept it, and they will take of it what they will.
114. "Shall I seek other than God as a judge when He has sent down to you this Scripture fully detailed?" Those to whom We have given the Scripture know it is sent down from your Lord with truth; so do not be of those who have doubt.

115.And the word of your Lord has been completed with truth and justice; there is no changing His words. He is the Hearer, the Knower.

116.And if you obey the majority of those on Earth they will lead you away from God's path; that is because they follow conjecture, and that is because they only guess.

117.Your Lord is fully aware of who strays from His path, and He is fully aware of the guided ones.

118.So eat from that on which God's name has been mentioned, if you indeed believe in His revelations.

119.And why should you not eat that on which God's name has been mentioned, when He has fully detailed to you what has been made forbidden; except what you are forced to? Many misguide by their desires without knowledge; your Lord is fully aware of the transgressors.

120.And leave what is openly a sin as well as what is discreet; those who earn sin will be punished for what they have taken.

121.And do not eat from that which God's name has not been mentioned, for it is vile. And the devils they inspire their supporters to argue with you; and if you obey them, then you have set up partners.

122.Is one who was dead and to whom We gave life, and We made for him a light to walk with amongst the people, as one whose example is in darkness and he will not exit from it? It is such that the work of the rejecters has been adorned for them.

123.And as such, We have permitted in every town the influential from its criminals, to scheme in it. They only scheme their own souls without perceiving.

124.And if a sign comes to them they Say: "We will not believe until we are given the same as what God's messengers were given!" God is fully aware where He makes His message; those criminals will have debasement with God and a painful retribution for what they had schemed.

125.Whoever God wishes to guide, He will open his chest towards submission; and whoever He wishes to misguide, He will make his chest tight and constricted, as one who is climbing towards the sky. It is such that God afflicts those who do not believe.

126.And this is your Lord's straight path. We have fully detailed the revelations to a people who remember.

127.They will have the abode of peace with their Lord; He is their supporter because of what they used to do.

128.And the Day We gather them all: "O tribes of Jinn, you have managed to take many humans." Their supporters from the humans said: "Our Lord, we have indeed enjoyed one another, and we have reached our destiny to which You delayed us." He said: "The Fire is your dwelling, in it you shall abide eternally, except as your Lord wishes." Your Lord is Wise, Knowledgeable.

129. It is such that We make the wicked as supporters to one another for what they had earned.

130. "O you tribes of Jinn and humans, did not messengers come to you from amongst you and relate to you My revelations, and warn you of the meeting of this Day?" They said: "Yes, we bear witness upon ourselves;" and the worldly life deceived them, and they bore witness on themselves that they were rejecters.

131. That is because your Lord was not to destroy any town because of its wickedness while its people were unaware.

132. But there are degrees for what they had done; and your Lord is not unaware of what they do.

133. And your Lord is Rich with Mercy. If He wished, He could remove you and bring after you whom He pleases, just like He established you from the seed of another people.

134. What you have been promised will come, you cannot escape it.

135. Say: "My people, work as you see fit, and I will work. You will then know to whom will be the punishment of the Hereafter. The wicked will not succeed."

136. And they made for God a portion of what He provided them of crops and the livestock; they said: "This is for God," by their claims, "And this is for our partners." So what was for their partners did not reach God, and what was for God, it reached their partners! Miserable is how they judged.

137. And it was adorned for those who set up partners, by such partners, to kill their unborn children in order to turn them and to confuse their system for them. Had God willed they would not have done this, so ignore them and what they invent.

138. And they said: "These are livestock and crops that are restricted, and none shall eat from them except as we please," by their claims; and livestock whose backs are forbidden, and livestock over which they do not mention God's name as invention against Him. He will recompense them for what they invented.

139. And they said: "What is in the bellies of these livestock is purely for our males and forbidden for our wives, and if comes out dead, then they will be partners in it." God will recompense them for what they describe. He is Wise, Knowledgeable.

140. Losers are those who have killed their unborn children foolishly, without knowledge, and they forbade what God had granted them by lying about God. They have strayed and they were not guided.

141. And He is the One Who initiated gardens; both trellised and untrellised; and palm trees, and plants, all with different taste; and olives and pomegranates, similar and not similar. Eat from its fruit when it blossoms and give its due on the day of harvest; and do not waste. He does not like the wasteful.

142. And from the livestock are those for burden, and also for clothing. Eat from what God has provided you and do not follow the footsteps of the devil; he is to you a clear enemy.

143. Eight pairs: from the lambs two, and from the goats two; Say: "Is it the two males that He forbade or the two females, or what the womb of the two females bore? Inform me if you are truthful!"

144. And from the camels two, and from the cattle two; Say: "Is it the two males that He forbade or the two females, or what the womb of the two females bore? Or were you witnesses when God ordered you with this?" Who is more wicked than one who invents lies about God to misguide the people without knowledge. God does not guide the wicked people.

145. Say: "I do not find in what is inspired to me forbidden except that it be already dead, or blood, or the meat of pig, for it is foul; or what is corruptly dedicated to other than God." Whoever is forced without seeking disobedience or transgression, then your Lord is Forgiving, Merciful.

146. And for the Jews We have forbidden all that have claws; and from the cattle and the sheep We forbade their fat except what is attached to the back, or entrails, or mixed with bone. That is a punishment for their rebellion, and We are truthful.

147. If they deny you, then Say: "Your Lord has vast Mercy, but His Might will not be turned away from the criminal people."

148. Those who have set up partners will Say: "If God wished, we would not have set up partners, nor would have our fathers, nor would we have forbidden anything." Those before them lied in the same way, until they tasted Our might. Say: "Do you have any knowledge to bring out to us? You only follow conjecture, you only guess."

149. Say: "With God is the greatest argument. If He wished He would have guided you all."

150. Say: "Bring forth your witnesses who bear witness that God has forbidden this." If they bear witness, then do not bear witness with them, nor follow

the desires of those who deny Our revelations, and those who do not believe in the Hereafter; and they make equals with their Lord!

151. Say: "Come let me recite to you what your Lord has forbidden for you: that you should not set up anything with Him; and be kind to your parents; and do not kill your unborn children for fear of poverty, We provide for you and for them; and do not come near lewdness, what is plain of it or subtle; and do not kill the soul which God has forbidden, except in justice. That is what He enjoined you that you may comprehend."

152. "And do not come near the money of the orphan, except for what is best, until he reached his maturity; and give honestly full measure and weight equitably. We do not burden a soul except by what it can bear, and if you speak then be just even if against a relative; and regarding the pledges made to God, you shall observe them. This He has enjoined you that you may remember."

153. And this is My path, a Straight One. "So follow it, and do not follow the other paths lest they divert you from His path. That is what He has enjoined you to that you may be righteous."

154. Then We gave Moses the Scripture, to complete for those who do right, and to fully detail all things, and a guide and mercy that they may believe in the meeting of their Lord.

155. And this is a Scripture that We have sent down which is blessed, so follow it and be aware, that you may receive mercy.

156. Lest you Say: "The Scripture was only sent down to two groups before us, and we were unaware of their study!"

157. Or you Say: "If the Scripture was sent to us we would have been more guided than they!" Clarity has come to you from your Lord, and a guidance and a mercy. Who is more wicked than one who denies God's revelations and turns away from them? We will punish those who turn away from Our revelations with the pain of retribution for what they turned away.

158. Do they wait until the Angels will come to them, or your Lord comes, or some signs from your Lord? The day some signs come from your Lord, it will do no good for any soul to believe if it did not believe before, or it gained good through its belief. Say: "Wait, for we are waiting."

159. Those who have divided their system and become sects, you are not with them in anything. Their matter will be with God, then He will inform them of what they had done.

160. Whoever comes with a good deed, he will receive ten times its worth, and whoever comes with a sin, he will only be recompensed its like; they will not be wronged.

161. Say: "My Lord has guided me to a Straight Path, an upright system, the creed of Abraham the monotheist; he was not from those who set up partners."

162. Say: "My oath, and my offerings, and my life, and my death, are all to God the Lord of the worlds."

163. "He has no partner, and it is to this that I was commanded, and I am the first of those who have submitted."

164. Say: "Shall I seek other than God as a Lord when He is the Lord of everything?" And every soul earns what is for it, and none will bear the burden of another. Then to your Lord is your return and He will inform you of what you disputed in.

165. And He is the One who made you inheritors on Earth, and He raised some of you over others in grades, to test you with what He had given you. Your Lord is quick to punishment, and He is Forgiving, Merciful.

Chapter 7

بسم الله الرحمن الرحيم

In the name of God, the Almighty, the Merciful.

1. A.L.M.S'

2. A Scripture that has been sent down to you, so let there not be any burden in your chest from it, that you may warn with it; and a reminder to the believers.

3. Follow what was sent down to you all from your Lord, and do not follow besides Him any supporters. Little do you remember!

4. And how many a town have We destroyed; for Our punishment came to them while sleeping, or while resting.

5. Then their only saying when Our punishment came to them was: "We were wicked!"

6. We will ask those to whom We have sent, and We will ask the messengers.

7. We will narrate to them with knowledge; We were not absent.

8. And the scales on that Day will be the truth. Whoever has heavy weights, then these are the successful ones.

9. And whoever has light weights, then these are the ones who lost their souls for what they transgressed of Our revelations.

10. And We granted you dominion on Earth, and made for you in it a habitat; little do you give thanks!

11. And We created you, then We shaped you, then We said to the Angels: "Yield to Adam;" so they yielded except for Satan, he was not of those who yielded.

12. He said: "What has prevented you from yielding when I have ordered you?" He said: "I am far better than him, You created me from fire and created him from clay!"

13. He said: "Descend from it, it is not for you to be arrogant here; depart, for you are disgraced."
14. He said: "Grant me respite until the Day they are resurrected?"
15. He said: "You are granted."
16. He said: "For that which You have caused me to be misled, I will stalk for them on Your Straight Path."
17. "Then I will come to them from between their hands, and from behind them, and from their right, and from their left; You will find most of them are unappreciative."
18. He said: "Get out from this, you are despised and banished. As for those of them who follow you, I will fill Hell with you all!"
19. "And Adam, reside with your mate in the paradise, and eat from wherever you please; but do not approach this tree or you will be of the wicked."
20. But the devil whispered to them, to reveal their lusts which was kept from them; and he said: "Your Lord did not forbid you from this tree except that you would become Angels, or you would be immortal."
21. And he swore to them: "I am giving good advice."
22. So he misled them with deception; and when they tasted the tree, their lusts became apparent to them, and they rushed to cover themselves with the leaves of the paradise; and their Lord called to them: "Did I not forbid you from that tree, and tell you that the devil is your clear enemy?"
23. They said: "Our Lord, we have wronged ourselves and if You do not forgive us and have mercy on us, then we will be of the losers!"
24. He said: "Descend; for you are enemies to one another; and on Earth you will have residence and provisions until the appointed time."
25. He said: "In it you will live and in it you will die, and from it you will be brought forth."
26. O Children of Adam, We have sent down for you garments to alleviate your sin, as well as feathers; and the garment of righteousness is the best. That is from God's signs, perhaps they will remember.
27. O Children of Adam, do not let the devil afflict you as he evicted your parents from the paradise; he removes from them their garments to show them their lusts. He and his tribe see you from where you do not see them. We have made the devils as allies for those who do not believe.
28. And if they commit evil acts, they Say: "We found our fathers doing such, and God ordered us to it." Say: "God does not order evil! Do you say about God what you do not know?"

29. Say: "My Lord orders justice, and that you be devoted at every temple, and that you call on Him, while being faithful to Him in the system; as He initiated you, so you will return."

30. A group He has guided and a group have deserved misguidance; that is because they have taken the devils as allies besides God; and they think they are guided!

31. O Children of Adam, dress nicely at every temple, and eat and drink and do not indulge; He does not like the indulgers.

32. Say: "Who has forbidden the nice things that God has brought forth for His servants and the good provisions?" Say: "They are meant for those who believe during this worldly life, and they will be exclusive for them on the Day of Resurrection." It is such that We explain the revelations for those who know.

33. Say: "My Lord has forbidden all lewd action, what is obvious from them and what is subtle, and sin, and aggression without cause, and that you set up partners with God that which He has never authorized, and that you say about God what you do not know."

34. And for every nation will be an allotted time; when their time is reached, they will not delay by one hour nor advance.

35. O Children of Adam, when messengers come to you from amongst yourselves and narrate My revelations to you; then for those who are aware, and upright, there will be no fear over them nor will they grieve.

36. As for those who reject Our revelations, and become arrogant towards them; then these are the dwellers of the Fire, in it they will abide"

37. Who is more wicked than one who invents lies about God, or denies His revelations? These will receive their recompense from the record; so that when Our messengers come to take them, they will Say: "Where are those whom you used to call on besides God?" they said: "They have abandoned us!" and they bore witness upon themselves that they were rejecters.

38. He said: "Enter with the multitude of nations before you from humans and Jinn to the Fire!" Every time a nation entered, it cursed its sister nation, until they are all gathered inside it; then the last of them says to the first: "Our Lord, these are the ones who have misguided us, so give them double the retribution of the Fire!" He replied: "Each will receive double, but you do not know."

39. And the first of them said to the last: "You have no preference over us, so taste the retribution for what you earned!"

40. Those who have denied Our revelations, and became arrogant towards them, the gates of the sky will not open for them, nor will they enter Paradise until the camel passes through the eye of a needle. It is such that We recompense the criminals.

41. They will have Hell as an abode, and from above them will be barriers. It is thus We recompense the wicked.

42. As for those who believe and do good; We do not burden a soul beyond its means; those are the dwellers of Paradise, in it they will abide.

43. And We removed what was in their chests of hate; rivers will flow beneath them; and they will Say: "Praise be to God who has guided us to this, and we would not have been guided unless God guided us. The messengers of our Lord had come with truth." And it was called to them: "This is Paradise; you have inherited it for what you have done."

44. And the dwellers of Paradise called the dwellers of the Fire: "We have found what our Lord promised us to be true; did you find what your Lord promised to be true?" They said: "Indeed!" Then a caller announced between them: "God's curse is on the wicked."

45. "The ones who hinder from the path of God, and sought to make it crooked; and with regard to the Hereafter they were rejecters."

46. And between them is a barrier, and on the elevated platform are men who recognized others by their features. And they called out to the dwellers of Paradise: "Peace be upon you!" They have not yet entered it, but they are hoping.

47. And when their eyes are turned towards the dwellers of the Fire, they Say: "Our Lord, do not make us with the wicked people!"

48. And the people standing on the elevated platform called on men they recognized by their features, they said: "What good did your large number do for you, or what you were arrogant for?"

49. Weren't these the ones whom you swore God would not grant them of His mercy? "Enter Paradise, there is no fear for you nor will you grieve."

50. And the dwellers of the Fire called on the dwellers of Paradise: "Give us some water, or what God has provided for you?" They said: "God has forbidden it for the rejecters."

51. The ones who took their system as amusement and games, and were preoccupied with this worldly life. Today We forget them as they forgot their meeting on this Day, and they did not heed Our revelations.

52. And We have come to them with a Scripture which We have detailed with knowledge; a guide and a mercy to those who believe.

53. Are they waiting for what it says to come true? On the day it comes true, those who previously forgot it will Say: "Our Lord's messengers have come with truth! Are there any intercessors to intercede for us? or can we be sent back and we will work differently than what we did?" They have lost their souls and what they have invented has abandoned them.

54. Your Lord is God who created the heavens and Earth in six days, then He settled upon the throne. The night runs from the day, which seeks it continually; and the sun and the moon and the stars are all subjected by His command; to Him is the creation and the command. Glory be to God, the Lord of the worlds.

55. Call on your Lord openly and in secret. He does not like the aggressors.

56. And do not corrupt the Earth after it has been made right; and call on Him out of fear and want. God's mercy is near to the righteous.

57. He is the One who sends the winds to be dispersed between His hands of mercy; so when it carries a heavy cloud, We drive it to a dead town, and We send down the water with it and We bring forth fruits of all kind. It is thus that We will bring out the dead, perhaps you will remember.

58. And the good town, its plants are brought forth by its Lord's leave. And for the one that is evil, it does not bring forth except very little. It is such that We cite the revelations for a people who are thankful.

59. We have sent Noah to his people, so he said: "My people, serve God, you have no god besides Him. I fear for you the retribution of a great Day!"

60. The leaders from his people said: "We see that you are clearly misguided."

61. He said: "My people, I am not misguided, but I am a messenger from the Lord of the worlds."

62. "I deliver to you my Lord's messages, and I advise you, and I know from God what you do not know."

63. "Are you surprised that a reminder has come to you from your Lord through a man from amongst you to warn you, and that you may receive mercy?"

64. They denied him, so We saved him and those with him in the Ship, and We drowned those who denied Our revelations; they were a blind people.

65. And to 'Aad We sent their brother Hud, he said: "My people, serve God, you have no god besides Him. Will you not be righteous?"

66. The leaders who rejected from among his people said: "We see you in foolishness, and we think you are one of the liars"

67. He said: "My people, there is no foolishness in me, but I am a messenger from the Lord of the worlds."

68. "To deliver to you my Lord's messages, and to you I am a trustworthy advisor."

69. "Are you surprised that a reminder has come to you from your Lord through a man from amongst you to warn you? And recall that he made you successors after the people of Noah, and He increased you in status. So recall God's grace, that you may succeed."

70. They said: "Have you come to us to serve God alone and abandon what our fathers had served? Bring us what you promise if you are of the truthful ones!"

71. He said: "An affliction and wrath shall befall you from your Lord. Do you argue with me over names which you and your fathers have created with no authority being sent down by God? Wait then, and I will wait with you."

72. We saved him and those with him by a mercy from Us, and We destroyed the remnant of those who rejected Our revelations, they were never believers.

73. And to Thamud, We sent their brother Saleh, he said: "My people, serve God, you have no god besides Him; clarity has come to you from your Lord, this is God's camel, in her you have a sign, so leave her to eat in God's land, and do not harm her, else the painful retribution will take you."

74. "And recall that He made you successors after 'Aad, and He established you in the land so that you make palaces on its plains, and you carve homes in the mountains. So recall God's grace, and do not roam the Earth as corrupters."

75. The leaders who were arrogant from among his people said to those who were weak and believed from amongst them: "How do you know that Saleh was sent from his Lord?" They said: "We believe in what he has been sent with."

76. Those who were arrogant said: "In that which you believe, we reject!"

77. They thus killed the camel and defied their Lord's command, and they said: "O Saleh, bring us what you promised us if you are of the messengers!"

78. The Earthquake took them, so they became lifeless in their homes.

79. Thus he turned away from them, and said: "My people, I had delivered to you the message of my Lord and advised you; but you do not like the advisers."

80. And Lot, he said to his people: "Do you commit lewdness such as none of those of the worlds had done before?"

81. "You come to men with desire instead of women; you are a transgressing people."

82. The only response of his people was: "Drive them out of your town; they are a people who wish to be pure!"

83. We saved him and his family, except for his wife; she was of those who were destroyed.

84. And We rained down upon them a rain, so see how was the punishment for the criminals.

85. And to Median, their brother Shu'ayb, he said: "My people, serve God, you have no god besides Him. Clarity has come to you from your Lord, so give full weight and measure, and do not hold back from the people what belongs to them, and do not make corruption on the Earth after it has been set-right. That is better for you if you believe."

86. "And do not stand on every road, robbing, and turning away from the path of God those who believe in Him, and you seek to make it crooked. And recall that you were few and He multiplied you; and see how is the retribution of the corrupters."

87. "And if a group of you believes in what I have been sent with, and a group disbelieves, then wait until God judges between us. He is the best of judges."

88. And the leaders who became arrogant form among his people said: "We will drive you out of our town Shu'ayb, along with those who believed with you, or else you will return to our creed!" He said: "Would you force us?"

89. "We would then be inventing lies about God if we return to your creed after God had saved us from it; and we would not return to it except if God our Lord wishes, our Lord encompasses everything with knowledge, in God we put our trust. Our Lord, open between us and between our people with truth, you are the best opener."

90. And the leaders who rejected from among his people said: "If you follow Shu'ayb, then you are losers."

91. The Earthquake took them, thus they became lifeless in their homes.

92. Those who denied Shu'ayb, it is as if they never prospered therein. Those who denied Shu'ayb, they were the losers.

93. Thus he turned away from them, and said: "My people, I had delivered to you the messages of my Lord and advised you. How can I feel sorry over a rejecting people?"

94. And We do not send a prophet to any town, except afterwards We would afflict its people with hardship and adversity that they may implore.

95. Then We replace the bad with good, until they have plenty, then they Say: "Our fathers were the ones afflicted by hardship, and adversity." We then take them suddenly, while they are unaware.

96. And if the town's people had only believed and been aware, then We would have opened for them blessings from the sky and the land; but they denied, so We took them for what they used to earn.

97. Are the people of the towns sure that Our punishment will not come to them at night while they are sleeping?

98. Or are the people of the towns sure that Our punishment will not come to them during the late morning while they are playing?

99. Have they become sure about God's scheming? None are sure about God's scheming except the people who are losers.

100. Is it not a guide for those who inherited the land after them, that if We wished We could have punished them immediately for their sins? And We stamp on their hearts, so they do not hear.

101. These are the towns whose stories We relate to you; their messengers had come to them with proofs, but they would not believe in what they had denied before. It is such that God stamps on the hearts of the rejecters.

102. And We did not find most of them up to their pledge, rather, We found most of them corrupt.

103. Then after them We sent Moses with Our signs to Pharaoh and his leaders. But they did wrong in them, so see how is the end of the corrupters.

104. And Moses said: "O Pharaoh, I am a messenger from the Lord of the worlds."

105. "It is not proper for me to say about God except the truth; I have come to you with proof from your Lord. So send with me the Children of Israel."

106. He said: "If you have come with a sign then bring it, if you are of the truthful?"

107. He threw down his staff and it manifested into a serpent.

108. And he drew out his hand, and it became pure white for the onlookers.

109. The commanders from among the people of Pharaoh said: "This is a knowledgeable magician!"

110. "He wishes to drive you out of your land; what is your command?"

111. They said: "Delay him and his brother, and send gatherers to the cities."

112. "They will come to you with every knowledgeable magician."

113. And the magicians came to Pharaoh, they said: "We require a reward if we are the victors."

114. He said: "Yes, and you will be made close to me."

115. They said: "O Moses, either you cast, or we will cast?"

116. He said: "You cast." So when they cast, they bewitched the eyes of the people, and struck terror in them, and they came with a great magic.

117.And We inspired Moses: "Throw down your staff;" and it swallowed what they invented.

118.Thus the truth was set, and what they did was made of no effect.

119.They were thus defeated there and then, and they turned in disgrace.

120.And the magicians went down prostrating.

121.They said: "We believe in the Lord of the worlds."

122."The Lord of Moses and Aaron."

123.Pharaoh said: "Have you become believers before I have given you permission? This is surely some scheme which you have schemed in the city to drive its people out; you will reveal what you know."

124."I will cut off your hands and feet from alternate sides, then I will crucify you all."

125.They said: "It is to our Lord that we will return."

126."And you are only seeking revenge on us because we believed in our Lord's signs when they came to us. Our Lord, provide us with patience and let us die having submitted."

127.And the commanders from among the people of Pharaoh said: "Will you let Moses and his people corrupt the land, and abandon you and your gods?" He said: "We will kill their children and rape their women; we will be supreme over them."

128.Moses said to his people: "Seek help with God, and be patient; for the land is God's, He will inherit it to whom He pleases of His servants; and the end will be to the righteous."

129.They said: "We were being harmed before you came to us and since you have come to us." He said: "Perhaps your Lord will destroy your enemy, and make you successors in the land, so He sees how you act?"

130.And We afflicted the people of Pharaoh with years of drought, and a shortage in crops, perhaps they will remember.

131.When any good comes to them, they Say: "This is ours," and when any bad afflicts them, they blame it on Moses and those with him. Their blame is with God, but most of them do not know.

132.And they said: "No matter what you bring us of a sign to bewitch us with, we will never believe in you."

133.So We sent them the flood, and the locust, and the lice, and the frogs, and the blood; all detailed signs; but they turned arrogant, they were a criminal people.

134.And when the plague befell them, they said: "O Moses, call on your Lord for what pledge He gave you, that if you remove this plague from us, then we will believe you and we will send with you the Children of Israel."

135.So when We removed from them the plague until a future time; they broke their pledge.

136.We thus took vengeance upon them by drowning them in the sea, for their denial of Our signs, and their disregard of them.

137.And We let the people who were weak inherit the east of the land and the west of it which We have blessed in it. And the good word of your Lord was completed towards the Children of Israel for their patience; and We destroyed what Pharaoh and his people were doing, and what they contrived.

138.And We let the Children of Israel cross the sea, then they came upon a people who were devoted to idols made for them; they said: "O Moses, make for us a god like they have gods?" He said: "You are an ignorant people!"

139."These people are ruined for what they are in, and evil is what they do."

140.He said: "Shall I seek other than God as a god for you when He has preferred you over the worlds?"

141.And We have saved you from the people of Pharaoh, they were afflicting you with the worst punishment; they used to kill your children and rape your women; and in that was a great trial from your Lord.

142.And We appointed for Moses thirty nights and completed them with ten, so the appointed time of his Lord was completed at forty nights. And Moses said to his brother Aaron: "Be my successor with my people and be upright, and do not follow the path of the corrupters."

143.So when Moses came to Our appointed time, and his Lord spoke to him, he said: "My Lord, let me look upon you." He said: "You will not see Me, but look upon the mountain, if it stays in its place then you will see Me." So when his Lord revealed Himself to the mountain, He caused it to crumble; thus Moses fell unconscious. When he awoke, he said: "Glory be to You, I repent to You and I am the first of those who believe."

144.He said: "O Moses, I have chosen you over the people with My message and My words; so take what I have given you and be of the thankful."

145.And We wrote for him on the tablets from everything a lesson, and detailing all things. Take it with strength and order your people to take the best from it. I will show you the abode of the corrupt.

146.I will turn away from My revelations those who are arrogant on Earth without right, and if they see every sign they do not believe in it, and if they see the path of guidance they do not take it as a path; and if they see the path of mischief, they take it as a path. That is because they have denied Our revelations and were heedless of them.

147. And those who deny Our revelations and the meeting of the Hereafter, their work has collapsed. Will they not be rewarded except for what they used to do?

148. And the people of Moses, in his absence, made from their ornaments the image of a calf which made a sound. Did they not see that it could not speak to them, nor guide them to any way? They took it and they were wicked.

149. And when they realized what their hands had done, and they saw that they had gone astray, they said: "If our Lord will not have mercy on us and forgive us, then we will be of the losers!"

150. And when Moses returned to his people, angry and grieved, he said: "Miserable is what you have done after I was gone; do you wish to hasten the action of your Lord?" And he cast down the tablets, and took his brother by his head dragging him towards him. He said: "Son of my mother, the people overpowered me and nearly killed me, so do not make the enemies rejoice over me, and do not make me with the wicked people."

151. He said: "My Lord, forgive me and my brother, and admit us in Your mercy; and you are the Most Merciful of those who show mercy."

152. Those who took-up the calf will be dealt with a wrath from their Lord and a humiliation in this worldly life. It is such that We punish the fabricators.

153. As for those who commit sin but then repent afterwards and believe; your Lord after that is Forgiving, Merciful.

154. And when the anger subsided from Moses, he took the tablets; and in its inscription was a guidance and mercy for those who revere their Lord.

155. And Moses selected from his people seventy men for Our appointed time; so when the Earthquake seized them, he said: "My Lord, if You wished You could have destroyed them before this, and me as well. Will you destroy us for what the foolish amongst us have done? It is all Your test, You misguide with it whom You please and You guide with it whom You please. You are our supporter, so forgive us and have mercy on us; You are the best forgiver."

156. "And decree for us good in this world, and in the Hereafter; we have been guided towards You." He said: "My punishment, I afflict with it whom I chose, and My mercy encompasses all things. I will thus decree it for those who are aware and contribute towards betterment, and those who believe in Our revelations."

157. "Those who follow the Gentile messenger prophet whom they find written for them in the Torah and the Injeel; he orders them to goodness, and deters

them from evil, and he makes lawful for them the good things, and he forbids for them the evil, and he removes their burden and the shackles that are upon them. So those who believe in him, and support him, and help him persevere, and follow the light that was sent down with him; these are the successful."

158. Say: "O mankind, I am God's messenger to you all. The One who has the sovereignty of heavens and Earth, there is no god but He; He gives life and causes death." So believe in God and His Gentile messenger prophet, who believes in God and His words; and follow him that you may be guided.

159. And from among the people of Moses are a nation who guide with truth and with it they become just.

160. And We separated them into twelve tribes as nations; and We inspired Moses when his people wanted to drink: "Strike the rock with your staff," thus twelve springs burst forth. Every group knew where from to drink. And We shaded them with clouds and We sent down to them manna and quail: "Eat from the good things that We have provided for you." They did not wrong Us, but it was their souls that they wronged.

161. And they were told: "Reside in this town and eat from it as you please, and Say: "Our load is removed," and enter the passageway by crouching, We will forgive for you your wrong doings, and We will increase for the good doers."

162. Those who were wicked amongst them altered what was said to them with something different; so We sent to them an affliction from the sky because they were wicked.

163. And ask them about the town which was by the sea, after they had transgressed the Sabbath; their fish would come to them openly on the day of their Sabbath, and when they are not in Sabbath, they do not come to them! It is such that We afflicted them for what they corrupted.

164. And a nation from amongst them said: "Why do you preach to a people whom God will destroy or punish a painful retribution?" They said: "A plea to your Lord, and perhaps they may be aware."

165. So when they forgot that which they were reminded of, We saved those who prohibited evil, and We took those who transgressed with a grievous retribution for what they were corrupting.

166. When they persisted in that which they had been prohibited from, We said to them: "Be despicable apes!"

167. And your Lord has sworn that He will send upon them, until the Day of Resurrection, people who would inflict severe punishment on them. Your Lord is quick to punish, and He is Forgiving, Merciful.

168. And We divided them through the land as nations. From them are the upright, and from them are other than that. And We tested them with good things and bad, perhaps they will return.

169. A generation came after them who inherited the Scripture, but they took the materialism of this world, which is lower; and they Say: "It will be forgiven for us." And if materialism again comes to them they take it; was not the covenant of the Scripture taken on them that they would only say the truth about God? And they studied what was in it; but the abode of the Hereafter is better for those who are aware. Do you not comprehend?

170. As for those who adhere to the Scripture, and they honour the oath of allegiance; We will not waste the reward of the righteous.

171. And We raised the mountain above them as if it were a cloud, and they thought it would fall on them: "Take what We have given you with strength and remember what is in it that you may be righteous."

172. And your Lord took for the children of Adam from their backs, their progeny; and He made them witness over themselves: "Am I not your Lord?" They said: "Yes, we bear witness." Thus you cannot say on the Day of Resurrection that you were unaware of this.

173. Nor can you Say: "It was our fathers who set up partners before and we were simply a progeny who came after them. Would You destroy us for what the innovators did?"

174. It is such that We explain the revelations, perhaps they will revert.

175. And recite to them the story of the person whom Our revelations were given to him, but he removed himself from them, and thus the devil followed him, and He became of those who went astray.

176. Had We wished, We could have elevated him by it, but he stuck to the Earth and he followed his desire. His example is like the dog, if you scold him he pants, and if you leave him he pants; such is the example of the people who deny Our revelations. Relate the stories, perhaps they will think.

177. Miserable is the example of the people who denied Our revelations, and it was their souls that they had wronged.

178. Whoever God guides, then he is the guided one; and whoever He misguides, then these are the losers.

179. And We have committed to Hell many Jinn and humans; they had hearts with which they did not comprehend, and they had eyes with which they did not see, and they had ears with which they did not hear. They are like cattle; no, they are even more astray. These are the unaware ones.

180. And to God belong the beautiful names, so call Him by them; and ignore those who blaspheme in His names. They will be punished for what they used to do.

181. And from among those We created is a community who guides with truth, and with it they are just.

182. As for those who deny Our revelations, We will entice them from where they do not know.

183. And I will encourage them, for My scheming is formidable.

184. Do they not reflect? Their companion has no madness; but he is a clear warner.

185. Did they not look at the dominion of heavens and Earth, and all that God has created? Perhaps their time is drawing near; so in which narrations after this one will they believe?

186. Whoever God misguides, then there is none to guide him; and He leaves them blindly wandering in their transgression.

187. They ask you regarding the Hour: "When will be its time?" Say: "Its knowledge is with my Lord, none can reveal its coming except Him. It is heavy through the heavens and the Earth; it will not come to you except suddenly." They ask you, as if you are responsible for it! Say: "Its knowledge is with God, but most people do not know."

188. Say: "I do not posses for myself any benefit or harm, except what God wills. And if I could know the future, then I would have increased my good fortune, and no harm would have come to me. I am but a warner and a bearer of good news to a people who believe."

189. He is the One who created you from one person, and He made from it its mate to reside with. When he dwelled with her, she became pregnant with a light load, and she continued with it; then when it became heavy, they called on God, their Lord: "If You give us an upright child, then we will be among the thankful."

190. But when He gave them an upright child, they made partners with Him in what He had given them. God be exalted above what they set up as partners.

191. Do they set up those who do not create anything, while they are created?

192. And they cannot give them aid, nor can they aid themselves?

193. And if you invite them to the guidance they will not follow you. It is the same whether you invite them or simply keep quiet.

194. Those whom you call on besides God are servants like you; so let them answer for you if you are truthful.

195. Do they have feet with which to walk?, or do they have hands with which to strike?, or do they have eyes with which to see?, or do they have ears with which to hear? Say: "Call on your partners, then scheme against me. You will not be given respite."

196. "My supporter is God who sent down the Scripture; and He takes care of the righteous."

197. As for those whom you call on beside Him, they cannot aid you, nor can they aid themselves.

198. And if you invite them to the guidance, they do not listen. And you see them looking at you, while they do not see.

199. Take to pardoning, and order with what is good, and turn away from the ignorant ones.

200. And if the devil harms you in any way, then seek refuge with God. He is the Hearer, the Knower.

201. Those who are pious, when any evil from the devil touches them, they remember, then they can see.

202. And their brethren attempt to drive them towards error, they do not cease.

203. And because you do not bring them a sign, they Say: "If only you had brought one." Say: "I only follow what is inspired to me from my Lord. This is an evidence from your Lord, and a guide and mercy to a people who believe."

204. And if the Quran is being related, then listen to it and pay attention, that you may receive mercy.

205. And remember your Lord in yourself out of humility and fear and without being too loud during the morning and the evening. And do not be of the careless ones.

206. Those who are at your Lord, they are never too proud to serve Him, and they glorify Him, and to Him they yield.

Chapter 8

بسم الله الرحمن الرحيم

In the name of God, the Almighty, the Merciful.

1. They ask you regarding the spoils of war, Say: "The spoils of war are for God and the messenger." So be aware of God, and be upright in matters between you; and obey God and His messenger if you are believers.

2. The believers are those whom, when God is mentioned, their hearts reverence; and when His revelations are recited to them, it increases their faith; and they put their trust in their Lord.

3. They honour the oath of allegiance, and from Our provisions to them they spend.

4. These are the true believers; they will have grades with their Lord and a forgiveness and a generous provision.

5. As your Lord made you go out from your home with the truth, but a party from among the believers disliked this.

6. They argue with you about the truth when it has been made clear to them; as if they were being herded towards death while they are watching!

7. And God promises you that one of the two parties will be defeated by you; and you wish that the one least armed be the one. But God wishes that the truth be manifest with His words, and that He eliminates the remnant of the rejecters.

8. So that truth will be manifest, and the falsehood will be confounded; even if the criminals dislike it.

9. You called on help from your Lord and He answered you: "I will provide you with one thousand Angels as defenders."

10. And God did not do this except to give you good news, and that your hearts may be assured by it. And victory is only from God; God is Noble, Wise.

11. Sleep overcame you from Him to give you peace; and He sent down to you water from the sky to cleanse you with it and cause the affliction of the devil to leave you; and so that He may strengthen your hearts and set firm your feet.

12. Your Lord inspired to the Angels: "I am with you so keep firm those who believe. I will cast terror into the hearts of those who have rejected; so strike above the necks, and strike from them every one standing."

13. That is because they have aggressed against God and His messenger. And whoever aggresses against God and His messenger, then God is severe in retribution.

14. This is for you to sample, and for the rejecters will be a retribution of Fire.

15. O you who believe; when you encounter those who have rejected on the battlefield, then do not flee from them.

16. And whoever on that day flees from them; unless it is part of the battle strategy or if he is retreating back to his group; then he has drawn God's wrath upon him, and his abode will be Hell. What a miserable destiny.

17. It was not you who killed them, but it was God who killed them. And it was not you who launched when you did, but it was God who launched. And so that the believers would be tested well by Him. God is Hearer, Knowledgeable.

18. That, and God weakens the plots of the rejecters.

19. If you sought conquest, then conquest has come to you, but if you cease, then it is better for you. And if you return again, then We will also return, and your group will avail you nothing even if it is many. God is with the believers.

20. O you who believe, obey God and His messenger, and do not turn away from him while you have heard.

21. And do not be like those who have said: "We hear," but they do not hear.

22. The worst creatures with God are the deaf and dumb who do not understand.

23. And if God had found any good in them, then He would have made them listen. But if He makes them listen, they would still turn away, averse.

24. O you who believe, answer the call of God and His messenger when he calls you to what will grant you life. And know that God comes between a person and his heart, and that to Him you will be gathered.

25. And be aware of a test that will not only afflict those of you who were wicked; and know that God is severe in retribution.

26. And recall when you were but a few who were weak in the land, you were fearful that the people might capture you. But He sheltered you, and He supported you with His victory, and He provided you with good provisions, so that you may be thankful.

27. O you who believe, do not betray God and the messenger, nor betray your trust, while you know.

28. And know that your money and your children are a test, and that God has the greatest reward.

29. O you who believe, if you are aware of God, He will make for you a criterion, and He will cancel your sins and forgive you. God is possessor of great favour.

30. And the rejecters plot against you to arrest you, or to kill you, or to expel you. And they plot, and God plots, and God is the best of plotters.

31. And if Our revelations are recited to them, they Say: "We have listened, and if we wish, we could have said the same thing. This is nothing but tales of the ancients!"

32. And they said: "Our god, if this is the truth from You, then send down upon us a rain of stones from the sky or bring on us a painful retribution."

33. But God was not to punish them while you are with them, nor will God punish them while they continue to seek forgiveness.

34. And why should God not punish them when they are turning others away from the Restricted Temple, and they were never its protectors! Its protectors are the righteous; but most of them do not know.

35. And their oath that they made at the Sanctuary was nothing but noise and aversion. Taste the retribution for what you have rejected.

36. Those who have rejected, they spend their money to turn others away from the path of God. They will spend it, then it will become an anguish for them, then they are defeated. Those who rejected will be gathered to Hell.

37. This is so that God will distinguish the bad from the good, and so that the bad will be gathered together into one heap then He will cast it all into Hell. These are the losers.

38. Say to the rejecters: "If they cease, then what has passed before will be forgiven to them, and if they return to it, then the example of the previous generations has already been given."

39. And fight them all until there is no more oppression, and so that the entire system is God's. But if they cease, then God is watcher over what they do.

40. And if they turn away, then know that God is your Patron. What an excellent Patron, and what an excellent Victor.

41. You should know: "Of anything you gain, that one-fifth shall go to God and the messenger, and the relatives, and the orphans, and the poor, and the wayfarer." You will do this if you believe in God and in what We revealed to Our servant on the day of the Criterion, the day the two armies clashed. God is able to do all things.

42. When you were on the near side, and they were on the far side, then the supply line became directly beneath you. And had you planned for this meeting, you would have disagreed on its timing, but God was to enforce a command that was already done. So that He would destroy those to be destroyed with proof, and to let those who will live be alive with proof. God is Hearer, Knowledgeable.

43. God shows them to you as being few in your dream, and had He shown them to be many, then you would have failed and you would have disputed in the matter; it was God who saved you. He is the Knower of what is inside the chests.

44. And He showed them to you when you met as being few to your eyes, and He made you appear as being fewer to their eyes. That was so God's decree would come to be; and to God all matters are returned.

45. O you who believe, when you meet a force, stand firm and mention God excessively, that you may succeed.

46. And obey God and His messenger, and do not dispute else you will fail and your momentum will depart, and be patient. God is with the patient ones.

47. And do not be like those who came out from their homes to boast and to be seen by the people, and they repel others away from the path of God. God is aware of what they do.

48. And the devil adorned their work for them, and he said: "No people can defeat you today, and I am by your side." But when the two forces came together, he turned on his heels to flee and he said: "I am innocent from you! I see what you do not see. I fear God, and God is severe in punishment."

49. The hypocrites and those who have a disease in their hearts said: "These people have been deceived by their system." But whoever puts his trust in God, then God is Noble, Wise.

50. And if you could only see as the Angels take those who have rejected, they strike their faces and their backs: "Taste the punishment of the blazing Fire!"

51. "This is for what your hands have put forth, and God does not wrong the servants."

52. Like the behaviour of the people of Pharaoh, and those before them; they rejected God's signs, so God took them for their sins. God is Strong, severe in punishment.
53. That is because God was not to change anything He bestowed to a people, unless they change what is in themselves. God is Hearer, Knowledgeable.
54. Like the behaviour of Pharaoh's people and those before them. They denied the signs of their Lord, so We destroyed them by their sins, and We drowned the people of Pharaoh; all of them were wicked.
55. The worst creatures to God are those who reject, for they do not believe.
56. The ones whom you made a pledge with them, then they break their pledge every time, and they do not care.
57. So, when you encounter them in battle, set them as an example to those who would come after them; perhaps they may remember.
58. And if you are being betrayed by a people, then you shall likewise move against them. God does not like the betrayers.
59. And let not those who have rejected think that they have escaped; they will never avail themselves.
60. And prepare for them all that you can of might, and from the steeds of war, that you may instil fear with it towards God's enemy and your enemy, and others beside them whom you do not know but God knows them. And whatever you spend in the cause of God will be returned to you, and you will not be wronged.
61. And if they seek peace, then you also seek it, and put your trust in God. He is the Hearer, the Knowledgeable.
62. And if they wish to deceive you, then God is sufficient for you. He is the One who supported you with His victory and with the believers.
63. And He made unity between their hearts. And had you spent all that is on Earth, you would not have united between their hearts, but God united between them. He is Noble, Wise.
64. O prophet, God is sufficient for you, and whoever followed you from the believers.
65. O prophet, urge the believers to fight. If there are twenty of you who are patient, they will defeat two hundred. And if there are one hundred of you, they will defeat one thousand from amongst those who reject; that is because they are a people who do not comprehend.
66. Now, God has lightened for you, for He knows that there is weakness in you. If there are one hundred of you who are patient, they will defeat two

hundred. And if there are one thousand of you, they will defeat two thousand by God's leave. God is with the patient.

67. And it was not for any prophet to take prisoners unless it was in battle. You desire the materials of this world, while God wants the Hereafter for you. God is Noble, Wise.

68. Had it not been previously ordained from God, then a severe punishment would have afflicted you for what you took.

69. So consume what you have gained, lawful and good, and be aware of God. God is Forgiving, Merciful.

70. O prophet, say to those prisoners whom you hold: "If God finds in your hearts any good, He will grant you better than what He took from you, and He will forgive you. God is Forgiving, Merciful."

71. And if they want to betray you, they have already betrayed God before, and He overpowered them. God is Knowledgeable, Wise.

72. Those who have believed and emigrated and strived with their money and lives in the cause of God, and those who sheltered and supported; these are the allies of one another. And those who believed but did not emigrate, you do not owe them any obligation until they emigrate. But if they seek your help in the system, then you must support them, except if it is against a people with whom there is a treaty between you. God is watcher over what you do.

73. As for those who reject, they are allies to one another. If you do not do this, then there will be oppression on Earth and great corruption.

74. And those who have believed and emigrated and strived in the cause of God, and those who sheltered and supported, these are truly the believers. They will have a forgiveness and a generous provision.

75. And those who believed afterwards and emigrated and strived with you, then they are from you. And the relatives by birth are also supportive of one another in God's record. God is aware of all things.

Chapter 9

1. This is a revocation from God and His messenger to those with whom you have made a treaty from among those who have set up partners.
2. Therefore, roam the land for four months and know that you will not escape God, and that God will humiliate the rejecters.
3. And a declaration from God and His messenger to the people, on this, the peak day of the Pilgrimage: "That God and His messenger are innocent from all those who set up partners." If you repent, then it is better for you, and if you turn away, then know that you will not escape God. And give news to those who have rejected of a painful retribution.
4. Except for those with whom you had a treaty from among those who have set up partners if they did not reduce anything from it nor did they plan to attack you; you shall continue the treaty with them until its expiry. God loves the righteous.
5. So when the restricted months have passed, then you may kill those who have set up partners wherever you find them, and take them, and surround them, and stand against them at every point. If they repent, and honour the oath of allegiance, and contribute towards betterment, then you shall leave them alone. God is Forgiving, Merciful.
6. And if any of those who have set up partners seeks your protection, then you may protect him so that he may hear the words of God, then let him reach his sanctity. This is because they are a people who do not know.
7. How can those who have set up partners have a pledge with God and with His messenger? Except for those with whom you made a pledge near the Restricted Temple, as long as they are upright with you, then you are upright with them. God loves the righteous.
8. How is it that when they come upon you they disregard all ties, either those of kinship or of pledge. They seek to please you with their words, but their hearts deny, and most of them are wicked.

9. They purchased with God's revelations a small price, so they turn others from His path. Evil indeed is what they used to do.

10. They do not respect those who are believers, nor a kinship, nor a pledge. These are the transgressors.

11. If they repent, and they honour the oath of allegiance, and they contribute towards betterment, then they are your brothers in the system. We explain the revelations for a people who know.

12. And if they break their oaths after making them, and they denounce the authority of your system; then you may kill the chiefs of rejection. Their oaths are nothing to them, perhaps they will then cease.

13. Would you not fight a people who broke their oaths and intended to expel the messenger, especially while they were the ones who attacked you first? Do you fear them? It is God who is more worthy to be feared if you are believers.

14. Fight them; perhaps God will punish them by your hands and humiliate them and grant you victory over them and heal the chests of the believing people.

15. And to remove the anger from their hearts; God pardons whom he pleases. God is Knowledgeable, Wise.

16. Or did you think that you would be left alone? God will come to distinguish those of you who strived and did not take other than God and His messenger and the believers as helpers. God is Expert in what you do.

17. It was not for those who have set up partners to maintain God's temples while they bear witness over their own rejection. For these, their works have fallen, and in the Fire they will abide.

18. Rather, the temples of God are maintained by he who believes in God and the Last Day, and he honours the oath of allegiance, and he contributes towards betterment, and he does not fear except God. It is these that will be of the guided ones.

19. Have you made the watering of the pilgrim and the maintenance of the Restricted Temple the same as one who believes in God and the Last Day and he strives in the cause of God? They are not the same with God. And God does not guide the wicked people.

20. Those who believed and emigrated and strived in the cause of God with their wealth and their lives are in a greater degree with God. These are the winners.

21. Their Lord gives them good news of a Mercy from Him, and acceptance, and estates that are for them in which there is permanent bliss.

22. They will abide in it eternally. God has a great reward.
23. O you who believe, do not take your fathers nor brothers as allies if they prefer rejection to belief. And whoever of you takes them as such, then these are the wicked.
24. Say: "If your fathers, and your sons, and your brothers, and your wives, and your clan, and money which you have gathered, and a trade which you would fear if it declines, and homes which you find pleasing; if these are dearer to you than God and His messenger and striving in His cause, then wait until God brings His decision. And God does not guide the wicked people."
25. God has granted you victory in many battles. And on the day of Hunayn when you were pleased with your great numbers but it did not help you at all, and the land became tight around you for what it held, then you turned to flee.
26. Then God sent down tranquility upon His messenger and the believers, and He sent down soldiers which you did not see, and He punished those who disbelieved. Such is the recompense of the rejecters.
27. Then God will accept the repentance of whom He pleases after that. God is Forgiving, Merciful.
28. O you who believe, those who have set up partners are impure, so let them not approach the Restricted Temple after this year of theirs; and if you fear poverty, then God will enrich you from His blessings if He wills. God is Knowledgeable, Wise.
29. Fight those who do not believe in God or the Last Day, and they do not forbid what God and His messenger have forbidden, and they do not uphold the system of truth; from among the people who have been given the Scripture; until they pay the fine, willingly or unwillingly.
30. The Jews said: "Ezra is God's son," and the Nazarenes said: "The Messiah is God's son." Such is their utterances with their mouths, they imitate the sayings of those who rejected before them. God will fight them. They are deluded from the truth!
31. They took their Priests and Monks to be patrons besides God, and the Messiah son of Mary, while they were only commanded to serve One god, there is no god but He, be He glorified for what they set up.
32. They want to extinguish God's light with their mouths, but God refuses such and lets His light continue, even if the rejecters hate it.

33. He is the One who sent His messenger with guidance and the system of truth, to make it expose all other systems, even if those who set up partners hate it.

34. O you who believe, many of the Priests and Monks consume people's money in falsehood, and they turn away from the path of God. And those who hoard gold and silver, and do not spend it in the cause of God, give them news of a painful retribution.

35. On the Day when they will be seared in the fires of Hell, and their foreheads and sides and backs will be branded with it: "This is what you have hoarded for yourselves, so taste what you have hoarded!"

36. The count of the months with God is twelve months in God's record the day He created the heavens and the Earth; four of them are restricted. This is the correct system; so do not wrong yourselves in them; and fight those who set up partners collectively as they fight you collectively. And know that God is with the righteous.

37. Know that the use of the additional month causes an increase in rejection, for it is used by those who have rejected that they may misguide with it by making it lawful one year and forbidding it one year, so as to circumvent the count that God has made restricted; thus they make lawful what God made forbidden! Their evil works have been adorned for them, and God does not guide the rejecting people.

38. O you who believe, what is wrong with you when you are told: "March forth in the cause of God," you become heavy on Earth. Have you become content with this worldly life over the Hereafter? The enjoyment of this worldly life compared to the Hereafter is nothing.

39. If you do not march forth, then He will punish you with a painful retribution, and He will replace you with another people, and you do not bother Him in the least. God is capable of all things.

40. If you do not help him, then God has helped him. When those who rejected expelled him, he was one of only two, and when they were in the cave, he said to his friend: "Do not grieve, for God is with us." So God sent down calmness over him and He supported him with soldiers that you did not see, and He made the word of those who rejected be the lowest, and God's word be the highest. God is Noble, Wise.

41. March forth in light gear or heavy gear, and strive with your money and lives in the cause of God. That is best if you knew.

42. If it were a near gain, or an easy journey, they would have followed you; but the distance was too much for them. And they will swear by God: "If we

could have, we would have come with you." They destroy themselves, and God knows they are liars.

43. God pardons you; why did you give them leave before it became clear to you who are truthful, and who are lying?

44. Those who believe in God and the Last Day will not ask leave. They strive with their money and their lives. And God is aware of the righteous.

45. Those who ask leave are the ones who do not believe in God and the Last Day, and their hearts are in doubt. In their doubts they are wavering.

46. And if they had gone with you then they would have taken all precautions for it, but God disliked them coming forth, so He made them lag behind, and they were told: "Stay with those who have stayed."

47. Had they come out with you they would have added nothing but disruption, and they would have hurried about seeking to cause for you an ordeal; and there are some amongst you who listen to them. God is aware of the wicked.

48. They wanted to cause an ordeal from before, and they turned matters upside down for you until the truth came and God's command was revealed, while they hated it.

49. And from them are those who Say: "Grant me leave, and do not test me." But it is in the test that they have indeed fallen, and Hell is surrounding the rejecters.

50. When any good befalls you, it upsets them, and if any bad befalls you, they Say: "We have made our precautions beforehand," and they turn away happy.

51. Say: "Nothing will befall us except what God has decreed for us, He is our Patron." And in God the believers shall put their trust.

52. Say: "You can only expect for us one of two good things; while we wait for you to be afflicted by God with a retribution from Him, or by our hands. So wait, we are with you waiting."

53. Say: "Spend willingly or unwillingly, it will not be accepted from you. You are a wicked people."

54. And what prevented what they would spend from being accepted from them except that they rejected God and His messenger, and they do not attend the oath of allegiance except lazily, and they do not spend except unwillingly.

55. So do not be impressed by their wealth or children; God only wishes to punish them with it in the worldly life, and so that their lives will end while they are rejecters.

56. And they swear by God that they are with you, while they are not with you; but they are a people who are indecisive.

57. If they find a refuge, or cave, or any place to enter, then they would have run to it while they are in haste.

58. And from them are those who criticize you regarding the charities. If they are given from it, they are content; and if they are not given from it, they become enraged!

59. And if they had only been content with what God and His messenger had given them, and they had said: "God suffices; God will give us from His bounty, and His messenger; it is to God that we desire."

60. The charities are to go to the poor, and the needy, and those who work to collect them, and those whose hearts have been united, and to free the slaves, and those in debt, and in the cause of God, and the wayfarer. A duty from God, and God is Knowledgeable, Wise.

61. And from them are those who harm the prophet, and they Say: "He only listens!" Say: "What he listens to is best for you. He believes in God, and he has trust for the believers, and he is a mercy to those who believe among you." And those who harm God's messenger will have a painful retribution.

62. They swear to you by God in order to please you; while God and His messenger are more worthy to be pleased if they are believers.

63. Did they not know that whoever is hostile towards God and His messenger, he will have the Fire of Hell to abide in. Such is the greatest humiliation.

64. The hypocrites fear that a chapter will be sent down which will expose what is in their hearts. Say: "Mock, for God will bring out what you fear."

65. And if you ask them they Say: "We were only jesting and playing." Say: "Is it in God and His verses and His messenger you were mocking?"

66. Do not apologize, for you have rejected after your belief. If We pardon one group from you, We will punish another group. That is because they were criminals.

67. The hypocrite men and women, they are to each other. They order evil and deter from good, and they close their hands. They forgot God, so He forgot them; the hypocrites are the wicked.

68. God has promised the hypocrite men and women and the rejecters a Fire in Hell, in it they will abide; it will be enough for them. And God has cursed them and they will have a lasting retribution.

69. Like those before them, they were more powerful than you, and with more wealth and offspring. They enjoyed their lives, and you enjoyed your lives as those before you enjoyed their lives; and you jested as they jested. They had their work crumble in this world and the next, and they were the losers.

70. Did the news not come to them of those before them, the people of Noah and 'Aad and Thamud. And the people of Abraham, and the dwellers of Median, and those overthrown. Their messengers came to them with clarity; it was not God who wronged them, but it was themselves that they wronged.

71. And the believing men and women, they are allies to one another. They order good and deter from evil, and they honour the oath of allegiance, and they contribute towards betterment and they obey God and His messenger. God will have mercy on them; God is Noble, Wise.

72. God has promised the believing men and women estates with rivers flowing beneath it, in which they will abide, and pleasing homes in the gardens of Eden. And the acceptance from God is the most important; such is the greatest success.

73. O prophet, strive against the rejecters and the hypocrites and be firm against them. Their dwelling is Hell, what a miserable destiny!

74. They swear by God that they did not say it, while they had said the word of rejection, and they rejected after they had submitted, and they were concerned with what they could not possess; and they could not find any fault except that God and His messenger had enriched them from His bounty. If they repent it is better for them, and if they turn away, then God will punish them severely in this world and the next. They will not have on Earth any ally or supporter.

75. And from them are those who pledged to God: "If He gives us from His bounty, then we will believe and we will be amongst the upright."

76. So when He gave them of His bounty, they became stingy with it, and they turned away while they were averse.

77. Thus, hypocrisy followed in their hearts until the Day they meet Him; that is for breaking what they promised God, and for what they were lying.

78. Did they not know that God knows their secrets, and their conspiracies, and that God is the knower of all the unseen?

79. Those who criticize the volunteers among the believers in charities; that they only have their effort to give; so they mock them. God mocks them, and they will have a painful retribution.

80. Whether you seek forgiveness for them, or do not seek forgiveness for them. If you seek forgiveness for them seventy times, God will not forgive them. That is because they have rejected God and His messenger; and God does not guide the wicked people.

81. Those who have remained behind are content with their position behind God's messenger, and they disliked to strive with their wealth and lives in the

cause of God; and they Say: "Do not march out in the heat." Say: "The fire of Hell is far hotter," if they could only understand.

82. Let them laugh a little, and cry a lot, a recompense for what they had earned.

83. If God returns you to a group of them, and they ask your permission to come with you, then Say: "You will not come with me ever; nor will you fight any enemy with me. You had accepted staying behind the first time, so stay with those who remain behind."

84. And do not approach any of them who have died, nor stand at their grave. They have rejected God and His messenger and died while they were wicked.

85. And do not be impressed by their wealth and their children; God only wishes to punish them with it in this world, and so their souls will be taken to death while they are rejecters.

86. And if a chapter is sent down: "That you shall believe in God and strive with His messenger," those with wealth and influence ask your permission and they Say: "Let us be with those who remain behind."

87. They were content to stay with those who remained behind, and it was stamped on their hearts, for they do not comprehend.

88. But the messenger and those who believe with him have strived with their money and their lives. For them will be the good things, and they are the successful ones.

89. God has prepared for them estates with rivers flowing beneath, in them they shall abide. Such is the great gain.

90. And those who had an excuse from among the Nomads came so permission would be given to them, and those who denied God and His messenger simply stayed behind. Those who rejected from them will be inflicted with a painful retribution.

91. There is no blame to be placed upon the weak, or the sick, or those who do not find anything to spend on, if they are sincere to God and His messenger. There is no argument against the good doers; and God is Forgiving, Merciful.

92. Nor upon those who come to ride out with you, while you said: "I do not have any mounts for you;" they turned away while their eyes were flooded with tears out of sadness, for they could not find anything to contribute.

93. Indeed, the argument is against those who sought your permission to stay while they were rich. They accepted to be with those who remained behind, and God stamps their hearts, for they do not know.

94. They will apologize to you when you return to them, Say: "Do not apologize, we will not believe you, for God has told us of your news." And God will see your work, as will His messenger, then you will be returned to the knower of the unseen and the seen, He will inform you of what you did.

95. They will swear by God to you, when you return to them, so that you would let them be. So let them be, for they are foul, and their destiny is Hell as a recompense for what they earned.

96. They swear to you so that you would accept them. Even if you accept them, God does not accept the wicked people.

97. The Nomads are the worst in rejection and hypocrisy, and more likely not to know the limits of what God has sent down upon His messenger. God is Knower, Wise.

98. And from the Nomads are some who look upon what they spend as a fine, and wait for misfortune upon you. They will have the misfortune of evil, and God is Hearer, Knowledgeable.

99. And from the Nomads are those who believe in God and the Last Day, and he looks upon what he spends to make him closer to God, and the allegiances to the messenger. It indeed makes them closer. God will admit them in His mercy; God is Forgiving, Merciful.

100. And those who came early and quickly from amongst the emigrants and the supporters, and those who followed them in kindness; God has accepted them, and they have accepted Him; and He prepared for them estates with rivers flowing beneath in which they will abide eternally. Such is the great success.

101. And from the Nomads around you are hypocrites, as well as from the city people, they persist in hypocrisy. You do not know them, but We know them. We will punish them twice, then they will be returned to a great punishment.

102. And others who have acknowledged their sins, they have mixed good work with bad. Perhaps God will pardon them. God is Forgiving, Merciful.

103. Take from their money a charity to purify them and develop them with it, and give allegiance to them; for your allegiances are a tranquility for them; and God is Hearer, Knowledgeable.

104. Did they not know that it is God who accepts repentance from His servants, and He takes the charities, and that God is the Pardoner, Merciful.

105. And Say: "Work, and God will see your work and His messenger and the believers. And you will be sent back to the knower of the unseen and the seen, and He will inform you of what you did."

106.And others will wait for God's decision; either He will punish them, or He will pardon them. God is Knowledgeable, Wise.

107.And there are those who establish a temple to do harm and cause rejection, and to divide between the believers, and as an outpost for those who fought God and His messenger before. They will swear that they only wanted to do good, and God bears witness that they are liars.

108.Do not maintain in it ever. A temple that is founded on righteousness from the first day is more worthy that you maintain in it; in it are men who love to be cleansed. And God loves the cleansed.

109.Is one who lays his foundation on obtaining righteousness from God and His acceptance better, or one who lays his foundation on the edge of a cliff which is about to crumble, so that it crumbled with him into the fires of Hell? God does not guide the wicked people.

110.Such a structure that they erect will continue to cause doubt in their hearts, until their hearts are severed. God is Knowledgeable, Wise.

111.God has purchased from the believers their very lives and their wealth, that they will have Paradise; they fight in the cause of God so they kill and are killed; a promise that is true upon Him in the Torah and the Injeel and the Quran. And whoever fulfills this vow with God, then have good news of the pledge which you are concluded with. Such is the supreme success.

112.Those who repent, those who serve, those who thank, those who wander in devotion, those who kneel, those who prostrate, those who order good and deter from evil, and those who keep the boundaries of God. And give good news to the believers.

113.It is not for the prophet and those who believe that they should seek forgiveness for those who have set up partners, even if they are relatives, after it has been made clear to them that they are the dwellers of Hell.

114.And Abraham seeking forgiveness for his father was only because of a promise he made to him. But when it became clear that he was God's enemy, he disowned him. Abraham was kind, compassionate.

115.And it is not for God to misguide a people after He guided them, until He makes clear to them what they should avoid. God is aware of all things.

116.To God is the sovereignty of heavens and Earth, He brings life and death. You have none besides God as a supporter or victor.

117.God has pardoned the prophet and the emigrants and the supporters that followed him in the darkest hour, even though the hearts of some of them nearly deviated, but then He pardoned them. He is towards them Compassionate, Merciful.

118.And upon the three who were left behind until the land, as vast as it is, became strained to them, and their very souls became strained, and they thought there is no shelter from God except to Him. Then He pardoned them that they might repent. God is the Redeemer, the Merciful.

119.O you who believe, be aware of God and be with the truthful.

120.It is not advisable for the city dwellers and those around them of the Nomads that they should lag behind after God's messenger, nor should they yearn for themselves above him. That is because any thirst that will come to them, or fatigue, or hunger in the cause of God, or any step that they take which will annoy the rejecters, or any gain they have over any enemy; it will be recorded as a good deed for them. God does not waste the reward of the good doers.

121.And anything small or large they spend, or any valley they cross, it will be recorded for them. God will recompense them with the best of what they did.

122.And it is not advisable for the believers to march out in their entirety. For every battalion that marches out, let a group remain to study the system, and warn their people when they return to them, perhaps they will be aware.

123.O you who believe, fight those who around you of the rejecters, and let them find strength in you; and know that God is with the righteous.

124.And when a chapter is revealed, some of them Say: "Who has been strengthened in faith by this?" For those who believe, it increased their faith, and they rejoice.

125.As for those who have a disease in their hearts, it only increased foulness to their foulness, and they died as rejecters.

126.Do they not see they are tested every year once or twice?, but then they do not repent, nor do they remember.

127.And when a chapter is revealed, they look at one another: "Does anyone see you?", then they turn away. God turns away their hearts, for they are a people who do not comprehend.

128.A messenger has come to you from yourselves, concerned over your suffering, anxious over you, towards the believers he is compassionate, merciful.

129.If they turn away, then Say: "God is enough for me, there is no god but He, in Him I put my trust and He is the Lord of the great throne."

Chapter 10

بسم الله الرحمن الرحيم

In the name of God, the Almighty, the Merciful.

1. A.L.R, these are the signs of the Scripture of wisdom.

2. Is it a surprise for the people that We would inspire a man from amongst them: "Warn the people and give good news to those who believe, that they will have a footing of truth with their Lord." The rejecters said: "This is clearly magic!"

3. Your Lord is God who created the heavens and the Earth in six days, then He settled over the throne; He handles all affairs. There is no intercessor except after His leave. Such is God your Lord, so serve Him. Would you not remember?

4. To Him is your return, all of you, for God's promise is true. He initiates the creation then He returns it to recompense with justice those who believed and did good work. As for those who rejected, they will have a boiling drink, and a painful retribution for what they had rejected.

5. He is the One who made the sun to emit light, and the moon to reflect it, and He measured its phases; that you may know the number of the years and the count. God has not created this except for truth. He details the revelations for a people who know.

6. In the difference between night and day and what God has created in heavens and Earth are signs for a people who are aware.

7. As for those who do not wish to meet Us, and they are content with the worldly life, and they became relieved with it, and they are unaware of Our signs.

8. To these will be the destiny of the Fire for what they earned.

9. Those who believe and do good work, their Lord will guide them by their faith. Rivers will flow beneath them in the gardens of Paradise.

10. Their prayer in it is: "Glory be to our god!" and their greeting in it is: "Peace," and the end of their prayer is: "Praise be to God, the Lord of the worlds!"

11. And if God were to hasten for the people the evil as He hastens for them the good, then they would have been ruined. We thus leave those who do not wish to meet Us wandering in their transgression.

12. And if any adversity inflicts mankind, then he calls upon Us on his side or sitting or standing. But when We remove his adversity from him, he goes on as if he never called upon Us to an adversity which touched him! It is thus that what the carefree have done was made to appear good to them.

13. We have destroyed the generations before you when they transgressed, and their messengers came to them with clear proofs, but they were not to believe. It is such that We will recompense the criminal people.

14. Then We made you successors on Earth after them to see how you would perform.

15. And when Our clear revelations are recited to them, those who do not wish to meet Us said: "Bring a Quran other than this, or change it!" Say: "It is not for me to change it from my own accord, I merely follow what is inspired to me. I fear if I disobey my Lord the retribution of a great day!"

16. Say: "Had God wished, I would not have recited it to you, nor would you have known about it. I have been residing amongst you for nearly a lifetime before this; do you not understand?"

17. Who is more wicked than one who invents lies about God or denies His revelations? The criminals will never succeed.

18. And they serve besides God what does not harm them or benefit them, and they Say: "These are our intercessors with God." Say: "Are you informing God of what He does not know in the heavens or in the Earth?" Be He glorified and high from what they set up.

19. The people were but one nation, then they differed. And had it not been for a previous command from your Lord, the matter would have been immediately judged between them for what they differed.

20. And they Say: "If only a sign was sent down to him from His Lord." Say: "The future is with God, so wait, and I will wait with you."

21. And if We let the people taste a mercy after some harm had afflicted them, they take to scheming against Our revelations! Say: "God is faster in scheming;" Our messengers record what you scheme.

22. He is the One who carries you on land and on the sea. And when you are on the ships and We drive them with a good wind which they rejoice with, a strong gust comes to it and the waves come to them from all sides, and they think that they are finished, they implore God with loyalty and devotion to His system: "If You save us from this, we will be of the thankful."

23. But when He saves them, they then traverse through the land with injustice. "O mankind, what you seek out is only the luxury of this worldly life, then to Us is your return and We will inform you of all that you had done."

24. The example of the worldly life is like a water which has come down from the sky, so it mixed with the plants of the Earth from what the people and the livestock eat. Then the Earth takes its shape and becomes beautiful and its inhabitants think that they have mastered it; then Our judgment comes by night or by day, so We make it a wasteland as if it never prospered by the yesterday! It is such that We clarify the revelations to a people who think.

25. God calls to the abode of peace, and He guides those whom He wishes to a Straight Path.

26. To those who do good work will be good and more, and their faces will not be darkened or humiliated. These are the people of Paradise, in it they will abide.

27. As for those who earn evil, the recompense of evil will be evil like it, and they will be humiliated. They do not have any besides God as a helper. It is as if their faces have been covered by a piece of darkness from the night. These are the people of the Fire, in it they will abide.

28. And on the Day We gather them all, We will say to those who have set up partners: "Stop where you are, you and your partners," then We separate between them, and their partners will Say: "It was not us that you served."

29. "God is sufficient as a witness between us and you, we were unaware of you serving of us."

30. It is then that every soul will know what it has done, and they are returned to God their true patron, and what they had invented has left them.

31. Say: "Who provides for you from the sky and the land? Who possesses the hearing and the eyesight?, and who brings forth the living from the dead and brings forth the dead from the living, and who controls all affairs?" They will Say: "God." Say: "Will you not be righteous!"

32. Such is God, your true Lord. So what is after the truth except straying! Why then do you turn away?

33. It was thus that your Lord's command came against those who were wicked, for they do not believe.

34. Say: "Are there any from those whom you have set up as partners who can initiate the creation and then return it?" Say: "God initiates the creation and then returns it." How are you deluded!

35. Say: "Are there any of those whom you set up as partners who can guide to the truth?" Say: "God guides to the truth. Is He who guides to the truth more worthy of being followed, or the one who does not guide except after he is guided? What is wrong with you, how do you judge?"

36. Most of them only follow conjecture. While conjecture does not avail against the truth in anything. God is aware of what they do.

37. This Quran could not have been produced without God, but it is to authenticate what is already present, and to give detail to the Scripture in which there is no doubt, from the Lord of the worlds.

38. Or do they say he invented it? Say: "Then bring a chapter like it, and call upon whoever you can besides God if you are truthful!"

39. No, they have lied about that which they did not have knowledge of, nor has its explanation come to them. It is also how those before them denied, so see how was the retribution of the wicked!

40. And there are some of them who believe in it, and some of them do not believe in it. Your Lord is better aware of the transgressors.

41. And if they deny you, then Say: "I have my deeds, and you have your deeds. You are innocent from what I do, and I am innocent from what you do."

42. And there are some of them who listen to you; but can you make the deaf hear, if they do not comprehend?

43. And there are some of them who look at you; but can you guide the blind, if they do not see?

44. God does not wrong the people in the least, but it is the people who wrong themselves.

45. And the Day We gather them, it will be as if they have slept for only an hour of a day. They will get to know one another. Losers are those who denied meeting God, and they were not guided.

46. And if We show you some of what We promise them, or We let you pass away, then to Us is their return and God is witness over what they do.

47. And for every nation is a messenger; so when their messenger comes, the matter is decreed between them with justice, and they are not wronged.

48. And they Say: "When is this promise if you are truthful?"

49. Say: "I do not posses for myself any harm or benefit except what God wills. For every nation is a time. When their time comes, they cannot delay it one hour nor advance it."

50. Say: "Do you see if His retribution will come to you by night or by day, then which portion would the criminals hasten in?"
51. "Would you then, when it occurs, believe in it? While now you are hastening it on!"
52. Then it will be said to those who were wicked: "Taste the everlasting retribution. You are only recompensed for what you have earned!"
53. And they seek news from you: "Is it true?" Say: "Yes, by my Lord it is true, and you cannot escape from it."
54. And if every soul that wronged had possessed all that is on Earth, it would have attempted to ransom it. And they declared their regret when they saw the retribution, and it was judged between them with fairness. They were not wronged.
55. To God is what is in the heavens and the Earth. God's promise is true, but most of them do not know.
56. He gives life, and He brings death, and to Him you will return.
57. O mankind, advice has come to you from your Lord and a remedy for what is in the chests, and a guidance and mercy for the believers.
58. Say: "By God's grace and His mercy." For that let them rejoice, that is better than all that they gather.
59. Say: "Have you seen what God has sent down to you from provisions, then you made some of it forbidden and some lawful?" Say: "Did God authorize you, or did you invent lies against God?"
60. And what will those who invent lies against God think on the Day of Resurrection? God is with great bounty to the people, but most of them are not thankful.
61. And any matter you are in, or any recitation you do of the Quran, or any work you do; We are witnesses over you when you undertake it. Nothing is hidden from your Lord, not even an atoms weight on Earth or in the heavens, nor smaller than that nor larger, but is in a clear record.
62. For God's allies, there is no fear over them nor will they grieve.
63. Those who believed and were aware.
64. For them are glad tidings in the worldly life and in the Hereafter. There is no changing the words of God. Such is the great success.
65. And do not be saddened by their speech, for all glory is to God. He is the Hearer, the Knowledgeable.
66. Certainly, to God belongs all who are in the heavens and those who are on Earth. As for those who call on partners besides God, they only follow conjecture, and they only guess.

67. He is the One who made the night for you to reside in, and the day to see. In that are signs for a people who listen.

68. They said: "God has taken a son." Be He glorified! He is the Rich. To Him is what is in the heavens and what is in the Earth. Do you have proof for this? Or do you say about God what you do not know?

69. Say: "Those who invent lies about God, they will not be successful."

70. A short pleasure in this world, then to Us is their return and We will make them taste the severe retribution for what they were rejecting.

71. And recite for them the news of Noah as he said to his people: "My people, if my position has become too troublesome for you, and my reminding you of God's signs, then in God I place my trust. So gather your evidence and your partners, then make certain your evidence does not become against you, then come to judge me, and do not hold back."

72. "But if you turn away, then I have not asked you for any reward, for my reward is with God. And I have been commanded to be of those who have submitted."

73. They denied him, so We saved him and those with him in the Ship, and We made them to succeed each other, and We drowned those who denied Our revelations. So see how was the punishment of those who were warned!

74. Then, after him, We sent messengers to their own people, so they came to them with proofs. But they did not want to believe in what they had already denied beforehand. It is such that We stamp on the hearts of the transgressors.

75. Then, after them, We sent Moses and Aaron with Our signs to Pharaoh and his leaders, but they turned arrogant, they were a criminal people.

76. So when the truth came to them from Us, they said: "This is clearly magic!"

77. Moses said: "Would you say this about the truth when it came to you? Is this magic? The magicians will not be successful."

78. They said: "Have you come to us to turn us away from that which we found our fathers upon, and so that you two would have greatness in the land? We will not believe in you."

79. And Pharaoh said: "Bring me every knowledgeable magician."

80. So, when the magicians came, Moses said to them: "Cast what you will cast."

81. So when they cast, Moses said: "What you have brought is magic, God will disable it. God does not set right the work of the corrupters."

82. "And so that God will set the truth with His words, even if the criminals hate it."

83. But none believed in Moses from his people except some from their descendants, because of their fear from Pharaoh and his leaders that he would persecute them. Pharaoh was high in the land, and he was of the tyrants.

84. And Moses said: "O my people, if you believe in God, then put your trust in Him if you have submitted."

85. They said: "In God we put our trust. Our Lord, do not make us a test for the wicked people."

86. "And save us by Your mercy from the rejecting people."

87. And We inspired to Moses and his brother: "Let your people leave their homes in Egypt, and let these homes be your focal point, and perform the oath of allegiance. And give good news to the believers."

88. And Moses said: "Our Lord, you have given Pharaoh and his commanders adornments and wealth in this worldly life so that they will misguide from Your path. Our Lord, wipe-out their wealth and bring grief to their hearts; for they will not believe until they see the painful retribution."

89. He said: "I have answered your prayer, so keep straight and do not follow the path of those who do not know."

90. And We helped the Children of Israel cross the sea, and Pharaoh and his soldiers followed them out of hatred and animosity. But when he was certain to drown, he said: "I believe that there is no god except the One in whom the Children of Israel believe, and I am of those who have submitted."

91. Now you say this?, while before you disobeyed and were of the corrupters!

92. This day, We will preserve your body, so that you become a sign for those after you. But most of the people are unaware of Our signs!

93. And We helped the Children of Israel reach a place of sanctity, and We provided them from the good things, and they did not differ until the knowledge came to them. Your Lord will judge between them on the Day of Resurrection for what they differed in.

94. If you are in doubt regarding what We have sent down to you, then ask those who have been reading the Scripture from before you. The truth has come to you from your Lord, so do not be of those who doubt.

95. And do not be of those who denied God's revelations, for you will be of the losers.

96. Those who have deserved your Lord's retribution do not believe.

97. Even if every sign were to come to them; until they see the painful retribution.

98. If there was any town that benefited from its belief, then that would be the people of Jonah. When they believed, We removed from them the retribution of disgrace in this worldly life, and We let them enjoy until a time.

99. And had your Lord willed, all the people on Earth in their entirety would have believed. Would you force the people to make them believe?

100. And it is not for a soul to believe except by God's leave. And He makes the affliction upon those who do not comprehend.

101. Say: "Look at all that is in the heavens and the Earth." But what good are the signs and warnings to a people who do not believe?

102. Are they waiting for the days like those who passed away before them? Say: "Wait, for I am with you waiting."

103. Then We will save Our messengers and those who believe. It is thus binding upon Us that We save the believers.

104. Say: "O people, if you are in doubt of my system, then I do not serve those that you serve besides God. But I serve God who takes me, and I have been commanded to be of the believers."

105. And set your direction to the system of monotheism, and do not be of those who set up partners.

106. And do not call upon other than God what does not benefit you or harm you; if you do, then you are of the wicked.

107. And if God afflicts you with any harm, then none can remove it except Him; and if He wanted good for you, then none can turn away His grace, He brings it to whom He wishes of His servants. And He is the Forgiver, the Merciful.

108. Say: "O people, the truth has come to you from your Lord, so whosoever is guided is being guided for himself, and whosoever is misguided will remain so, and I am not a caretaker over you."

109. And follow what is being inspired to you and be patient until God judges. And He is the best of judges.

Chapter 11

بسم الله الرحمن الرحيم

In the name of God, the Almighty, the Merciful.

1. A.L.R, a Scripture whose verses have been made firm, then detailed, from One who is Wise, Expert.

2. "That you shall serve none other than God. I am to you from Him a warner and a bearer of good news."

3. "And seek forgiveness from your Lord, then repent to Him; He will make you enjoy an enjoyment until a predetermined period. And He gives His grace to those who are of grace. And if you turn away, then I do fear for you the retribution of a great day!"

4. "To God is your return, and He is capable of all things."

5. Alas, they folded their chests to hide from it. Even when they hide themselves under their outer garments, He knows what they keep secret and what they declare. He is the knower of all that is in the chests.

6. And there is not a creature on Earth except that its provision is due from God. And He knows where it dwells and where it hides. All is in a clear record.

7. He is the One who created the heavens and Earth in six days, and His throne was upon the water, and to test who from amongst you works the best. And when you Say: "You will be resurrected after death." those who rejected will Say: "This is but clear magic!"

8. And if We delay for them the retribution to a near period, they will Say: "What has kept it?" Alas, on the day it comes to them, nothing will turn it away from them, and what they used to mock will catch-up with them.

9. And if We give man a taste of mercy from Us, then We withdraw it from him; he becomes despairing, rejecting.

10. And if We give him the taste of a blessing after hardship had afflicted him, he will Say: "Evil has gone from me!"; he becomes happy, boastful.

11. Except for those who are patient and do good work; these will have a pardon, and a great reward.

12. So perhaps you wish to ignore some of what has been inspired to you, and you are depressed by it, because they Say: "If only a treasure was sent down with him, or an Angel had come with him!" You are but a warner, and God is caretaker over all things.

13. Or do they Say: "He invented it!" Say: "Bring ten invented chapters like it, and call on whom you can besides God if you are truthful."

14. So, if they do not respond to you, then know that it was sent down with God's knowledge, and that there is no god but He. Will you then submit?

15. Whoever wants the worldly life and its adornments, then We will grant them their works in it, and they will not be short changed in it.

16. These will have nothing but fire in the Hereafter, and what they have done will be put-down, and evil is what they have worked.

17. For those who are on a clarity from their Lord, and are followed by a testimony from Him; and before it was the Scripture of Moses as a guide and a mercy; they will believe in it. And whoever rejects it from amongst the parties, then the Fire is his meeting place. So do not be in any doubt about it. It is the truth from your Lord, but most people do not believe.

18. And who is more wicked than one who invents lies about God? They will be displayed before their Lord, and the witnesses will Say: "These are the ones who lied about their Lord." Alas, God's curse will be upon the wicked.

19. Those who block others from the path of God and they seek to twist it; and regarding the Hereafter they are in denial.

20. These are the ones who will not escape on Earth, nor do they have besides God any allies. The retribution will be doubled for them. They were not able to hear, nor could they see.

21. They are the ones who lost themselves, and what they had invented has abandoned them.

22. There is no doubt, that in the Hereafter they are the greatest losers.

23. Those who believe and do good works, and are humble towards their Lord; they are the dwellers of Paradise, in it they will remain.

24. The example of the two groups is like the blind and deaf, and the seer and hearer. Are they the same when compared? Do you not take heed?

25. And We had sent Noah to his people: "I am to you a clear warner!"

26. "Do not serve except God. I fear for you the retribution of a painful day."

27. The leaders who rejected from amongst his people said: "We do not see you except as a human like us, and we see that only the lowest amongst our people who have no opinion have followed you. And we do not see anything that makes you better than us; in fact, we think you are liars."

28. He said: "My people, do you not see that I have clarity from my Lord and He gave me mercy from Himself, but it has been blinded to you? Shall we compel you to it while you have a hatred to it?"

29. "And my people, I do not ask you for money, my reward is with God. Nor will I turn away those who believe, for they will meet their Lord. But I see that you are a people who are ignorant."

30. "And my people, who will give me victory against God if I turn them away? Will you not remember!"

31. "Nor do I say to you that I have the treasures of God, nor do I know the future, nor do I say that I am an Angel, nor do I say to those whom your eyes look down upon that God will not grant them any good. God is more aware of what is in their souls; in such case I would be among the wicked."

32. They said: "O Noah, you have argued with us, and continued arguing with us, so bring us what you promise us if you are of the truthful ones."

33. He said: "It is God who will bring it to you if He wishes; you will not have any escape."

34. "And my advice will not benefit you if I wanted to advise you and God wanted that you should stray. He is your Lord, and to Him you will return."

35. Or do they Say: "He invented it?" Say: "If I invented it, then I am responsible for my crime, and I am innocent from your crimes"

36. And it was inspired to Noah: "No more of your people will believe except those who have already believed. So do not be saddened by what they have done."

37. "And construct the Ship under Our eyes and Our inspiration, and do not speak to Me regarding those who are wicked. They will be drowned."

38. And as he was constructing the Ship, every time any cluster from his people passed by, they mocked him. He said: "If you mock us, then we also mock you as you mock."

39. "You will know to whom the retribution will come to disgrace him, and upon him will be a lasting punishment."

40. So, when Our command came and the volcano erupted. We said: "Carry in it two from every pair, and your family; except those against whom the word has been issued; and whoever believed." But those who believed with him were few.

41. He said: "Climb inside, in the name of God shall be its sailing and its anchorage. My Lord is Forgiving, Merciful."

42. And while it was running with them in waves like mountains, Noah called to his son, who was in an isolated place: "My son, ride with us, and do not be with the rejecters!"

43. He said: "I will take refuge to the mountain which will save me from the water." He said: "There is no saviour from God's decree except to whom He grants mercy." And the wave came between them, so he was one of those who drowned.

44. And it was said: "O land, swallow your water, and O sky, cease." And the water was diminished, and the matter concluded. And it came to rest on the Judi, and it was said: "Away with the wicked people."

45. And Noah called on his Lord, and he said: "My Lord, my son is from my family, and your promise is the truth, and you are the Wisest of all Judges."

46. He said: "O Noah, he is not from your family, he was fathered illicitly, so do not ask what you have no knowledge of. I advise you not to be of the ignorant."

47. He said: "My Lord, I seek refuge with You that I would ask You what I did not have knowledge of. And if You do not forgive me and have mercy on me, I will be of the losers!"

48. It was said: "O Noah, descend in peace from Us and blessings upon you and upon nations to come from those with you; and nations whom We will grant pleasure, then a painful retribution will reach them from Us."

49. This is from the news of the unseen that We inspire to you. Neither did you nor your people know this, so be patient. The ending is always in favour of the righteous.

50. And to 'Aad was sent their brother Hud. He said: "My people, serve God, you have no god besides Him; you are simply conjecturing."

51. "My people, I do not ask you for any wage, my wage is from the One who initiated me. Will you not understand?"

52. "And my people, seek forgiveness from your Lord, then repent to Him; He will send the sky to you abundantly, and He will increase might to your might. So do not turn away as criminals."

53. They said: "O Hud, you have not come to us with any proof, nor will we leave our gods based on what you say. We will not believe in you."

54. "All we can say is that perhaps some of our gods have seized you with evil." He said: "I make God my witness, and all of you witness, that I disown what you have set up as partners."

55. "Besides Him, so scheme against me all of you, then do not give me respite."

56. "I have put my trust in God, my Lord and your Lord. There is not a creature except He will seize it by frontal lobe. My Lord is on a Straight Path."

57. "So, if you turn away, then I have delivered what I was sent to you with. And my Lord will bring after you a people who are not like you, and you will not harm Him the least. My Lord is Guardian over all things."

58. And when Our command came, We saved Hud and those who believed with him by a mercy from Us, and We saved them from a mighty retribution.

59. Such was the case of 'Aad. They disregarded the revelations of their Lord, and they disobeyed His messengers, and they followed the lead of everyone powerful and stubborn.

60. And they were followed by a curse in this world and on the Day of Judgment, for 'Aad rejected their Lord. There is no more 'Aad, the people of Hud.

61. And to Thamud was sent their brother Saleh. He said: "My people, serve God, you have no god besides Him. He established you in the land and gave you control over it, so seek His forgiveness, then repent to Him. My Lord is Near, Responsive."

62. They said: "O Saleh, you were well liked amongst us before this. Do you deter us from serving what our fathers served? We are in serious doubt as to what you are inviting us."

63. He said: "My people, what do you think if I was on clear evidence from my Lord, and He gave me from Him a mercy. Who would then support me against God if I disobey Him? You would only increase me in loss!"

64. "And my people, this is God's camel, in her you have a sign. So leave her to eat from God's land freely, and do not harm her, or else a close retribution will take you."

65. But they slaughtered her. So he said: "You will only have three days of enjoyment in your homes. This is a promise that will not be denied."

66. So, when Our command came, We saved Saleh and those who believed with him by a mercy from Us against the disgrace of that day. Your Lord is the Powerful, the Noble.

67. And those who wronged were taken by the scream, thus they lay motionless in their homes.

68. It is as if they never lived there. For Thamud rejected their Lord. There is no more Thamud.

69. And Our messengers came to Abraham with good news, they said: "Peace" He said: "Peace," and it was not long before he came back with a roasted calf.

70. But when he saw that their hands did not go towards it, he mistrusted them, and he began to have fear of them. They said: "Have no fear, we have been sent to the people of Lot."

71. And his wife was standing, so she laughed when We gave her good news of Isaac, and after Isaac, Jacob.

72. She said: "O my!, how can I give birth while I am an old woman, and here is my husband an old man? This is indeed a strange thing!"

73. They said: "Do you wonder at the decree of God? God's Mercy and Blessings are upon you O people of the Sanctuary. He is Praiseworthy, Glorious."

74. So when the shock left Abraham, and the good news was delivered to him, he began to argue with Us for the people of Lot.

75. Abraham was compassionate, kind.

76. O Abraham, turn away from this. Your Lord's command has come, and a retribution that will not be turned back is coming for them.

77. And when Our messengers came to Lot, he was grieved on their account and he felt discomfort for them and said: "This is a distressful day."

78. And his people came rushing towards him, and before it they were committing sin, he said: "My people, these are my daughters, they are purer for you, so be aware of God and do not disgrace me regarding my guests. Is there no sane man among you?"

79. They said: "You know we have no interest in your daughters, and you are aware of what we want!"

80. He said: "If only I had strength against you, or I could find for myself some powerful support."

81. They said: "O Lot, we are your Lord's messengers; they will not be able to harm you, so travel with your family during the cover of the night and let not any of you look back except for your wife, she will be afflicted with what they will be afflicted. Their appointed time will be the morning. Is the morning not near?"

82. So when Our command came, We turned it upside down, and We rained on it with hardened fiery projectiles.

83. Marked from your Lord, and they are never far from the wicked.

84. And to Median was their brother Shu'ayb, he said: "My people, serve God, you have no god besides Him, and do not give short in the measure and

weight. I see you in prosperity, and I fear for you the retribution of a day that is surrounding."

85. "And my people, give full measure and weight with justice, and do not hold back from the people what is theirs, and do not roam the land corrupting."

86. "What will remain for you with God is far better if you are believers. And I am not a guardian over you."

87. They said: "O Shu'ayb, does your oath order you that we leave what our fathers served, or that we do not do with our money as we please? You are the compassionate, the sane!"

88. He said: "O my people, do you see that if I am on clear evidence from my Lord, and He has provided me with good provision from Him, then I would not want to contradict by doing what I am deterring you from. I only want to fix what I can, and my guidance is only with God. To Him I place my trust, and to Him I repent."

89. "And my people, let not your hatred towards me incriminate you that you suffer the fate of what afflicted the people of Noah, or the people of Hud, or the people of Saleh; and the people of Lot were not far off from you."

90. "And seek forgiveness from your Lord then repent to Him. My Lord is Merciful, Loving."

91. They said: "O Shu'ayb, we do not understand most of what you say, and we see you as weak amongst us; and if it were not for who your family is, we would have stoned you, and you would not be proud against us."

92. He said: "My people, is who my family is more important to you than God, while you have cast Him away behind your backs? My Lord is encompassing what you do."

93. "And my people, continue to act as you do, and I will act. You will then come to know to whom the retribution will come to humiliate him and who is the liar. Watch then, and I will watch with you."

94. And when Our command came, We saved Shu'ayb and those who believed with him by a mercy from Us; and the scream took those who had wronged, so they lay motionless in their homes.

95. It is as if they never lived there. Away with Median as it was away with Thamud.

96. And We sent Moses with Our signs and a clear authority.

97. To Pharaoh and his leaders; but they followed the command of Pharaoh, and Pharaoh's command was not wise.

98. He will be at the head of his people on the Day of Resurrection, and he will lead them to the Fire. What a miserable place they are brought in!

99. And they were followed by a curse in this, and on the Day of Resurrection. What a miserable path to follow!

100. That is from the news of the towns which We relate to you; some are still standing and some have been wiped-out.

101. We did not wrong them, but they wronged themselves; their gods that they called on besides God did not rescue them at all when your Lord's command came, and they only added to their destruction.

102. Such is the taking of your Lord when He takes the towns while they are wicked. His taking is painful, severe.

103. In this is a sign for he who fears the retribution of the Hereafter. That is a Day to which all the people will be gathered, and that is a Day which will witnessed.

104. And We do not delay it except to a term already prepared for.

105. On the Day it comes, no person will speak to another except by His leave. Some of them will be distraught, some will be happy.

106. As for those who are distraught, they will be in the Fire; in it for them is a sighing and a wailing.

107. They will abide in it as long as the heavens and Earth exist, except for what your Lord wishes. Your Lord does as He pleases.

108. As for those who are fortunate, they will be in Paradise; in it they will abide as long as the heavens and Earth exist, except for what your Lord wishes, a giving without end.

109. So do not be in doubt as to what these men serve. They serve nothing but what their fathers before them served. We will give them their recompense in full.

110. We have given Moses the Scripture, yet they disputed in it; and had it not been for a word which was already given by your Lord, their case would have been judged immediately. They are in grave doubt concerning it.

111. And to each your Lord will recompense their works. He is expert in what they do.

112. So stand straight as you were commanded and those who repented with you and do not transgress. He is watcher over what you do.

113. And you shall not lean towards those who have wronged else you will incur the Fire; and you will not have besides God any allies, and you will not be victorious.

114. And you shall perform the oath of allegiance at the two edges of the day, and at the near part of the night. The good deeds take away the bad. This is a reminder to those who remember.

115.And be patient, for God does not waste the reward of the good doers.

116.If only there was from the previous generations a people with wisdom who deterred from the corruption on Earth, except the few that We saved of them. And those who were wicked followed the enjoyment they were in, and they were criminal.

117.And your Lord would not destroy the towns wrongfully, while its people were good doers.

118.And had your Lord wished, He could have made all the people one nation, but they still would continue to disagree.

119.Except whom your Lord has mercy upon; and for that He has created them. And the word of your Lord came true: "I will fill Hell with the Jinn and the people together!"

120.And from each We relate to you the news of the messengers with which We strengthen your heart. In this has come to you the truth and a lesson and a reminder for the believers.

121.And say to those who do not believe: "Continue to do what you will, we will also do."

122."And wait, for we are also waiting."

123.And to God is the unseen of heavens and Earth, and to Him all matters return. So serve Him and put your trust in Him. Your Lord is not unaware of what you all do.

Chapter 12

بسم الله الرحمن الرحيم

In the name of God, the Almighty, the Merciful.

1. A.L.R, these are the signs of the clarifying Scripture.
2. We have sent it down an Arabic compilation, perhaps you will comprehend.
3. We relate to you the best stories through what We have inspired to you in this Quran; and before it you were of those who were unaware.
4. When Joseph said to his father: "My father, I have seen eleven planets and the sun and the moon, I saw them yielding to me."
5. He said: "O my son, do not relate your vision to your brothers, or they will scheme against you. The devil is to man a clear enemy."
6. And as such, your Lord has chosen you, and He teaches you the interpretation of dreams, and He completes His blessings upon you and upon the descendants of Jacob, as He completed it for your fathers before that, Abraham and Isaac. Your Lord is Knowing, Wise.
7. It is thus that in Joseph and his brothers are signs for those who seek.
8. For they said: "Joseph and his brother are more loved by our father than us, while we are a numerous group. Our father is clearly misguided."
9. "Kill Joseph or cast him in the land, then your father's favour will be all yours, and after that you will be an upright people."
10. One amongst them said: "Do not kill Joseph, but if you are going to do anything, then cast him into the bottom of the well, so that anyone traveling by will pick him up."
11. They said: "Our father, why do you not trust us with Joseph, we are to him well wishers."
12. "Send him with us tomorrow to enjoy and play, and we will take care of him."

13. He said: "It saddens me that you should take him, and I fear that the wolf would eat him if you would be absent of him."
14. They said: "If the wolf eats him, while we are a numerous group, then we are the losers."
15. So, when they went with him they had agreed to place him at the bottom of the well. And We inspired to him: "You will inform them of this act of theirs while they will not expect it."
16. And they came to their father in the evening crying.
17. They said: "Our father, we went to race and left Joseph by our things, and the wolf ate him! But you would not believe us even if we are truthful."
18. And they came with his shirt stained in false blood. He said: "You have invented this tale yourselves. Patience is good, and God's help is sought against what you describe."
19. And a traveling caravan came and they sent their man to draw water, but when he drew he said: "Good news, there is a boy!" So they hid him as merchandise. And God is aware of what they do.
20. And they sold him for a low price, a few silver coins, and they regarded him as insignificant.
21. And the one from Egypt who bought him said to his wife: "Make his stay generous, perhaps he will benefit us or we may take him as a son." And it was thus that We established Joseph in the land and to teach him the interpretation of dreams. And God has full power over matters, but most of the people do not know.
22. And when he reached his maturity, We gave him position and knowledge. It is thus that We reward the good doers.
23. And the woman, in whose house he was staying, attempted to seduce him away from himself. And she closed the doors and said: "I have prepared myself for you." He said: "I seek refuge with God, He is my Lord, He made good my residence; the wicked do not succeed."
24. And she desired him and he desired her, had it not been that he saw His Lord's proof; it was thus that We turned evil and lewdness away from him; he is of Our loyal servants.
25. And as they rushed towards the door, she tore his shirt from behind; and they found her master at the door. She said: "What is the punishment of he who wanted to molest your family? Is it not that he be jailed or punished painfully?"

26. He said: "She is the one who seduced me from myself," and a witness from her family gave testimony: "If his shirt was torn from the front, then she is truthful, and he is the liar."

27. "And if his shirt is torn from behind, then she is lying, and he is truthful."

28. So when he saw that his shirt was torn from behind, he said: "This is from your female scheming, your female scheming is indeed great!"

29. "Joseph, turn away from this. And you woman, seek forgiveness for your sin; you were of the wrongdoers."

30. And some women in the city said: "The wife of the Governor is trying to seduce her young man from himself; she is taken by love. We see her clearly misguided."

31. So when she heard of their scheming, she sent for them and prepared a banquet for them, and she gave each one of them a knife. And she said: "Come out to them," so when they saw him they exalted him and cut their hands, and they said: "God be praised, this is not a human, but a blessed Angel!"

32. She said: "This is the one whom you blamed me for, and I have seduced him from himself but he refused. And if he does not do as I command him, he will be imprisoned, and he will be one of those disgraced."

33. He said: "My Lord, prison is better to me than what they are inviting me to do. And if You do not turn their scheming away from me, I will fall for them and be of the ignorant."

34. So his Lord responded to him, and He turned away their scheming from him. He is the Hearer, the Knowledgeable.

35. But it appealed to them, even after they had seen the signs, to imprison him until a time.

36. And with him in the prison entered two young men. One of them said: "I dreamt that I was pressing wine," and the other said: "I dreamt that I was carrying bread on top of my head, and that the birds were eating from it." "Tell us what this means, for we see that you are of the good doers."

37. He said: "There is not any provision of food that will come to you except that I will tell you of its interpretation before it comes. That is from what my Lord has taught me. I have just left the creed of a people who do not believe in God, and they are rejecting the Hereafter."

38. "And I followed the creed of my fathers: Abraham, and Isaac, and Jacob. It was not for us to set up partners with God at all. That is God's blessings over us and over the people, but most of the people are not thankful."

39. "O my fellow inmates, are various lords better, or God, the One, the Omniscient?"

40. "What you serve besides Him are nothing but names which you have created you and your fathers, God did not send down any authority for such. The judgment is for none but God. He ordered that none be served but He. That is the true system, but most of the people do not know."

41. "My fellow inmates, one of you will be serving wine for his lord, while the other will be crucified so that the birds will eat from his head. The matter which you have sought is now concluded."

42. And he said to the one whom he thought would be saved of them: "Mention me to your lord." But the devil made him forget to mention to his lord, so He remained in prison for a few years.

43. And the King said: "I continue to dream of seven fat cows which are being eaten by seven thin ones, and seven green pods and others which are dry. O you commanders, tell me what my vision means if you are able to interpret the visions."

44. They said: "It is nothing but bad dreams; and we are not knowledgeable in the interpretation of dreams."

45. And the one of them who had been saved and remembered after all this time said: "I will tell you of its interpretation, so have me dispatched."

46. "Joseph, O man of truth, explain to us the matter regarding seven fat cows being eaten by seven thin ones, and seven green pods and others which are dry? Then perhaps I may go back to the people so they will know."

47. He said: "You will plant regularly for seven years, and whatever you harvest you must leave it in its pods, except for the little that you will eat."

48. "Then will come seven after that which are severe in drought and which will consume all that you plant except for what you have stored."

49. "Then after that will come a year in which the people will have abundant rain and which they will be able to produce once again."

50. And the King said: "Bring him to me." So when the messenger came to him, he said: "Go back to your lord and ask him what was the matter regarding the women that cut their hands? My Lord is well aware of their scheming."

51. He said: "What is your plea that you tried to seduce Joseph from himself?" They said: "God forbid that we would do any harm to him." The wife of the Governor said: "Now the truth must be known, I did seek to seduce Joseph from himself and he is of the truthful ones."

52. "That is so he knows that I will not betray him while he is not present and that God does not guide the scheming of the betrayers."

53. "And I do not make myself free of blame, for the soul is inclined to sin, except what my Lord has mercy on. My Lord is Forgiving, Merciful."

54. And the King said: "Bring him to me so that I may employ him to my person." So when he spoke to him, he said: "Today you are with us in high rank and trusted."

55. He said: "Make me keeper over the granaries of the land, for I know how to keep records and I am knowledgeable."

56. And it was such that We gave Joseph authority in the land, to travel in it as he pleases. We bestow Our mercy upon whom We please, and We do not waste the reward of the good doers.

57. And the reward of the Hereafter is better for those who believe and were aware.

58. And Joseph's brothers came and entered upon him, and he recognized them, but they did not recognize him.

59. So, when he furnished them with their provisions, he said: "Bring me a stepbrother of yours who is from your father. Do you not see that I give full measure of grain and that I am the best of hosts?"

60. "But if you do not bring him to me, then there shall be no measure of grain for you with me, and do not come near me."

61. They said: "We will try to get him away from his father, and we shall be successful."

62. And he said to his servants: "Return their goods back into their bags, so that they will recognize it when they return to their family and they will come back again."

63. So when they returned to their father, they said: "Our father, we have been banned from getting anymore measure of grain, so send our brother with us so we may be given measure of grain, and we will be his guardians."

64. He said: "Shall I trust him with you as I trusted you with Joseph before that? God is the best guardian, and He is the Most Merciful of those who show mercy."

65. So when they opened their bags, they found their goods had been returned to them, and they said: "Our father, what more can we desire, this is our goods returned to us, so we can get more for our family, and be guardians over our brother, and increase a measure of grain to load a camel. That is truly an easy measure!"

66. He said: "I will not send him with you until you come to me with a covenant to God that you will bring him back unless you are completely overtaken." So when they brought him the covenant, he said: "God is placed in trust over what we say."

67. And he said: "My sons, do not enter from one gate, but enter from separate gates; and I cannot avail you anything against God, for the judgment is to God. In Him I put my trust, and in Him those who put their trust should trust."

68. And when they entered from where their father had commanded them, it would not have availed them in the least against God, but it was out of a concern in Jacob's soul that he brought out. And he is with knowledge for what We have taught him, but most of the people do not know.

69. And when they entered upon Joseph, he called his brother to himself and said: "I am your brother, so do not be saddened by what they have done."

70. So when he furnished them with their provisions, he placed the measuring bowl in his brothers bag, then a caller cried out: "O you in the caravan, you are thieves!"

71. They said, while coming towards him: "What is it you are missing?"

72. He said: "We are missing the measuring bowl of the King, and for whomever can produce it, we will give a camel's load, and I will be bound by this."

73. They said: "By God, you know we did not come to cause corruption in the land, and we are no thieves!"

74. He said: "What shall be the punishment, if you are not truthful?"

75. They said: "The punishment is that whomever it is found in his bags, then to compensate is his punishment. It is such that we punish the wicked."

76. So he began with their bags before his brother's bag. Then he brought it out of his brother's bag. It was such that We planned for Joseph, for he would not have been able to take his brother under the King's system, except that God wished it so. We raise the degrees of whom We please, and over every one of knowledge is the All Knowledgeable.

77. They said: "If he has stolen, there was a brother of his before who also had stolen." Joseph kept this all inside himself, and did not reveal anything to them. He said: "You are in an awkward position, and God best knows what you describe."

78. They said: "O Governor, he has an elderly father, so take one of us in his place. Indeed we see you as one of the good doers."

79. He said: "God forbid that we would take anyone except he whom we found our belongings with. Indeed, we would then be wrong doers."

80. So when they gave-up from him, they held a conference in private. The eldest of them said: "Did you not know that your father has taken a covenant over you with God, and before this you also failed in your duty with Joseph?

I will not leave this land until my father permits me to do so or that God will judge for me. He is the best of judges."

81. "Return to your father, and tell him: "Our father, your son has stolen, and we did not witness except what we learned, and we could not know the unseen!"

82. "And ask the people of the town which we were in, and the caravan which we have returned with. We are being truthful."

83. He replied: "No, for it is your own souls that have conspired you to this. So patience is most fitting, perhaps God will bring them all to me. He is the Knowledgeable, the Wise."

84. And he turned away from them and said: "Oh, my sorry over Joseph." And his eyes turned white from sadness, and he became blind.

85. They said: "By God, will you never cease to remember Joseph until you become senile or you are dead!"

86. He said: "I merely complain my grief and sorrow to God, and I know from God what you do not know."

87. "My sons, go and inquire about Joseph and his brother, and do not give-up from God's Spirit. The only people who would give-up from God's Spirit are the rejecters of faith."

88. So when they entered upon him, they said: "O Governor, we have been afflicted with harm, us and our family, and we have come with poor goods to trade, so give us a measure of grain, and be charitable towards us, for God does reward the charitable."

89. He said: "Do you know what you have done with Joseph and his brother, while you are ignorant?"

90. They said: "Are you indeed Joseph?" He said: "I am Joseph, and this is my brother. God has been gracious to us. For anyone who reveres and is patient, then God will not waste the reward of the good doers."

91. They said: "By God, God has indeed preferred you over us and we were wrongdoers."

92. He said: "There is no blame on you this day, may God forgive you, and He is the Most Merciful of those who show mercy."

93. "Take this shirt of mine and cast it over my fathers face, and he will become with sight; and bring to me all your family."

94. And when the caravan departed, their father said: "I do indeed feel the scent of Joseph, except that you may think me senile."

95. They said: "By God, you are back to your old misguidance."

96. Then, when the bearer of good news came, he cast it over his face and he returned clear with sight. He said: "Did I not tell you that I know from God what you do not know?"

97. They said: "Our father, ask forgiveness for our sins, indeed we have been wrong."

98. He said: "I will ask forgiveness for you from my Lord, He is the Forgiving, the Merciful."

99. So when they entered upon Joseph, he took his parents to him and he said: "Enter Egypt, God willing, in security."

100. And he raised his parents on the throne, and they fell in prostration to Him. And he said: "My father, this is the interpretation of my vision from before. My Lord has made it true, and He has been good to me that he took me out of prison and brought you out of the wilderness after the devil had placed a rift between me and my brothers. My Lord is kind to whom He wills. He is the Knowledgeable, the Wise."

101. "My Lord, You have given me sovereignty and taught me the interpretations of what is narrated. Initiator of the heavens and Earth, You are my protector in this world and the Hereafter. Let me die as one who has submitted, and join me with the good doers."

102. That is from the news of the unseen that We inspire to you. You were not amongst them when they arranged their plan and were scheming.

103. And most of the people, even if you are diligent, will not believe.

104. And you do not ask them for a wage for it, it is but a reminder to the worlds.

105. And how many a sign in the heavens and the Earth do they pass by, while they are turning away from it.

106. And most of them will not believe in God except while setting-up partners.

107. Are they secure against the coming of a cover of retribution from God, or that the Hour would come to them suddenly while they do not perceive?

108. Say: "This is my way, I invite to God in full disclosure, myself and whomever follows me. And glory be to God. And I am not of those who set up partners."

109. And We have not sent before you except men, to whom We gave inspiration, from the people of the towns. Would they not roam the Earth and see how was the punishment of those before them? And the abode of the Hereafter is far better for those who are aware. Do you not comprehend?

110. Then, when the messengers gave up, and they thought that they have been denied, Our victory came to them. We then save whom We wish, and Our punishment cannot be swayed from the wicked people.

111. In their stories is a lesson for the people of intelligence. It was not a narration that was invented, but an authentication of what was already revealed and a detailing of all things, and a guidance and mercy to a people who believe.

Chapter 13

بسم الله الرحمن الرحيم

In the name of God, the Almighty, the Merciful.

1. A.L.M.R, these are the signs of the Scripture. And what has been sent down to you from your Lord is the truth; but most of the people do not believe.

2. God, Who raised the skies without any pillars that you can see, then He settled to the throne, and He commissioned the sun and the moon; each running to a fixed destiny. He manages all affairs, and He details the signs so that you will be aware of the meeting with your Lord.

3. And He is the One who stretched-out the land, and made in it stabilizers and rivers, and from every fruit He made a pair of two; the night covers the day. In that are signs for a people who will think.

4. And on Earth are neighbouring pieces of land with gardens of grape and plants and palm trees, some of which may be twin sharing the same root, or single, even though they are being watered with the same water source; and We make preference for some of them over others in what they consume. In that are signs for a people who comprehend.

5. And if you are surprised, then what is more surprising is their saying: "Can it be that when we are dust, we will be created anew!" These are the ones who rejected their Lord, and they will have chains around their necks, and they are the dwellers of the Fire, in it they will abide.

6. And they hasten towards you with sin before good, and the examples of those before them have already been given. Your Lord is with great forgiveness to the people for their transgression, and your Lord is severe in retribution.

7. And those who reject Say: "If only a sign was sent down to him from his Lord." You are but a warner, and to every nation is a guide.

8. God knows what every female carries, and how short her pregnancy or how long. And everything with Him is measured.

9. The knower of the unseen and the seen, the Great, the Most High.

10. It is the same whether any of you openly declares what he says, or conceals it; whether he is hiding in the night or going openly in the day.

11. Present with him and behind him are retainers, they guard him by God's command. God is not to change what is in a people until they change what is within themselves. And if God wanted to harm a people, then there is no turning Him back, nor will they have any protector against Him.

12. He is the One who shows you the lightning, giving you fear and hope. And He establishes the heavy clouds.

13. And the thunder glorifies with His praise, and the Angels are in awe of Him, and He sends the thunderbolts, and strikes with it whom He will. Yet they are still arguing regarding God, while He is severe in punishment.

14. To Him is the call of truth. And those who are called on besides Him, they will not respond to them in anything; like one who places his hands openly in the water to drink, but it never reaches his mouth. The call of the rejecters is nothing but in misguidance.

15. And to God prostrate all who are in the heavens and the Earth, willingly and unwillingly, as do their shadows in the morning and the evening.

16. Say: "Who is the Lord of the heavens and Earth," Say: "God." Say: "Have you taken besides Him allies who do not posses for themselves any benefit or harm?" Say: "Is the blind and the seer the same?, or does the darkness and the light equate? Or have they made partners with God who have created like His creation, so the creations all seemed the same to them?" Say: "God has created all things, and He is the One, the Supreme."

17. He sent down water from the sky, so valleys flowed according to their capacity, and the flood produces foam. And from what they burn to smelt jewellery or goods is produced a similar foam. It is in such a manor that God strikes the falsehood with the truth. As for the foam, it passes away, and as for what benefits the people, it remains in the Earth. It is such that God cites the examples.

18. For those who responded to their Lord is goodness. As for those who did not respond to Him, if they had all that is in the Earth twice over, they would offer it to be saved. To these will be a terrible reckoning, and their abode is Hell; what a miserable abode.

19. Is one who knows that the truth has been sent down to you from your Lord like one who is blind? Only those with understanding will remember.

20. Those who fulfill God's pledge, and they do not break the Covenant.
21. And those who deliver what God has ordered be delivered, and they revere their Lord and they fear the terrible reckoning.
22. And those who are patient seeking their Lord's direction; and they honour the oath of allegiance, and they spend from what We bestowed upon them secretly and openly, and they counter sin with good; these will have an excellent abode.
23. The gardens of Eden, they will enter it with those who are good doers from their fathers and their mates and their progeny. And the Angels will enter upon them from every gate.
24. "Peace be upon you for what you have been patient for. Excellent indeed is the final abode."
25. As for those who break the pledge of God after making its covenant, and they sever what God ordered that it be delivered, and they corrupt in the Earth; to those is a curse and they will have a miserable abode.
26. God gives the provisions for whom He wishes, and He is able. And they were happy with the worldly life, but the worldly life compared to the Hereafter was nothing but a brief enjoyment.
27. And those who have rejected Say: "If only a sign were sent down to him from his Lord!" Say: "God misguides whom He wishes and guides to Him whoever is repenting."
28. The ones who believed and their hearts are relieved by the remembrance of God; for in God's remembrance the hearts are relieved.
29. And those who believed, and did good works, there will be happiness for them and a good abode.
30. And as such, We have sent you to a nation as other nations that have come before, so that you may recite for them that which has been inspired to you; while they are still rejecting the Almighty. Say: "He is my Lord, there is no god but He, in Him I place my trust and to Him is my repentance."
31. And if a compilation were to be used to move mountains, or to slice the Earth, or the dead were spoken to with it. No, to God is all matters. Did not those who believe know that if God wished He would have guided all the people? As for those who reject, they continue to be stricken with disaster or it comes near to their homes, until God's promise comes true. God does not break the appointment.
32. And messengers before you were ridiculed, but I gave time to those who rejected, then I took them. Then how was My punishment?

33. The One who is standing over every soul for what it has earned; yet they make partners with God. Say: "Name them?, or are you informing Him of what He does not know on Earth or is it just a show of words?" But to the rejecters, their scheming is made to appear clever, and they are turned away from the path. And whoever God misguides will have no guide.
34. They will have a punishment in the worldly life, and the punishment of the Hereafter is more difficult. And they will have no defender against God.
35. The example of Paradise that the righteous have been promised, is that rivers flow beneath it, and its provisions are continuous as is its shade. Such is the abode of those who were righteous, while the abode of the rejecters is the Fire.
36. And those to whom We have previously given the Scripture rejoice at what has been sent down to you, but there are some of the groups that reject parts of it. Say: "I am only ordered to serve God and not join any partner with Him. To Him I pray and to Him is the return."
37. And as such, We have sent it down a law in Arabic. And if you follow their desires after what has come to you of the knowledge, then you will not have any ally or defender against God.
38. And We have sent messengers before you and We have made for them mates and offspring. It was not for a messenger to come with any sign except by God's leave, but for every time there is a decree.
39. God erases what He wishes and affirms, and with Him is the source of the Scripture.
40. And if We show you some of what We promise them or if We let you pass away, then you are only to deliver while for Us is the reckoning.
41. Do they not see that We come to the land and reduce it from its ends? And God gives judgment and there is none to override His judgment. And He is quick to reckoning.
42. And those before them have schemed, but to God is all scheming. He knows what every soul earns and the rejecters will come to know to whom is the better abode.
43. And those who reject Say: "You are not a messenger." Say: "God is sufficient as a witness between me and you, the One who has the knowledge of the Scripture."

Chapter 14

In the name of God, the Almighty, the Merciful.

1. A.L.R, a Scripture which We have sent down to you so that you may take the people out of the darkness and into the light by their Lord's leave, to the path of the Noble, the Praiseworthy.

2. God, to whom belongs all that is in the heavens, and all that is in the Earth. And woe to the rejecters from a painful retribution.

3. The ones who have preferred the worldly life over the Hereafter, and they repel away from the path of God, and they seek to make it crooked. Those are the ones who are in misguidance.

4. And We have not sent any messenger except in the language of his people, so he may clarify to them. But God misguides whom He wills, and He guides whom He wills. And He is the Noble, the Wise.

5. And We have sent Moses with Our signs, that you should bring your people out from the darkness and into the light, and remind them of God's days. In this are signs for any who are patient and thankful.

6. And Moses said to his people: "Remember God's blessings upon you that He saved you from the people of Pharaoh. They used to inflict the worst punishment upon you, and they used to murder your children, and rape your women. And in that was a great trial from your Lord."

7. And your Lord proclaimed: "If you give thanks, then I will increase for you, but if you are rejecting, then My retribution is severe."

8. And Moses said: "If you reject, you and all who are on Earth together, then know that God is Rich, Praiseworthy."

9. Did not news come to you of those before you: the people of Noah, and 'Aad, and Thamud, and those after them whom none know but God? Their

messengers came to them with clarity, but they placed their hands to their mouths and said: "We are rejecting what you have been sent with, and we are in grave doubt as to what you are inviting us to."

10. Their messengers said: "Is there doubt regarding God, the initiator of the heavens and the Earth? He invites you so that He may forgive some of your sins, and grant you until a predetermined time." They said: "You are but humans like us, you wish to turn us away from what our fathers used to serve. So come to us with clear proof."

11. Their messengers said: "We are but humans like you, but God will bestow His grace upon whom He pleases from His servants. And it is not up to us to bring you proof except by God's leave. And in God the believers should place their trust"

12. "And why should we not place our trust in God, when He has guided us our path. And we will be patient to the harm you inflict upon us. And in God those who trust should put their trust."

13. And those who rejected said to their messengers: "We will drive you out of our land, or you will return to our creed." It was then that their Lord inspired to them: "We will destroy the wicked."

14. "And We will let you reside in the land after them. That is for those who fear My station and fear My deliverance."

15. And they sought victory, and every arrogant tyrant was then made to lose.

16. From behind him is Hell, and he will be served boiling water.

17. He tries to drink it, but it cannot be swallowed, and death comes to him from everywhere, but he will not die; and from behind him is a powerful retribution.

18. The example of those who reject their Lord is that their works are like ashes, on which the wind blows strongly on a stormy day, they cannot get anything of what they earned. Such is the farthest misguidance.

19. Did you not see that God created the heavens and the Earth with truth? If He wished, He would do away with you and bring a new creation.

20. And that for God is not difficult to do.

21. And they appeared before God, all of them. And the weak ones said to those who were arrogant: "We were following you, so will you avail us anything from God's retribution?" They said: "If God had guided us, then we would have guided you. It makes no difference if we cry out or are patient, for we have no refuge."

22. And the devil said when the matter was complete: "God had promised you the promise of truth, and I promised you and broke my promise. And I had

no power over you except that I invited you and you responded to me. So do not blame me, but blame yourselves; I cannot help you nor can you help me. I reject that you have set me as a partner before this; the wicked will have a painful retribution."

23. And admission was given to those who believed and did good works to estates with rivers flowing beneath them. In them they will abide by the leave of their Lord. Their greeting therein is "Peace."

24. Have you not seen how God cites the example of a good word is like a good tree, whose root is firm and its branches in the sky.

25. It bears its fruit every so often by its Lord's leave. And God cites the examples for the people, perhaps they will remember.

26. And the example of a bad word is like a tree which has been uprooted from the surface of the Earth, it has nowhere to settle.

27. God makes firm those who believe with firm sayings in the worldly life, and in the Hereafter. And God misguides the wicked, and God does what He wishes.

28. Did you not see those who replaced God's blessings with rejection, and they caused their people to dwell in the abode of destruction?

29. Hell is where they will burn, what a miserable place to settle.

30. And they made to God equals in order that they may misguide from His path. Say: "Enjoy, for your destiny is to the Fire."

31. Say to My servants who believe, that they should honour the oath of allegiance, and spend from what provisions We granted them secretly and publicly, before a Day comes when there is no trade therein, nor will there be any friends.

32. God is the One who created the heavens and the Earth, and He sent down water from the sky and brought out fruits as provisions for you, and He committed for you the ships to run in the sea by His command, and He committed for you the rivers.

33. And He committed for you the sun and the moon, both in continuity; and He committed for you the night and the day.

34. And He gave you all that you have asked Him. And if you were to count God's blessings, you will never fathom them. The human is indeed transgressing, disbelieving.

35. And Abraham said: "My Lord, make this town a sanctity, and keep me and my sons away from serving idols."

36. "My Lord, they have misguided many from amongst the people. So, whoever follows me, then he is of me, and whoever disobeys me, then You are Forgiving, Merciful."

37. "Our Lord, I have resided part of my progeny in an uncultivated valley near your Restricted Sanctuary. My Lord, so that they may honour the oath of allegiance. So let the hearts of the people incline towards them and give provisions to them of the fruits that they may give thanks."

38. "Our Lord, you know what we hide and what we declare. And nothing is hidden from God at all in the Earth or in the heavens."

39. "Praise be to God who has granted me in my old age Ishmael and Isaac. My Lord is the hearer of prayers."

40. "My Lord, let me honour the oath of allegiance, and also from my progeny. Our Lord, accept my prayer."

41. "Our Lord, forgive me and my parents, and the believers on the Day the judgment is called."

42. And do not think that God is unaware of what the wicked do. He is merely delaying them to a Day when all eyes are watching.

43. They will approach with their heads bowed, and their eyes will not blink, and their hearts will be void.

44. And warn the people of the Day when the retribution will come to them, and those who were wicked will Say: "Our Lord, delay this for us until a short time, and we will heed your call and follow the messengers!" Did you not swear before this that you would last forever?

45. And you resided in the homes of those who had wronged themselves, and it was made clear to you what We did to them. And We had cited the examples to you.

46. And they schemed their scheming, and their scheming is known to God; and their scheming was enough to make the mountains cease to exist.

47. So do not think that God will fail to keep His promise to His messengers. God is Noble, able to seek revenge.

48. The Day the Earth is replaced with another Earth, as are the heavens, and they will appear before God, the One, the Irresistible.

49. And you will see the criminals on that Day held by restraints.

50. Their clothes will be of tar, and the fire will overwhelm their faces.

51. Thus God will recompense every soul by what it earned. God is quick to reckoning.

52. This is a proclamation for the people and so that they are warned with it, and so that they know that there is but One god, and so that those with intelligence will remember.

Chapter 15

بسم الله الرحمن الرحيم

In the name of God, the Almighty, the Merciful.

1. A.L.R, these are the signs of the Scripture, and a clear Quran.
2. Ultimately, those who have rejected will wish they had submitted!
3. Leave them to eat and enjoy, and let them be preoccupied with hope. They will come to know.
4. We have not destroyed any town except that it had an appointed time.
5. No nation can quicken its fate, nor can they delay.
6. And they said: "O you upon whom the Reminder has been sent down, you are crazy."
7. "Why not bring us the Angels if you are of the truthful ones?"
8. We do not send down the Angels except with truth, and then they would have no more delay.
9. Indeed it is We who have sent down the Reminder, and indeed it is We who will preserve it.
10. And We have sent before you to the groups of old.
11. And any messenger that came to them, they would mock him.
12. It is such that We let it seep into the hearts of the criminals.
13. They do not believe in it, while the examples of the early generations has been brought to them.
14. And if We opened for them a gate in the heaven and they were to continue ascending to it,
15. They would have said: "Our sight has been fogged. No, we are a people who are being bewitched!"
16. And We have placed towers in the heavens and We have made them pleasant to the onlookers.

17. And We have guarded them from every outcast devil.
18. Except he who manages to eavesdrop, he will be pursued clearly by a flaming meteor.
19. And the land We have stretched, and placed stabilizers in it, and We have planted in it everything in balance.
20. And We made for you in it a habitat, as well as those whom you are not required to provide for.
21. And there is not a thing, except that We have vaults of it, yet We only send it down in a measured amount.
22. And We have sent the winds to pollinate, and We sent down water from the sky for you to drink. And it is not you who are keeping it in storage.
23. And it is indeed We who give life and death, and We are the inheritors.
24. And We have known those who came early amongst you, and We have known those who came late.
25. And it is your Lord that will gather them. He is Wise, Knowledgeable.
26. And We have created man from a clay hardened and shaped.
27. And the Jinn, We created him before that from the flames of fire.
28. And your Lord said to the Angels: "I am creating a human being from a hardened clay."
29. "So when I perfect him, and blow of My spirit in him, you shall yield to him."
30. Thus, all of the Angels yielded.
31. Except for Satan, he refused to be with those who yielded.
32. He said: "O Satan, what is the matter that you are not with those who have yielded?"
33. He said: "I am not to yield to a human You have created from a hardened clay."
34. He said: "Exit from here, you are cast out."
35. "And a curse shall be upon you until the Day of Judgment."
36. He said: "My Lord, respite me until the Day they are resurrected."
37. He said: "You are given respite."
38. "Until the Day of the appointed time."
39. He said: "My Lord, for that which I have been misled by, I will make the Earth appear beautiful for them, and I will mislead them all."
40. "Except for Your servants who are devoted."
41. He said: "This shall be a Straight Path to Me."
42. "For My servants, you shall have no authority over them, except those who are misled and follow you."

43. "And Hell, for all of those, shall be the appointed place."
44. "It has seven gates, for every gate will be an assigned segment from them."
45. The righteous will be in paradises and springs.
46. "Enter it in peace and security."
47. And We removed what sadness was in their chests, they are brothers in quarters facing one another.
48. No fatigue shall touch them, nor will they be made to leave from it.
49. Inform My servants that I am the Forgiver, the Merciful.
50. And that My punishment is a painful retribution.
51. And inform them of Abraham's guests.
52. That they entered upon him, they said: "Peace." He said: "We are worrisome of you."
53. They said: "Do not worry, we bring you good news of a knowledgeable son."
54. He said: "What good news can you bring me when old age has come upon me? Is that your good news?"
55. They said: "We have brought you good news with truth, so do not be of those in denial."
56. He said: "And who would deny the mercy of his Lord except the misguided ones!"
57. He said: "What then is your business here, O messengers?"
58. They said: "We have been sent to a people who are criminals."
59. "Except for the family of Lot, we will save them all."
60. "Except for his wife, we have measured that she will be with those destroyed."
61. So when the messengers came to the family of Lot.
62. He said: "You are a people unknown to me."
63. They said: "Alas, we have come to you with that which they are doubting."
64. "And we have come to you with the truth, and we are forthcoming."
65. "So let your family leave during the last hours of the night, and you follow just behind them, and do not let any of you look back, and go to where you are commanded."
66. And We made it known to him, that the seed of these people will be cut off in the morning.
67. And the people of the city came seeking good news.
68. He said: "These are my guests, so do not embarrass me!"
69. "And be aware of God, and do not disgrace me!"
70. They said: "Did we not forbid you from outsiders?"
71. He said: "Here are my daughters if it is your intention."

72. By your life, they are in their drunkenness, blundering.
73. So the scream took them at sunrise.
74. Thus We turned it upside down, and rained upon them with fiery projectiles.
75. In this are signs for those who see.
76. And it was on an established path.
77. In that is a sign for the believers.
78. And the dwellers of the forest were wicked.
79. So, We sought revenge from them. And they were both on an open plain.
80. And the dwellers of the cavern disbelieved the messengers.
81. And We gave them Our signs, but they turned away from them.
82. And they used to sculpt from the mountains dwellings that were secure.
83. So the scream took them in the morning.
84. What benefit did what they earn make for them?
85. And We have not created the heavens and the Earth and what is in between except with the truth. And the Hour is coming, so overlook their faults gracefully.
86. Your Lord is the Creator, the Knower.
87. And We have given you seven of the pairs and the great Quran.
88. So do not linger with your eyes on what We have bestowed upon some couples from them, and do not grieve for them, and lower your wing for the believers.
89. And Say: "I am the clarifying warner."
90. As We have sent down on the dividers.
91. The ones who have taken the Quran as obsolete.
92. By your Lord, We will ask them all.
93. Regarding what they use to do.
94. So proclaim what you have been commanded and turn away from those who set up partners.
95. We will relieve you from those who mocked.
96. Those who placed with God another god. They will come to know.
97. And We know that your chest is strained by what they say.
98. So glorify with the praise of your Lord, and be of those who prostrate.
99. And serve your Lord until certainty comes to you.

Chapter 16

بسم الله الرحمن الرحيم

In the name of God, the Almighty, the Merciful.

1. God's command will come, so do not hasten it. Glorified is He and High above the partners they have set up.

2. He sends down the Angels with the Spirit by His command upon whom He wishes of His servants: "That you shall warn that there is no god but I, so be aware of Me."

3. He created the heavens and the Earth with the truth. He is High above the partners they have set up.

4. He created man from a seed, but then he becomes clearly in opposition.

5. And the livestock He created them for you, in them is warmth and benefits, and from them you eat.

6. And for you in them is beauty, when you relax and when you travel.

7. And they carry your loads to a place you would not have been able to reach except with great strain. Your Lord is Compassionate, Merciful.

8. And the horses, and mules, and donkeys, that you may ride them and as an adornment. And He creates what you do not know.

9. And to God shall be the path, but some are mislead. And if He wished, He could have guided you all.

10. He is the One who sent down water from the sky for you, from it you drink, and from it emerge the trees that you wander around in.

11. He brings forth with it vegetation and olives and palm trees and grapes and from all the fruits. In that are signs for a people who think.

12. And He committed for you the night and the day, and the sun and the moon, and the stars are committed by His command. In that are signs for a people who comprehend.

13. And what He has placed for you on Earth in various colors. In that are signs for a people who remember.

14. And He is the One who committed the sea, that you may eat from it a tender meat, and that you may extract from it pearls that you wear. And you see the ships flowing through it, so that you may seek from His bounty, and that you may be thankful.

15. And He has cast into the Earth stabilizers so that it does not sway with you, and rivers, and paths, perhaps you will be guided.

16. And landmarks, and by the stars they use to guide.

17. Is the One who creates the same as one who does not create? Will you not remember?

18. And if you count the blessings of God you will not be able to fathom them. God is Forgiving, Merciful.

19. And God knows what you hide and what you declare.

20. As for those they call on besides God, they do not create anything, but are themselves created!

21. They are dead, not alive, and they will not know when they are resurrected.

22. Your god is One god. Those who do not believe in the Hereafter, their hearts are denying, and they are arrogant.

23. Certainly, God knows what they hide and what they reveal. He does not like the arrogant.

24. And if they are told: "What has your Lord sent down?" They Say: "Fairytales of old."

25. They will carry their burdens in full on the Day of Resurrection, and also from the burdens of those whom they misguided without knowledge. Evil indeed is what they bear.

26. Those before them have schemed, but God came to their buildings from the foundation, thus the roof fell on top of them, and the retribution came to them from where they did not know.

27. Then, on the Day of Resurrection He will humiliate them, and Say: "Where are My partners whom you used to dispute regarding them?" Those who have received the knowledge said: "The humiliation today and misery is upon the rejecters."

28. Those whom the Angels take while they had wronged their souls: "Amnesty, we did not do any evil!" "Alas, God is aware of what you had done."

29. "So enter the gates of Hell, in it you shall reside; such is the abode of the arrogant."

30. And it was said to those who were righteous: "What has your Lord sent down?" They said: "All goodness." For those who have done good in this world there is good, and the Hereafter is even better. Excellent indeed is the home of the righteous.
31. The gardens of Eden, which they will enter, with rivers flowing beneath, in it they will have what they wish. It is such that God rewards the righteous.
32. Those whom the Angels take, while they had been good, they will Say: "Peace be upon you, enter Paradise because of that which you have done."
33. Are they waiting for the Angels to come for them, or a command from your Lord? It was exactly the same as what those before them did. God did not wrong them, but it was their own selves that they wronged.
34. Thus, the evil of their work afflicted them, and they were surrounded by that which they used to make fun of!
35. And those who set up partners said: "If God had wished it, we would not have served anything besides Him; neither us nor our fathers; nor would we have forbidden anything without Him." Those before them did the exact same thing; so are the messengers required to do anything but deliver with clarity?
36. And We have sent a messenger to every nation: "You shall serve God and avoid evil." Some of them were guided by God, and some of them deserved to be misguided. So travel in the land, and see how the punishment was of those who denied.
37. If you are concerned for their guidance, God does not guide whom He misleads. And they will have no victors.
38. And they swore by God, in their strongest oaths, that God will not resurrect whoever dies. No, it is a promise of truth upon Him, but most people do not know.
39. So that He will make clear for them that in which they have disputed, and so that those who have rejected will know that they were liars.
40. It is Our saying to a thing if We want it, to say to it: "Be," and it is.
41. And those who have emigrated for God, after they were oppressed, We will grant them good in the world, and the reward of the Hereafter will be greater, if they knew.
42. Those who are patient, and put their trust in their Lord.
43. And We did not send any except men before you whom We inspired, so ask the people who received the Reminder if you do not know.
44. With clarity and the Psalms. And We sent down to you the Reminder to make clear to the people what was sent to them, and perhaps they will think.

45. Have those who schemed evil guaranteed that God will not make the Earth swallow them, or the retribution come to them from where they do not expect?
46. Or that He will take them in their sleep?, for they cannot stop it.
47. Or that He will take them while they are in fear? Your Lord is Compassionate, Merciful.
48. Did they not see that anything God creates, its shadow inclines to the right and the left in prostration to God, while they may resent it?
49. And to God prostrate all those in the heavens and all those on the Earth, from the creatures as well as the Angels, and they are not arrogant.
50. They fear their Lord from above them, and they do what they are commanded.
51. And God said: "Do not take-up two gods, there is only One god, so it is Me that you shall reverence."
52. And to Him is what is in the heavens and the Earth, and the system shall be to Him. Is it other than God that you shall be aware of?
53. And any blessings that are with you are from God. Then, when harm afflicts you, to Him you cry out.
54. Then, when He removes the harm from you, a group of you set up partners with their Lord!
55. So they reject what We have given them. Enjoy, for you will come to know.
56. And they allocate a portion from what We provide to them to that which they did not have knowledge of. By God, you will be asked about the lies you have invented!
57. And they assign their daughters to God; be He glorified; and to them is what they desire.
58. And when one of them is given news of a female, his face becomes darkened and he is in grief!
59. He hides from his people because of the bad news he has received. Shall he keep her with dishonour, or bury her in the sand? Miserable indeed is how they judge!
60. For those who do not believe in the Hereafter is the worst example, and for God is the highest example, and He is the Noble, the Wise.
61. And if God were to call the people to account for their transgression, then He would not leave a single creature standing. But He delays them to a determined time; so when that time comes to any of them, they cannot delay it by one hour or advance it.

62. And they assign to God what they hate, and their tongues describe with lies that they will have what is good. No doubt they will have the Fire, for they have rebelled.

63. By God, We have sent others to nations before you, but the devil adorned their work for them. So he is their ally today, and they will have a painful retribution.

64. And We did not send down the Scripture to you except that you may clarify to them that in which they disputed, and as a guidance and mercy to a people who believe.

65. And God has sent down water from the sky, so He revives the land with it after its death. In that is a sign for a people who listen.

66. And for you there is a lesson in the livestock; We give you to drink from what is in its stomach between the digested food and the blood, a pure milk which is relieving for the drinkers.

67. And from the fruits of the palm trees and the grapes you make wine and a good provision. In that is a sign for a people who comprehend.

68. And your Lord inspired to the bees: "You shall take homes of the mountains and of the trees and of what they erect."

69. Then you shall eat from every fruit, so seek the path your Lord has made easy. From its stomach will emerge a liquid that has different colors, in it is a healing for the people. In that is a sign for a people who will think.

70. And God created you then He will take you. And some of you will continue to old age so that he will not know anything more after his knowledge. God is Knowing, Capable.

71. And God has preferred some of you over others in provision. Those who have been preferred will not relinquish their provision to those who are still dependant, so they may become equal in it. Are they denying the favour of God?

72. And God has made for you mates from amongst yourselves, and He has made from your mates children and grandchildren, and He has provided you from the good provisions. Do they believe in falsehood, while in God's favour they are denying?

73. And they serve besides God that which does not and cannot possess anything of the provisions from the sky or the land.

74. So do not give parables to God. God knows while you do not know.

75. God puts forth the example of a slave who is owned and cannot achieve anything, against one whom We have provided a good provision which he

spends of it secretly and openly. Are they the same? God be praised, but most of them do not know.

76. And God puts forth the example of two men, one of them is mute and he cannot achieve anything, and he is a burden to his guardian. Wherever he points him, he does not come with any good. Is he the same as one who orders good and he is upon a straight path?

77. And to God is the unseen of the heavens and the Earth, and the matter of the Hour is like the blink of the eye or nearer. God is capable of all things.

78. And God brought you out of your mothers wombs while you knew nothing. And He made for you the hearing and the eyesight and the heart, perhaps you would be thankful.

79. Did they not look to the birds held in the atmosphere of the sky? No one holds them up except God. In that are signs for a people who believe.

80. And God has made your homes a habitat, and He made for you from the hides of the livestock shelter which you find light for travel and when you stay, and from its wool, fur, and hair you make furnishings and goods, for a while.

81. And God has made for you shade from what He created, and He made from the mountains a refuge for you, and He made for you garments which protect you from the heat, and garments which protect you from attack. It is such that He completes His blessing upon you, that you may submit.

82. So if they turn away, then you are only required to deliver clearly.

83. They recognize God's blessings, then they deny them. And most of them are rejecters.

84. And the Day We send from every nation a witness, then those who have rejected will not be given leave, nor will they be allowed to repent.

85. And then those who were wicked will see the retribution; it will not be lightened for them, nor will they be given respite.

86. And when those who set up partners saw the partners they made, they said: "Our Lord, these are our partners that we used to call upon besides You." But they returned in answer to them: "You are liars!"

87. And they gave in to God on that Day, and what they had invented abandoned them.

88. Those who rejected, and repelled others from the path of God, We have increased the retribution for them over the retribution for what they had corrupted.

89. And the Day We send to every nation a witness against them from themselves, and We have brought you as a witness against these. And We have

sent down to you the Scripture as a clarification for all things, and a guide and mercy and good tidings to those who have submitted.

90. God orders justice and goodness and that you shall help your relatives, and He deters from evil, vice, and transgression. He warns you that you may remember.

91. And fulfill your pledge to God when you pledge so, and do not break your oath after making it, for you have made God a sponsor over you. God is aware of what you do.

92. And do not be like she who unravelled her knitting after it had become strong, by breaking your oaths as a means of deception between you. That a nation shall be more numerous than another nation, for God puts you to the test by it. And He will show you on the Day of Resurrection that which you were disputing in.

93. And had God wished, He would have made you one nation, but He misguides whom He wishes, and He guides whom He wishes. And you will be asked about what you used to do.

94. And do not use your oaths as a means of deception between you, that a foot will falter after it had been firm, and you will taste the evil of turning away from the path of God, and you will have a great retribution.

95. And do not purchase with God's pledge a cheap price. What is with God is far better for you if you know.

96. What you have will run out, while what God has will remain. And We will deliver to those who are patient their reward for the best of what they used to do.

97. Whoever does good work, be he male or female, and is a believer, We will give him a good life and We will reward them their dues with the best of what they used to do.

98. When you read the Quran, you shall seek refuge with God from Satan the outcast.

99. He has no authority over those who believe, and who put their trust in their Lord.

100. His authority is over those who follow him, and set him up as a partner.

101. And if We exchange a verse in place of another verse; and God is more aware of what He is revealing; they Say: "You are making this up!" Alas, most of them do not know.

102. Say: "The holy Spirit has sent it down from your Lord with truth, so that those who believe will be strengthened, and as a guidance and good news for those who have submitted."

103. And We are aware that they Say: "A human is teaching him." The language of the one they refer to is foreign, while this is a clear Arabic language.

104. Those who do not believe in God's revelations, God will not guide them, and they will have a painful retribution.

105. Making-up lies is only done by those who do not believe in God's revelations, and these are the liars.

106. Whoever rejects God after having believed; except for one who is forced while his heart is still content with belief; and has opened his chest to rejection, then they will have a wrath from God and they will have a great retribution.

107. That is because they preferred the worldly life over the Hereafter, and God does not guide the rejecting people.

108. Those are the ones whom God has stamped on their hearts, and their hearing, and their sight, and these are the unaware ones.

109. Without doubt, in the Hereafter they are the losers.

110. And your Lord is to those who emigrated after they were persecuted, then they strived and were patient; your Lord after that is Forgiving, Merciful.

111. The Day every soul will come to argue for itself, and every soul will be paid in full for what it did, and they will not be wronged.

112. And God cites the example of a town which was peaceful and content, its provisions were coming to it bountifully from all places, but then it rebelled against God's blessings and God made it taste hunger and fear for what they used to do.

113. And a messenger came to them from themselves, but they denied him, so the punishment took them while they were wicked.

114. So eat from what God has provided for you, that which is good and lawful, and thank the blessings of God, if it is indeed He whom you serve.

115. He only made forbidden for you what is already dead, and blood, and the meat of pig, and what was sacrificed to any other than God. But whoever is forced to, without disobedience or transgression, then God is Forgiving, Merciful.

116. And do not say regarding what your tongues describe with lies: "This is lawful and that is forbidden;" that you seek to invent lies about God. Those who invent lies about God will not succeed.

117. A small enjoyment, and they will have a painful retribution.

118. And for those who are Jews, We forbade what We narrated to you before. We did not wrong them, but it was themselves they used to wrong.

119. Then your Lord to those who do evil out of ignorance, then they repent after that and they make right, your Lord after that is Forgiving, Merciful.

120. Abraham was a nation, devoted to God, a monotheist, and he was not of those who set up partners.

121. Thankful for His blessings. He chose him and guided him to a Straight Path.

122. And We gave him good in this world, and in the Hereafter he is of the upright ones.

123. Then We inspired to you: "You shall follow the creed of Abraham, monotheism, and he was not of those who set up partners."

124. The Sabbath was only decreed for those who disputed in it, and your Lord will judge between them for that which they disputed in.

125. Invite to the path of your Lord with wisdom and good advice, and argue with them in that which is better. Your Lord is fully aware of who is misguided from His path, and He is fully aware of the guided ones.

126. And if you punish, then punish with equivalence to that which you were punished. And if you are patient then it is better for the patient ones.

127. And be patient, for your patience is on none but God. And do not grieve for them, and do not be depressed by what they scheme.

128. God is with those who are aware and are good doers.

Chapter 17

بسم الله الرحمن الرحيم

In the name of God, the Almighty, the Merciful.

1. Glory be to the One who took His servant by night from the Restricted Temple to the most distant temple which We had blessed around, so that We may show him of Our signs. Indeed, He is the Listener, the Seer.

2. And We gave Moses the Scripture and We made it a guidance for the Children of Israel: "Do not believe in any besides Me."

3. The progeny of those whom We carried with Noah, he was a thankful servant.

4. And We decreed to the Children of Israel in the Scripture, that you will make corruption twice on Earth, and that you will become very high and mighty.

5. So, when the promise of the first one comes to pass, We would send against you servants of Ours who are very powerful, thus they managed to breach your very homes, and this was a promise which has come to pass.

6. Then We gave back to you your independence from them, and We supplied you with wealth and children, and We made you more influential.

7. If you do good, then it will be good for you, and if you do bad, then so be it. But when the promise of the second time comes, they will make your faces filled with sorrow and they will enter the Temple as they did the first time, and they will strike down all that was raised up.

8. Perhaps your Lord will have mercy on you, and if you revert then so will We. And We made Hell a gathering place for the rejecters.

9. This Quran guides to that which is more upright, and it gives glad tidings to the believers who do good work that they will have a bountiful reward.

10. And for those who do not believe in the Hereafter, We have prepared for them a painful retribution.

11. And man calls to evil as much as he calls to good, and man was always hasty.

12. And We made the night and the day as two signs, so We erased the sign of night and We made the sign of day to see-in, that you may seek bounty from your Lord, and that you may know the number of the years and the count. And everything We have detailed completely.

13. And We have attached to every person's neck his deeds, and We bring forth for him a record on the Day of Resurrection which he will find on display.

14. Read your record! It is enough for you that you are aware of yourself today.

15. Whoever is guided is guided for himself, and whoever is misguided is for his own loss. And no person shall carry the load of another, and We were not to punish until We send a messenger.

16. And if We wish to destroy a town, We allow its carefree to rule it, then they commit evil in it, then it deserves the punishment, then We destroy it completely.

17. And how many a generation have We destroyed after Noah? And it is enough for your Lord to have knowledge and sight over the sins of His servants.

18. Whoever seeks the life of haste, We will make for Him what he wishes, then We will make Hell for him a place which he will reach disgraced and rejected.

19. And whoever seeks the Hereafter and strives for it as it deserves, and is a believing person, then to those what they have sought is given in thanks.

20. For both groups We will bestow from the bounty of your Lord. And the bounty of your Lord is never restricted.

21. See how We have preferred some of them over the others; and in the Hereafter are greater levels, and greater preference.

22. Do not make with God another god, or you will find yourself disgraced, abandoned.

23. And your Lord decreed that you shall not serve except Him, and do good to your parents. When one of them or both of them reaches old age, do not say to them a word of disrespect nor raise your voice at them, but say to them a kind saying.

24. And lower for them the wing of humility through mercy, and Say: "My Lord, have mercy upon them as they have raised me when I was small."

25. Your Lord is fully aware of what is in your souls. If you are good, then He is to the obedient a Forgiver.

26. And give the relative his due, and the poor, and the wayfarer; and do not waste excessively.
27. Those who waste excessively are brothers to the devils, and the devil was to his Lord a rejecter.
28. And if you turn away from them to seek a mercy from your Lord which you desire, then say to them a gentle saying.
29. And do not make your hand stingy by holding it to your neck, nor shall you lay it fully open so you become in despair and regret.
30. Your Lord lays out openly the provision for whom He wishes, and He is able to do so. He is Expert and Watcher to His servants.
31. And do not kill your unborn children out of fear of poverty; We shall provide for you and them. The killing of them was a big mistake.
32. And do not come near adultery, for it is a sin and an evil path.
33. And do not kill, for God has made this forbidden, except in the course of justice. And whoever is killed unjustly, then We have given his heir authority, so let him not transgress in the taking of a life, for He will be given victory.
34. And do not come near the orphan's money, except for that which is best, until he reaches maturity. And fulfill your oath, for the oath brings responsibility.
35. And give full measure when you deal, and weigh with a balance that is straight. That is good and better in the end.
36. And do not uphold what you have no knowledge of. For the hearing, eyesight, and mind, all these you are responsible for.
37. And do not walk in the land arrogantly, for you will not penetrate the Earth, nor will you reach the mountains in height.
38. All of this is bad, and disliked by your Lord.
39. That is from what your Lord has inspired to you of the wisdom. And do not make with God another god, or you will be cast into Hell, blameworthy and regretting.
40. Has your Lord preferred for you the males, while He takes the females as Angels? You are indeed saying a great thing!
41. And We have cited in this Quran so they may remember, but it only increases their aversion!
42. Say: "If there had been gods with Him as they say, then they would have tried to gain a way to the throne."
43. Be He glorified and High from what they say, a great falsehood.

44. He is glorified by the seven universes and the Earth and who is in them, and there is not a thing but it glorifies His praise, but you do not comprehend their glorification. He is Compassionate, Forgiving.

45. And when you read the Quran, We place between you and those who do not believe in the Hereafter an invisible barrier.

46. And we place shields over their hearts, that they should not understand it, and a deafness in their ears. And if you mention your Lord in the Quran alone, they run away turning their backs in aversion.

47. We are fully aware of what they are listening to, for they are listening to you but while they are in council the wicked Say: "You are but following a man bewitched!"

48. See how they cite the examples for you. They have gone astray, and cannot come to the path.

49. And they said: "When we are bones and fragments, will we then be resurrected to a new creation?"

50. Say: "Even if you be stones or metal."

51. "Or a creation that is held dear in your chests." They will Say: "Who will return us?" Say: "The One who initiated you the first time." They will shake their heads to you and Say: "When is this?" Say: "Perhaps it is near."

52. The Day He calls you and you respond by His grace, and you think that you only stayed a little while.

53. And say to My servants to speak that which is best. The devil plants animosity between them. The devil was to mankind a clear enemy.

54. Your Lord is fully aware of you, if He wishes He will have mercy on you, or if He wishes He will punish you. And We have not sent you as a guardian over them.

55. And your Lord is fully aware of who is in the heavens and the Earth. And We have preferred some prophets over others, and We gave David the Psalms.

56. Say: "Call on those you have claimed besides Him. For they have no power to remove harm from you or shift it."

57. The ones you call on, they are themselves seeking a path to their Lord which is nearer, and they desire His mercy, and they fear His retribution. The retribution of your Lord is to be feared!

58. And there is not a town before the Day of Resurrection that We will not destroy it, or punish it a severe punishment. This has been written in the record.

59. And what stopped Us from sending the signs except that the previous people disbelieved in them. And We sent to Thamud the camel with foresight, but

they did her wrong. And We do not send the signs except to make them fearful.

60. And when We said to you: "Your Lord has encompassed the people." And We did not make the vision that We showed you except as a test for the people, and tree that was cursed in the Quran. And We are making them fearful, but it only increases their transgression.

61. And We said to the Angels: "Yield to Adam." So they yielded except for Satan, he said: "Shall I yield to one you have created from mud!"

62. He said: "Shall I show You this one whom You have preferred over me, that if You respite me until the Day of Resurrection, I will seize his progeny, except for a few."

63. He said: "Go, and whoever follows you from them. Hell shall be the reward to you all, a reward well deserved."

64. "And entice whoever you can of them with your voice, and mobilize all your forces and men against them, and you may share with them in their money and children, and promise them." But the devil promises nothing but deceit.

65. "As for My servants, you will have no power over them." And your Lord suffices as a Caretaker.

66. Your Lord is the One Who drives the ships for you in the sea so that you may seek of His bounty. He is Merciful towards you.

67. And if harm should afflict you at sea, then all those whom you called on besides Him suddenly vanish from you except for Him. So when He saves you to dry land, you turn away. Mankind is ever ungrateful.

68. Are you confident that He will not cause this side of the land to swallow you up, or that He would not send a violent storm against you? Then you will find no caretaker for yourselves.

69. Or are you confident that He would not send you back again in it, then He would send against you a violent wind and cause you to drown for your rejection? Then you will not find a second chance with Us.

70. And We have honoured the Children of Adam and carried them in the land and the sea, and We have provided for them of the good things, and We have preferred them over many of those We created in a marked preference.

71. The Day We call every people by their Scripture. Then, whoever are given their record by their right, they will relate their record, and they will not be wronged in the least.

72. And whosoever is blind in this, then he will be blind in the Hereafter and more astray from the path.

73. And they nearly diverted you from what We inspired to you so that you would fabricate something different against Us, and then they would have taken you as a friend!

74. And if We had not made you stand firm, you were about to lean towards them a little bit.

75. Then, We would have made you taste double the retribution in this life and double the retribution in death. And then you would not find for yourself any victor against Us.

76. And they nearly frightened you to drive you out of the land. But in that case, they would have shortly been destroyed after you were gone.

77. This is the way of those whom We sent before you of Our messengers. And you will not find any change in Our way.

78. You shall perform the oath of allegiance at the setting of the sun till the twilight; and the Quran at dawn; the Quran at dawn is witnessed.

79. And from the night you shall reflect upon it additionally for yourself, perhaps your Lord would grant you to a high rank.

80. And Say: "My Lord, admit me an entrance of truth and let me exit an exit of truth, and grant me from Yourself a support to victory."

81. And Say: "The truth has come and falsehood has perished. Falsehood is always bound to perish!"

82. And We send down from the Quran what is a healing and mercy to the believers. And it only increases the wicked in their loss.

83. And if We bless mankind, he turns away and turns his side. But when adversity touches him, he is ever in despair!

84. Say: "Let each work according to his own. Your Lord is fully aware of who is best guided to the path."

85. And they ask you concerning the Spirit. Say: "The Spirit is from the command on my Lord, and the knowledge you were given was but very little."

86. And if We wished, We would take away that which We have inspired to you. Then you would not find for yourself with it against Us a caretaker.

87. Except for a mercy from your Lord. His favour upon you has been great.

88. Say: "If all the humans and the Jinn were to gather to bring a Quran like this, they could not come with its like, even if they were helping one another."

89. And We have cited to the people in this Quran from every example, but most people refuse to be anything but a rejecter!

90. And they said: "We will not believe to you until you cause a spring of water to burst from the land"

91. "Or that you have an estate of palm trees and grapes, and you cause gushing rivers to burst through it."

92. "Or that you make the heaven fall upon us in pieces as you claimed, or that you bring God and the Angels before us."

93. "Or that you have a luxurious mansion, or that you can ascend into the heavens. And we will not believe in your ascension unless you bring for us a record that we can read." Say: "Glory be to my Lord. Am I anything other than a human messenger!"

94. And what stopped the people from believing when the guidance came to them, except that they said: "Has God sent a human messenger?"

95. Say: "If the Earth had Angels walking about in security, We would have sent down to them from heaven an Angel as a messenger."

96. Say: "God suffices as a witness between me and you. He is Expert and Watcher over His servants."

97. Whomever God guides is the truly guided one. And whomever He misguides then you will not find for them any allies except for Him. And We gather them on the Day of Resurrection on their faces, blind, mute, and deaf; their abode will be Hell. Every time it dies down, We increase for them the fire.

98. Such is their recompense that they rejected Our revelations, and they said: "If we are bones and fragments, will we be sent into a new creation?"

99. Did they not see that God who has created the heavens and the Earth is able to create their like? And He has made an appointed time for them in which there is no doubt. But the wicked refuse anything except rejection.

100. Say: "If you were the ones possessing the vaults of my Lord's mercy, you would have held back for fear of spending. And man was always stingy!"

101. And We had given Moses nine clear signs. So ask the Children of Israel, when he came to them, then Pharaoh said: "I think that you Moses are bewitched!"

102. He said: "You know that no one has sent these down except for the Lord of the heavens and the Earth as visible proofs. And I think that you Pharaoh are doomed!"

103. So he wanted to entice them out of the land. But We drowned him and all those with him.

104. And We said after him to the Children of Israel: "Dwell in the land, then, when the time of the second promise comes, We will bring you all together as a mixed crowd."

105.And it is with truth that We have sent it down, and with truth it came down. And We have not sent you except as a bearer of good news and a warner.

106.And a compilation that We have separated, so that you may relate it to the people over time; and We have brought it down gradually.

107.Say: "Believe in it or do not believe in it. Those who have been given the knowledge before it, when it is recited to them, they fall to their chins prostrating."

108.And they Say: "Praise be to our Lord. Truly, the promise of our Lord was fulfilled."

109.And they fall upon their chins crying, and it increases them in humility.

110.Say: "Call on God or call on the Almighty. Whichever it is you call on, for to Him are the best names." And do not be too loud in making your oath, nor too quite; but seek a path in between.

111.And Say: "Praise be to God who has not taken a son, nor does He have a partner in sovereignty, nor does He have an ally out of weakness." And glorify Him greatly.

Chapter 18

بسم الله الرحمن الرحيم

In the name of God, the Almighty, the Merciful.

1. Praise be to God who sent down the Scripture to His servant, and He did not make in it any crookedness.

2. It is valuable, giving warning of the severe punishment from Him; and it gives glad tidings to the believers who do good works, that they will have a fair reward.

3. In which they will abide eternally.

4. And to warn those who said: "God has taken a son."

5. They have no knowledge of this, nor do their fathers. Tremendous indeed is the word coming out of their mouths. They are but saying a lie!

6. Perhaps you will torment yourself in grief over them, because they will not believe in this saying at all.

7. We have made what is on Earth an adornment for them, so that We will test them as to who is better in deeds.

8. And We will then make what is on it a barren wasteland.

9. Did you perceive that the dwellers of the cave and the numbers related were of Our wondrous signs?

10. When the youths hid in the cave, and they said: "Our Lord, bring us a mercy from Yourself, and help us in our affair!"

11. So We sealed upon their ears in the cave for a number of years.

12. Then We sent them to know which of the two groups had remained for as long as they stayed.

13. We narrate to you their news with truth. They were youths who believed in their Lord, and We increased them in guidance.

14. And We made firm their hearts when they stood and said: "Our Lord, the Lord of heavens and Earth, we will not call besides Him any god. If we have done so then it was in error."

15. "Here are our people, they have taken gods besides Him, while they do not come with any clear authority. Who then is more wicked than one who invents lies about God?"

16. So when you withdraw from them and what they serve besides God, seek refuge in the cave, and your Lord will distribute His mercy upon you and prepare for your problem a solution.

17. And you see the sun when it rises, it visits their cave from the right, and when it sets, it touches them from the left, while they are in an enclosure from it. That is from God's signs. Whomever God guides is the guided one, and whomever He misguides, you will not find for him any ally to lead.

18. And you would think they are awake while they are asleep. And We turn them on the right-side and on the left-side, and their dog has his legs outstretched in their midst. If you looked upon them you would have run away from them and you would have been filled with terror from them!

19. And it was thus that We delivered them so they would ask themselves. A speaker from amongst them said: "How long have you stayed?" They said: "We stayed a day or part of a day." He said: "Your Lord is surely aware how long you stayed, so send one of you with these stamped coins of yours to the city, and let him see which is the tastiest food, and let him come with a provision of it. And let him be careful and let no one take notice of you."

20. "If they discover you, they will stone you or return you to their creed. Then you will never be successful."

21. And as such, We revealed their case so that they would know that God's promise is true and that there is no doubt regarding the Hour. They argued amongst themselves regarding them, so they said: "Erect a monument for them!" Their Lord is fully aware of them, those who managed to win the argument said: "We will construct a temple over them."

22. They will Say: "Three, the fourth is their dog." And they Say: "Five, the sixth is their dog," guessing at what they do not know. And they Say: "Seven, and the eighth is their dog." Say: "My Lord is fully aware of their number, none know them except for a few." So do not debate in them except with proof, and do not seek information regarding them from anyone.

23. And do not simply say of something: "I will do this tomorrow."

24. "Except if God wills." And remember your Lord if you forget and Say: "Perhaps my Lord will guide me to what is nearer to this in wisdom."

25. And they remained in their cave for three hundred years, and increased by nine.
26. Say: "God is fully aware how long they remained, to Him is the unseen of heavens and Earth, He sees and hears. They do not have besides Him any ally, nor does He share in His judgment with anyone."
27. And recite what has been inspired to you from your Lord's Scripture, there is no changing His words, and you will not find besides Him any refuge.
28. And have patience upon yourself regarding those who call on their Lord at dawn and dusk seeking His presence, and let not your eyes overlook them that you seek the beauty of this worldly life. And do not obey the one whom We have made his heart heedless of Our remembrance and he followed his desire, and his fate was lost.
29. And Say: "The truth is from your Lord, so let whomever desires believe, and whomever desires reject." We have prepared for the wicked a Fire whose walls will be surrounding them. And if they cry out, they are given a water like boiling oil which burns their faces. What a miserable place!
30. Those who believe and do good works, We do not waste the reward of those who have done well.
31. They will have the gardens of Eden with rivers flowing beneath them, and they will be adorned with bracelets of gold and they will wear green garments of fine silk. They will sit in it on raised thrones. Beautiful is the reward, and beautiful is the dwelling place.
32. And give them the example of two men: We made for one of them two gardens of grapes, and We surrounded them with palm trees, and We made between them a green field.
33. Both gardens brought forth their fruit, and none failed in the least. And We caused a river to pass through them.
34. And he had abundant fruit, so he said to his friend while discussing with him: "I am better off than you financially, and of great influence."
35. And he went back into his garden while he had wronged himself. He said: "I do not think that this will ever perish."
36. "And I do not think that the Hour is coming. And if I am indeed returned to my Lord, then I will surely find even better things for me."
37. His friend said to him while discussing with him: "Have you disbelieved in the One who created you from dirt, then from a seed, then He evolved you into a man?"
38. "But He is God, my Lord, and I do not place any partners at all with my Lord."

39. "And if you enter your garden, you should have said: "This is what God has given, there is no power except by God." You see me as being less than you in wealth and in children?"

40. "Perhaps my Lord will give me better than your garden, and He should send upon it a violent storm from the sky, so it becomes completely barren."

41. "Or that its water becomes deep under-ground, so you will not be able to seek it."

42. So his fruits were ruined, and he began turning his hands at that which he has spent on it while it remained destroyed upon its foundations. And he said: "I wish I did not make any partner with my Lord!"

43. And he had no group which could help against God, and he would not have had victory.

44. Such is the true authority of God. He is best to reward, and best to punish.

45. And give them the parable of this worldly life is like a water which We have sent down from the sky, so that the plants of the Earth mix with it and it becomes murky being moved by the wind. And God is capable of all things.

46. Wealth and buildings are the beauty of this life. But the good deeds that remain behind are better with your Lord for a reward, and better for hope.

47. And the Day We move the mountains, and you see the Earth barren, and We gather them. We did not forget anyone of them.

48. And they are displayed before your Lord as a column: "You have come to Us as We had created you the first time. No, you claimed We would not make for you an appointed time!"

49. And the record was displayed, so you see the criminals fearful of what is in it. And they Say: "Woe to us!, what is wrong with this record that it does not leave out anything small or large except that it has counted it." And they found what they had done present. And your Lord does not wrong anyone.

50. And We said to the Angels: "Yield to Adam." So they all yielded except for Satan, he was of the Jinn, so he disobeyed the order of his Lord. "Will you take him and his progeny as allies besides Me, while they are your enemy?" Miserable for the wicked is the substitute!

51. I did not make them witness the creation of heavens and Earth, nor the creation of themselves. Nor do I take the misleaders as helpers.

52. The Day when He says: "Call on your partners that you had claimed." So they called them, but they did not respond to them. And We made between them a barrier.

53. And the criminals saw the Fire, and they realized they will be placed in it, and they did not find any way to avert it.

54. And We have cited in this Quran every example for the people. But man was always most argumentative.

55. And what prevented the people from believing when the guidance came to them, and to seek forgiveness from their Lord? Are they waiting for what happened to the people of old to come to them, or that the retribution be brought to them face to face?

56. And We do not send the messengers except as bearers of good news and warners. But those who reject will argue using falsehood to overshadow the truth with it. And they took My revelations and what they have been warned by as a joke!

57. And who is more wicked than one who is reminded of his Lord's verses but he turned away from them, and he forgot what his hands had done. We have made veils upon their hearts from understanding them, and a deafness in their ears. And if you invite them to the guidance, they will never be guided.

58. And your Lord is forgiving, with mercy. If He were to judge the people for what they had already earned, He would hasten for them the retribution. No, they have an appointment, beyond which they will find no escape.

59. And such are the towns which We had destroyed when they transgressed. And We made for their destruction an appointed time.

60. And Moses said to his youth: "I will not stop until I reach the junction of the two seas, or I spend a lifetime trying."

61. But when they did reach the junction between, they forgot their fish, and it was able to make its way back to the sea in a stream.

62. And when they had passed further on, he said to his youth: "Bring us our lunch; we have found much fatigue in this journey of ours."

63. He said: "Do you remember when we rested upon the rock? I forgot the fish, and it was the devil that made me forget to remember it. It made its way back to the sea amazingly!"

64. He said: "That is what we have been seeking!" So they went back retracing their steps.

65. So they came upon a servant of Ours whom We had given him mercy from Us and We taught him knowledge from Us.

66. Moses said to him: "Can I follow you so that you will teach me from the guidance you have been taught?"

67. He said: "You will not be able to have patience with me."

68. "And how can you be patient about that which you have not been given any news?"

69. He said: "You will find me, God willing, to be patient. And I will not disobey any command of yours."
70. He said: "If you follow me, then do not ask about anything until I relate it to you."
71. So they ventured forth until they rode in a boat and he made a hole in it. He said: "Did you make a hole in it to drown its people? You have done something dreadful!"
72. He said: "Did I not tell you that you will not be able to have patience with me?"
73. He said: "Forgive me for what I forgot, and do not be hard upon my request with you."
74. So they ventured forth until they came upon a youth, and he killed him. He said: "Have you killed an innocent person without justice? You have truly come with something awful!"
75. He said: "Did I not tell you that you will not be able to have patience with me?"
76. He said: "If I ask you about anything after this, then do not keep me in your company. You will then have a reason over me."
77. So they ventured forth until they came to the people of a town. They requested food from its people but they refused to host them. Then they found a wall which was close to collapsing, so he built it. He said: "If you wished, you could have asked a wage for it!"
78. He said: "For this, we will now part ways. I will inform you of the meanings of those things that you could not have patience over."
79. "As for the boat, it belonged to some poor people who were working the sea, so I wanted to damage it as there was a king coming who takes every boat by force."
80. "And as for the youth, his parents were believers, so we feared that he would oppress them by his transgression and disbelief."
81. "So we wanted their Lord to replace for them with one who is better than him in purity and closer to mercy."
82. "And as for the wall, it belonged to two orphaned boys in the city, and underneath it was a treasure for them, and their father was a good man, so your Lord wanted that they would reach their maturity and take out their treasure as a mercy from your Lord. And none of what I did was of my own accord. That is the meaning of what you could not have patience for."
83. And they ask you about the one who is from Two Eras, Say: "I will recite to you a memory from him."

84. We had facilitated for him in the land, and We had given him the means of everything.
85. So he followed the means.
86. Until he reached the setting of the sun, and he found it setting at a hot spring, and he found near it a people. We said: "O Two Eras, either you are to punish, or you are to do them good."
87. He said: "As for he who has transgressed, we will punish him then he will be returned to his Lord and He will punish him an awful punishment."
88. "And as for he who believes and does good, then he will have the reward of goodness, and we will speak to him simply of our plan."
89. Then he followed the means.
90. So when he reached the rising of the sun, he found it rising on a people whom We did not make for them any cover except it.
91. So it was, and We knew ahead of time about what he intended.
92. Then he followed the means.
93. Until he reached the area between the two barriers, he found no one beside it except a people who could barely understand anything said.
94. They said: "O Two Eras, Gog and Magog are destroyers of the land, so shall we make a tribute for you that you will make between us and them a barrier?"
95. He said: "What my Lord has given me is far better. So help me with strength and I will make between you and them a barrier."
96. "Bring me iron ore." Until he levelled between the two walls, he said: "Blow," until he made it a furnace, he said: "Bring me tar so I can pour it over."
97. So they could not come over it, and they could not make a hole in it.
98. He said: "This is a mercy from my Lord. But when the promise of my Lord comes, He will make it rubble. And the promise of my Lord is truth."
99. And We left them till that day to surge like waves on one another. And the horn was blown so We gathered them together.
100. And We displayed Hell on that Day to the disbelievers openly.
101. Those whose eyes were closed from My remembrance, and they were unable to hear.
102. Did those who reject think that they can take My servants as allies besides Me? We have prepared Hell for the rejecters as a dwelling place.
103. Say: "Shall we inform you of the greatest losers?"
104. "Those whose efforts in the worldly life were wasted while they thought they were doing good!"

105. These are the ones who rejected the revelations of their Lord and His meeting. So their works were in vain, and We will not give them any value on the Day of Resurrection.
106. That is their recompense, Hell; for what they rejected and for taking My revelations and My messengers for mockery!
107. Those who believe and do good works, they will have estates of Paradise as a dwelling place.
108. Abiding therein. They will not want to be moved from it.
109. Say: "If the sea were an inkwell for the words of my Lord, then the sea would run out before the words of my Lord run out;" even if We were to bring another like it for its aid.
110. Say: "I am but a human being like you, being inspired that your god is One god. So whoever looks forward to meeting his Lord, then let him do good works and not set up any partner in the service of his Lord."

Chapter 19

بسم الله الرحمن الرحيم

In the name of God, the Almighty, the Merciful.

1. K.H'.Y.A'.S'

2. A reminder of your Lord's mercy to His servant Zachariah.

3. When he called out to his Lord secretly.

4. He said: "My Lord, my bones have gone frail, and my hair has turned white, and I have never been mischievous in calling to You my Lord."

5. "And I fear the kinfolk after I am gone, and my wife is infertile, so grant me from Yourself an ally."

6. "To inherit from me, and inherit from the descendants of Jacob. And make him my Lord, well pleasing."

7. "O Zachariah, We give you glad tidings of a son whose name is John. We have not given that name before to anyone."

8. He said: "My Lord, how can I have a son when my wife is infertile, and I have reached a very old age?"

9. He said: "It is such that your Lord has said. It is an easy thing for Me. And I had created you before when you were not even anything."

10. He said: "My Lord, make for me a sign." He said: "Your sign is that you will not speak to the people for three nights consecutively."

11. So he went out amongst his people from the temple enclosure, and he indicated to them that they should glorify Him at dawn and dusk.

12. "O John, take the Scripture with confidence." And We gave him authority while in his youth.

13. And he had kindness from Us and purity, and he was ever righteous.

14. And dutiful to his parents, and never was he a tyrant or disobedient.

15. And peace be upon him the day he was born, and the day he dies, and the Day he is resurrected alive.
16. And relate in the Scripture Mary, when she withdrew herself from her family to a place which was to the east.
17. She took to a barrier which separated her from them, so We sent Our spirit to her, and he took on the shape of a human being in all similarity.
18. She said: "I seek refuge with the Almighty from you if you are a person of faith."
19. He said: "I am the messenger of your Lord, to grant you the gift of a pure son."
20. She said: "How can I have a son when no human being has been with me, nor have I desired such?"
21. He said: "It is such that your Lord has said, it is easy for Me. And We shall make him a sign for the people and a mercy from Us. It is a matter already ordained."
22. So she was pregnant with him, and she went to deliver in a far place.
23. Then the birth pains came to her, by the trunk of a palm tree. She said: "I wish I had died before this, and became totally forgotten!"
24. But then he called to her from beneath her: "Do not be sad, your Lord has made below you a stream."
25. "And shake the trunk of this palm tree, it will cause ripe dates to fall upon you."
26. "So eat and drink and be happy. If you see any human being, then Say: "I have declared a fast for the Almighty, and I will not talk today to any of mankind.""
27. Then she came to her people carrying him. They said: "O Mary, you have come with something totally unexpected!"
28. "O sister of Aaron, your father was not a bad man, and your mother was never unchaste!"
29. So she pointed to him. They said: "How can we talk to someone who is a child in a cradle?"
30. He said: "I am God's servant, He has given me the Scripture and made me a prophet."
31. "And He made me blessed wherever I was, and He charged me with the oath of allegiance and towards betterment as long as I am alive."
32. "And to be dutiful to my mother, and He did not make me a rebellious tyrant."

33. "And peace be upon me the day I was born, and the day I die, and the Day I am resurrected alive."

34. Such was Jesus, the son of Mary, and this is the truth of the matter in which they doubt.

35. God was never to take a son, be He glorified. If He decrees a matter, then He simply says to it: "Be," and it is.

36. And God is my Lord and your Lord, so serve Him. This is a straight path.

37. So the parties disputed between them. Therefore, woe to those who have rejected from the scene of a terrible Day.

38. Listen to what they say and watch on the Day they come to Us. But the wicked today are in clear misguidance.

39. And warn them of the Day of remorse. When the matter is decided while they are oblivious, and they do not believe.

40. It is We who will inherit the Earth and all that is on it. And to Us they will return.

41. And recall in the Scripture Abraham; he was a man of faith, a prophet.

42. When he said to his father: "O father, why do you serve what does not hear or see, nor help you in anything?"

43. "My father, knowledge has come to me which did not come to you. So follow me that I will guide you to a good path."

44. "My father, do not serve the devil. For the devil was ever disobedient to the Almighty."

45. "My father, I fear that a retribution will inflict you from the Almighty and that you will become an ally to the devil."

46. He said: "Have you abandoned my gods O Abraham? If you do not stop this, I will stone you. Leave me alone."

47. He said: "Peace be upon you, I will ask forgiveness for you from my Lord. He has been most kind to me."

48. "And I will abandon you and what you call on besides God. And I will call on my Lord. I hope that I will not be mischievous in calling upon my Lord."

49. So when he abandoned them and what they serve besides God, We granted him Isaac and Jacob, and We made each a prophet.

50. And We granted them from Our mercy, and We made for them a tongue of truth to be heard.

51. And recall in the Scripture Moses; he was loyal, and he was a messenger prophet.

52. And We called him from the right side of the mount, and We brought him close to talk with.

53. And We granted him from Our mercy his brother Aaron as a prophet.

54. And recall in the Scripture Ishmael; he was truthful to his promise, and he was a messenger prophet.

55. And he used to instruct his family with the oath of allegiance and towards betterment, and his Lord was pleased with him.

56. And recall in the Scripture Enoch; he was a man of truth, a prophet.

57. And We raised him to a high place.

58. Those are the ones whom God has blessed from amongst the prophets from the progeny of Adam, and those We carried with Noah, and from the progeny of Abraham and Israel, and from whom We have guided and chosen. When the revelations of the Almighty are recited to them, they fall down prostrating, and in tears.

59. Then generations came after them who lost the oath of allegiance, and followed the desires. They will find their consequences.

60. Except for whoever repents and believes and does good work; they will be admitted to Paradise, and they will not be wronged in the least.

61. The gardens of Eden, which the Almighty had promised His servants in the unseen. His promise must come to pass.

62. They will not hear in it any nonsense, only peace. And they will have their provision in it morning and evening.

63. Such is Paradise that We inherit to any of Our servants who are righteous.

64. "And we are not sent except by the command of your Lord. To Him is our present and our future, and all that is in-between. And your Lord was never to forget."

65. "The Lord of the heavens and the Earth and what is in-between them. So serve Him and be patient in His service. Do you know anything that is like Him?"

66. And man says: "Can it be that when I am dead, I will be brought out alive?"

67. Does man not remember that We created him before that and he was nothing at all?

68. By your Lord, We will gather them and the devils, then We will place them around Hell on their knees.

69. Then We will drag out from every group which of them was the worst opposition to the Almighty.

70. Then, it is We who are best aware of those who deserve to be burnt therein.

71. And every single one of you must pass by it. This for your Lord is a certainty that will come to pass.

72. Then We will save those who were righteous, and We leave the wicked in it on their knees.

73. And when Our clear revelations were recited to them, those who rejected said to those who believed: "Which of the two groups of ours is more in authority and more prosperous?"

74. And how many generations have We destroyed before them? They had more wealth and more influence.

75. Say: "Whoever is in misguidance, then the Almighty will lead them on." Until they see what they have been promised, either the retribution or the Hour. Then they will know who is in a worst place and weaker in power.

76. And God increases the guidance of those who are guided. And what remains of good is better with your Lord as a reward and a far better return.

77. Did you see the one who rejected Our revelations and said: "I will be given wealth and children."

78. Did he look into the future? Or has he taken a pledge with the Almighty?

79. No, We will record what he says, and We will increase for him the retribution significantly.

80. Then We inherit from him all that he said, and he shall come to Us all alone.

81. And they have taken gods besides God to be for them their glory.

82. On the contrary, they will reject their service of them and they will be standing against them.

83. Did you not see that We send the devils upon the rejecters to drive them into evil?

84. So do not be impatient; for We are preparing for them a preparation.

85. The Day We gather the righteous to the Almighty as a delegation.

86. And We drive the criminals to Hell as a herd.

87. None will posses intercession, except for he who has taken a pledge with the Almighty.

88. And they said the Almighty has taken a son!

89. You have come with a gross blasphemy.

90. The heavens are about to shatter from it, and the Earth crack open, and the mountains fall and crumble.

91. That they claimed that the Almighty had a son!

92. And what need does the Almighty have to take a son?

93. When all there is in the heavens and the Earth will but come to the Almighty as servants.

94. He has encompassed them, and counted them one by one.

95. And all of them will come to Him on the Day of Resurrection, all alone.

96. Those who believe and do good works, the Almighty will bestow them with love.

97. Thus We have made this easy in your tongue so that you may give good news with it to the righteous and that you may warn with it the quarrelsome people.

98. And how many a generation have We destroyed before them? Do you perceive any of them or hear from them a sound?

Chapter 20

بسم الله الرحمن الرحيم

In the name of God, the Almighty, the Merciful.

1. T'.H'

2. We did not send down to you the Quran so you may suffer.

3. It is but a reminder for the one who takes heed.

4. Sent down from the One who created the Earth and the heavens above.

5. The Almighty, on the throne He settled.

6. To Him is what is in the heavens and what is in the Earth, and what is in between, and what is underneath the soil.

7. And if you declare openly what you say, He knows the secret and what is hidden.

8. God, there is no god but He, to Him are the beautiful names.

9. And did the news of Moses come to you?

10. When he saw a fire, he said to his family: "Stay here, I have seen a fire, perhaps I can bring a piece from it, or find at the fire some guidance."

11. So when he came to it he was called: "O Moses."

12. "I am your Lord, so take off your slippers, you are in the holy valley Tawa."

13. "And I have chosen you, so listen to what is being inspired."

14. "I am God, there is no god but Me, so serve Me and perform the oath of allegiance for My remembrance."

15. "The Hour is coming, I am nearly keeping it hidden, so that every soul will be recompensed with what is strived."

16. "So do not be deterred from it by he who does not believe in it and followed his desire and perished."

17. "And what is in your right hand O Moses?"

18. He said: "It is my staff, I lean on it, and I guide my sheep with it, and I have other uses in it."
19. He said: "Cast it down O Moses."
20. So he cast it down, and it became a moving serpent!
21. He said: "Take it and do not be fearful, We will turn it back to its previous form."
22. "And place your hand under your arm, it will come out white without blemish, as another sign."
23. "This is to show you Our great signs."
24. "Go to Pharaoh, for he has transgressed."
25. He said: "My Lord, relieve for me my chest."
26. "And make my mission easy."
27. "And remove the knot in my tongue."
28. "So they can understand what I say."
29. "And allow for me an advisor from my family."
30. "Aaron, my brother."
31. "So that I may strengthen my resolve through him."
32. "And share with him my mission."
33. "So that we may glorify You plenty."
34. "And remember You plenty."
35. "You Have been watcher over us."
36. He said: "You have been given what you asked O Moses."
37. "And We Have graced you another time."
38. "When We inspired to your mother what was inspired."
39. "That she should cast him in the basket, and cast the basket in the sea, so the sea will place him on the shore, where an enemy of Mine and his will take him. And I placed upon you a love from Me. And that you shall be raised under My eye."
40. "That your sister should follow, and Say: "Shall I guide you to a person who will nurse him" Thus We returned you to your mother, so that she may be pleased and not be sad. And you killed a person, but We saved you from harm and We tested you greatly. So it was that you stayed with the people of Median for many years, then you came here by fate O Moses."
41. "And I Have raised you for Myself."
42. "Go, you and your brother with Our signs, and do not linger from My remembrance."
43. "Go, both of you, to Pharaoh, for he has transgressed."
44. "So say to him soft words, perhaps he will remember or take heed."

45. They said: "Our Lord, we fear that he would let loose upon us, or transgress."
46. He said: "Do not fear, I am with you, I hear and I see."
47. So come to him and Say: "We are messengers from your Lord, so send with us the Children of Israel, and do not punish them. We have come to you with a sign from your Lord, and peace be upon those who follow the guidance."
48. "It has been inspired to us that the retribution will be upon he who denies and turns away."
49. He said: "So who is the lord of you both O Moses?"
50. He said: "Our Lord is the One who gave everything its creation, then guided."
51. He said: "What then has happened to the previous generations?"
52. He said: "It's knowledge is with my Lord, in a record. My Lord does not err or forget."
53. The One who made for you the Earth habitable and He made ways for you in it, and He brought down water from the sky, so We brought out with it pairs of vegetation of all types.
54. Eat and raise your livestock, in that are signs for those of thought.
55. From it We created you and in it We return you, and from it We bring you out another time.
56. And We showed him Our signs, all of them, but he denied and refused.
57. He said: "Have you come to us to take us out of our land with your magic O Moses?"
58. "We will bring you a magic like it, so let us make an appointment between us and you which neither of us will break, a place where we both agree."
59. He said: "Your appointment is the day of festival, and when the people start crowding during the late morning."
60. So Pharaoh went away, and he gathered his scheming then he came.
61. Moses said to them: "Woe to you, do not invent lies about God, else the retribution will take you, and miserable is the one who invents."
62. So they disputed in their matter between themselves, and they kept secret their council.
63. They said: "These are but two magicians who want to take you out of your land with their magic, and they want to do away with your ideal way."
64. "So agree your scheme, then come as one front. Whoever wins today will succeed."

65. They said: "O Moses, either you cast down or we will be the first to cast down."

66. He said: "No, you cast down." So their ropes and staffs appeared from their magic as if they were moving.

67. And Moses held some fear in himself.

68. We said: "Do not fear, you will best them."

69. "And cast down what is in your right hand it will consume what they have made. They have only made the work of a magician, and the magician will not succeed no matter what he does."

70. So the magicians went down in prostration. They said: "We believe in the Lord of Aaron and Moses."

71. He said: "Have you believed to him before taking my permission? He is surely your great one who has taught you magic. So, I will cut off your hands and feet from alternate sides, and I will crucify you on the trunks of the palm trees, and you will come to know which of us is greater in retribution and more lasting!"

72. They said: "We will not prefer you over the proofs that have come to us, and over the One who initiated us. So issue whatever judgment you have, for you only issue judgment in this worldly life."

73. "We have believed in our Lord that He may forgive us our sins, and what you had forced us into doing of magic. And God is better and everlasting."

74. He who comes to his Lord as a criminal, he will have Hell, where he will neither die in it nor live.

75. And he who comes to Him as a believer doing good works, for those will be the highest ranks.

76. The gardens of Eden with rivers flowing beneath them, abiding therein. Such is the reward of he who is developed.

77. And We inspired to Moses: "Take My servants out, and make for them through the sea a path. You shall not fear being overtaken, nor be afraid."

78. So Pharaoh followed them with his soldiers, but the sea came-over them and covered them.

79. Thus, Pharaoh misled his people and he did not guide.

80. O Children of Israel, We have saved you from your enemy, and We summoned you at the right side of the mount, and We sent down to you manna and quail.

81. Eat from the good things that We have provided for you and do not transgress in this else My wrath will be upon you. Whomever has incurred My wrath is lost.

82. And I am forgiving for whomever repents and does good work, then is guided.
83. "And what has caused you to rush ahead of your people O Moses?"
84. He said: "They are coming in my tracks, and I came quickly to you my Lord so you would be pleased."
85. He said: "We have tested your people after you left, and the Samarian misguided them."
86. So Moses returned to his people angry and disappointed. He said: "My people, did not your Lord promise you a good promise? Has the waiting been too long, or did you want that the wrath of your Lord be upon you? Thus you broke the promise with me."
87. They said: "We did not break the promise by our own will, but we were loaded down with the jewellery of the people so we cast them down, and it was such that the Samarian suggested."
88. He then produced for them a statue of a calf that emitted a sound. So they said: "This is your god and the god of Moses, but he had forgotten!"
89. Did they not see that it did not respond to them? Nor did it possess for them any harm or benefit?
90. And Aaron said to them before: "My people, you are being tested with it. Your Lord is the Almighty, so follow me and obey my command!"
91. They said: "We will remain devoted to it until Moses comes back to us."
92. He said: "O Aaron, what prevented you when you saw them being astray?"
93. "Do you not follow me? Have you disobeyed my command?"
94. He said: "O son of my mother, do not grab me by my beard nor by my head. I feared that you would say that I separated between the Children of Israel, and that I did not follow your orders."
95. He said: "So what do you have to say O Samarian?"
96. He said: "I noticed what they did not notice, so I took a handful from where the messenger was standing, and I cast it in. This is what my soul inspired me to do."
97. He said: "Then be gone, for you will have it in this life to Say: "I am not to be touched" And you will have an appointed time which you will not forsake. And look to your god that you remained devoted to, we will burn him, then we will destroy him in the sea completely."
98. Your god is God; whom there is no god but He. His knowledge encompasses all things.
99. And it is such that We relate to you the news of what has passed. And We have given you from Us a remembrance.

100. Whoever turns away from it, then he will carry a load on the Day of Resurrection.

101. They will remain therein, and miserable on the Day of Resurrection is what they carry.

102. The Day the horn is blown, and We gather the criminals on that Day white eyed.

103. They whisper amongst themselves: "You have only been away for a period of ten."

104. We are fully aware of what they say, for the best in knowledge amongst them will Say: "No, you have only been away for a day."

105. And they ask you about the mountains, Say: "My Lord will annihilate them completely."

106. "Then He will leave it as a smooth plain."

107. "You will not see in it any crookedness or curves."

108. On that Day, they will follow the caller, there is no crookedness to him. And all voices will be humbled for the Almighty, you will not be able to hear except whispers.

109. On that Day, no intercession will be of help, except for he whom the Almighty allows and accepts what he has to say.

110. He knows their present and their future, and they do not have any of His knowledge.

111. And the faces shall be humbled for the Eternal, the Living. And whoever carried wickedness with him has failed.

112. And whoever does any good works, while he is a believer, then he should not fear injustice nor being given less than his due.

113. And it was such that We sent it down as an Arabic compilation, and We cited in it many warnings, perhaps they will become aware or it will cause for them a remembrance.

114. Then High above all is God, the King, the True. And do not be hasty with the Quran before its inspiration is completed to you, and Say: "My Lord, increase my knowledge."

115. And We had made a pledge to Adam from before, but he forgot, and We did not find in him the will power.

116. And We said to the Angels: "Yield to Adam." They all yielded except for Satan, he refused.

117. So We said: "O Adam, this is an enemy to you and your mate. So do not let him take you out from the paradise, else you will have hardship."

118. "You will have in it that you will not go hungry nor need clothes."

119. "And you will have in it that you will not go thirsty nor suffer from heat."

120. But the devil whispered to him, he said: "O Adam, shall I lead you to the tree of immortality and a kingdom which will not waste away?"

121. So they both ate from it, and their lusts became apparent for them, and they began to place leaves on themselves from the paradise. Adam had disobeyed his Lord, and had gone astray.

122. Then his Lord recalled him, and He forgave him, and gave guidance to him.

123. He said: "Descend from this, all of you, for you are enemies to one another. So, when My guidance comes to you, then, whoever follows My guidance, he will not go astray nor suffer."

124. "And whoever turns away from My remembrance, then he will have a miserable life, and We will raise him blind on the Day of Resurrection."

125. He said: "My Lord, you have raised me blind while I used to be able to see?"

126. He said: "It was the same when Our revelations came to you, you forgot them, and similarly today you will be forgotten."

127. And it is such that We recompense he who transgresses, and did not believe in His Lord's revelations. And the retribution of the Hereafter is more severe and lasting.

128. Is it not a guide to them how many generations We had destroyed before them, which they are walking now in their homes? In that are signs for the people of understanding.

129. And had it not been for a word already given by your Lord, they would have been held to account immediately.

130. So be patient to what they are saying and glorify the grace of your Lord before the rising of the sun, and before its setting, and during the night glorify; and at various parts of the day perhaps you may be content.

131. And do not strain your eyes on what We have given other people as luxuries of this worldly life so as to test them with it; and the provision of your Lord is better and more lasting.

132. And instruct your family with the oath of allegiance, and be patient for it. We do not ask you for provision, for We provide for you. And the good end is for the righteous.

133. And they said: "If only he would bring us a sign from his Lord!" Did not proof come to them from what is in the previous Scriptures?

134. And if We had destroyed them with retribution before this, they would have said: "Our Lord, if only You had sent us a messenger so we could follow Your revelations before we are humiliated and shamed!"

135. Say: "All are waiting, so wait, and you will come to know who are the people upon the even path and who are guided."

Chapter 21

بسم الله الرحمن الرحيم

In the name of God, the Almighty, the Merciful.

1. The judgment for the people has come near, while they are turning away unaware.

2. When a reminder comes to them from their Lord that is new, they listen to it while playing.

3. Their hearts are preoccupied, and those who are wicked confer privately: "Is he not a human being like you? Would you accept this magic while you know?"

4. Say: "My Lord knows what is said in the heavens and in the Earth, and He is the Hearer, the Knower."

5. They said: "No, these are just bad dreams; no, he made it up; no, he is a poet. So let him bring us a sign like those who were sent before."

6. None of the towns which We destroyed before them had believed. Will they believe?

7. And We did not send before you except men whom We inspired to. So ask the people of the remembrance if you do not know.

8. And We did not make for them bodies that do not need to eat, nor were they immortal.

9. Then We fulfilled the promise to them, so We saved them and whom We pleased, and We destroyed those who transgressed.

10. We have sent down to you a Scripture in which is your remembrance. Do you not comprehend?

11. And how many a town have We destroyed because of its wrong doing, and We established after them a different people?

12. So it was that when they perceived Our power, they were running from it.

13. "Do not run, and come back to that which you were living lavishly in and your homes; so that you will be questioned."
14. They said: "Woe to us, we have been wicked!"
15. So that remained as their cry until We took them all, and they became still.
16. And We did not create the heavens and the Earth and what is between them for entertainment.
17. If We wanted to be amused, We could have done so from what is already with Us, if that is what We wished to do.
18. No, We cast with the truth upon the falsehood, so it disrupts it, and then it retreats. And woe to you for what you have described.
19. And to Him is whoever is in the heavens and in the Earth. And those who are near Him are not too proud to serve Him, nor do they complain.
20. They glorify in the night and the day, they do not cease.
21. Or have they taken gods from the Earth who can resurrect?
22. If there were gods in them except for God, then they would have been ruined. Glory be to God, the Lord of the throne from what they describe.
23. He is not questioned about what He does, while they will be questioned.
24. Or have they taken gods besides Him? Say: "Bring your proof. This is a reminder of those with me and a reminder of those before me." But, most of them do not know the truth, so they turn away.
25. And We did not send any messenger before you except that We inspired him that: "There is no god but Me, so serve Me."
26. And they said: "The Almighty has taken a son!" Be He glorified, they are all but honoured servants.
27. They do not speak ahead of Him, and on His command they act.
28. He knows their present and their future, and they cannot intercede unless it is for those whom He is pleased with. And they stand in awe and reverence of Him.
29. And whoever of them says: "I am a god besides Him," then that person We will punish with Hell. It is such that We punish the wicked.
30. Did those who reject not see that the heavens and the Earth were one piece and We tore them apart? And that We made from the water everything that lives. Will they not believe?
31. And We made on the Earth stabilizers so that it would not tumble with you, and We made in it wide paths that they may be guided.
32. And We made the sky a protective ceiling. And yet they are turning away from Our signs!

33. He is the One who created the night and the day, and the sun and the moon, each swimming in an orbit.
34. And We did not give immortality to any human being that came before you. If you are going to die, would they be immortal?
35. Every soul will taste death. And We burden you with evil and good as a test, and it is to Us that you will return.
36. And when those who reject see you, they take you for mockery: "Is this the one who speaks about your gods!" While in the remembrance of the Almighty they are rejecters!
37. Mankind has been created from haste. I will show you My signs, so do not be hasty.
38. And they Say: "When will this promise come to pass if you are truthful?"
39. If only those who reject knew, that they will not be able to ward off the fire from their faces, nor from their backs, nor will they be helped.
40. No, it will come to them suddenly. And they will not be able to turn it away, nor will they be delayed.
41. And messengers before you have been mocked, but those who mocked were then surrounded by that which they were mocking!
42. Say: "Who can protect you during the night and the day from the Almighty?" No, they are turning away from the remembrance of their Lord.
43. Or do they have gods that will protect them from Us? They cannot help themselves, nor can they be protected from Us.
44. It was Us who gave luxury to these and their fathers, until they grew old with age. Do they not see that We come to the land and make it shrink from its edges? Will they be able to win?
45. Say: "I am merely warning you with the inspiration." But the deaf do not hear the call when they are being warned.
46. And if a breath of your Lord's torment touches them, they will Say: "Woe to us, we have been wicked!"
47. And We will place the scales of justice for the Day of Resurrection, so that no soul will be wronged in the least. Even if it was the weight of a mustard seed, We will bring it. And We are sufficient as a Reckoner.
48. And We had given Moses and Aaron the Criterion, a shining light, and reminder for the righteous.
49. Those who reverence their Lord, even when unseen, and they are weary for the Hour.
50. And this is a blessed reminder which We have sent down. Will you be deniers of it?

51. And before that We gave Abraham his understanding, and We were aware of him.
52. As he said to his father and people: "What are these statues to which you are devoted?"
53. They said: "We found our fathers worshipping them."
54. He said: "You and your fathers have been clearly misguided."
55. They said: "Have you come to us with the truth, or are you simply playing?"
56. He said: "No, your lord is the Lord of heavens and Earth, the One who initiated them. And I bear witness to such."
57. "And by God, I will scheme against your statues after you have gone away and given your backs."
58. So he broke them into pieces except for the biggest of them, so that they may turn to him.
59. They said: "Who has done this to our gods? He is surely one of the wicked."
60. They said: "We heard a young man mentioning them. He was called Abraham."
61. They said: "Bring him before the eyes of the people so that they may be witness."
62. They said: "Did you do this to our gods O Abraham?"
63. He said: "It was the biggest one of them here who did it, so ask them, if they do speak!"
64. So they turned and said to themselves: "It is indeed ourselves who have been wicked!"
65. Then they reverted to their old ideas: "You know that they do not speak!"
66. He said: "Do you serve besides God that which does not benefit you at all nor harm you?"
67. "I am fed-up of you and to what you serve besides God! Do you not comprehend?"
68. They said: "If you are to do anything, then burn him, and give victory to your gods."
69. We said: "O fire, be cool and safe upon Abraham."
70. And they wanted to harm him, but We made them the losers.
71. And We saved him and Lot to the land which We have blessed in for the worlds.
72. And We granted him Isaac and Jacob afterward, and each of them We made a good doer.

73. And We made them leaders who guide by Our command, and We inspired them to do good work and honour the oath of allegiance and contribute towards betterment, and they were in service to Us.

74. And Lot, We gave him wisdom and knowledge, and We saved him from the town that used to do vile things. They were a people of evil, corrupt.

75. And We admitted him into Our mercy. He was of the good doers.

76. And Noah when he called out before that, thus We responded to him, and We saved him and his family from the great distress.

77. And We granted him victory against the people that denied Our revelations. They were a people of evil, so We drowned them all.

78. And David and Solomon, when they gave judgment in the case of the crop that was damaged by the sheep of the people, and We were witness to their judgment.

79. So We gave Solomon the correct understanding, and both of them We have given wisdom and knowledge. And We committed the mountains with David to praise as well as the birds. This is what We did.

80. And We taught him the making of armour for you to protect you from your enemy. Are you then thankful?

81. And to Solomon the gusting winds run by his command all the way to the land which We have blessed in. And We were aware of everything.

82. And from the devils are those who dive for him, and they perform other tasks, and We were guardian over them.

83. And Job when he called his Lord: "I have been afflicted with harm, and you are the Most Merciful of those who show mercy!"

84. So We answered him, and We removed what was afflicting him, and We brought him back his family and others with them as a mercy from Us and a reminder to those who serve.

85. And Ishmael and Enoch and Isaiah, all of them were patient.

86. And We admitted them in Our mercy, they were of the good doers.

87. And Jonah, when he went off in anger, and he thought that We would not be able to take him. Then he called out in the darkness: "There is no god but You! Glory to You, I was of the wicked!"

88. So We responded to him and We saved him from distress. And it is such that We save the faithful.

89. And Zachariah when he called out to his Lord: "My Lord, do not leave me without an heir, and You are the best inheritor."

90. So We responded to him, and We granted him John, and We cured his wife. They used to hasten to do good, and they would call to Us in joy and in fear. And to Us they were reverent.

91. And the one who protected her chastity, so We blew into her from Our Spirit, and We made her and her son a sign for the worlds.

92. This is your nation, one nation, and I am your Lord so serve Me.

93. And they disputed in the matter amongst themselves. Each of them will be returned to Us.

94. So whosoever does good work and he is a believer, then his efforts will not be rejected and We will record it for him.

95. It is forbidden for a town that We destroy that they would return!

96. Until Gog and Magog is opened, and from every elevated place they will race forth.

97. And the promise of truth draws near. Then, when it is seen by the eyes of those who rejected: "Woe to us, we have been oblivious to this. Indeed, we were wicked!"

98. Both you and what you serve besides God shall be fuel for Hell; you will enter it.

99. If these were gods, then they would not have entered it! And all will abide therein.

100. They will be breathing heavily in it, and they will not be heard therein.

101. As for those who deserved good from Us, they will be removed far away from it.

102. They shall not hear the slightest sound from it, and they will be in what their soul desires abiding therein.

103. The great horror will not sadden them, and the Angels will receive them: "This is your Day which you have been promised."

104. On the Day when We roll up the heavens like the scroll of a scripture is rolled up. As We initiated the first creation, so shall We return it. It is a promise of Ours that We will do this.

105. And We have written in the Psalms: "After the remembrance, that the Earth will be inherited by My servants who do good."

106. In this is a proclamation for a people who serve.

107. And We have not sent you except as a mercy to the worlds.

108. Say: "It is inspired to me that your god is but One god, so will you submit to Him?"

109. So if they turn away, then Say: "I have given you notice sufficiently, and I do not know if what you are promised is near or far."

110. "He knows that which is spoken publicly and He knows that which you keep secret."
111. "And for all I know, it may be a test for you and an enjoyment for a while."
112. He said: "My Lord, judge with truth. And our Lord, the Almighty, is sought for what you describe."

Chapter 22

بسم الله الرحمن الرحيم

In the name of God, the Almighty, the Merciful.

1. O mankind, be aware of your Lord, for the quaking of the Hour is a terrible thing.

2. The moment you see it, every nursing mother will leave her suckling child, and every pregnant one will miscarry, and you will see the people drunk while they are not drunk, but the retribution of God is most severe.

3. And from mankind is he who argues regarding God without knowledge, and he follows every rebellious devil.

4. It was decreed for him that any who follow him, he will mislead him, and guide him to the retribution of Fire.

5. O mankind, if you are in doubt as to the resurrection, then We have created you from dirt, then from a seed, then from an embryo, then from a fetus developed and undeveloped so that We make it clear to you. And We settle in the wombs what We wish to an appointed time, then We bring you out a child, then you reach your maturity, and of you are those who will pass away, and of you are those who are sent to an old age where he will not be able to learn any new knowledge after what he already has. And you see the land still, but when We send down the water to it, it vibrates and grows, and it brings forth of every lovely pair.

6. That is because God is the truth, and He gives life to the dead, and He is capable of all things.

7. And the Hour is coming, there is no doubt in it, and God will resurrect those who are in the graves.

8. And from the people are those who argue regarding God with no knowledge nor guidance nor enlightening Scripture.

9. Bending his side to misguide from the path of God. He will have humiliation in the world and We will make him taste on the Day of Resurrection the retribution of burning.

10. That is for what your hands have brought forth, and God does not wrong the servants.

11. And from the people there is he who serves God nervously. So if good comes to him, he is content with it; and if an ordeal comes to him, he makes an about-face. He has lost this world and the Hereafter. Such is the clear loss.

12. He calls upon besides God what will not harm him and what will not benefit him. Such is the far straying.

13. He calls on those who harm him more than they benefit him. What a miserable patron, and what a miserable companion.

14. God admits those who believe and do good works to estates with rivers flowing beneath them. God does as He wishes.

15. Whosoever thinks that God will not grant him victory in this world and the Hereafter, then let him extend his request to the heavens, then let him stop and see whether this action has removed his obstacles.

16. And as such, We have sent down clear revelations, and God guides whomever He wishes.

17. Surely those who believe; and those who are Jewish, and the Sabiens, and the Nazarenes, and the Majoos; and those who have set up partners; God will separate between them on the Day of Resurrection. For God is witness over all things.

18. Did you not see that to God yields what is in the heavens and what is in the Earth, and the sun and the moon and the stars and the mountains and the trees and what moves, and many of the people, and many who have deserved the retribution. And whoever God disgraces, then none can honour him. God does what He pleases.

19. Here are two opponents who have disputed regarding their Lord; as for those who rejected, outer garments made from fire are cut out for them, and boiling water is poured from above their heads.

20. It melts the inside of their stomachs and their skin.

21. And they will have hooked rods of iron.

22. Every time they want to escape the anguish, they are returned to it. Taste the retribution of the burning!

23. God will admit those who believe and do good works to estates with rivers flowing beneath them, wherein they will be adorned with bracelets of gold and pearl, and their garments will be of silk.

24. And they are guided to the good sayings, and guided to the path of the Praiseworthy.

25. Those who have rejected and repel from the path of God and the Restricted Temple that We have made for the people, for the dweller or the visitor to it; and whoever inclines to evil action in it, We will let them taste a painful retribution.

26. And We have appointed to Abraham the location of the Sanctuary: "Do not set up anyone with Me, and purify My Sanctuary for those who will partake, and those who will enforce, and those who kneel and prostrate."

27. And call out to the people with the Pilgrimage, they will come to you walking and on every transport, they will come from every deep enclosure.

28. So that they may witness benefits for themselves and recall God's name in the appointed days over what He has provided for them of the animal livestock. So eat from it and feed the needy and the poor.

29. Then let them complete their duties and fulfill their vows, and let them traverse at the ancient Sanctuary.

30. Thus, and whosoever honours God's restrictions, then it is better for him with His Lord. And the livestock is made lawful for you except what is recited upon you. So avoid the foulness of idols and avoid saying false statements.

31. Monotheists to God, not setting up anything with Him. And whosoever sets-up partners with God, then it is as if he has fallen from the sky and the birds snatch him or the wind takes him to a place far off.

32. Thus, and whoever honours the symbols of God, then it is from the piety of the hearts.

33. In them are benefits to an appointed time, then their place is to the ancient Sanctuary.

34. And for every nation We have made a rite that they may mention God's name over what He has provided for them of the animal livestock. So your god is One god, so to Him submit and give good tidings to those who obey.

35. Those who, when God is mentioned, their hearts revere, and they are patient to what befalls them, and they honour the oath of allegiance, and from what We provide them they spend.

36. And the livestock heavy with child, We have made them for you as symbols from God, in them is benefit for you. So mention God's name upon the newborns; then, when they have matured, you may eat from them and feed with them the poor and the needy. It was thus that We have made them in service to you, that you may be thankful.

37. Neither their meat nor their blood reaches God, but what reaches Him is the righteousness from you. It was thus that He made them in service to you, so that you may glorify God for what He has guided you to, and give news to the good doers.

38. God defends those who believe. God does not like any betrayer, rejecter.

39. It is permitted for those who have been persecuted to fight. And God is able to give them victory.

40. The ones who were driven out of their homes without justice, except that they said: "Our Lord is God!" And if it were not for God defending the people against themselves, then many places of gathering, and markets, and allegiances, and temples where the name of God is frequently mentioned, would have been destroyed. God will give victory to those who support Him. God is Powerful, Noble.

41. Those whom if We allow them authority in the land, they honour the oath of allegiance, and they contribute towards betterment, and deter from evil. And to God is the conclusion of all matters.

42. And if they deny you, then denied also before them did the people of Noah and 'Aad and Thamud.

43. And the people of Abraham and the people of Lot.

44. And the dwellers of Median; and Moses was denied. So I granted respite to the rejecters then I took them, how then was My punishment?

45. So how many a town have We destroyed while it was doing wrong, so that it is lying in ruins with its wells abandoned, and empty palaces.

46. Have they not roamed the land and had hearts with which to comprehend and ears with which to hear? No, it is not the sight which is blind, but it is the hearts that are in the chests that are blind.

47. And they seek you to hasten the retribution; and God will not break His promise. And a day with your Lord is like one thousand of the years you count.

48. And many a town I have given it respite while it was doing wrong, then I seized it! And to Me is the destiny.

49. Say: "O people, I am but a clear warner to you!"

50. As for those who believe and do good work, for them is a forgiveness and a great provision.

51. And those who seek to obstruct Our revelations, those are the dwellers of Hell.

52. And We did not send before you any messenger or prophet, without having the devil interfere with his wishes. God then overrides what the devil has cast, and God secures His revelations. And God is Knower, Wise.

53. That He may make what the devil has cast as a tests for those who have a disease in their hearts and those whose hearts are hardened. And the wicked are far away in opposition.

54. And to let those who have been given knowledge know that it is the truth from your Lord, and they will believe in it, and their hearts will soften to it. And God will guide those who believe to a straight path.

55. And those who have rejected will remain to be in doubt from it until the Hour comes to them suddenly, or the retribution will come to them on a Day which will stand still.

56. The sovereignty on that Day is to God, He will judge between them. So as for those who have believed and did good works, they are in the gardens of Paradise.

57. And those who rejected and disbelieved Our revelations, those will have a humiliating retribution.

58. And those who emigrated in the cause of God, then they were killed or died, God will provide them with a good provision, and God is the best of providers.

59. He will admit them an entrance that they will be pleased with, and God is Knowledgeable, Compassionate.

60. It is decreed that whoever retaliates with equal measure as was retaliated against him, then he was persecuted for this, God will give him victory. God is Pardoning, Forgiving.

61. That is because God merges the night in the day, and He merges the day in the night. And God is Hearer, Seer.

62. That is because God is the truth, and what they call on besides Him is falsehood. And God is the Most High, the Great.

63. Did you not see that God sends down water from the sky, and then the land becomes green? God is Compassionate, Expert.

64. To Him is what is in the heavens and what is in the Earth. And God is the Rich, the Praiseworthy.

65. Did you not see that God commits to you what is in the land, and the ships which sail in the sea by His leave? And He holds the sky so that it would not collapse upon the Earth, except by His leave. Indeed, God is Kind towards the people, Merciful.

66. He is the One who gave you life, then He makes you die, then He gives you life. But mankind is always rejecting!

67. For every nation We have made rites which they will fulfill. So do not let the matter fall into dispute. And call upon your Lord, for you are on a guidance which is straight.

68. And if they argue with you, then Say: "God is fully aware of what you do."

69. "God will judge between you on the Day of Resurrection in what you dispute therein."

70. Did you not know that God knows what is in the heavens and the Earth? All is in a record. All that for God is easy.

71. And they serve besides God what He did not send any authority upon, and what they have no knowledge of. And the wicked will not have any helper.

72. And if Our clear revelations are recited to them, you see hatred in the faces of those who have rejected. They are nearly close to attacking those who are reciting to them Our revelations! Say: "Shall I inform you of what is worse than this? The Fire, which God has promised to those who have rejected. What a miserable destiny!"

73. O mankind, an example is being cited so listen to it: those you call upon besides God will not create a fly even if they all gathered to do so. And if the fly takes anything from them, they will not be able to return it from him. Weak is both the seeker and the sought!

74. They have truly underestimated God's power. God is Powerful, Noble.

75. God chooses messengers from amongst the Angels and from amongst the people. God is Hearer, Seer.

76. He knows their present and their future. And to God all matters are returned.

77. O you who believe, kneel and prostrate and serve your Lord and do good that you may succeed.

78. And strive in the cause of God its truly deserved striving. He is the One who has chosen you, and He has made no hardship for you in the system, the creed of your father Abraham; He is the One who named you 'those who have submitted' from before as well as in this. So let the messenger be witness over you and you be witness over the people. So honour the oath of allegiance and contribute towards betterment and hold tight to God, He is your patron. What an excellent Patron, and what an excellent Supporter.

Chapter 23

بسم الله الرحمن الرحيم

In the name of God, the Almighty, the Merciful.

1. The believers are indeed successful.
2. Those who are humble when making their oath.
3. And they abstain from vain talk.
4. And they are active towards betterment.
5. And they cover their private parts.
6. Except around their mates, or those who are their dependants, they are free from blame.
7. But whosoever seeks anything beyond this, then these are the transgressors.
8. And those who are true to what they have been entrusted and their pledges.
9. And those who maintain their allegiances.
10. These are the inheritors.
11. The ones who shall inherit Paradise, in it they will abide.
12. We have created mankind from a structure derived from mud.
13. Then We made him a seed in a safe lodging.
14. Then We created the seed into an embryo, then We created the embryo into a fetus, then We created the fetus into bone, then We covered the bone with flesh, then We brought forth a new creation. So glory be to God, the best of creators.
15. Then after that, you will die.
16. Then you will be resurrected on the Day of Resurrection.
17. And We have created above you seven paths; and We are never, with regards to the creation, unaware.
18. And We sent down from the sky water in due measure, then We let it reside in the land, and We are capable of taking it away.

19. So We brought forth for you gardens of palm trees and grapes, for which you will find many fruits and from it you will eat.

20. And a tree which emerges from the mount of Sinai, it grows oil and is a relish for those who eat.

21. And in the livestock are lessons for you. We give you to drink from what is in its bellies, and you have many other benefits from them, and of them you eat.

22. And on them and on the ships you are carried.

23. And We have sent Noah to his people, so he said: "O my people, serve God, you have no other god besides Him. Will you not take heed?"

24. But the leaders who rejected from among his people said: "What is this but a human like you? He wants to make himself better than you! And if it was indeed God's will, He would have sent down Angels. We did not hear such a thing among our fathers of old."

25. "He is no more than a man who has madness in him. So keep watch on him for a while."

26. He said: "My Lord, grant me victory for what they denied me."

27. So We inspired him: "Construct the Ship under Our eyes and Our inspiration. Then, when Our command comes and the volcano erupts, then you shall take on the Ship two from every pair, and your family; except for those of them upon whom the word has come. And do not address Me regarding those who have done wrong, for they will be drowned."

28. So when you and those who are with you have embarked on the ship, then Say: "All praise is due to God who has saved us from the wicked people."

29. And Say: "My Lord, cause me to embark upon a blessed place, for You are the best for those who embark."

30. In this are signs, and We will always test.

31. Then We raised after them a different generation.

32. So We sent a messenger to them from amongst them: "Serve God, you have no other god besides Him. Will you not take heed?"

33. And the leaders from amongst his people who rejected and denied the meeting of the Hereafter; and We indulged them in this worldly life; said: "What is this but a human like you? He eats from what you eat and he drinks from what you drink."

34. "And if you obey a human being like you, then you will indeed be losers."

35. "Does he promise you that if you die and become dust and bones that you will be brought out?"

36. "Far fetched is what you are being promised."

37. "There is nothing but our worldly life, we die and we live, and we will not be resurrected."
38. "He is but a man who has invented a lie against God, and we will not believe in him."
39. He said: "My Lord, grant me victory for what they denied me."
40. He replied: "In a little while they will be in regret."
41. So the scream took them with justice, and We made them as dead plants. So away with the wicked people.
42. Then We raised after them different generations.
43. No nation can hasten its appointed time, nor can it delay.
44. Then We sent Our messengers in succession. Every time there came to a nation their messenger, they denied him. So We made them follow one another, and We made them history. So away with a people who do not believe!
45. Then We sent Moses and his brother Aaron with Our signs and a clear authority.
46. To Pharaoh and his leaders. But they became arrogant, for they were a high and mighty people.
47. So they said: "Shall we believe to two human beings like us, while their people are servants to us?"
48. So they denied them, and they became of those who were destroyed.
49. And We have given Moses the Scripture, so that they may be guided.
50. And We made the son of Mary and his mother a sign, and We gave them refuge on high ground, a place for resting and with a flowing stream.
51. "O messengers, eat from what is good, and do righteous work. I am aware of what you do."
52. "And this is your nation, one nation, and I am your Lord so be aware."
53. But the affair was disputed between them into segments. Every group happy with what it had.
54. So leave them in their error until a time.
55. Do they not think why We are extending them with wealth and children?
56. We are quick to give them the good things. But they do not perceive.
57. As for those who are in reverence from the awareness of their Lord.
58. And they believe in the revelations of their Lord.
59. And they do not set up anything with their Lord.
60. And they give of what they were given, and their hearts are full of reverence that they will return to their Lord.
61. These are the ones who race in doing good, and they are the first to it.

62. And We do not burden a soul except with what it can bear. And We have a record that speaks with the truth, they will not be wronged.
63. No, their hearts are unaware of this! And they have deeds besides this which they are doing.
64. Until We take their carefree people with the retribution, then they will shout for help.
65. Do not shout for help today, for you will not be helped against Us.
66. My revelations were recited to you, but you used to turn back on your heels.
67. You were too proud from it, talking evil about it; and you defiantly disregarded it.
68. Did they not ponder the words, or has what come to them not come to their fathers of old?
69. Or did they not know their messenger? For they are in denial of him.
70. Or do they say that there is a madness in him? No, he has come to them with the truth, but most of them are hateful of the truth.
71. And if the truth were to follow their desires, then the heavens and the Earth and all who are in them would have been corrupted. No, We have come to them with their reminder, but from their reminder they are turning away.
72. Or do you ask them for a wage? The wage of your Lord is best, and He is the best of providers.
73. And you are inviting them to a Straight Path.
74. And those who do not believe in the Hereafter, they are deviating away from the path.
75. And if We were to have mercy on them and remove what distress was upon them, they would still return to persist in their transgression, wandering blindly.
76. And when We seized them with the punishment, they did not humble themselves to their Lord nor did they invoke Him.
77. Until We open for them a door of immense retribution, then they become in sorrow and despair.
78. And He is the One who established for you the hearing, and the sight, and the hearts. Little do you give thanks.
79. And He is the One who multiplied you on the Earth, and to Him you will be returned.
80. And He is the One who gives life and brings death, and to Him is the alteration of the night and the day. Do you not comprehend?
81. No, they have said the same as what the people of old had said.

82. They said: "If we are dead and become dust and bones, will we then be resurrected?"
83. "We, as well as our fathers, have been promised this from before. This is nothing but the tales of the ancients."
84. Say: "To whom is the Earth and whosoever is in it if you know?"
85. They will Say: "To God." Say: "Will you then not remember!"
86. Say: "Who is the Lord of the seven universes and the Lord of the great throne?"
87. They will Say: "To God." Say: "Will you then not take heed?"
88. Say: "In whose hand is the sovereignty of all things, and He protects while there is no protector against Him, if you know?"
89. They will Say: "To God." Say: "Then why are you deceived?"
90. No, We have come to them with the truth, and they are truly liars.
91. God has not taken a son, nor is there with Him any god. If it were so, then every god would have taken what He created and they would have tried to overtake each other. God be glorified against what they describe!
92. The knower of the unseen and the seen. Be He exalted above what they set up.
93. Say: "My Lord, if You show me what they are promised."
94. "My Lord, then do not leave me amongst the wicked people."
95. And We are able to show you what We promise them.
96. Push away evil with that which is better. We are better aware of what they describe.
97. And Say: "My Lord, I seek refuge with you from the whispers of the devils."
98. "And I seek refuge with you O Lord that they should come near."
99. Until death comes to one of them, he says: "My Lord, send me back."
100. "So that I may do good in that which I have left behind." No, it is but a word he is speaking. And there is a barrier to prevent them from going back until the Day they are all resurrected.
101. So when the horn is blown, then there will be no kinship between them on that Day, nor will they ask for one another.
102. So, those whose weight is heavy on the scales, then those are the successful ones.
103. And those whose weight is light on the scales, those are the ones who lost their souls, in Hell they will abide.
104. The Fire will scorch their faces, and in it their grin will be with displaced lips.
105. "Were My revelations not recited to you, then you denied them?"

106.They said: "Our Lord, our wickedness overcame us, and we were a misguided people."

107."Our Lord, bring us out of it, and if we return to this then we are wicked."

108.He said: "Be humiliated therein and do not speak to Me."

109.There was a group from among My servants who used to Say: "Our Lord, we have believed, so forgive us, and have mercy upon us, for You are the best of those who show mercy."

110.But you mocked them, so much so that they made you forget My remembrance, and you used to laugh at them.

111.I have rewarded them today for their patience, they are indeed the winners.

112.Say: "How long have you stayed on Earth in terms of years?"

113.They said: "We remained for a day, or for part of a day. So ask those who kept count."

114.He said: "You have remained for very little, if you knew."

115."Did you think that We have created you without purpose, and that you would not return to Us?"

116.So, exalted is God, the true King, there is no god but He, the Lord of the supreme throne.

117.And whosoever calls on another god with God when he has no proof for such, then his judgment is with his Lord. The rejecters will never succeed.

118.And Say: "My Lord, forgive and have mercy, and you are the best of those who are merciful."

Chapter 24

بسم الله الرحمن الرحيم

In the name of God, the Almighty, the Merciful.

1. A chapter which We have sent down and imposed, and We have sent down in it clear revelations that you may remember.

2. The adulteress and the adulterer, you shall lash each of them one hundred lashes, and do not let any pity take you over God's system if you believe in God and the Last Day. And let a group of the believers witness their punishment.

3. The adulterer will only marry an adulteress or one who is an idolatress. And the adulteress, she will only be married to an adulterer or an idolater. And this has been forbidden for the believers.

4. And those who accuse the independent women and they do not bring forth four witnesses, then you shall lash them eighty lashes and do not ever accept their testimony. Those indeed are the evildoers.

5. Except those who repent after this and do right, then God is Forgiving, Merciful.

6. And those who accuse their wives, but they have no witnesses except for themselves, then the testimony of one of them is to be equivalent to that of four witnesses if he is swearing by God that he is being truthful.

7. And the fifth shall be God's curse upon him if he is one of those lying.

8. And the punishment will be averted from her if she testifies four times by God that he is of the liars.

9. And the fifth shall be that God's curse is upon her if he is speaking the truth.

10. All this is from God's favour upon you and His mercy. And God is Forgiving, Wise.

11. Those who have brought forth the false accusation were a group from within you. Do not think it is bad for you, for it is good for you. Every person amongst them will have what he deserves of the sin. And as for he who had the greatest portion of it, he will have a great retribution.

12. If only when you heard it the believing men and women should have thought good of their own selves and said: "This is an obvious lie!"

13. If only they had brought four witnesses to it. If they did not have the witnesses, then these with God are the liars.

14. And had it not been for God's favour upon you and His mercy upon you in this world and the Hereafter, a great retribution would have touched you for what you have spoken.

15. For you have cast it with your tongues, and you say with your mouths what you have no knowledge of, and you think it is a minor issue, while with God it was great.

16. And when you heard it you should have said: "It was not right for us to speak of this. Glory to You, this is a great lie."

17. God warns you not to repeat something similar to this ever, if you are believers.

18. And God clarifies for you the revelations; and God is Knower, Wise.

19. As for those who enjoy that immorality spreads amongst those who have believed, they will have a painful retribution in the world and the Hereafter. And God knows while you do not know.

20. And all this is from God's favour upon you and His mercy. And God is Compassionate, Merciful.

21. O you who believe, do not follow the footsteps of the devil. And whosoever follows the footsteps of the devil should know that he advocates immorality and evil. And had in not been for God's favour upon you and His mercy, not one of you would have ever been purified, but God purifies whom He wishes, and God is Hearer, Knower.

22. And let not those amongst you who have been blessed with abundance refuse to give to the relatives, and the needy, and those who have immigrated in the cause of God. Let them pardon and forgive. Would you not like God to forgive you? And God is Forgiving, Merciful.

23. Those who accuse the independent chaste believing women, they will be cursed in this world and the Hereafter, and they will have a painful retribution.

24. On the Day when their tongues, and their hands, and their feet will bear witness against them for what they used to do.

25. On that Day, God will pay them what they are owed in full, and they will know that God is the Truth Manifested.

26. The wicked women are for the wicked men, and the wicked men are for the wicked women, and the good women are for the good men, and the good men are for the good women. These people are innocent from what statements have been made, and for them is forgiveness and a generous provision.

27. O you who believe, do not enter any homes except your own unless you are invited and you greet the people in them. This is best for you, perhaps you will remember.

28. But, if you do not find anyone in them then do not enter until you are given permission. And if you are told to go back, then return for it is purer for you. And God is aware of what you do.

29. There is no sin upon you that you enter homes which are abandoned if in them there are belongings of yours. And God knows what you reveal and what you conceal.

30. Tell the believing men to lower their gaze and keep covered their private parts, for that is purer for them. God is fully aware of what you do.

31. And tell the believing women to lower their gaze and keep covered their private parts, and that they should not show-off their beauty except what is apparent, and let them cast their shawls over their cleavage. And let them not show-off their beauty except to their husbands, or their fathers, or fathers of their husbands, or their sons, or the sons of their husbands, or their brothers, or the sons of their brothers, or the sons of their sisters, or their children that come after them, or those who are still their dependants, or the male servants who are without need, or the child who has not yet understood the composition of women. And let them not strike with their feet in a manner that reveals what they are keeping hidden of their beauty. And repent to God, all of you believers, that you may succeed.

32. And marry off those among you that are single, and the good from among your male and female servants. If they are poor, then God will grant them from His grace. And God is Encompassing, Knowledgeable.

33. And let those who are not able to marry continue to be chaste until God enriches them of His Bounty. And if those who are still dependants seek marriage, then marry them off if you find that they are ready, and give them from the wealth of God which He has bestowed upon you. And do not force your daughters into marriage when they have desired independence, in order that you may make a gain in the goods of this worldly life. But if anyone has compelled them, then for their compulsion, God is Forgiving, Merciful.

34. And We have sent down to you clarifying revelations and an example of those who came before you and a lesson for the righteous.

35. God is the Light of the heavens and the Earth. The example of His light is like a concave mirror within a lamp, the lamp is within a glass, the glass is like a radiant planet, which is lit from a blessed olive tree that is neither of the east nor of the west, its oil nearly gives off light even if not touched by fire. Light upon light, God guides to His light whom He pleases. And God sets forth parables for the people, and God is aware of all things.

36. In sanctuaries that God has allowed to be raised and His name mentioned in them. He is glorified therein day and night.

37. Men who are not distracted by trade or sale from the remembrance of God and performing the oath of allegiance, and contributing towards betterment. They fear a Day when the hearts and sight will be overturned.

38. God will reward them for the best of what they did, and He will increase them from His grace. And God provides for whom He pleases without any price.

39. As for those who reject, their works are like a mirage in the desert. A thirsty person thinks it is water, until he reaches it, he finds it is nothing; and he finds God there and He pays him his due, and God is swift in judgment.

40. Or like the darkness out in a deep ocean in the midst of violent waves, with waves upon waves and dark clouds. Darkness upon darkness, if he brings out his own hand, he could barely see it. And for whomever God does not make a light, he will have no light.

41. Do you not see that everything in the heavens and the Earth glorifies God? Even the birds in formation, each knows its allegiance and its glorification. And God is fully aware of everything they do.

42. And to God is the sovereignty of the heavens and the Earth, and to God is the final destiny.

43. Do you not see that God drives the clouds, then He gathers them together, then He piles them upon each other, then you see the soft rain coming out of them? And He sends down hail from the sky from the mountains to afflict whomever He wills, and He diverts it from whomever He wills, the brightness of the snow almost blinds the eyes.

44. God rotates the night and the day. In that is a lesson for those who have insight.

45. And God created every moving creature from water. So some of them move on their bellies, and some walk on two legs, and some walk on four. God creates whatever He wills. God is capable of all things.

46. We have sent down to you clarifying revelations, and God guides whoever He wills to a straight path.
47. And they Say: "We believe in God and in the messenger, and we obey," but a group of them turn away after that. These are not believers.
48. And if they are invited to God and His messenger to judge between them, a party of them turn away.
49. However, if the judgment is in their favour, they come to it willingly with submission!
50. Is there a disease in their hearts, or are they doubtful? Or do they fear that God and His messenger would wrong them in the judgment? In fact, they are the wrong doers.
51. The utterance of the believers when they are invited to God and His messenger to judge in their affairs is to Say: "We hear and obey." These are the winners.
52. And whosoever obeys God and His messenger, and he fears God and is aware of Him, then these are the winners.
53. And they swear by God with their strongest oaths that if you would only command them they would mobilize. Say: "Do not swear, for obedience is an obligation. God is Expert over what you do."
54. Say: "Obey God, and obey the messenger." But if they turn away, then he is only responsible for his obligation, and you are responsible for your obligations. And if you obey him, you will be guided. The messenger is only required to deliver clearly.
55. God promises those among you who believe and do good works, that He will make them successors on Earth, as He made successors of those before them, and He will enable for them their system which He has approved for them, and He will substitute security for them in place of fear, that they serve Me and do not associate anything with Me. And as for those who reject after that, they are the wicked.
56. And honour the oath of allegiance and contribute towards betterment, and obey the messenger, that you may attain mercy.
57. Do not think that those who disbelieve will remain in the land. Their abode is Hell. What a miserable destiny!
58. O you who believe, let those who are your dependants and have not yet attained puberty request your permission regarding three times: Before the dawn oath of allegiance, and should you put off your attire from being outdoors, and after the evening oath of allegiance. These are three private times for you. Other than these times, it is not wrong for you or them to intermin-

gle with one another. God thus clarifies the revelations for you. And God is Knowledgeable, Wise.

59. And when the children among you reach puberty, then let permission be sought from them like it was sought from those before them. God thus clarifies His revelations for you. And God is Knowledgeable, Wise.

60. And the women who are past child bearing and who do not seek to get married have no sin upon them if they put-off their garments, provided they are not adorned for beauty. And if they remain as they were, then it is better for them. God is Hearer, Knower.

61. There is no blame upon the blind, nor is there any blame upon the crippled, nor is there any blame upon the ill, nor is there any blame upon yourselves, if you eat at your homes, or the homes of your fathers, or the homes of your mothers, or the homes of your brothers, or the homes of your sisters, or the homes of your uncles, or the homes of your aunts, or the homes of your mothers' brothers, or the homes of your mothers' sisters, or that which you possess their keys, or that of your friends. You commit nothing wrong by eating together or as individuals. When you enter any home, you shall greet each other a greeting from God that is blessed and good. God thus explains the revelations for you that you may understand.

62. The believers are those who believe in God and His messenger, and when they are with him in a meeting, they do not leave him without permission. Those who ask permission are the ones who do believe in God and His messenger. If they ask your permission, in order to tend to some of their affairs, you may grant permission to whomever you wish, and ask God to forgive them. God is Forgiver, Merciful.

63. Do not let the calling of the messenger between you be as if you are calling each other. God is fully aware of those among you who slip away under lame excuses. Let those who oppose his command beware, for an ordeal may strike them, or a severe retribution.

64. Certainly, to God belongs all that is in the heavens and the Earth. Surely, He knows what your condition is; and on the Day when they are returned to Him, He will inform them of everything they had done. God is aware of all things.

Chapter 25

بسم الله الرحمن الرحيم

In the name of God, the Almighty, the Merciful.

1. Blessed is the One who sent down the Statute Book to His servant, so he can be a warner to the world.

2. The One to whom belongs the sovereignty of the heavens and the Earth, and He did not take a son, and He does not have any partner in kingship. And He created everything and measured it precisely.

3. And they took besides Him gods that do not create anything and are themselves created! And they do not possess for themselves any harm or benefit, nor do they possess death or life, nor resurrection.

4. And those who rejected said: "This is but a falsehood that he invented and other people have helped him with it; for they have come with what is wrong and fabricated."

5. And they said: "Tales of the people of old, he wrote them down while they were being dictated to him morning and evening."

6. Say: "It was sent down by the One who knows the secrets in the heavens and the Earth. He is always Forgiving, Merciful."

7. And they said: "What is with this messenger that he eats the food and walks in the market places? If only an Angel were sent down to him so that he would jointly be a warner."

8. "Or that a treasure is given to him, or that he has a paradise that he eats from." And the wicked said: "You are but following a man bewitched!"

9. See how they cited the examples for you, for they have strayed, and they cannot find a path.

10. Blessed is the One who if He wishes can make for you better than that. Paradises with rivers flowing beneath them, and He will make for you palaces.

11. But they have denied the Hour, and We have prepared for those who deny the Hour a flaming Fire.
12. When it sees them from a far place, they hear its raging and roaring.
13. And when they are cast into it from a tight crevice, in chains, they call out their remorse.
14. Do not call out one remorse today, but call out many remorses.
15. Say: "Is that better or the Paradise of eternity that the righteous have been promised?" It is their reward and destiny.
16. In it they will have what they wish eternally. It is upon your Lord an obligated promise.
17. And on the Day when We gather them together with what they served besides God; then He will Say: "Did you misguide My servants here, or did they stray from the path?"
18. They said: "Glory be to You, it was not for us to take besides You any allies; indeed You gave them and their fathers luxury until they forgot the remembrance, and they were a lost people."
19. They have refuted what you claimed, so you will not find any excuse nor any victor. And whosoever has done wrong among you, We will let him taste a great retribution.
20. And We have not sent before you any messengers except that they ate the food and walked in the market places. And We have made some of you as a trial for others to see if you will have patience. And your Lord was ever seeing.
21. And those who do not expect to meet Us said: "If only the Angels were sent down upon him, or that we see our Lord." They have become arrogant in their souls, and they have produced a great blasphemy!
22. On the Day they see the Angels, that is not good news for the criminals. And they will Say: "Away to a place that is sealed off."
23. And We turned to the works that they did, and We made it dust in the wind.
24. The dwellers of Paradise on that Day are in the best abode and the best destiny.
25. And the Day when the sky will be filled with clouds, and the Angels will be sent down in succession.
26. The true kingship on that Day will be to the Almighty. And it is a Day which will be very hard on the rejecters.
27. And that Day the wrongdoer will bite on his hand and Say: "I wish I had taken the path with the messenger!"

28. "Woe unto me, I wish I did not take so and so as a friend!"
29. "He has misguided me from the remembrance after it came to me, and the devil was always a betrayer of mankind!"
30. And the messenger said: "My Lord, my people have deserted this Quran."
31. And it is such that We make for every prophet enemies from among the criminals. And your Lord suffices as a Guide and a Victor.
32. And those who rejected said: "If only the Quran was sent down to him in one go!" It was done as such so We could strengthen your heart with it, and We arranged it accordingly.
33. And for every example they come to you with, We bring you the truth and the best explanation.
34. Those who will be gathered to Hell on their faces, these are the most evil and the most strayed from the path.
35. And We gave Moses the Scripture and We made his brother Aaron a minister with him.
36. So We said: "Go both of you to the people who have denied Our signs." So We then destroyed them utterly.
37. And the people of Noah, when they denied the messengers We drowned them, and We made them a lesson for mankind. And We have prepared for the wicked a painful retribution.
38. And 'Aad and Thamud and the dwellers of Arras, and many generations in between.
39. And for each We cited the examples, and each We destroyed utterly.
40. And they have come upon the town that was showered with a miserable shower. Did they not see it? No, they do not expect any resurrection.
41. And if they see you they take you for a mockery: "Is this the one that God sent as a messenger?"
42. "He nearly diverted us from our gods had we not been patient for them." They will learn when they see the retribution who is on a path most astray.
43. Have you seen the one who has taken his ego as his god? Will you be a caretaker over him?
44. Or do you think that most of them hear or understand? They are just like cattle. No, they are worse off.
45. Did you not see to your Lord how He casts the shadow? And if He wished, He could have made it still, then We would have made the sun as a guide to it.
46. Then We retract it to us a simple retraction.

47. And He is the One who made for you the night as a cover, and sleep for resting, and He made the day to move about in.
48. And He is the One who sent the winds to spread between the hands of His mercy. And We sent down from the sky water which is pure.
49. So that We can revive a dead land with it and We give to drink to Our creation of many of the livestock and mankind.
50. And We have distributed it amongst them so that they may remember, but most people refuse to be anything but rejecters.
51. And if We wish, We could send to every town a warner.
52. So do not obey the rejecters, and strive against them with it in a great striving.
53. And He is the One who merges the two bodies of water. This is fresh and palatable and this is salty and bitter. And He made between them a partition and an inviolable barrier.
54. And He is the One who created from the water a human being, so He made for him blood kin and mates. And your Lord is Capable.
55. And they serve besides God what does not benefit them nor harm them. And the rejecter is always set-against his Lord.
56. And We have not sent you except as a bearer of good news and a warner.
57. Say: "I do not ask you for a wage; but for whoever chooses to make a path to his Lord."
58. And put your trust in the Eternal Who does not die, and glorify His praise. It is enough for Him that He is expert in the sins of His servants.
59. The One who created the heavens and the Earth and what is between them in six days, then He settled to the throne. The Almighty; so ask Him for He is Expert.
60. And if they are told: "Prostrate to the Almighty." They Say: "And what is the Almighty? Shall we prostrate to what you order us?" And it increases their aversion.
61. Blessed is the One Who made towers in the universe and He made in it a beacon and a shining moon.
62. And He is the One Who made the night and the day in succession, for those who wish to remember or wish to be thankful.
63. And the servants of the Almighty who walk on the Earth in humility and if the ignorant speak to them, they Say: "Peace."
64. And those who stay awake for their Lord, in prostration and standing.
65. And those who Say: "Our Lord, avert from us the retribution of Hell. Its retribution is terrible."

66. "It is a miserable abode and dwelling."
67. And those who when they give they are not excessive nor stingy, but they are in a measure between that.
68. And those who do not call on any other god with God, nor do they kill the life that God has made forbidden except in justice, nor do they commit adultery; and whosoever does that will receive the punishment.
69. The retribution will be doubled for him on the Day of Judgment and he will abide in it eternally in disgrace.
70. Except for the one who repents and believes and does good work, for those God will replace their sins with good, and God is Forgiving, Merciful.
71. And whosoever repents, and does good, then he shall repent towards God a true repentance.
72. And those who do not bear false witness, and if they pass by vein talk they pass by with dignity.
73. And those who when they are reminded of their Lord's verses, they do not fall on them deaf and blind.
74. And those who Say: "Our Lord, grant us from our mates and our progeny what will be the comfort of our eyes, and make us role models the righteous."
75. These will be rewarded with a dwelling for what they have been patient for, and they will find in it a greeting and peace.
76. In it they will abide, what an excellent dwelling and position.
77. Say: "My Lord would not care about you except for your imploring. But you have denied, so it will be your destiny."

Chapter 26

بسـم الله الرحمن الرحيم

In the name of God, the Almighty, the Merciful.

1. T'.S.M.
2. These are the signs of the Scripture of clarity.
3. Perhaps you are grieving yourself that they do not become believers.
4. If We wish, We could send down for them from the heavens a sign, to which they would bend their necks in humility.
5. And not a reminder comes to them from the Almighty, except that they turn away from it.
6. They have denied, thus the news will come to them of what they used to ridicule.
7. Did they not look to the Earth, how many plants have We raised in it, from each a good pair.
8. In that is a sign, but most of them are not believers.
9. And your Lord is the Noble, the Merciful.
10. And when your Lord called Moses: "Go to the people who are wicked."
11. "The people of Pharaoh. Will they not be righteous?"
12. He said: "My Lord, I fear that they would deny me."
13. "And my chest would become tight, and my tongue would not be able to express; so send for Aaron."
14. "And they have charges of a crime against me, so I fear they will kill me."
15. He said: "It will not be. Go both of you with Our signs. I am with you listening."
16. "So both of you go to Pharaoh and Say: "We are messengers of the Lord of the worlds"
17. "So send with us the Children of Israel""

18. He said: "Did we not raise you amongst us as a new born, and you stayed with us for many of your years?"
19. "And you did what deed you did, and you are of the rejecters."
20. He said: "I did it, and I was of those misguided."
21. "So I ran away from you all when I feared you. So my Lord granted me judgment, and made me of the messengers."
22. "And that was a favour that you held against me, so you could continue to enslave the Children of Israel."
23. Pharaoh said: "And what is the Lord of the worlds?"
24. He said: "The Lord of the heavens and the Earth and all that is between them, if you are aware."
25. He said to those around him: "Do you hear that?"
26. He said: "Your Lord and the Lord of your forefathers!"
27. He said: "This messenger of yours who has been sent to you is mad!"
28. He said: "The Lord of the east and the west, and what is between them, if you understand."
29. He said: "If you take a god other than me, then I will put you among the prisoners."
30. He said: "What if I brought you proof?"
31. He said: "Then bring it forth if you are of the truthful ones."
32. So he cast his staff, then it manifested into a serpent.
33. And he drew out his hand, then it became white to the onlookers.
34. He said to the commanders around him: "This is a knowledgeable magician."
35. "He wants to bring you out of your land with his magic. So what will you decide?"
36. They said: "Delay him and his brother, and send people in the cities to gather."
37. "They will come to you with every knowledgeable magician."
38. So the magicians were gathered to an appointed day.
39. And it was said to the people: "Will you also gather?"
40. "Perhaps we can follow the magicians if they are the winners."
41. So when the magicians came, they said to Pharaoh: "We should be rewarded if we are the winners."
42. He said: "Yes, and you shall also be near to me."
43. Moses said to them: "Cast down what it is you will cast."
44. So they cast down their ropes and staffs and they said: "By the might of Pharaoh, we will be the winners."

45. So Moses cast down his staff, then it was eating-up all that they showed!
46. So the magicians went down prostrating.
47. They said: "We believe in the lord of the worlds!"
48. "The Lord of Moses and Aaron."
49. He said: "Have you believed to him before I permitted you? He is surely your great one who has taught you magic. So you shall come to know. I will cut-off your hands and feet from alternate sides, and I will crucify you all."
50. They said: "There is no worry, for we are all returning to our Lord."
51. "We hope that our Lord will forgive us our sins, as we are the first to believe."
52. And We inspired Moses: "Take away My servants, for you will be followed."
53. So Pharaoh sent gatherers to the cities.
54. "These are but a small band."
55. "And they have done what has enraged us."
56. "And We are all gathered and forewarned."
57. So, We evicted them out of gardens and springs.
58. And treasures and an honourable dwelling.
59. As such, We gave it to the Children of Israel.
60. So they were pursued at sunrise.
61. But when the two groups saw each other, the companions of Moses said: "We are caught!"
62. He said: "No, my Lord is with me and He will guide me."
63. So We inspired to Moses: "Strike the sea with your staff." So it split into two, each side like a great mountain.
64. And We then brought them to the other side.
65. And We saved Moses and all those with him.
66. Then We drowned the others.
67. In that is a sign, but most of them are not believers.
68. And your Lord is the Noble, the Merciful.
69. And recite to them the news of Abraham.
70. When he said to his father and his people: "What do you worship?"
71. They said: "We worship statues, thus we remain devoted to them."
72. He said: "Do they hear you when you pray to them?"
73. "Or do they benefit you or harm you?"
74. They said: "No, but we found our fathers doing the same."
75. He said: "Do you see that which you have been worshipping."
76. "You and your fathers of old."
77. "They are enemies to me, except for the Lord of the worlds."

78. "The One who created me, He will guide me."
79. "And He is the One who feeds me and gives me to drink."
80. "And if I am sick, He is the One who cures me."
81. "And the One who will make me die and then bring me to life."
82. "And the One whom I hope will forgive my faults on the Day of Judgment."
83. "My Lord, grant me authority and join me with the good doers."
84. "And give me a tongue that is true for those who will follow."
85. "And make me of the inheritors of the gardens of bliss."
86. "And forgive my father, for he was of those misguided."
87. "And do not disgrace me on the Day when they are resurrected."
88. "The Day when no money or children can help."
89. "Except for he who comes to God with a pure heart."
90. And Paradise was made near for the righteous.
91. And Hell was displayed for the wrongdoers.
92. And it was said to them: "Where is what you used to worship?"
93. "Without God, can they help you or help themselves?"
94. So they were thrown in it on their faces, them and the wrongdoers.
95. As well as all the soldiers of Satan.
96. They said, while they were disputing therein:
97. "By God, we were clearly misguided."
98. "For we equated you with the Lord of the Worlds!"
99. "And none misled us except the criminals."
100. "So we have none to intercede for us."
101. "Nor a close friend."
102. "If only we could have another chance, we would be among the believers."
103. In that is a sign, but most of them are not believers.
104. And your Lord is the Noble, the Merciful.
105. The people of Noah disbelieved the messengers.
106. When their brother Noah said to them: "Will you not be righteous?"
107. "I am to you a trustworthy messenger."
108. "So be aware of God and obey me."
109. "And I do not ask you for a wage, for my reward is upon the Lord of the worlds."
110. "So be aware of God and obey me."
111. They said: "Shall we believe to you when the lowest type of people have followed you?"
112. He said: "And what knowledge do I have of what they used to do?"
113. "Their judgment is on my Lord, if you could know."

114."And I will not drive away the believers."

115."I am but a clear warner."

116.They said: "If you do not cease, O Noah, you will be among those who are stoned."

117.He said: "My Lord, my people have denied me!"

118."So open between me and them a rift, and save me and those who are with me of the believers."

119.So We saved him and those who were with him in the charged Ship.

120.Then after that We drowned the rest.

121.In that is a sign, but most of them are not believers.

122.And your Lord is the Noble, the Merciful.

123.'Aad denied the messengers.

124.For their brother Hud said to them: "Will you not be righteous?"

125."I am to you a clear messenger."

126."So be aware of God and obey me."

127."And I do not ask you for a wage, for my reward is upon the Lord of the worlds."

128."Do you build on every high place a symbol, for the sake of vanity!"

129."And you take for yourselves strongholds, perhaps you will live forever?"

130."And if you attack, you strike ruthlessly?"

131."So be aware of God and obey me."

132."And be aware of the One who provided you with what you know."

133."He provided you with livestock and shelters."

134."And gardens and springs."

135."I fear for you the retribution of a great day"

136.They said: "It is the same whether you preach or do not preach."

137."This is nothing but an invention by the people of old."

138."And we are not going to be punished."

139.So they denied him, and We destroyed them. In that is a sign, but most are not believers.

140.And your Lord is the Noble, the Merciful.

141.Thamud denied the messengers.

142.For their brother Saleh said to them: "Will you not be righteous?"

143."I am to you a clear messenger."

144."So be aware of God and obey me."

145."And I do not ask you for a wage, for my reward is upon the Lord of the worlds."

146."Will you be left secure in that which you have here?"

147. "In gardens and springs."
148. "And green crops and palm trees laden with fruit."
149. "And you carve homes out of the mountains with great skill?"
150. "So be aware of God and obey me."
151. "And do not obey the command of the carefree."
152. "The ones who corrupt in the land and are not reformers."
153. They said: "You are but one of those bewitched!"
154. "You are but a human being like us. So bring a sign if you are of the truthful ones."
155. He said: "This is a female camel which will have to drink and you will drink on a different day."
156. "And do not afflict her with harm, else the retribution of a great day will seize you."
157. But they slaughtered her, and they became regretful.
158. So the retribution took them. In that is a sign, but most of them are not believers.
159. And your Lord is the Noble, the Merciful.
160. The people of Lot denied the messengers.
161. For their brother Lot said to them: "Will you not be righteous?"
162. "I am to you a trustworthy messenger."
163. "So be aware of God and obey me."
164. "And I do not ask you for a wage, for my reward is upon the Lord of the worlds."
165. "Do you approach the males of the worlds?"
166. "And you leave what your Lord has created for you of mates? You are an intrusive people!"
167. They said: "If you do not cease O Lot, you will be among those driven out."
168. He said: "I am in severe opposition to your acts!"
169. "My Lord, save me and my family from what they do."
170. So We saved him and his entire family.
171. Except for an old woman who remained.
172. Then We destroyed the others.
173. And We rained upon them a rain. Miserable was the rain to those who had been warned.
174. In that is a sign, but most of them are not believers.
175. And that your Lord is the Noble, the Merciful.
176. The dwellers of the Woods disbelieved the messengers.
177. For Shu'ayb said to them: "Will you not be righteous?"

178. "I am to you a trustworthy messenger."
179. "So be aware of God and obey me."
180. "And I do not ask you for a wage, for my reward is upon the Lord of the worlds."
181. "Give full measure and do not be of those who cause losses."
182. "And weigh with the balance that is straight."
183. "And do not defraud the people of their belongings, and do not venture into the land corrupting."
184. "And be aware of the One who created you and the generations of old."
185. They said: "You are but one of those bewitched."
186. "And you are nothing but a human being like us, and we think you are one of those who lie."
187. "So let pieces from the sky fall upon us if you are of those who are truthful!"
188. He said: "My Lord is most aware of what you do."
189. But they denied him, so the retribution of the day of shadow took them. It was the retribution of a terrible day.
190. In that is a sign, but most of them are not believers.
191. And your Lord is the Noble, the Merciful.
192. And this is a revelation from the Lord of the worlds.
193. It was sent down with the trusted Spirit.
194. Upon your heart, so that you would be of the warners.
195. In a clear Arabic tongue.
196. And it is in the Psalms of old.
197. Was it not a sign for them that the scholars of the Children of Israel knew it?
198. And had We sent it down upon some of the foreigners,
199. And he related it to them, they would not have believed in it.
200. As such, We diverted it from the hearts of the criminals.
201. They do not believe in it until they see the painful retribution.
202. So it will come to them suddenly, while they do not perceive it.
203. Then they would Say: "Can we be given more time?"
204. Was it not their wish that Our punishment be hastened?
205. Do you see that if We gave them luxury for years.
206. Then what they were promised came to them.
207. All they luxury they were given will not avail them.
208. And We have not destroyed any town except after having warners.
209. By way of a reminder, and We were never unjust.
210. And it is not the devils who have brought this down.
211. Nor would they, nor could they.

212. They are blocked from overhearing.
213. So do not call upon any other god with God, else you will be with those punished.
214. And warn your closest kin.
215. And lower your wing for any who follow you of the believers.
216. Then if they disobey you, then Say: "I am innocent from what you do."
217. And put your trust in the Noble, the Merciful.
218. The One who sees you when you stand.
219. And your movements amongst those who prostrate.
220. He is the Hearer, the Knowledgeable.
221. Shall I inform you on whom the devils descend?
222. They descend on every sinful liar.
223. They claim to listen, but most of them are liars.
224. And the poets, are followed by the strayers.
225. Do you not see that they traverse in every valley.
226. And that what they say, is not what they do!
227. Except for those who believe, and do good works, and remember God greatly, and were victorious after they were wronged. As for those who did wrong, they will know which fate they will meet.

Chapter 27

بسم الله الرحمن الرحيم

In the name of God, the Almighty, the Merciful.

1. T'.S, these are the signs of the Quran and a clear Scripture.
2. A guide and good news to the believers.
3. Those who honour the oath of allegiance, and contribute towards betterment, and regarding the Hereafter they are certain.
4. As for those who do not believe in the Hereafter, We have made their work appear pleasing to them, so they walk around blind.
5. They will have the worst retribution, and in the Hereafter they are the biggest losers.
6. And you are receiving the Quran from One who is Wise, Knowledgeable.
7. And Moses said to his family: "I have seen a fire, I will bring you from there some news or I will bring you a burning piece so that you may be warmed."
8. So when he came to it he was called: "Blessed is the One at the fire and whoever is around it, and glory be to God, the Lord of the worlds."
9. "O Moses, it is I God, the Noble, the Wise."
10. "And throw down your staff." So when he saw it vibrate as if it were a Jinn, he ran away and would not turn back. "O Moses, do not fear, for My messengers shall have no fear from Me."
11. "Except one who transgresses. But then if he replaces the evil deed with good, then I am Forgiving, Merciful."
12. "And place your hand into your pocket; it will come out white with no blemish, one of nine signs to Pharaoh and his people."
13. So when Our signs came to them for all to see, they said: "This is clearly magic!"

14. And they rejected them out of their souls' transgression and arrogance. So see how it ended for the wicked.

15. And We bestowed upon David and Solomon knowledge, and they both said: "Praise be to God who preferred us over many of His believing servants."

16. And Solomon inherited from David, and he said: "O people, we have been taught how to understand the speech of the creatures that fly, and we have been given from everything. This is indeed an evident grace."

17. And Solomon's soldiers were gathered, comprising of humans and Jinn and birds, for they were to be spread out.

18. Until they came to a valley of ants, a female ant said: "O ants, enter your homes else you will be crushed by Solomon and his soldiers while they do not notice."

19. He then smiled, amused by what she said. And he said: "My Lord, help me to be thankful for the blessings You have bestowed upon me and upon my parents, and that I may do good work that pleases You, and admit me by Your Mercy with Your righteous servants."

20. And he inspected the birds, then said: "Why do I not see the hoopoe, or is he among those absent?"

21. "I will punish him severely, or I will kill him, else he should have an clear excuse."

22. But the hoopoe did not stay away long, then he said: "I have seen what you do not know, and I have come to you from Sheba with news which is certain."

23. "I found them ruled by a woman, and she was given all possession, and she had a great throne."

24. "And I found her and her people prostrating to the sun instead of God! And the devil had made their work appear good to them, so he kept them away from the path, for they are not being guided."

25. "Will they not prostrate to God who brings out what is hidden in the heavens and the Earth, and He knows what you hide and what you declare?"

26. "God, there is no god but He, the Lord of the great throne."

27. He said: "We will see if you are being truthful or are one of those who lie."

28. "Take this letter of mine and deliver it to them, then withdraw from them and observe what they respond with."

29. She said: "O commanders, a noble letter has been delivered to me."

30. "It is from Solomon, and it reads: "In the name of God, the Almighty, the Merciful""

31. ""Do not be arrogant toward me and come to me as submitters""

32. She said: "O commanders, advise me in this matter of mine, for I will not take a decision until you give testimony."

33. They said: "We are people of strength and mighty in power. But the decision is yours, so see what you will command."

34. She said: "When the kings enter a town they destroy it and make its most noble people humiliated. It is such that they do."

35. "And I will send to them a gift, then I will see with what the messengers will return."

36. So when they came to Solomon he said: "Are you providing me with wealth? What God has provided for me is far better than what He has given you. Now you are happy with your gift!"

37. "Return to them. For we shall come to them with soldiers the like of which they have never seen, and we will drive them out humiliated, while they are feeble."

38. He said: "O commanders, which of you can bring me her throne before they come to me in submission?"

39. A powerful being from among the Jinn said: "I will bring it to you before you rise from your station. For I am strong and trustworthy."

40. And one who had knowledge from the Scripture said: "I will bring it to you before you blink." So when he saw it resting before him, he said: "This is from the grace of my Lord, so that He tests me whether I am thankful or whether I reject. As for he who is thankful, he is thankful for himself, and as for he who rejects, then my Lord is Rich, Bountiful."

41. He said: "Disguise her throne so we may see if she will be guided or if she will be of those who are not guided."

42. So when she came, it was said: "Is your throne like this?" She said: "It appears to be similar." And we were given knowledge before her, and we had submitted.

43. And she was prevented by that which she served besides God. She was of the people who were rejecters.

44. It was said to her: "Enter the palace." So when she saw it she thought there was a pool, and she uncovered her legs. He said: "It is a palace paved with crystal." She said: "My Lord, I have wronged myself; and I submit with Solomon to God, the Lord of the worlds."

45. And We have sent to Thamud their brother Saleh: "You shall serve God." But they became two disputing groups.

46. He said: "My people, why do you hasten with evil ahead of good? If you would only seek God's forgiveness, perhaps you will receive mercy."

47. They said: "You have an ill omen with you and those with you." He said: "Your ill omen is with God, but you are a people that are being tested."
48. And in the city were nine ruffians who were causing corruption in the land, and they were not reforming.
49. They said: "Swear by God to one another that we will attack him and his family at night, and we will then say to his supporters: "We did not witness who murdered his family, and we are being truthful""
50. And they schemed a scheme and We schemed a scheme, while they did not notice.
51. So see what the result of their planning was! We destroyed them and their people together.
52. So these are their homes, ruined, for what they transgressed. In that is a sign for a people who know.
53. And We saved those who believed and were righteous.
54. And Lot, when he said to his people: "Are you committing lewdness while you can clearly see?"
55. "You are approaching the men out of lust instead of the women! No, you are an ignorant people!"
56. But the reply of his people was that they said: "Expel the family of Lot from your town, for they are a people who are being pure!"
57. So We saved him and his family, except for his wife, for We found her to be of those who will remain.
58. And We rained down a rain upon them. Miserable was the rain of those warned.
59. Say: "Praise be to God, and peace be upon His servants whom He has selected." Is God better, or that which you set up?
60. The One who created the heavens and the Earth, and He sent down water from the sky for you, so We cause gardens to grow with it that are full of beauty. It is not your ability to cause the growth of its trees. Is there a god with God? No. But they are a people who ascribe equals!
61. The One who made the Earth a habitat, and He made in it rivers and He made for it stabilizers, and He made between the two seas a barrier. Is there a god with God? No. But most of them do not know.
62. The One who answers the distressed when he calls Him, and He removes the evil, and He makes you successors on Earth. Is there a god with God? Little do you remember!

63. The One who guides you in the darkness of the land and the sea, and He sends the winds to spread between the hands of His mercy. Is there a god with God? God be exalted above what they set up!

64. The One who initiates the creation then He returns it, and He provides for you from the sky and the land. Is there a god with God? Say: "Bring your proof if you are being truthful."

65. Say: "None in the heavens or the Earth know the unseen except God. And they do not perceive when they will be resurrected."

66. No, they have no knowledge of the Hereafter. No, they are in doubt regarding it. No, they are blind to it.

67. And those who rejected said: "When we have become dust, as our fathers, shall we be brought out?"

68. "We have been promised this, both us and our fathers before. This is nothing but tales of the ancients!"

69. Say: "Roam the Earth and see how was the end of the criminals."

70. And do not be saddened for them, and do not be distraught for what they plot.

71. And they Say: "When is this promise if you are truthful?"

72. Say: "It may already upon you by some of that which you hasten."

73. And your Lord has given favour to the people, but most of them are not thankful.

74. And your Lord knows what is concealed in their chests and what they reveal.

75. And there is not a thing hidden in the heavens or the Earth, but is in a clear record.

76. This Quran narrates to the Children of Israel most of that which they are in dispute over.

77. And it is a guidance and mercy for the believers.

78. Your Lord decides between them by His judgment. And He is the Noble, the Knowledgeable.

79. So put your trust in God, for you are clearly on the truth.

80. You cannot make the dead hear, nor can you make the deaf hear the call when they turn their backs and flee.

81. Nor can you guide the blind from their misguidance. You can only make those who believe in Our revelations hear you, for they have submitted.

82. And when the punishment has been deserved by them, We will bring out for them a creature from the Earth, it will speak to them that the people have been unaware regarding Our revelations.

83. And the Day We gather from every nation a party that denied Our revelations, then they will be driven.

84. Until they have come, He will Say: "Have you denied My revelations while you had no explicit knowledge of them? What were you doing?"

85. And the punishment was deserved by them for what they transgressed, for they did not speak.

86. Did they not see that We made the night for them to rest in, and the day to see in? In that are signs for a people who have faith.

87. And on the Day when the horn is blown, then those in the heavens and the Earth will be in terror except for whom God wills. And all shall come to Him humbled.

88. And you see the mountains, you think they are solid, while they are passing by like the clouds. The making of God who perfected everything. He is Expert over what you do.

89. Whoever comes with a good deed will receive better than it, and from the terror of that Day they will be safe.

90. And whoever comes with the bad deed, their faces will be cast in Hell. Are you not being rewarded for what you used to do?

91. "I have been ordered to serve the Lord of this town that He has made restricted, and to Him are all things, and I have been ordered to be of those who submit."

92. "And that I recite the Quran." He who is guided is guided for himself, and to he who is misguided, Say: "I am but one of the warners."

93. Say: "Praise be to God, He will show you His signs and you will know them. And your Lord is not unaware of what you do."

Chapter 28

بسم الله الرحمن الرحيم

In the name of God, the Almighty, the Merciful.

1. T'.S.M.
2. These are the signs of the clear Scripture.
3. We recite to you from the news of Moses and Pharaoh with truth, for a people who believe.
4. Pharaoh became mighty in the land, and he turned its people into factions, he oppressed a group of them by killing their children and raping their women. He was of those who corrupted.
5. And We wanted to help those who were oppressed in the land, and to make them role models, and to make them the inheritors.
6. And to enable them in the land, and to show Pharaoh and Haamaan and their troops what they had feared.
7. And We inspired to Moses' mother: "Suckle him, and when you become fearful for him, then cast him off in the sea, and do not fear nor grieve. We will return him to you and We will make him of the messengers."
8. Then the family of Pharaoh picked him up, so he would be an enemy to them and a source of sadness. Certainly, Pharaoh and Haamaan and their troops were doing wrong.
9. And Pharaoh's wife said: "A pleasure to my eye and yours, so do not kill him, perhaps he will benefit us or we may take him as a son!", while they did not perceive.
10. And Moses' mother's heart became anxious, that she nearly revealed her identity. But We strengthened her heart, so that she would be of the believers.

11. And she said to his sister: "Follow his path." So she watched him from afar, while they did not notice.

12. And We forbade him from accepting all the nursing mothers. Then his sister said: "Shall I lead you to a family that can nurse him for you, and take good care of him?"

13. Thus, We returned him to his mother, so that she may be pleased and not be saddened, and to let her know that God's promise is the truth. However, most of them do not know.

14. And when he reached his maturity and strength, We bestowed him with wisdom and knowledge. We thus reward the good doers.

15. And he entered the city unexpectedly, without being noticed by the people. He found in it two men who were fighting, one was from his own race, and the other was from his enemy's. So the one who was from his own race called on him for help against his enemy, whereby Moses punched him, killing him. He said: "This is from the work of the devil; he is an enemy that clearly misleads."

16. He said: "My Lord, I have wronged my soul, so forgive me." He then forgave him, for He is the Forgiver, the Merciful.

17. He said: "My Lord, for what blessings you have bestowed upon me, I will never be a supporter for the criminals."

18. So he spent the night in the city, afraid and watchful. Then the one who sought his help yesterday, was asking again for his help. Moses said to him: "You are clearly a trouble maker."

19. But when he was about to strike their common enemy, he said: "O Moses, do you want to kill me, as you killed that person yesterday? Obviously, you wish to be a tyrant on Earth; you do not wish to be of the righteous."

20. And a man came running from the far side of the city, saying: "O Moses, the commanders are plotting to kill you, so leave immediately. I am giving you good advice."

21. He exited the city, afraid and watchful. He said: "My Lord, save me from the wicked people."

22. And as he traveled towards Midyan, he said: "Perhaps my Lord will guide me to the right path."

23. When he arrived at the watering hole of Midyan, he found a crowd of people watering, and he noticed two women waiting on the side. He said: "What is holding you back." They said: "We cannot draw water until the shepherds finish, and our father is an old man."

24. So he drew water for them, then he turned to a shaded area, and he said: "My Lord, I am poor, lacking any provisions You may have sent down."

25. So one of the two women approached him, shyly, and said: "My father invites you to reward you for watering for us." So when he came to him, and told him his story, he said: "Do not fear, for you have been saved from the wicked people."

26. One of the two women said: "O my father, hire him. For the best to be hired is one who is strong and honest."

27. He said: "I wish you to marry one of my two daughters, on condition that you work for me through eight pilgrimage periods; if you complete them to ten, it will be voluntary on your part. I do not wish to make this matter too difficult for you. You will find me, God willing, of the righteous."

28. He said: "It is then an agreement between me and you. Whichever period I fulfill, you will not be averse to either one. And God is entrusted over what we said."

29. So after Moses fulfilled his obligation and was traveling with his family, he saw a fire on the slope of the mount. He said to his family: "Stay here, I have seen a fire, perhaps I can bring you from there some news or a burning piece of the fire so that you may be warmed."

30. So when he reached it, he was called from the edge of the right side of the valley at the blessed area of the tree: "O Moses, it is I, God, the Lord of the worlds."

31. "Now, throw down your staff." So when he saw it vibrate as if it were a Jinn, he turned around to flee and would not return. "O Moses, come forward and do not be afraid. You are of those who are safe."

32. "Place your hand into your pocket. It will come out white without any blemish, and fold your hand close to your side against fear. These are two proofs from your Lord, to Pharaoh and his leaders. They have been a wicked people."

33. He said: "My Lord, I have killed a person from them, so I fear that they will kill me."

34. "And my brother Aaron is more eloquent in speech than I. So send him with me to help and to confirm me. For I fear that they will deny me."

35. He said: "We will strengthen you with your brother, and We will provide you both with authority. Thus, they will not be able to touch either one of you. With Our signs, the two of you, along with those who follow you, will be the victors."

36. So when Moses went to them with Our clear signs, they said: "This is nothing but fabricated magic; nor did we hear of this from our fathers of old!"

37. And Moses said: "My Lord is fully aware of who has brought the guidance from Him, and who will have the best deal in the Hereafter. The wicked never succeed."

38. And Pharaoh said: "O commanders, I have not known of any god for you other than me. Therefore, O Haamaan, fire-up the bricks and build me a platform, so perhaps I may take a look at the god of Moses! And I am certain he is a liar."

39. And he and his soldiers were arrogant in the land without any right, and they thought that they would not be returned to Us.

40. So We took him and his soldiers, and We cast them into the sea. So see how was the end of the wicked!

41. We made them role models for inviting to the Fire. And on the Day of Resurrection, they will not be supported.

42. And We made them followed by a curse in this world, and on the Day of Resurrection they will be despised.

43. We had given Moses the Scripture after We had destroyed the earlier generations; as an example for the people and a guidance and mercy, perhaps they will take heed.

44. And you were not on the western slope when We decreed the command to Moses. You were not a witness.

45. And We established many generations, and many ages passed them by. And you were not living among the people of Midyan, reciting Our revelations to them. But We did send messengers.

46. And nor were you on the side of the mount when We called. But it is a mercy from your Lord, so that you may warn a people who received no warner before you, perhaps they may take heed.

47. Thus, if any disaster strikes them as a consequence of their own deeds they cannot Say: "Our Lord, if only You sent a messenger to us, so that we would follow Your revelations, and we would be of the believers."

48. But when the truth came to them from Us, they said: "If only he was given the same that was given to Moses!" Had they not rejected what was given to Moses before? They had said: "Two magicians assisting one another." And they said: "We reject all these things."

49. Say: "Then bring forth a scripture from God that is better in guidance so I may follow it, if you are truthful."

50. But if they fail to respond to you, then know that they follow only their desires. And who is more astray than one who follows his desire, without guidance from God? God does not guide the wicked people.
51. And We have delivered the message, perhaps they may take heed.
52. Those whom We gave the Scripture to before this, they will believe in it.
53. And if it is recited to them, they Say: "We believe in it. It is the truth from our Lord. Indeed, we had submitted before it."
54. To these We grant twice the reward for that they have been patient. And they counter evil with good, and from Our provisions to them, they give.
55. And if they come across vain talk, they disregard it and Say: "To us are our deeds, and to you is your deeds. Peace be upon you. We do not seek the ignorant."
56. You cannot guide whom you love. But it is God who guides whom He wills; and He is fully aware of those who receive the guidance.
57. And they said: "If we follow the guidance with you, we will be deposed from our land." Did We not establish for them a safe territory, to which all kinds of fruits are offered, as a provision from Us? Indeed, most of them do not know.
58. And how many a town have We destroyed for turning unappreciative of their lives. So here are their homes, nothing but uninhabited ruins after them, except a few. We were the inheritors.
59. And your Lord never annihilates the towns without sending a messenger to their capital, to recite Our revelations to them. And We never annihilate the towns unless its people are wicked.
60. And anything that is given to you is only the materialism of this world, and its glitter. And what is with God is far better, and everlasting. Do you not comprehend?
61. Is one whom We promised a good promise, and it will come to pass, equal to one whom We provided with the goods of this life, then on the Day of Resurrection he is of those who will suffer?
62. And on the Day when He calls upon them, saying: "Where are My partners whom you used to claim?"
63. Those who have deserved the retribution will Say: "Our Lord, these are the ones we misled; we misled them only because we ourselves were misled. We seek to absolve ourselves to You, it was not us that they worshipped."
64. And it will be said: "Call upon your partners," but they will not respond to them. And they will see the retribution. If only they were guided!

65. On that Day, He will ask them and Say: "What was the answer you gave to the messengers?"
66. They will be shocked by the news on that Day, they will be speechless.
67. As for the one who repents, believes, and does good works; perhaps he will be with the winners.
68. And your Lord creates what He wills, and He selects; it is not for them to select. Glory be to God, He is far above the partners they set up.
69. And your Lord knows what is concealed in their chests and what they declare.
70. And He is God, there is no god but He. To Him belongs all praise in the first and in the last, and judgment belongs with Him, and to Him you will be returned.
71. Say: "Have you noted: what if God made the night eternal, until the Day of Resurrection? Which god, other than God, can bring you with light? Do you not listen?"
72. Say: "Have you noted: what if God made the daylight eternal, until the Day of Resurrection? Which god, other than God, can provide you with a night for your rest? Do you not see?"
73. And from His mercy is that He created for you the night and the day, in order to rest in it, and that you may seek of His provisions. And perhaps you may be appreciative.
74. And the Day He will call them and Say: "Where are My partners whom you had claimed?"
75. And We will extract from every nation a witness, then We will Say: "Bring forth your proof." They will then realise that all truth belongs with God, and what they had invented will abandon them.
76. Qaaroon was from among Moses' people, but he betrayed them. And We gave him such treasures that the keys thereof were almost too heavy for the strongest person. His people said to him: "Do not become too happy, for God does not like such kind of joy."
77. "And seek with the provisions bestowed upon you by God the abode of the Hereafter, and do not forget your share in this world, and do good as God has done good to you. And do not seek corruption in the land. God does not like the corruptors."
78. He said: "I have attained all this only because of my own knowledge." Did he not realise that God had annihilated before him generations that were much stronger than he, and greater in riches? The transgressors were not asked about their crimes.

79. Then he came out among his people draped in his ornaments. Those who preferred this worldly life said: "Oh, if only we were given similar to what Qaaroon has been given. Indeed, he is very fortunate."

80. And those who were blessed with knowledge said: "Woe to you! The reward from God is far better for those who believe and do good works. And none attains it except the steadfast."

81. We then caused the Earth to swallow him and his mansion. He had no group that could protect him against God; nor would he be victorious.

82. And those who wished they were in his place the day before said: "Indeed it is God Who provides or restricts for whomever He chooses from among His servants. Had it not been for God's grace towards us, He could have caused the Earth to swallow us as well. We now realise that the rejecters never succeed."

83. Such will be the abode of the Hereafter; We reserve it for those who do not seek prestige on Earth, nor corruption. And the end belongs to the righteous.

84. Whoever brings forth a good deed, he will receive a better reward than it. And whoever brings forth a sin then the retribution for their sins will be to the extent of their deeds.

85. Surely, the One who decreed the Quran to you will summon you to a predetermined appointment. Say: "My Lord is fully aware of who it is that brings the guidance, and who has gone astray."

86. Nor did you expect this Scripture to come your way; but this is a mercy from your Lord. Therefore, you shall not side with the rejecters.

87. Nor shall you be diverted from God's revelations, after they have come to you. And invite to your Lord. And do not be of those who set up partners.

88. And do not call besides God any god, there is no god but He. Everything will fade away except His presence. To Him is the judgment, and to Him you will be returned.

Chapter 29

بسم الله الرحمن الرحيم

In the name of God, the Almighty, the Merciful.

1. A.L.M.
2. Did the people think that they will be left to Say: "We believe" without being put to the test?
3. While We had tested those before them, so that God would distinguish those who are truthful and so that He would know the liars.
4. Or did those who sinned think that they would be ahead of Us? Miserable indeed is their judgment!
5. Whosoever looks forward to meeting God, then God's meeting will come. And He is the Hearer, the Knowledgeable.
6. And whosoever strives then he is only striving for himself; for God is in no need of the worlds.
7. And those who believed and did good works, We will cancel their sins and We will reward them in the best for what they did.
8. And We instructed the human to be good to his parents. But if they strive to make you set up partners with Me, then do not obey them. To Me are all your destinies, and I will inform you of what you used to do.
9. And those who believed and did good works, We will admit them with the righteous.
10. And from among the people are those who Say: "We believe in God," but if he is harmed in the sake of God, he equates the persecution inflicted by the people with God's punishment! And if a victory comes from your Lord, he says: "We were with you!" Is God not fully aware of what is inside the chests of the worlds?

11. God is fully aware of those who believed, and He is fully aware of the hypocrites.
12. And those who rejected said to those who believed: "Follow our path and we will carry your sins." But they cannot carry anything from their sins, they are liars!
13. They will carry their own burdens as well as burdens with their burdens, and they will be asked on the Day of Resurrection regarding what they fabricated.
14. And We had sent Noah to his people, so he stayed with them one thousand less fifty years. Then the flood took them while they were wicked.
15. So We saved him and the people on the ship, and We made it a sign for the worlds.
16. And Abraham when he said to his people: "Serve God and be aware of Him, that is better for you if you knew."
17. "You are worshipping nothing but idols besides Him, and you are creating fabrications. Those that you worship besides God do not possess for you any provisions, so seek with God the provision and serve Him and be thankful to Him; to Him you will return."
18. "And if you disbelieve, then nations before you have also disbelieved." The messenger is only required to deliver clearly.
19. Did they not observe how God initiates the creation then He returns it? All that for God is easy to do.
20. Say: "Roam the Earth and observe how the creation was initiated. Thus God will establish the final creation. God is capable of all things."
21. "God will punish whom He wills and He will have mercy on whom He wills, and to Him you will return."
22. "And you will not be able to escape this fact, on Earth or in the heavens, nor do you have besides God any ally or victor."
23. And those who rejected God's revelations and in meeting Him, they have forsaken My mercy, and they will have a painful retribution.
24. But the only response from his people was their saying: "Kill him, or burn him." But God saved him from the fire. In this are signs for a people who believe.
25. And he said: "You have taken idols besides God in order to preserve some friendship among you in this worldly life. But then, on the Day of Resurrection, you will disown one another, and curse one another. Your destiny is Hell, and you will have no victors."

26. Thus, Lot believed with him and said: "I am emigrating to my Lord. He is the Noble, the Wise."

27. And We granted him Isaac and Jacob, and We made within his progeny the prophethood and the Scripture. And We gave him his reward in this world, and in the Hereafter he is among the righteous.

28. And Lot, when he said to his people: "You commit a lewdness that no others in the world have done before!"

29. "You sexually approach men, and you commit highway robbery, and you bring all vice to your society." But the only response from his people was to Say: "Bring us God's retribution, if you are being truthful!"

30. He said: "My Lord, grant me victory over the wicked people."

31. And when Our messengers came to Abraham with good news, they then said: "We are to destroy the people of such a town, for its people have been wicked."

32. He said: "But Lot is in it!" They said: "We are fully aware of who is in it. We will save him and his family, except his wife; she is of those doomed."

33. Thus when Our messengers came to Lot, they were mistreated, and he was embarrassed towards them. And they said: "Do not fear, and do not be saddened. We will save you and your family, except for your wife; she is of those doomed."

34. "We will send down upon the people of this town an affliction from the sky, as a consequence of their wickedness."

35. And We left remains of it as a clear sign for a people who understand.

36. And to Median was their brother Shu'ayb. He said: "O my people, serve God and seek the Last Day, and do not roam the Earth corrupting."

37. But they denied him, thus the Earthquake took them; they were then left dead in their homes.

38. And 'Aad and Thamud. Much was made apparent to you from their dwellings. The devil had adorned their works in their eyes, thus he diverted them from the path, even though they could see.

39. And Qaaroon, and Pharaoh, and Haamaan; Moses went to them with clear proofs. But they became arrogant in the land, and they were not the first.

40. We took each by his sins. Some of them We sent upon him violent winds, some of them were taken by the scream, some of them We caused the Earth to swallow, and some of them We drowned. God is not the One who wronged them; it is they who wronged themselves.

41. The example of those who take allies besides God is like the spider how it makes a home; and the weakest home is the home of the spider, if they only knew.

42. God knows that what they are calling on besides Him is nothing. He is the Noble, the Wise.

43. Such are the examples We cite for the people, but none comprehend except the knowledgeable.

44. God created the heavens and the Earth, with truth. In that is a sign for the faithful.

45. Recite what is inspired to you of the Scripture, and perform the oath of allegiance. For the oath of allegiance prohibits evil and vice, and the remembrance of God is the greatest. God knows everything you do.

46. And do not argue with the people of the Scripture except in the best manner; except for those who are wicked amongst them; and Say: "We believe in what was revealed to us and in what was revealed to you, and our god and your god is the same; to Him we submit."

47. And similarly, We have sent down to you the Book. Thus, those whom We have given the Scripture will believe in it. Also, some of your people will believe in it. The only ones who mock Our revelations are the rejecters.

48. You were not reciting any scripture before this, nor were you writing one down by your hand. In that case, the doubters would have had reason.

49. In fact, it is a clear revelation in the chests of those who have been given knowledge. And it is only the wicked who doubt Our revelations.

50. And they said: "If only signs would come down to him from his Lord!" Say: "All signs are with God, and I am but a clear warner."

51. Is it not enough for them that We have sent down to you the Scripture, being recited to them? In that is a mercy and a reminder for people who believe.

52. Say: "God is enough as a witness between me and you. He knows what is in the heavens and the Earth. As for those who believe in falsehood and reject God, they are the losers."

53. And they hasten you for the retribution! If it were not for a predetermined appointment, the retribution would have come to them. It will come to them suddenly, when they do not expect.

54. They hasten you for the retribution; while Hell surrounds the rejecters.

55. The Day will come when the retribution overwhelms them, from above them and from beneath their feet; and We will Say: "Taste the results of what you used to do!"

56. "O My servants who believed, My Earth is spacious, so serve only Me."

57. Every soul will taste death, then to Us you will be returned.

58. And those who believe and do good work, We will settle them in mansions in Paradise, with rivers flowing beneath. Eternally they abide therein. Excellent is the reward for the workers.

59. They are the ones who were patient, and put their trust in their Lord.

60. Many a creature does not carry its provision; God provides for it, as well as for you. He is the Hearer, the Knowledgeable.

61. And if you ask them: "Who created the heavens and the Earth, and put the sun and the moon in motion?" They will Say: "God." Why then did they deviate?

62. God expands the provision for whomever He chooses from among His servants, and withholds it. God is fully aware of all things.

63. And if you ask them: "Who sends down water from the sky, thus reviving the land after its death?" They will Say: "God," Say: "Praise be to God." But most of them do not understand.

64. This worldly life is no more than play and distraction, while the abode of the Hereafter is the reality, if they only knew.

65. When they ride on a ship, they call on God, devoting the system to Him. But as soon as He saves them to the shore, they set up partners.

66. Let them reject what We have given them, and let them enjoy; for they will come to know.

67. Have they not seen that We have established a safe territory, while all around them the people are in constant danger? Would they still believe in falsehood, and reject God's blessings?

68. Who is more evil than one who fabricates lies and attributes them to God, or denies the truth when it comes to him? Is there not a place in Hell for the rejecters?

69. As for those who strive in Our cause, We will guide them to Our paths. For God is with the pious.

Chapter 30

In the name of God, the Almighty, the Merciful.

1. A.L.M.
2. The Romans have won.
3. At the lowest point on the Earth. But after their victory, they will be defeated.
4. In a few more years. The decision before and after is for God, and on that day the believers will rejoice.
5. With God's victory. God gives victory to whom He wishes; He is the Noble, the Merciful.
6. Such is God's pledge, and God does not break His pledge, but most people do not know.
7. They only know the outside appearance of the worldly life; and regarding the Hereafter, they are ignorant.
8. Did they not reflect upon themselves? God did not create the heavens and the Earth and what is between them except by truth and an appointed term. But most of the people are in denial regarding their meeting with their Lord.
9. Did they not roam the Earth and see how it ended for those before them? They were more powerful than them, and they cultivated the land and they built in it far more than these have built, and their messengers came to them with the proofs. God was not to wrong them, but it was they who wronged themselves.
10. Then the end of those who did evil was evil, that is because they denied God's signs, and they used to mock them.
11. God initiates the creation, then He repeats it, then to Him you will return.

12. And the Day when the Hour will be established, the criminals will be in despair.
13. And they did not have any intercessors from the partners they set up, and they will reject such partners.
14. And on the Day the Hour is established, they will be separated.
15. Then as for those who believed and did good works, they will be delighted in a luxurious place.
16. And as for those who rejected and denied Our revelations and the meeting of the Hereafter, they shall be brought forth for the retribution.
17. So glory be to God when you retire and when you wake.
18. And to Him is all praise in the heavens and in the Earth, and in the evening and when you go out.
19. He brings the living out of the dead, and He brings the dead out of the living. And He revives the land after its death. And similarly you will be brought out.
20. And from His signs is that He created you from dust, then you became human beings spreading out.
21. And from His signs is that He created for you mates from yourselves that you may reside with them, and He placed between you affection and mercy. In that are signs for a people who reflect.
22. And from His signs is the creation of the heavens and the Earth, and the difference of your languages and your colors. In that are signs for the world.
23. And from His signs is your sleep by night and day, and your seeking of His bounty. In that are signs for a people who listen.
24. And from His signs is that He shows you the lightning, by way of fear and hope, and He sends down water from the sky, and He revives the land with it after its death. In that are signs for a people who understand.
25. And from His signs is that the heavens and the Earth will rise by His command. Then, when He calls you forth from the Earth, you will come out.
26. And to Him is all that is in the heavens and the Earth. All are subservient to Him.
27. And He is the One who initiates the creation, then He repeats it, and this is easy for Him. And to Him is the highest example in the heavens and the Earth. And He is the Noble, the Wise.
28. An example is cited for you from among yourselves: are there any from among those who are still dependant that are partners to you in what provisions We have given you that you become equal therein? Would you fear

them as you fear each other? It is such that We clarify the revelations for a people who have sense.

29. No, those who were wrong followed their desires without knowledge. So who can guide one whom God misguides? And they will have no victors.

30. So establish yourself to the system of monotheism. It is the inclination that God has nurtured the people on. There is no changing in God's creation. Such is the pure system, but most people do not know.

31. Turn to Him, and be aware of Him, and honour the oath of allegiance, and do not be of those who set up partners.

32. Or like those who split-up their system, and they became sects, each group happy with what it had.

33. And if harm afflicts the people, they call out sincerely to their Lord. But then, when He gives them a taste of His mercy, a group of them set up partners with their Lord!

34. So as to reject what We gave them. Enjoy then, for you will come to know.

35. Or have We sent down to them a proof, which speaks to them of that which they have set up?

36. And if We grant the people a taste of mercy, they become happy with it, but if evil afflicts them for what they have done, they become in despair!

37. Did they not see that God grants the provisions for whom He wills, and He is able? In that are signs for a people who believe.

38. So give the relative his due, and the poor, and the wayfarer. That is best for those who seek God's presence, and they are the successful ones.

39. And any financial interest you have placed to grow in the people's money, it will not grow with God. And any contribution that you have placed seeking His presence, then those will be multiplied.

40. God who created you, then He provided for you, then He puts you to death, then He brings you to life. Is there any among the partners you set up that can do any of this? Be He glorified and exalted above what they set up.

41. Pollution has appeared in the land and the sea by the hands of the people for what they earned. He will make them taste some of what they have done, perhaps they will revert.

42. Say: "Roam the Earth and see how the end was for those before. Most of them had set up partners."

43. So establish yourself to the system which is straight, before a Day comes from God that none can avert. On that Day they shall be separated.

44. Whosoever rejects, then he will suffer his rejection; and whosoever does good works, then it is for themselves that they are preparing a good place.

45. So that He will reward those that believe and do good works from His grace. He does not love the rejecters.
46. And from His signs is that He sends the winds with glad tidings, and to give you a taste of His mercy, and so that the ships may sail by His command, and that you may seek of His bounty; perhaps you will be thankful.
47. And We have sent before you messengers to their people, so they came to them with clear proofs, then We took revenge on those who were criminals, and it is an obligation for Us to grant victory to the believers.
48. God Who sends the winds, so they raise clouds, and He spreads them in the sky as He wishes, then He turns them into joined pieces, then you see the rain drops come forth from their midst. Then when He makes them fall on whomever He wills of His servants, they rejoice!
49. Even though just before He sent it down to them, they were in despair!
50. So look at the effects of God's mercy, how He revives the land after its death. Such is the One who will revive the dead, and He is capable of all things.
51. And if We chose to send a wind and they see it turn yellow, they will continue to be rejecters after it.
52. You cannot make the dead listen, nor can you make the deaf hear the call when they have turned their backs.
53. Nor can you enlighten the blind from their straying; but you can only make those who believe in Our revelations listen, for they have submitted.
54. God is the One Who created you from weakness, then He made strength after the weakness, then He makes after the strength a weakness and grey hair. He creates what He wills and He is the Knowledgeable, the Able.
55. And the Day the Hour is established, the criminals will swear that they have remained only for an hour! Thus they were deluded.
56. And those who were given knowledge and faith said: "You have remained according to God's decree until the Day of Resurrection; so this is the Day of Resurrection, but you did not know."
57. So on that Day, the excuses of those who transgressed will not help them, nor will they be allowed to revert.
58. And We have cited for the people in this Quran of every example. And if you come to them with a sign, those who rejected will Say: "You are bringing falsehood!"
59. It is thus that God seals the hearts of those who do not know.
60. So be patient, for God's promise is true, and do not be dissuaded by those who do not have certainty.

Chapter 31

بسم الله الرحمن الرحيم

In the name of God, the Almighty, the Merciful.

1. A.L.M.
2. These are the signs of the Scripture of wisdom.
3. A guide and a mercy for the good doers.
4. Those who honour the oath of allegiance, and contribute towards betterment and regarding the Hereafter they are certain.
5. These are on a guidance from their Lord, and they are the successful ones.
6. And from the people, there are those who accept baseless narrations to mislead from the path of God without knowledge, and they take it as entertainment. These will have a humiliating retribution.
7. And when Our revelations are recited to him, he turns away arrogantly as if he did not hear them, as if there is a deafness in his ears. So announce to him a painful retribution.
8. Those who believe and do good works, for them will be gardens of bliss.
9. Abiding eternally therein with certainty, as promised by God. He is the Noble, the Wise.
10. He created the skies without pillars that you can see. And He placed in the Earth firm stabilizers so that it would not tumble with you, and He spread on it all kinds of creatures. And We sent down water from the sky, thus We caused to grow all kinds of good plants.
11. This is God's creation, so show me what those besides Him have created? Indeed, the transgressors are far astray.
12. And We had given Luqmaan the wisdom: "You shall be thankful to God, and whoever is thankful is being thankful for his own good. As for whosoever rejects, then God is Rich, Praiseworthy."

13. And Luqmaan said to his son, while he was advising him: "O my son, do not set up any partners with God; for setting up partners is an immense wrong-doing."

14. And We enjoined the human being regarding his parents. His mother bore him with hardship upon hardship, and his weaning takes two years. You shall give thanks to Me, and to your parents. To Me is the final destiny.

15. If they strive to make you set up any partners besides Me, then do not obey them. But continue to treat them amicably in this world. You shall follow only the path of those who have sought Me. Ultimately, you all return to Me, then I will inform you of everything you have done.

16. "O my son, if it be anything even as the weight of a mustard seed, be it deep inside a rock, or be it in the heavens or the Earth, God will bring it. God is Sublime, Expert."

17. "O my son, perform the oath of allegiance and advocate righteousness and forbid evil, and bear with patience whatever befalls you. These are the most honourable traits."

18. "And do not turn your cheek arrogantly from people, nor shall you roam the Earth insolently. For God does not like the arrogant show offs."

19. "And be humble in how you walk and lower your voice. For the harshest of all voices is the donkey's voice."

20. Did you not see that God has committed in your service everything in the heavens and the Earth, and He has showered you with His blessings, both apparent and hidden? Yet from the people are some who argue about God without knowledge, without guidance, and without an enlightening Scripture.

21. And if they are told: "Follow that which God has sent down." They Say: "No, we will follow what we found our fathers doing." What if the devil had been leading them to the agony of Hell?

22. And whosoever submits himself completely to God, while he is righteous, then he has taken hold of the strongest bond. And to God all matters will return.

23. And whosoever rejects, then do not be saddened by his rejection. To Us is their ultimate return, then We will inform them of what they had done. God is fully aware of what is inside the chests.

24. We let them enjoy for a while, then We commit them to severe retribution.

25. And if you ask them: "Who created the heavens and the Earth?" They will Say: "God." Say: "Praise be to God." Yet, most of them do not know.

26. To God belongs everything in the heavens and the Earth. God is the Rich, the Praiseworthy.

27. And if all the trees on Earth were made into pens, and the ocean were supplied by seven more oceans, the words of God would not run out. God is Noble, Wise.

28. Your creation and your resurrection is all as one breath. God is Hearer, Seer.

29. Have you not seen that God merges the night into the day and merges the day into the night, and that He has committed the sun and the moon, each running to a predetermined term; and that God is expert of everything you do?

30. That is because God is the truth, and that which they call on besides Him is falsehood, and that God is the Most High, the Great.

31. Have you not seen the ships sailing the sea, carrying God's provisions, to show you some of His signs? In that are signs for every one who is patient, thankful.

32. And when waves surround them like mountains, they call on God, sincerely devoting the system to Him. But when He saves them to the shore, some of them revert. None discard Our signs except those who are betrayers, unappreciative.

33. O mankind, you shall reverence your Lord, and fear a Day when a father cannot help his own child, nor can a child help his father. Certainly, God's promise is truth. Therefore, do not be deceived by this worldly life; and do not be deceived from God by arrogance.

34. With God is the knowledge regarding the Hour. And He sends down the rain, and He knows what is inside the wombs. No soul knows what it may gain tomorrow, nor does any soul know in which land it will die. God is Knowledgeable, Expert.

Chapter 32

بسم الله الرحمن الرحيم

In the name of God, the Almighty, the Merciful.

1. A.L.M.
2. The sending down of this Scripture, without a doubt, from the Lord of the worlds.
3. Or do they Say: "He fabricated it!" No, it is the truth from your Lord, so that you may warn a people who never received a warner before you, in order that they may be guided.
4. God is the One who created the heavens and the Earth, and everything between them in six days, then He settled to the Throne. You do not have beside Him any Lord, nor intercessor. Will you not then remember?
5. He arranges matters from the heaven to the Earth, then it ascends to Him in a day which is equivalent to one thousand of the years which you count.
6. Such is the Knower of the unseen and the seen; the Noble, the Merciful.
7. The One who perfected everything He created and He began the creation of the human from mud.
8. Then He made his offspring from a structure derived from a lowly liquid.
9. Then He evolved him, and blew into him from His spirit. And He made for you the hearing, the eyesight, and the hearts; rarely are you thankful.
10. And they said: "When we are buried in the ground, will we be created anew?" Indeed, they reject the meeting of their Lord.
11. Say: "The Angel of death that has been assigned to you will take you, then to your Lord you will be returned."
12. And if only you could see the criminals when they bow down their heads before their Lord: "Our Lord, we have now seen and we have heard, so send us back and we will do good work. Now we have attained certainty!"

13. And if We had wished, We could have given every soul its guidance, but the word from Me has taken effect, that I will fill Hell with the Jinn and people all together.

14. So taste the consequences of your forgetting this Day; for We have now forgotten you. And taste the eternal retribution in return for what you used to do.

15. The only people who believe in Our revelations are those whom when they are reminded by them, they fall prostrating, and they glorify the praise of their Lord, and they are not arrogant.

16. Their sides readily forsake their beds, to call on their Lord out of fear and hope, and from Our provisions to them they give.

17. No person knows what is being hidden for them of joy, as a reward for what they used to do.

18. Is one who was a believer the same as one who was wicked? They are not the same.

19. As for those who believe and do good works, for them are eternal Paradises as an abode, in return for their works.

20. And as for those who were wicked, their abode is the Fire. Every time they try to leave it, they will be put back in it, and it will be said to them: "Taste the retribution of the Fire in which you used to deny."

21. And We will let them taste the worldly retribution before the greater retribution, perhaps they will revert.

22. And who is more wicked than one who is reminded of his Lord's revelations, then he turns away from them? We will exact a punishment from the criminals.

23. And We have given Moses the Scripture. So do not be in any doubt about meeting Him. And We made it a guide for the Children of Israel.

24. And We made from among them leaders who guided in accordance with Our command, for they were patient and had certainty regarding Our revelations.

25. Your Lord will separate between them on the Day of Resurrection regarding that which they disputed in.

26. Is it not a guide for them how many generations We have annihilated before them in whose homes they now walk? In that are signs. Do they not listen?

27. Have they not seen that We drive the water to the barren lands, and produce with it crops to feed their livestock, as well as themselves? Do they not see?

28. And they Say: "When is this victory, if you are being truthful?"

29. Say: "On the day of the victory, it will not benefit those who rejected if they believe, nor will they be given respite."
30. Therefore, turn away from them and wait, for they too are waiting.

Chapter 33

بسم الله الرحمن الرحيم

In the name of God, the Almighty, the Merciful.

1. O you prophet, you shall be aware of God, and do not obey the rejecters and the hypocrites. God is Knowledgeable, Wise.

2. And follow what is being revealed to you by your Lord. God is fully aware of all that you do.

3. And put your trust in God. God suffices as an advocate.

4. God did not make any man with two hearts in his body. Nor did He make your wives whom you estrange to be as your mothers. Nor did He make your adopted children to be your sons. Such is what you claim with your mouths, but God speaks the truth, and He guides to the path.

5. Name them by retaining their father's name. That is more just with God. But if you do not know their fathers, then, name them as your brothers in the system and your patrons. There is no sin upon you if you make a mistake in this respect; but you will be responsible for what your hearts deliberately intend. God is Forgiver, Merciful.

6. The prophet is closer to the believers than themselves, and his wives are mothers to them. And God's decree to the believers and the emigrants is that before they help their relatives, they have taken care of their own families first. Such has been decreed in the Scripture.

7. And when We took from the prophets their covenant. And from you, and from Noah, and Abraham, and Moses, and Jesus the son of Mary; We took from them a strong covenant.

8. So that the truthful may be asked about their truthfulness, and He has prepared for the rejecters a painful retribution.

9. O you who believe, remember God's favour upon you when soldiers attacked you and We sent upon them a wind and invisible soldiers. God is Seer of everything you do.

10. For they came from above you, and from beneath you; and your eyes were terrified, and the hearts reached to the throat, and you harboured doubts about God.

11. That is when the believers were truly tested; they were severely shaken up.

12. And the hypocrites and those who have a sickness in their hearts said: "God and His messenger promised us nothing but illusions!"

13. And a group of them said: "O people of Yathrib, you cannot make a stand; therefore, retreat." And a small party of them sought permission from the prophet, saying: "Our homes are exposed," while they were not exposed. They just wanted to flee.

14. And if the enemy had entered at them from all sides, and then they were asked to betray, they would do so with very little hesitation.

15. And indeed they had pledged to God before this that they would not turn around and flee. Making a pledge to God brings great responsibility.

16. Say: "It will not benefit you to flee away from death or from being killed, for you will only have the enjoyment for a short while."

17. Say: "Who can protect you from God if He intends to harm you, or He intends any blessing for you?" They will never find besides God any ally or victor.

18. God already knows which of you are the hinderers, and those who say to their brothers: "Come and stay with us." Rarely do they mobilize for battle.

19. They are miserable towards you. Then, when fear comes, you see their eyes rolling, as if death had already come to them. But once the fear is gone, they lash-out at you with sharp tongues. They are miserable towards doing any good. These have not believed, so God nullifies their works. This is easy for God to do.

20. They thought that the opponents had not yet mobilized. And if the opponents do appear, they wish that they were out in the desert, seeking out news for you. Even if they were among you, they would not have fought except very little.

21. Indeed, in the messenger of God a good example has been set for you for he who seeks God and the Last Day and thinks constantly about God.

22. And when the believers saw the opponents, they said: "This is what God and His messenger have promised us, and God and His messenger are truthful." This only increased their faith and their submission.

23. From among the believers are men who fulfilled their pledge to God. Thus, some of them died, while some are still waiting; but they never altered in the least.

24. That God may recompense the truthful for their truthfulness, and punish the hypocrites if He so wills, or accepts their repentance. God is Forgiver, Merciful.

25. And God drove back those who disbelieved with their rage, they left empty handed. God thus spared the believers any fighting. God is Powerful, Noble.

26. And He also brought down those who helped support them from among the people of the Scripture from their secure positions, and He threw terror into their hearts. Some of them you killed, and some you took captive.

27. And He inherited you their land, their homes, their money, and lands you had never stepped on. God is able to do all things.

28. O prophet, say to your wives: "If you are seeking this worldly life and its vanities, then come, I will make a provision for you and release you in an amicable manner."

29. "But if you are seeking God and His messenger, and the abode of the Hereafter, then God has prepared for the righteous among you a great reward."

30. O wives of the prophet, if any of you commits evident lewdness, then the retribution will be doubled for her. This is easy for God to do.

31. Any whosoever of you is obedient to God and His messenger, and does good works, We will grant her double the recompense, and We have prepared for her a generous provision.

32. O wives of the prophet, you are not like any other women. If you are righteous, then do not speak too softly, lest those with disease in their hearts will move with desire; you shall speak in an honourable manner.

33. You shall settle down in your homes, and do not be about like the olden days of ignorance. You shall perform the oath of allegiance, and contribute towards betterment, and obey God and His messenger. God wishes to remove any affliction from you, O people of the Sanctuary, and to purify you completely.

34. And mention all that is being recited in your homes of God's revelations and the wisdom. God is Sublime, Expert.

35. Surely, the submitting men, and the submitting women, the believing men, and the believing women, the obedient men, and the obedient women, the truthful men, and the truthful women, the patient men, and the patient women, the humble men, and the humble women, the charitable men, and the charitable women, the fasting men, and the fasting women, the men who

keep covered their private parts, and the women who similarly keep covered, and the men who commemorate God frequently, and the commemorating women; God has prepared for them a forgiveness and a great recompense.

36. It is not for a believing man or believing woman, if God and His messenger issue any command, that they have any choice in their decision. And anyone who disobeys God and His messenger, he has gone far astray.

37. And you said to the one who was blessed by God, and blessed by you: "Keep your wife and reverence God," and you hid inside yourself what God wished to proclaim. And you feared the people, while it was God you were supposed to fear. So when Zayd ended his relationship with his wife, We had you marry her, to establish that there is no wrongdoing for the believers in marrying the wives of their adopted sons if their relationship is ended. And God's command is always done.

38. There is no blame on the prophet in doing anything that God has decreed upon him. Such was God's way with the people of old. And God's command is a determined duty.

39. Those who deliver God's messages, and reverence Him, and they do not reverence anyone but God. God suffices as a Reckoner.

40. Mohammed was not the father of any man among you, but he is the messenger of God and the seal of the prophets. And God is fully aware of all things.

41. O you who believe, you shall remember God frequently.

42. And glorify Him morning and evening.

43. He is the One who gives allegiance to you, along with His Angels, to lead you out of darkness into the light. And He is ever Merciful towards the believers.

44. Their greeting the Day they meet Him is: "Peace" and He has prepared for them a generous recompense.

45. O prophet, We have sent you as a witness, and a bearer of good news, and a warner.

46. Inviting to God, by His leave, and a guiding beacon.

47. And give good news to the believers, that they have deserved from God a great blessing.

48. And do not obey the rejecters and the hypocrites, and ignore their insults, and put your trust in God; God suffices as an advocate.

49. O you who believe, if you marry the believing women, then divorced them before having intercourse with them, then there is no interim required of them. You shall compensate them, and let them go in an amicable manner.

50. O prophet, We have made lawful for you the wives to whom you have already given their dowry, and the one who is committed to you by oath, as granted to you by God, and the daughters of your father's brothers, and the daughters of your father's sisters, and the daughters of your mother's brothers, and the daughters of your mother's sisters, of whom they have emigrated with you. Also, the believing woman who had decreed herself to the prophet, the prophet may marry her if he wishes, as a privilege given only to you and not to the believers. We have already decreed their rights in regard to their spouses and those who are still dependant. This is to spare you any hardship. God is Forgiver, Merciful.

51. You may postpone whom you will of them, and you may receive whom you will. And whomsoever you seek of those whom you have set aside then there is no sin upon you. Such is best that they may be comforted and not grieve, and may all be pleased with what you give them. God knows what is in your hearts. God is Knowledgeable, Compassionate.

52. No women are lawful to you beyond this, nor that you change them for other wives, even though you may be attracted by their beauty, except those to whom you are committed by oaths. And God is watchful over all things.

53. O you who believe, do not enter the prophet's homes except if you are invited to a meal, without you forcing such an invitation. But if you are invited, you may enter. And when you finish eating, you shall leave, without staying to wait for news. This used to annoy the prophet, and he was shy to tell you. But God does not shy away from the truth. And if you ask his wives for something, ask them from behind a barrier. This is purer for your hearts and their hearts. And it is not for you to harm God's messenger, nor that you should marry his wives after him. This is indeed a gross offence with God.

54. If you reveal anything, or hide it, God is fully aware of all things.

55. There is no sin upon them before their fathers, or their sons, or their brothers, or the sons of their brothers, or the sons of their sisters, or their offspring yet to come, or their women, or those who are still their dependants. And be aware of God, for God is witness over all things.

56. God and His Angels give allegiance to the prophet. O you who believe, you shall give allegiance to him, and yield completely.

57. Surely those who harm God and His messenger, God will curse them in this life and in the Hereafter; and He has prepared for them a shameful retribution.

58. And those who harm the believing men and the believing women, with no just reason, they have brought upon themselves a slander and a gross sin.

59. O prophet, tell your wives, your daughters, and the wives of the believers that they should lengthen upon themselves their outer garments. That is better so that they would not be recognized and harmed. God is Forgiver, Merciful.

60. If the hypocrites, and those with disease in their hearts and those who spread lies in the city do not refrain, then We will let you overpower them, then they will not be able to remain as your neighbours except for a short while.

61. They are cursed wherever they are found, and they are taken and killed in numbers.

62. This is God's way with those who have passed away before, and you will not find any change in God's way.

63. The people ask you regarding the Hour. Say: "Its knowledge is with God. And for all that you know the Hour may be near!"

64. God has cursed the rejecters, and He has prepared for them Hell.

65. Eternally they abide therein. They will find no ally, or victor.

66. On the Day when their faces will be turned over in the Fire, they will Say: "Oh, we wish we had obeyed God, and obeyed the messenger"

67. And they will Say: "Our Lord, we have obeyed our leaders and our learned ones, but they misled us from the path."

68. "Our Lord, give them double the retribution, and curse them with a mighty curse."

69. O you who believe, do not be like those who harmed Moses, but then God cleared him of all they said, and he was honourable before God.

70. O you who believe, be aware of God and speak only the truth.

71. He will then direct your works, and forgive your sins. And whosoever obeys God and His messenger has triumphed a great triumph.

72. We have offered the trust to the heavens and the Earth, and the mountains, but they refused to bear it, and were fearful of it. But the human being accepted it; he was transgressing, ignorant.

73. So that God may punish the hypocrite men and the hypocrite women, and the men who set up partners and the women who set up partners. And God redeems the believing men and the believing women. And God is Forgiver, Merciful.

Chapter 34

بسم الله الرحمن الرحيم

In the name of God, the Almighty, the Merciful.

1. Praise be to God, to whom belongs everything in the heavens and the Earth; and to Him is the praise in the Hereafter. He is the Wise, the Expert.

2. He knows what goes into the Earth, and what comes out of it, and what comes down from the sky, and what climbs into it. He is the Merciful, Forgiver.

3. And those who rejected said: "The Hour will not come upon us!" Say: "Yes, by my Lord, it will come to you." He is the Knower of the unseen, not even an atom's weight or less than that or greater can be hidden from Him, be it in the heavens or the Earth. All are in a clear record.

4. That He may reward those who believe and do good works. To them will be a forgiveness and a generous provision.

5. As for those who sought against Our revelations to frustrate them, they will have a retribution of painful affliction.

6. And those that have been given knowledge will see that what has been sent down to you from your Lord is the truth, and that it guides to the path of the Noble, the Praiseworthy.

7. And those who rejected said: "Shall we lead you to a man who will tell you that after you are dismembered you will be created anew?"

8. "Has he invented a lie against God, or is there a madness in him?" Indeed, those who do not believe in the Hereafter will be in a retribution and far straying.

9. Have they not seen to all that is before them and behind them, in the heaven and the Earth? If We wished, We could cause the Earth to swallow them, or

cause pieces of the sky to fall on them. In this is a sign for every obedient servant.

10. And We granted David blessings from Us: "O mountains, glorify with him, as well as the birds." And We softened the iron for him.

11. That you may make armour coats that fit perfectly, and work righteousness. For I am Seer of what you do.

12. And for Solomon the wind was given, traveling one month coming and one month going, and We caused a spring of tar to flow for him. And from among the Jinn are those that worked for him by his Lord's leave; and any one of them who turns from Our commands, We shall cause him to taste the retribution of the Fire.

13. They made for him what he desired of enclosures, and statues, and pools of deep reservoirs, and heavy pots. "O family of David, work to show thanks." Only a few of My servants are appreciative.

14. Then, when We decreed death for him, nothing informed them of his death until a worm kept eating from his staff, so when he fell down, the Jinn realised that if they had known the unseen, they would not have remained in the humiliating retribution.

15. There was for Sheba a sign in their homeland, with two gardens on the right and the left. "Eat from the provisions of your Lord, and be thankful to Him." A good land, and a forgiving Lord.

16. But they turned away, so We sent them a destructive flash flood, and We substituted their two gardens into two gardens of rotten fruits, thorny plants, and a skimpy harvest.

17. We thus requited them for what they rejected. And We do not requite except the rejecter.

18. And We placed between them and between the towns that We blessed, towns that were easy to see; and We measured the journey between them: "Travel in them by night and day in complete security."

19. But they said: "Our Lord, make the measure between our journeys longer," and they wronged themselves. So We made them a thing of the past, and We scattered them into small groups. In this are signs for every person who is patient, thankful.

20. And Satan has been successful in his suggestions to them, for they followed him, except for a group of the believers.

21. And he did not have any authority over them except that We might know who believed in the Hereafter from those who are doubtful about it. And your Lord is Keeper over all things.

22. Say: "Call on those whom you have claimed besides God. They do not possess even a single atom's weight in the heavens, or the Earth. They possess no partnership therein, nor is there for Him any assistant among them."

23. Nor will intercession be of any help with Him, except for whom He has already given leave. Until when the fear has subsided from their hearts, they ask: "What did your Lord say?" They will Say: "The truth!" And He is the Most High, the Great.

24. Say: "Who provides for you from the heavens and the Earth?" Say: "God! And either we or you are guided, or are clearly astray."

25. Say: "You will not be asked about our crimes, nor will we be asked for what you do."

26. Say: "Our Lord will gather us together then He will judge between us with truth. He is the Judge, the Knowledgeable."

27. Say: "Show me those whom you have set up as partners with Him! No; He is but God, the Noble, the Wise."

28. And We have sent you to all people to be a bearer of good news, as well as a warner; but most people do not know.

29. And they Say: "When is this promise, if you are truthful?"

30. Say: "You have an appointed day, which you cannot delay by one hour, nor advance."

31. And those who rejected have said: "We will not believe in this Quran, nor in what is already with him." And if you could but see these transgressors when they stand before their Lord, how they will accuse one another back and forth. Those who were weak will say to those who were mighty: "If it were not for you, we would have been believers!"

32. Those who were mighty will say to those who were weak: "Did we turn you away from the guidance after it had come to you? No, it was you who were criminal."

33. And those who were weak will say to those who were mighty: "No, it was your scheming night and day, when you commanded us to reject God, and to set up equals to Him." And they will be filled with regret, when they see the retribution. And We will place shackles around the necks of those who rejected. Are they not being requited for what they used to do?

34. And We do not send a warner to any town, except its carefree ones would Say: "We reject what you have been sent with."

35. And they said: "We have more wealth and more children, and we will not be punished."

36. Say: "My Lord gives provisions to whomever He wishes, or He restricts them, but most people do not know."

37. And it is not your money or your children that will bring you closer to Us, but only those who believe and do good work, they will receive double the reward for their works, and they will reside in the high dwellings in peace.

38. As for those who sought against Our revelations, they will be brought to the retribution.

39. Say: "My Lord gives provisions for whom He wishes of His servants and He restricts. And anything you spend, He will replace it; and He is the Best of providers."

40. And on the Day when We gather them all, then We will say to the Angels: "Was it you that these people used to worship?"

41. They will Say: "Be You glorified. You are our Lord, not them. No, most of them were worshiping the Jinn; most were believers to them."

42. So today, none of you can help or harm one another. And We will say to the transgressors: "Taste the retribution of the Fire that you used to deny."

43. And when Our clear revelations were recited to them, they said: "This is but a man who wants to turn you away from what your parents were worshiping." And they also said: "This is nothing but a fabricated lie." And those who disbelieved say of the truth when it has come to them: "This is nothing but evident magic!"

44. We had not given to them any Scriptures to study, nor did We send to them before you any warner.

45. And those before them had also denied, while they did not reach one tenth of what We have given to this generation, so they denied My messengers, how severe was My retribution!

46. Say: "I advise you to do one thing: that you stand to God, in pairs or as individuals, then reflect. There is no madness in your friend, he is only a warner to you in the face of a severe retribution."

47. Say: "I have not asked you for any wage; you can keep it. My wage is from God, and He is witness over all things."

48. Say: "My Lord rebuts with the truth. He is the Knower of all secrets."

49. Say: "The truth has come; while falsehood can neither initiate anything, nor resurrect."

50. Say: "If I stray, then I stray to my own loss. And if I am guided, then it is because of what my Lord inspired to me. He is Hearer, Near."

51. And if you could but see, when they will be terrified with no escape, and they will be taken from a place that is near.

52. And they will Say: "We believe in it," but it will be far too late.
53. And they had rejected it in the past; and they conjectured about the unseen from a place far off.
54. And they will be separated from what they had desired, as was done for their counterparts before. They have been in grave doubt.

Chapter 35

بسم الله الرحمن الرحيم

In the name of God, the Almighty, the Merciful.

1. Praise be to God, Initiator of the heavens and the Earth; maker of the Angels as messengers with wings in two's, and three's, and four's. He increases in the creation as He wishes. God is able to do all things.

2. Whatever mercy God opens for the people, none can stop it. And what He holds back none can send it other than He. And He is the Noble, the Wise.

3. O mankind, remember God's blessing upon you. Is there any creator other than God who provides for you from the heaven and the Earth? There is no god besides Him, so why do you deviate?

4. And if they deny you, then also messengers before you have been denied. And to God will all matters be returned.

5. O mankind, God's promise is the truth; therefore, do not be overwhelmed by this worldly life, and do not let arrogance overwhelm you from God.

6. The devil is an enemy to you, so treat him as an enemy. He only invites his faction to be the dwellers of Hell.

7. Those who reject will have a painful retribution, and those who believe and do good works they will have a forgiveness and a great reward.

8. The one whose evil work is adorned and he sees it as being good. God thus misguides whom he wills, and He guides whom He wills. So do not let yourself grieve over them. God is fully aware of what they are doing.

9. And God is the One who sends the winds so it stirs up a cloud, then We drive it to a town that is dead, and We revive with it the land after it had died. Such is the resurrection.

10. Whosoever is seeking pride, then know that to God belongs all Pride. To Him ascend the good words, and they are exalted by the good deeds. And as

for those who scheme evil, they will have a painful retribution, and their scheming will fail.

11. And God created you from dust, then from a seed, then He made you into pairs. And no female becomes pregnant, nor gives birth, without His knowledge. Nor does anyone have his life extended, or his life is shortened, except in a record. This is easy for God.

12. Nor are the two seas the same. One is fresh and palatable, good to drink, while the other is salty and bitter. And from each of them you eat tender meat, and you extract jewellery to wear. And you see the ships sailing through them, seeking His provisions; and perhaps you may be appreciative.

13. He merges the night into the day, and merges the day into the night. And He has committed the sun and the moon, each runs for a predetermined period. Such is God your Lord; to Him is the sovereignty. And as for those whom you call on besides Him, they do not possess a seed's shell.

14. If you call on them, they cannot hear you. And even if they hear you, they cannot respond to you. And on the Day of Resurrection, they will reject your idolatry. And none can inform you like an Expert.

15. O mankind, you are the poor when it comes to God, while God is the Rich, the Praiseworthy.

16. If He wishes, He could do away with you and He would bring a new creation.

17. And this is not difficult for God.

18. And none can carry the load of another, and even if it calls on another to bear part of its load, no other can carry any part of it, even if they were related. You will only be able to warn those who fear their Lord while unseen, and they honour the oath of allegiance. And whoever contributes, is contributing for himself. And to God is the final destiny.

19. The blind and the seer are not equal.

20. Nor are the darkness and the light.

21. Nor are the shade and the heat.

22. Nor equal are the living and the dead; God causes whomever He wills to hear. And you cannot make those who are in the graves hear.

23. You are but a warner.

24. We have sent you with the truth, a bearer of good news, and a warner. There is not a nation but a warner came to it.

25. And if they deny you, then those before them have also denied. Their messengers went to them with proofs, and the Psalms, and the enlightening Scripture.

26. But then I seized those who rejected; how terrible was My retribution!
27. Do you not see that God sends down water from the sky, thus We produce with it fruits of various colors? And of the mountains are peaks that are white, red, or some other color and intense black.
28. And from the people, and the animals, and the livestock, are various colors. As such, only the knowledgeable among God's servants reverence Him. God is Noble, Forgiving.
29. Surely, those who recite God's Scripture, and honour the oath of allegiance, and spend secretly and openly from what We have provided them, they are seeking a trade that can never lose.
30. He will give them their recompense, and He will increase them from His blessings. He is Forgiving, Appreciative.
31. And what We inspired to you from the Scripture, it is the truth, authenticating what is present. God is Expert of His servants, Seer.
32. Then We inherited the Scripture to those whom We selected from Our servants. Subsequently, some of them wronged their souls, and others upheld it partly, while others were eager to work righteousness in accordance with God's will; this is the greatest triumph.
33. They will enter the gardens of Eden, where they will be adorned with bracelets of gold and pearls, and their garments in it will be of silk.
34. And they will Say: "Praise be to God who took away our sorrow. Our Lord is Forgiving, Appreciative."
35. "The One who admitted us into the abode of eternal bliss, out of His grace. In it, no boredom touches us, nor does any fatigue."
36. As for those who have rejected, for them is the fire of Hell, where they do not terminate and die, nor is its retribution ever reduced for them. It is such that We requite every rejecter.
37. And they will scream in it: "Our Lord, let us out, and we will work righteousness instead of the works we used to do." Did We not give you a long life so that he who would remember would take heed, and a warner came to you? Therefore, taste, for the transgressors will have no supporter.
38. God knows the unseen of the heavens and the Earth. He is knowledgeable of what is even inside the chests.
39. He is the One who made you successors on the Earth. Subsequently, whoever disbelieves, then to him is his disbelief. And the disbelief of the disbelievers only increases their Lord's abhorrence towards them. The disbelief of the disbelievers only increases their loss.

40. Say: "Do you see the partners whom you have called on besides God? Show me what they have created on Earth. Or do they possess any partnership in the heavens? Or have We given them a scripture wherein they are taking knowledge from it? Indeed, what the transgressors promise one another is no more than arrogance."

41. God is the One who holds the heavens and the Earth, lest they cease to exist. And they would certainly cease to exist if anyone else were to hold them after Him. He is Compassionate, Forgiving.

42. And they swore by God in their strongest oaths, that if a warner came to them, they would be the most guided of all nations, but when a warner came to them, it only increased their aversion!

43. Arrogance on Earth, and evil scheming. And the evil schemes only backfire on those who scheme them. Were they expecting anything different from the ways used on the people of the past? You will not find any change in God's way, and you will not find any bypass to God's way.

44. Did they not roam the Earth and note how was the consequence for those who were before them? And they were even more powerful than they in strength. But nothing can deter God be it in the heavens, or in the Earth. He is Knowledgeable, Omnipotent.

45. And if God were to punish the people for what they have earned, He would not leave a single creature standing. But He delays them to a predetermined time. Then, when their time comes, then God is Seer of His servants.

Chapter 36

بسم الله الرحمن الرحيم

In the name of God, the Almighty, the Merciful.

1. Y.S.
2. And the Quran of wisdom.
3. You are one of the messengers.
4. Upon a straight path.
5. The revelation of the Most Honourable, the Merciful.
6. To warn a people whose fathers were not warned, for they are unaware.
7. The retribution has been deserved by most of them, for they do not believe.
8. We have placed shackles around their necks, up to their chins, so that they are forced in direction.
9. And We have placed a barrier in front of them, and a barrier behind them, thus We shielded them so they cannot see.
10. And whether you warn them or do not warn them, they will not believe.
11. You can only warn him who follows the reminder, and reverences the Almighty while unseen. Give him good news of forgiveness and a generous reward.
12. It is indeed Us who resurrect the dead, and We record what they have done and left behind. And everything We have counted in a clear ledger.
13. And cite for them the example of the people of the town, when the messengers came to it.
14. Where We sent two to them, but they disbelieved in them, so We supported them with a third one, thus they said: "We are messengers to you."
15. They replied: "You are but human beings like us, and the Almighty did not send down anything, you are only telling lies."
16. They said: "Our Lord knows that we have been sent to you."

17. "And we are only required to give a clear delivery."
18. They replied: "We have welcomed you better than you deserve. If you do not cease, we will stone you, and you will receive a painful retribution from us!"
19. They said: "Keep your welcome with you, for you have been reminded. Indeed, you are transgressing people."
20. And a man came running from the farthest part of the city, saying: "O my people, follow the messengers."
21. "Follow those who do not ask you for any wage, and are guided."
22. "And why should I not serve the One who initiated me, and to Him is your ultimate return?"
23. "Shall I take gods besides Him? If the Almighty intends any harm for me, their intercession cannot help me in the least, nor can they save me."
24. "Then I would be clearly astray."
25. "I have believed in your Lord, so listen to me!"
26. It was said: "Enter Paradise." He said "Oh, how I wish my people only knew!"
27. "Of what my Lord has forgiven me, and made me of the honoured ones."
28. And We did not send down upon his people after him soldiers from the sky; for there was no need to send them down.
29. For all it took was one scream, whereupon they were stilled.
30. What sorrow for the servants. For every time a messenger went to them, they would ridicule him.
31. Did they not see how many generations We destroyed before them, do they not go back to them?
32. And how every one of them will be summoned before Us.
33. And a sign for them is the dead land, We revive it and produce from it seeds from which they eat.
34. And We made in it gardens of date palms, and grapes, and We cause springs to gush forth therein.
35. So that they may eat from its fruits, and what they manufacture with their own hands. Would they be thankful?
36. Praise be to the One who created all pairs from what the Earth sprouts out and from themselves, and from what they do not know.
37. And a sign for them is the night, We remove the daylight from it, whereupon they are in darkness.
38. And the sun runs to a specific destination, such is the design of the Noble, the Knowledgeable.

39. And the moon We have measured it to appear in stages, until it returns to being like an old curved sheath.
40. The sun is not required to overtake the moon, nor will the night precede the day; each of them is swimming in its own orbit.
41. And a sign for them is that We carried their ancestors on the charged Ship.
42. And We created for them of its similarity, to ride in.
43. And if We wished, We could drown them, so that their screaming would not be heard, nor could they be saved.
44. Except through a mercy from Us, and as an enjoyment for awhile.
45. And when they are told: "Be aware of your present and your past, that you may attain mercy."
46. And no matter what sign comes to them from the signs of their Lord, they turn away from it.
47. And when they are told: "Spend from what God has provisioned you." Those who reject say to those who believe: "Shall we feed those whom God could feed, if He so willed? You are clearly misguided!"
48. And they Say: "When is this promise to come, if you are truthful?"
49. They will not realize it when one scream overwhelms them, while they dispute.
50. They will not even be able to leave a will, nor will they be able to return to their people.
51. And the horn will be blown, whereupon they will rise from the graves massing towards their Lord.
52. They will Say: "Woe to us. Who has resurrected us from our resting place? This is what the Almighty had promised. The messengers were truthful!"
53. It only took one scream, whereupon they are summoned before Us.
54. On this Day, no soul will be wronged in the least. You will be recompensed precisely for whatever you did.
55. The dwellers of Paradise will be, on that Day, joyfully busy.
56. Both them and their spouses, they will be shaded, reclining on high furnishings.
57. They will have fruits therein; they will have in it whatever they ask for.
58. Saying of: "Peace" from a Merciful Lord.
59. "As for you, O criminals, you are singled out."
60. "Did I not pledge to you, O Children of Adam, that you should not serve the devil for he is your most ardent enemy?"
61. "And that you should serve Me? That is a straight path."

62. "He has misled mountain loads of you. Did you not possess any understanding?"

63. "This is Hell that you have been promised!"

64. "Burn in it today, as a consequence of your rejection."

65. Today, We shall seal their mouths, and their hands will speak to Us, and their feet will bear witness to everything they had done.

66. And if We wished, We can blind their eyes, and they would race towards the path, but how would they see?

67. And if We wished, We can freeze them in their place; thus, they can neither move forward, nor go back.

68. And for whomever We grant a long life, We weaken him in body. Do they not understand?

69. And We did not teach him poetry, nor does he need it. This is a reminder and a clear Quran.

70. To warn those who are alive, and so that the retribution will be deserved by the rejecters.

71. Did they not see that We created for them with Our own hands livestock which they own?

72. And they were subdued by Us for them. So some they ride, and some they eat.

73. And they have in them other benefits, as well as drinks. Would they not be appreciative?

74. And they have taken besides God other gods, perhaps they will help them!

75. They cannot help them. And they become to them as foot-soldiers.

76. So do not be saddened by what they say. We are fully aware of what they conceal and what they declare.

77. Has man not seen that We have created him from a seed, that he would become a clear enemy?

78. And he cites an example for Us, while forgetting his own creation! He says: "Who can resurrect the bones while they are dust?"

79. Say: "The One who made them in the first place will resurrect them. He is fully aware of every creation."

80. The One who initiated for you a forest fire, by which you learned to light.

81. Is not the One who created the heavens and the Earth able to create the like of them? Yes indeed; He is the Creator, the Knowledgeable.

82. His command, when He wants anything, is to say to it: "Be" and it is!

83. Therefore, praise be to the One in whose Hand is the sovereignty of all things, and to Him you will be returned.

Chapter 37

بسم الله الرحمن الرحيم

In the name of God, the Almighty, the Merciful.

1. By the columns in formation.
2. By the drivers of clouds.
3. By the remembrance which follows.
4. Your god is indeed One.
5. The Lord of the heavens and the Earth, and what lies between them, and Lord of the easts.
6. We have adorned this universe with the decoration of planets.
7. And to guard against every rebellious devil.
8. They cannot listen to the command up high; and they are bombarded from every side.
9. Outcasts; they will have an eternal retribution.
10. Any of them who snatches something away, he is pursued by a piercing flame.
11. So ask them: "Are they the more powerful creation, or the others We created?" We have created them from sticky mud.
12. While you were awed, they simply mocked.
13. And when they are reminded, they do not care.
14. And when they see a sign, they make fun of it.
15. And they said: "This is nothing but evident magic!"
16. "Can it be that after we die and become dust and bones, that we are resurrected?"
17. "What about our fathers of old?"
18. Say: "Yes, and then you will be humiliated."
19. All it takes is one sound, then they will be staring.

20. And they said: "Woe to us, this is the Day of Judgment!"
21. This is the Day of decisiveness that you used to deny.
22. Gather the transgressors, and their mates, and all they worshiped.
23. Beside God, and guide them to the path of Hell.
24. And let them stand and be questioned:
25. "Why do you not support one another?"
26. No, for today they have totally given up.
27. And some of them came to each other, questioning.
28. They said: "You used to entice us from the right side."
29. They replied: "No, it was you who were not believers."
30. "And we never had any power over you, but you were a wicked people."
31. "So our Lord's decree is now upon us, that we will suffer."
32. "We misled you, because we were astray."
33. Then, on that Day they will all share in the retribution.
34. This is how We deal with the criminals.
35. When it was said to them: "There is no god except God," they would be arrogant.
36. And they would Say: "Shall we leave our gods because of a crazy poet?"
37. No, he has come with the truth and he has confirmed the messengers.
38. You will taste the greatest of retribution.
39. And you are only recompensed for what you have done.
40. Except for God's servants who are faithful.
41. For them will be known provisions.
42. Fruits, and they will be honoured.
43. In the gardens of bliss.
44. On furnishings which are opposite one another.
45. They will be served with cups of pure drinks.
46. Clear and tasty for the drinkers.
47. There is no bitterness therein, nor will they tire from it.
48. And with them are attendants with wide eyes and a splendid look.
49. They are like fragile eggs.
50. So then they approached one another, questioning.
51. One of them said: "I used to have a friend."
52. "Who use to Say: "Are you among those who believe in this?"
53. "That if we die and turn into dust and bones, that we would be called to account?""
54. He said: "Can anyone find him?"
55. So when he looked, he saw him in the midst of Hell.

56. He said: "By God, you nearly ruined me!"
57. "And had it not been for my Lord's blessing, I would have been with you."
58. "Are we then not going to die,"
59. "Except for our first death, and we will not be punished?"
60. Such is the greatest triumph.
61. For this let those who will work endeavour.
62. Is that a better destination, or the tree of Bitterness?
63. We have made it a punishment for the transgressors.
64. It is a tree that grows in the midst of Hell.
65. Its shoots are like the devils' heads.
66. They will eat from it, so that their bellies are filled up.
67. Then they will have with it a drink of boiling liquid.
68. Then they will be returned to Hell.
69. They had found their parents astray.
70. So they too have hastened in their footsteps.
71. Most of the previous generations have strayed before them.
72. And We had sent to them warners.
73. Thus note the consequences for those who were warned.
74. Except for God's servants who are faithful.
75. And Noah had called upon Us, for We are the best to respond.
76. And We saved him and his family from the great disaster.
77. And We made his progeny the one that remained.
78. And We kept his history for those who came later.
79. Peace be upon Noah among the worlds.
80. It is such that We reward the righteous.
81. He is of Our believing servants.
82. Then We drowned the others.
83. And from among his descendants was Abraham.
84. For he came to his Lord with a pure heart.
85. When he said to his father and his people: "What are you worshiping?"
86. "Is it fabricated gods, instead of God, that you want?"
87. "What do you say of the Lord of the worlds?"
88. Then he looked towards the stars.
89. And he said: "I am ill!"
90. So they turned away from him and departed.
91. He then went to their idols and said: "Can you not eat?"
92. "What is the matter, you do not speak?"
93. So he then turned on them, striking with his hand.

94. Then they approached him outraged.
95. He said: "Do you worship what you carve?"
96. "While God has created you, and all that you make!"
97. They said: "Build for him a structure, and then throw him into its fire."
98. So they wanted to harm him, but We made them the losers.
99. And he said: "I am going to my Lord; He will guide me."
100. "My Lord, grant me from among the righteous."
101. So We gave him good news of a compassionate child.
102. And when he grew enough to work with him, he said: "My son, I am seeing in a dream that I am sacrificing you. What do you think?" He said: "O my father, do what you are commanded to do. You will find me, God willing, patient."
103. So when they both had surrendered, and he put his forehead down.
104. And We called him: "O Abraham,"
105. "You have believed the vision." It was such that We rewarded the righteous.
106. Surely, this was an exacting test.
107. And We ransomed him with a great animal sacrifice.
108. And We kept his history for those who came later.
109. Peace be upon Abraham.
110. It is thus that We reward the righteous.
111. He was of Our believing servants.
112. And We gave him the good news of the coming of Isaac, a prophet from among the righteous.
113. And We blessed him and Isaac. And from among their progeny, some are righteous, and some are clearly wicked.
114. And indeed, We have given Our grace to Moses and Aaron.
115. And We saved them and their people from the great disaster.
116. And We supported them, so that they became the winners.
117. And We gave both the clear Scripture.
118. And We guided them to the straight path.
119. And We kept their history for those who came later.
120. Peace be upon Moses and Aaron.
121. We thus reward the righteous.
122. Both of them were among Our believing servants.
123. And Elias was one of the messengers.
124. When he said to his people: "Would you not be righteous?"
125. "Would you call on Ba'al and forsake the best Creator?"
126. "God is your Lord, and the Lord of your fathers of old!"

127.But they denied him. Thus they were called to account.

128.Except for God's devoted servants.

129.And We kept his history for those who came later.

130.Peace be upon the family of Elias.

131.We thus reward the righteous.

132.He was one of our believing servants.

133.And Lot was one of the messengers.

134.When We saved him and all his family.

135.Except an old woman who remained.

136.Then, We destroyed the rest.

137.And you pass by their ruins in the morning;

138.And in the night. Do you not understand?

139.And Jonah was one of the messengers.

140.When he escaped to the charged ship.

141.And he was guilty, so he became among the losers.

142.Thus a whale swallowed him, and he was the one to blame.

143.And had it not been that he was one of those who implored,

144.He would have stayed in its belly until the Day of Resurrection.

145.So We threw him on the shore while he was sick.

146.And We caused seaweed to grow on him.

147.And We sent him to a hundred thousand, or more.

148.And they believed, so We gave them enjoyment for a time.

149.So ask them: "Are the daughters for your Lord, while the sons are for them?"

150.Or did We create the Angels as females while they witnessed?

151.Indeed, it is out of their falsehood that they Say:

152."The son of God." And they are liars.

153.Has He chosen the daughters over the sons?

154.What is wrong with you, how do you judge?

155.Will you not remember?

156.Or do you have a clear proof?

157.Bring forth your scripture, if you are truthful.

158.And they invented a kinship between Him and the Jinn. But the Jinn know that they will be gathered.

159.God be glorified from what they describe.

160.Except for God's servants who are faithful.

161.As for you and what you worship.

162.You cannot lead away from Him.

163.Except those who are destined to Hell.

164. Every one of us has a destined place.
165. And we are the ones who are in columns.
166. And we are the ones that glorify.
167. And they used to Say:
168. "If only we had received a reminder from the previous generations,"
169. "We would have surely been God's loyal servants."
170. But they rejected it. They will come to know.
171. Our word had been decreed to Our servants who were sent.
172. That they would be made victorious.
173. And that Our soldiers are the winners.
174. So turn away from them for awhile.
175. And observe them; for they will see.
176. Do they seek to hasten Our retribution?
177. Then, when it descends into their courtyard, evil will be the morning, for they have already been warned.
178. And turn away from them for awhile.
179. And observe; for they will see.
180. Glory be to your Lord, the Lord of greatness, for what they have described.
181. And peace be upon the messengers.
182. And praise be to God, Lord of the worlds.

Chapter 38

بسم الله الرحمن الرحيم

In the name of God, the Almighty, the Merciful.

1. S', and the Quran that contains the remembrance.
2. Indeed, those who have disbelieved are in false pride and defiance.
3. How many a generation have We destroyed before them. And they called out when it was far too late.
4. And they were surprised that a warner has come to them from among themselves. And the rejecters said: "This is a magician, a liar."
5. "Has he made the gods into One god? This is indeed a strange thing!"
6. And the leaders among them went out: "Walk away, and remain patient to your gods. This thing can be turned back."
7. "We never heard of this from the people before us. This is but an innovation."
8. "Has the remembrance been sent down to him, from between all of us!" Indeed, they are doubtful of My reminder. Indeed, they have not yet tasted My retribution.
9. Or do they have the treasures of mercy of your Lord, the Noble, the Grantor.
10. Or do they possess the dominion of the heavens and the Earth, and all that is between them? Then let them bring their own solutions.
11. The opposing troops they have gathered will be defeated.
12. Disbelieving before them were the people of Noah, 'Aad, and Pharaoh with the planks.
13. And Thamud, and the people of Lot, the dwellers of the Woods; such were the opponents.

14. Each of them disbelieved the messengers, therefore My retribution came to be.
15. And what these people are waiting for is a single scream, from which they will not recover.
16. And they said: "Our Lord, hasten for us our punishment, before the Day of Reckoning."
17. Be patient to what they say, and recall Our servant David, the resourceful. He was obedient.
18. We committed the mountains to glorify with him, during dusk and dawn.
19. And the birds were gathered; all were obedient to him.
20. And We strengthened his kingship, and We gave him the wisdom and the ability to make sound judgement.
21. Did the news come to you of the disputing party who came over into the temple enclosure?
22. When they entered upon David, he was startled by them. They said: "Have no fear. We are two who have disputed, and one has wronged the other, so judge between us with truth, and do not wrong us, and guide us to the right path."
23. "This is my brother and he owns ninety nine lambs, while I own one lamb; so he said to me: 'Let me take care of it' and he pressured me."
24. He said: "He has wronged you by asking to combine your lambs with his lambs. And many who mix their properties take advantage of one another, except those who believe and do good works, and these are very few." And David guessed that We had tested him, so he sought forgiveness from his Lord, and fell down kneeling, and repented.
25. So We forgave him in this matter. And for him with Us is a near position, and a beautiful abode.
26. O David, We have made you a successor on Earth. Therefore, you shall judge among the people with truth, and do not follow desire, lest it diverts you from the path of God. Indeed, those who stray off the path of God will have a severe retribution for forgetting the Day of Reckoning.
27. And We did not create the heaven and the Earth, and everything between them, in vain. Such is the thinking of those who rejected. Therefore, woe to those who have rejected from the Fire.
28. Or shall We treat those who believe and do good works as We treat those who make corruption on Earth? Or shall We treat the righteous as the wicked?

29. A Scripture that We have sent down to you, that is blessed, so that they may reflect upon its verses, and so that those with intelligence will take heed.

30. And to David We granted Solomon. What an excellent and obedient servant.

31. When, close to dusk, well trained horses were displayed before him.

32. He then said: "I have enjoyed materialism more than I enjoyed the remembrance of my Lord; now the sun has totally set!"

33. "Send them back." He then rubbed their legs and necks.

34. And We tested Solomon and placed a corpse on his throne, but he then repented.

35. He said: "My Lord, forgive me, and grant me a kingship that will never be attained by anyone after me. You are the Grantor."

36. So, We committed the wind to run by his command, raining gently where he directed it.

37. And the devils, building and diving.

38. And others, held by restraints.

39. "This is Our gift, so you may spend or withhold, without any repercussions."

40. And he has deserved a near position with Us, and a wonderful abode.

41. And recall Our servant Job, when he called upon his Lord: "The devil has afflicted me with an illness and pain."

42. "Strike with your foot, here is a cold spring to wash with and to drink."

43. And We restored his family to him along with a group like them, as a mercy from Us; and a reminder for those who possess intelligence.

44. "And take in your hand a bundle and travel with it, and do not break your oath." We found him steadfast. What a good servant! He was obedient.

45. And recall Our servants Abraham, Isaac, and Jacob. They were resourceful, and with vision.

46. We had chosen them to enforce awareness of the Hereafter.

47. And they are with Us of the elite, the best.

48. And recall Ishmael, Elisha, and Isaiah; all are among the best.

49. This is a reminder, and the righteous will have a wonderful abode.

50. The gardens of Eden, whose gates will be open for them.

51. Reclining therein, they will be invited to many fruits and drinks.

52. And with them are attendants with a splendid look and of equal age.

53. This is what you have been promised for the Day of Reckoning.

54. Such is Our provisions, it does not run out.

55. This is so, and for the transgressors is a miserable destiny.

56. Hell is where they burn. What a miserable abode!
57. This is so, and let them taste a boiling drink and bitter food.
58. And other multitudes that are similar to that.
59. Here is another group to be thrown into Hell with you. "We have no welcome for them, for they shall burn in the Fire."
60. They said: "No, you are the ones without welcome. It was you who misled us, so here is the result!"
61. They said: "Our Lord, whoever brought this upon us, then double their retribution in the Fire!"
62. And they said: "Why do we not see some men whom we used to count among the wicked?"
63. "Did we mock them erroneously, or have our eyes failed to find them?"
64. Surely, this is in truth the feuding of the people of Hell.
65. Say: "I am but a warner; and there is no god besides God, the One, the Supreme."
66. "The Lord of the heavens and the Earth, and everything between them; the Noble, the Forgiving."
67. Say: "It is an awesome news."
68. "From which you turn away."
69. "I had no knowledge of the command up high, that they had quarrelled."
70. "It is only inspired to me that I am a clear warner."
71. For your Lord said to the Angels: "I am creating a human being from clay."
72. "So when I have evolved him, and breathed into him from My spirit, then you shall yield to him."
73. The Angels yielded, all of them,
74. Except Satan; he turned arrogant, and became one of the rejecters.
75. He said: "O Satan, what prevented you from yielding to what I have created by My hands? Are you too arrogant? Or are you one of those exalted?"
76. He said: "I am better than he; You created me from fire, and created him from clay."
77. He said: "Therefore exit from it, you are outcast."
78. "And My curse will be upon you until the Day of Judgment."
79. He said: "My Lord, respite me till the Day they are resurrected."
80. He said: "You are respited."
81. "Until the appointed Day."
82. He said: "By Your majesty, I will mislead them all."
83. "Except for Your servants who are loyal."
84. He said: "The truth, and the truth is what I say."

85. "That I will fill Hell with you and all those who follow you."
86. Say: "I do not ask you for any wage, nor am I a fraud."
87. "It is but a reminder for the worlds."
88. "And you will come to know its news after awhile."

Chapter 39

بسم الله الرحمن الرحيم

In the name of God, the Almighty, the Merciful.

1. The sending down of the Scripture is from God, the Noble, the Wise.
2. We have sent down to you the Scripture with truth, so serve God while devoting the system to Him.
3. Absolutely, to God is the true system. And those who set up allies besides Him: "We only serve them so that they may bring us closer to God." God will judge between them in what they dispute. Surely, God does not guide him who is a liar, a rejecter.
4. If God wished to take a son, He could have exalted from among His creation what He pleases. Be He glorified; He is God, the One, the Supreme.
5. He created the heavens and the Earth with truth. He rolls the night over the day, and He rolls the day over the night. And He committed the sun and the moon, each running for an appointed term. Absolutely, He is the Noble, the Forgiving.
6. He created you from one person, then He made from it its mate. And He sent down to you eight pairs of the livestock. He creates you in the wombs of your mothers, a creation after a creation in three darkness's. Such is God your Lord. To Him belongs the sovereignty. There is no god besides Him. How is it then you deviate?
7. If you reject, then know that God is in no need of you, and He dislikes rejection for His servants. And if you are appreciative, He is pleased for you. And none shall bear the burdens of another. Then to your Lord is your return, and He will inform you of everything you had done. He is fully aware of what is inside the chests.

8. And when the human being is afflicted with adversity, he implores his Lord, turning in repentance to Him. But then, when He grants him a blessing from Him, he forgets his previous imploring, and sets up equals with God, in order to mislead others from His path. Say: "Enjoy your rejection for a while; for you are of the dwellers of the Fire."

9. Is one better who is meditating during the night, prostrating and standing, fearing the Hereafter, and seeking the mercy of his Lord? Say: "Are those who know equal to those who do not know?" Only those who possess understanding will remember.

10. Say: "O My servants who believed, be aware of your Lord." For those who worked righteousness in this world will be a good reward, and God's Earth is spacious. Those who steadfastly persevere will receive their recompense fully, without reckoning.

11. Say: "I have been commanded to serve God, devoting the system to Him."

12. "And I was commanded to be the first of those who submit."

13. Say: "I fear, if I disobeyed my Lord, the retribution of a great Day."

14. Say: "God is the One I serve, devoting my system to Him."

15. "Therefore, serve whatever you wish besides Him." Say: "The losers are those who lose their souls, and their families, on the Day of Resurrection. Indeed, such is the real loss."

16. They will have coverings of fire from above them and below them. It is as such that God makes His servants fearful: "O My servants, you shall reverence Me."

17. And for those who avoid serving evil, and turn to God in repentance, for them are glad tidings. So give the good news to My servants.

18. The ones who listen to what is being said, and then follow the best of it. These are the ones whom God has guided, and these are the ones who possess intelligence.

19. As for those who have deserved the retribution; can you save those who are in the Fire?

20. But those who reverence their Lord, they will have dwellings constructed upon dwellings, with rivers flowing beneath them. God's promise, and God does not break the promise.

21. Do you not see that God sends down water from the sky, and causes it to become streams through the land, then He produces with it plants of various colors, then they grow until they turn yellow, then He makes them dry and broken? In this is a reminder for those of understanding.

22. If God opens a person's chest to submission, then he will be on a light from his Lord. So woe to those whose hearts are hardened against remembering God. They have gone far astray.

23. God has sent down the best narration, a Scripture that is similar with two paths. The skins of those who reverence their Lord shiver from it, then their skins and their hearts soften up to the remembrance of God. Such is God's guidance; He guides with it whoever He wills. And for whomever God misguides, then none can guide him.

24. As for he who saves his face from the terrible retribution on the Day of Resurrection; and it will be said to the transgressors: "Taste for what you have earned."

25. Those before them have denied, and thus the retribution came to them from where they did not perceive.

26. So God made them taste the humiliation in this worldly life, but the retribution in the Hereafter is far greater, if only they knew.

27. And We have cited for the people in this Quran from every example, that they may take heed.

28. A compilation in Arabic, without any crookedness, that they may be righteous.

29. God cites the example of a man who has partners that dispute with each other, and a man who has given to dealing with only one man. Are they the same? Praise be to God; most of them do not know.

30. You will die, and they will die.

31. Then, on the Day of Resurrection, you will quarrel at your Lord.

32. Who then is more wicked than one who lies about God, and denies the truth when it comes to him? Is there not in Hell an abode for the rejecters?

33. And those who came with the truth, and believed in it, these are the righteous.

34. They shall have what they wish at their Lord. Such is the reward for the good doers.

35. So that God may cancel for them the worst that they did, and He may recompense them their reward for the best of what they used to do.

36. Is God not enough for His servant? And they frighten you with others beside Him. And whomever God sends astray, then for him there will be no guide.

37. And whomever God guides, then there will be none that can mislead him. Is God not Noble, with Vengeance?

38. And if you ask them: "Who created the heavens and the Earth?", they will Say: "God." Say: "Do you see what you call on besides God, If God wanted

any harm for me, can they alleviate His harm? Or if He wanted a mercy for me, can they hold back his mercy?" Say: "God is sufficient for me; in Him those who trust shall put their trust."

39. Say: "O my people, work according to your way, and I will work. You will come to know."

40. "To whom the humiliating retribution will come, and on whom descends the eternal retribution."

41. We have sent down to you the Scripture for the people with truth. Then, whoever is guided is guided for himself, and whoever goes astray goes astray to his own loss. And you are not a keeper over them.

42. God takes the souls when they die, and during their sleep. He then keeps those that have been overtaken by death, and He sends the others back until a predetermined time. In that are signs for a people who will think.

43. Or have they taken intercessors besides God? Say: "What if they do not possess any power, nor understanding?"

44. Say: "To God belong all intercessions." To Him belongs the sovereignty of the heavens and the Earth, then to Him you will be returned.

45. And when God Alone is mentioned, the hearts of those who do not believe in the Hereafter are filled with aversion; and when others are mentioned beside Him, they rejoice!

46. Say: "Our god, Initiator of the heavens and the Earth, Knower of the unseen and the seen, You will judge between Your servants regarding what they disputed in."

47. And if those who transgressed owned everything on Earth, and its equivalent again with it, they would ransom it to avoid the terrible retribution on the Day of Resurrection. They will be shown by God what they did not expect.

48. And the sinful works they had earned will be shown to them, and they will be surrounded by that which they used to mock!

49. So when the human is touched by adversity, he implores Us, then when We bestow a blessing upon him, he says: "I attained this because of knowledge I had!" Indeed, it is a test, but most of them do not know.

50. Those before them have said the same thing, yet what they earned did not help them in the least.

51. So, they suffered the evil of what they had earned. And those who transgressed from among these here will suffer the evil of what they earned; they cannot escape.

52. Do they not realise that God spreads the provision for whomever He chooses, and withholds? In that are signs for a people who believe.

53. Say: "O My servants who transgressed against themselves, do not despair of God's mercy. For God forgives all sins. He is the Forgiver, the Merciful."

54. And repent to your Lord, and submit to Him, before the retribution comes to you. Then you cannot be helped.

55. And follow the best of what has been sent down to you from your Lord, before the retribution comes to you suddenly when you least expect it.

56. Lest a soul will Say: "How sorry I am for disregarding God's path; and I was certainly one of those who mocked."

57. Or Say: "Had God guided me, I would have been among the righteous."

58. Or say, when it sees the retribution: "If only I could have another chance, I would be among the good doers."

59. Yes indeed, My revelations came to you, but you denied them and turned arrogant, and became one of the rejecters.

60. And on the Day of Resurrection you will see those who lied about God their faces will be blackened. Is there not an abode in Hell for the arrogant ones?

61. And God will save those who were righteous as their reward. No harm will touch them, nor will they grieve.

62. God is the Creator of all things, and He is Guardian over all things.

63. To Him belongs the keys of the heavens and the Earth. And those who rejected God's revelations, they are the losers.

64. Say: "Do you order me to serve other than God, O you ignorant ones?"

65. And He has inspired to you and to those before you, that if you set up partners, He will nullify all your work, and you will be of the losers.

66. Therefore, you shall serve God, and be among the appreciative.

67. And they have not given God His true worth; and the whole Earth is within His fist on the Day of Resurrection, and the heavens will be folded in His right hand. Be He glorified; He is much too high above what they set up.

68. And the horn will be blown, whereupon everyone in the heavens and the Earth will be struck unconscious, except those spared by God. Then it will be blown another time, whereupon they will all rise up, looking.

69. And the Earth will shine with the light of its Lord, and the record will be placed, and the prophets and the witnesses will be brought forth; and it will then be judged between them with truth, and they will not be wronged.

70. And every soul will be paid for whatever it did, for He is fully aware of everything they have done.

71. And those who rejected will be driven to Hell in groups. When they reach it, and its gates are opened, its guards will say to them: "Did you not receive messengers from among you, who recited to you the revelations of your

Lord, and warned you about meeting this Day?" They said: "Yes, but the promise of retribution was destined to be upon the rejecters."

72. It was said: "Enter the gates of Hell, wherein you will abide. What a miserable destiny for the arrogant."

73. And those who reverenced their Lord will be driven to Paradise in groups. When they reach it, and its gates are opened, its guards will say to them: "Peace be upon you. You have done well, so enter to abide herein."

74. And they said: "Praise be to God who has fulfilled His promise to us, and He made us inherit the Earth, enjoying Paradise as we please. What a beautiful recompense for the workers!"

75. And you will see the Angels surrounding the throne, glorifying the praise of their Lord. And it will be judged between them with truth, and it will be said: "Praise be to God, Lord of the worlds"

Chapter 40

In the name of God, the Almighty, the Merciful.

1. H.M.
2. The revelation of the Scripture is from God, the Noble, the Knowledgeable.
3. Forgiver of sins, and acceptor of repentance, severe in retribution, with ability to reach. There is no god other than Him, to Him is the ultimate destiny.
4. None dispute in God's revelations except those who have rejected. So do not be impressed by their influence through the land.
5. Denial had come before them from the people of Noah and the opponents after them, and every nation plotted against their messenger to seize him, and they disputed by means of falsehood to defeat with it the truth. So I took them; how then was My punishment!
6. And as such, the word of your Lord has come to pass upon those who rejected, that they are the dwellers of the Fire.
7. Those who carry the throne and all those around it glorify the praise of their Lord, and believe in Him, and they seek forgiveness for those who have believed: "Our Lord, You encompass all things with mercy and knowledge, so forgive those who repented and followed Your path, and spare them the agony of Hell."
8. "Our Lord, and admit them into the gardens of Eden which You had promised for them and for those who did good of their fathers, their spouses, and their progeny. You are the Noble, the Wise."
9. "And save them from the sins. And whomever You save from the sins, on that Day, You have granted him mercy. And that is the greatest triumph."

10. Those who had rejected will be told: "God's abhorrence towards you is greater than your abhorrence towards yourselves, for you were invited to believe, but you chose to reject."

11. They will Say: "Our Lord, You have made us die twice, and You have given us life twice. Now we have confessed our sins. Is there any way out of this path?"

12. This is because when God Alone was mentioned, you rejected, but when partners were associated with Him, you believed. Therefore, the judgment is for God, the Most High, the Great.

13. He is the One who shows you His signs, and He sends down to you provisions from the sky. But none do remember except those who repent.

14. Therefore, call on God while being pure to His system, even if the rejecters dislike it.

15. Possessor of the highest ranks, the One with the Throne. He sends the Spirit with His command upon whom He wills from His servants, that they may warn of the Day of Summoning.

16. The Day when they will be exposed. None of them will hide anything from God. To whom is the sovereignty on this Day? To God, the One, the Supreme.

17. Today, every soul will be recompensed for what it had earned. There will be no injustice today. Truly, God is swift in reckoning.

18. And warn them of the imminent Day, when the hearts will reach the throats, and many will be remorseful. The transgressors will have no friend nor intercessor to be obeyed.

19. He knows what the eyes have seen, and what the chests conceal.

20. And God judges with the truth, while those they call on besides Him do not judge with anything. Certainly, God is the Hearer, the Seer.

21. Have they not roamed the Earth and seen how was the consequence of those who were before them? They used to be stronger than they, and had built more in the land. But God seized them for their sins, and they had no protector against God.

22. That is because their messengers used to come to them with proofs, but they rejected. Thus God seized them; for He is Mighty, severe in punishment.

23. And We had sent Moses with Our signs, and a clear authority.

24. To Pharaoh, Haamaan, and Qaaroon. But they said: "A lying magician!"

25. Then, when the truth came to them from Us, they said: "Kill the children of those who believed with him, and rape their women." But the scheming of the rejecters is always in error.

26. And Pharaoh said: "Leave me to kill Moses, and let him call upon his Lord. I fear that he may change your system, or that he will cause evil to spread throughout the land."

27. And Moses said: "I seek refuge in my Lord and your Lord from every arrogant one who does not believe in the Day of Reckoning"

28. And a believing man from among Pharaoh's people, who had concealed his belief, said: "Will you kill a man simply for saying: 'My Lord is God', and he has come to you with proofs from your Lord? And if he is a liar, then his lie will be upon him, and if he is truthful, then some of what he is promising you will afflict you. Surely, God does not guide any transgressor, liar."

29. "O my people, you have the kingship today throughout the land. But then who will save us against God's torment, should it come to us?" Pharaoh said: "I am showing you that which I see, and I am guiding you in the right path."

30. And the one who believed said: "O my people, I fear for you the same fate as the day of the opponents."

31. "Like the fate of the people of Noah, 'Aad, and Thamud, and those after them. And God does not wish any injustice for the servants."

32. "And, O my people, I fear for you the Day of mutual blaming."

33. "A Day when you will turn around and flee, you will have no protector besides God, and whomever God sends astray, then there is none who can guide him."

34. "And Joseph had come to you before with proofs, but you remained in doubt regarding what he came to you with, until when he died, you said: "God will not send any messenger after him." It is such that God sends astray he who is a transgressor, doubter."

35. Those who dispute about God's signs without any authority that has come to them, it is greatly abhorred with God and with those who believe. God thus seals the hearts of every arrogant tyrant.

36. And Pharaoh said: "O Haamaan, build for me a high platform that I may uncover the secrets."

37. "The secrets of the heavens, and that I can take a look at the god of Moses, although I think he is a liar." Thus the evil works of Pharaoh were made to appear correct to him, and he was blocked from the path. And Pharaoh's scheming brought nothing but regret.

38. And the one who believed said: "O my people, follow me, and I will guide you to the right path."

39. "O my people, this worldly life is but an enjoyment, while the Hereafter is the permanent abode."

40. "Whosoever does an evil deed, he will not be requited except for its equivalent, and whosoever does good, whether male or female and is a believer, then those will be admitted to Paradise, where they will receive provision without limit."

41. "And, O my people, why is it that I invite you to salvation, while you invite me to the Fire!"

42. "You invite me to reject God, and place partners beside Him that I have no knowledge of, and I am inviting you to the Noble, the Forgiver."

43. "There is no doubt that what you invite me to has no basis in this world, nor in the Hereafter. And our ultimate return will be to God, and that the transgressors will be the dwellers of the Fire."

44. "You will come to remember what I am telling you, and I leave my affair in this matter to God; God is the Seer of the servants."

45. So God protected him from the evil of what they schemed, while the people of Pharaoh have incurred the worst retribution.

46. The Fire, which they will be exposed to morning and evening, and on the Day when the Hour is established: "Admit the people of Pharaoh into the most severe of the retribution."

47. And when they argue in Hell, the weak will say to those who were arrogant: "We used to be your followers, can you take from us any portion of the Fire?"

48. Those who were arrogant will Say: "We are all in it together, for God has passed judgment upon the servants."

49. And those who are in Fire will say to the guardians of Hell: "Call upon your Lord to reduce for us the retribution, by just one day!"

50. They will Say: "Did not your messengers come to you with proofs?" They will reply: "Yes." They will Say: "Then call out, for the call of the rejecters is nothing but in vain."

51. We will indeed grant victory to Our messengers and to those who believed in the worldly life, and on the Day when the witnesses will rise.

52. A Day when excuses will be of no help to the transgressors, and they will be cursed, and they will have the worst abode.

53. And We have given Moses the guidance, and We made the Children of Israel inherit the Scripture.

54. A guide and a reminder for those who possess intelligence.

55. So be patient, for the promise of God is true, and seek forgiveness for your sin, and glorify and praise your Lord evening and morning.

56. Surely, those who dispute about God's revelations without any authority given to them, there is nothing but arrogance in their chests, which they do not perceive. Therefore, seek refuge in God; He is the Hearer, the Seer.

57. The creation of the heavens and the Earth is greater than the creation of the people, but most of the people do not know.

58. And not equal are the blind and the seer, nor those who believe and do good works, and those who do evil. Little do you remember.

59. Surely the Hour is coming, there is no doubt in it, but most people do not believe.

60. And your Lord said: "Call on Me and I will respond to you." Surely, those who are too arrogant to serve Me, they will enter Hell, forcibly.

61. God, it is He Who has made for you the night to reside in and the day to see in. Surely, God provides many blessings upon the people, but most people are not thankful.

62. That is God, your Lord, Creator of all things. There is no god except He, so why do you deviate?

63. Thus, those who used to deny God's Revelations were deviated.

64. God is the One who made the Earth a habitat for you, and the sky as a structure, and He designed you, and has perfected your design. And He provided you with good provisions. Such is God your Lord. Most Exalted is God, Lord of the worlds.

65. He is the Living; there is no god except He. So call on Him while devoting the system for Him. Praise be to God, Lord of the worlds.

66. Say: "I have been forbidden from serving those whom you are calling upon besides God, since the proofs have come to me from my Lord. And I have been commanded to submit to the Lord of the worlds."

67. He is the One who created you from dust, then from a seed, then from an embryo, then He brings you out as a child, then He lets you reach your maturity, then you become old, and some of you may pass away before this, and so that you may reach an appointed term, in order that you may understand.

68. He is the One who gives life and causes death. And when He decides upon anything, He simply says to it: "Be" and it is.

69. Did you not see those who dispute about God's revelations, how they have deviated?

70. Those who deny the Scripture, and what We have sent Our messengers with. Therefore, they will come to know.

71. When the collars will be around their necks and in chains they will be dragged off.
72. To the boiling water, then in the Fire they will be burned.
73. Then it will be said to them: "Where are those that you have set up as partners"
74. "Beside God?" They will Say: "They have abandoned us. No, we did not used to call on anything before!" Thus God leads the rejecters astray.
75. That was because you used to gloat on Earth without any right, and for what you used to rejoice.
76. Enter the gates of Hell, abiding therein. What a miserable abode for the arrogant ones.
77. So be patient, for the promise of God is true. Either We will show you some of what We have promised them, or We will let you die, then it is to Us that they will be returned.
78. And We have sent messengers prior to you. Some of them We mentioned to you, and some We did not mention to you. And it was not given to any messenger that he should bring a sign except by God's leave. So, when God's judgment is issued, the matter is decided with truth, and the followers of falsehood will be lost.
79. God is the One who made the livestock for you that you may ride on some of them, and some of them you eat.
80. And you have other benefits in them. And that you may reach by them what is desired in your chests. And on them and on the ships, you are carried.
81. And He shows you His signs. So which of God's signs do you deny?
82. Have they not roamed the Earth and noted the consequences for those who were before them? They used to be greater in number than them and mightier in strength, and they had built more in the land. Yet, all that they had earned could not avail them.
83. Then, when their messengers came to them with clear proofs, they were content with what they already had of the knowledge. And that which they ridiculed became their doom.
84. So when they saw Our might, they said: "We believe in God Alone, and we reject all the partners we used to set up!"
85. But their belief could not help them once they saw Our might. Such is God's way that has been established with His servants. And the rejecters were then totally in loss.

Chapter 41

بسم الله الرحمن الرحيم

In the name of God, the Almighty, the Merciful.

1. H.M.

2. A revelation from the Almighty, the Merciful.

3. A Scripture whose verses are detailed, a compilation in Arabic for a people who know.

4. A bearer of good news, and a warner. But most of them turn away; they do not hear.

5. And they said: "Our hearts are sealed from what you invite us to, and in our ears is a deafness, and there is a barrier between us and you. So do what you will, and so will we."

6. Say: "I am no more than a human being like you. It is inspired to me that your god is One god, therefore you shall be upright towards Him and seek His forgiveness. And woe to those who set up partners."

7. "The ones who do not contribute towards betterment, and with regards to the Hereafter, they are disbelievers."

8. Surely, those who believe and do good works, they will receive recompense without limit.

9. Say: "You are rejecting the One who created the Earth in two days, and you set up equals with Him. This is Lord of the worlds."

10. And He placed in it stabilizers from above it, and He blessed it and established its provisions in four equal days, to satisfy those who ask.

11. Then He settled to the heaven, while it was still smoke, and He said to it, and to the Earth: "Come willingly or unwillingly." They said: "We come willingly."

12. Thus, He then made them into seven universes in two days, and He inspired to every universe its affair. And We adorned the lowest universe with lamps, and for protection. Such is the design of the Noble, the Knowledgeable.

13. But if they turn away, then Say: "I have warned you of a destruction like the destruction of 'Aad and Thamud."

14. When the messengers came to them, publicly and privately: "You shall not serve except God." They said: "Had our Lord willed, He would have sent Angels. We are rejecting what you have been sent with."

15. As for 'Aad, they turned arrogant on Earth, without any right, and they said: "Who is mightier than us in strength?" Did they not see that God, who created them, was mightier than they in strength? And they were denying Our revelations.

16. Consequently, We sent upon them violent wind, for a few miserable day, that We may let them taste the humiliating retribution in this life, and the retribution of the Hereafter is more humiliating; they can never win.

17. And as for Thamud, We provided them with guidance, but they preferred blindness over guidance. Consequently, the blast of humiliating retribution annihilated them, because of what they earned.

18. And We saved those who believed and were righteous.

19. And the Day when the enemies of God will be gathered to the Fire, forcibly.

20. When they come to it, their own hearing, eyes, and skins will bear witness to everything they had done.

21. And they will say to their skins: "Why did you bear witness against us?" They will reply: "God made us speak; He is the One who causes everything to speak. He is the One who created you the first time, and to Him you return."

22. And there was no way you could hide from the testimony of your own hearing, or your eyes, or your skins. In fact, you thought that God was unaware of much of what you do.

23. And this is the kind of thinking about your Lord that has caused you to fail, and thus you became of the losers.

24. If they wait, then the Fire will be their destiny, and if they beg to be excused, they will not be excused.

25. And We assigned to them companions who adorned their present and past actions. Thus, the retribution has been deserved by them the same as previous nations of Jinn and humans; all of them were losers.

26. And those who rejected said: "Do not listen to this Quran and talk over it that you may succeed."

27. We will let those who have rejected taste a severe retribution. And We will recompense them for the evil that they used to do.

28. Such is the recompense for God's enemies; the Fire shall be their eternal abode, as a recompense for their discarding Our revelations.

29. And those who have rejected will Say: "Our Lord, show us those who have misled us from among the Jinn and humans so we can trample them under our feet, and render them the lowliest."

30. Surely, those who have said: "Our Lord is God," then they did right, the Angels will descend upon them: "You shall not fear, nor shall you grieve. Rejoice in the good news of Paradise that you have been promised."

31. "We are your allies in this worldly life and in the Hereafter. In it you will have anything your soul desires, and in it you will have anything you ask for."

32. "A dwelling, from a Forgiver, Merciful."

33. And who is better in saying than one who invites to God, and does good works, and says: "I am one of those who have submitted."

34. Not equal are the good and the bad response. You shall resort to the one which is better. Thus, the one who used to be your enemy, may become your best friend.

35. And none can attain this except those who are patient. And none can attain this except those who are extremely fortunate.

36. And if the devil misleads you in anything, then you shall seek refuge with God. He is the Hearer, the Knowledgeable.

37. And from among His signs are the night and the day, and the sun and the moon. Do not prostrate to the sun, nor the moon; you shall prostrate to God who created them, if it is truly Him you serve.

38. So, if they become arrogant, then those who are with your Lord glorify Him night and day, and they never despair.

39. And from among His signs is that you see the land still, then, as soon as We send down the water upon it, it shakes and grows. Surely, the One who revived it can revive the dead. He is capable of all things.

40. Surely, those who distort Our revelations are not hidden from Us. Is one who is thrown into Hell better, or one who comes secure on the Day of Resurrection? Do whatever you wish; He is Seer of everything you do.

41. Surely, those who have rejected the Reminder when it came to them; and it is an Honourable Scripture.

42. No falsehood could enter it, presently or afterwards; a revelation from a Most Wise, Praiseworthy.

43. What is being said to you is the same that was said to the messengers before you. Your Lord has forgiveness, and a painful retribution.

44. And had We made it a non-Arabic compilation, they would have said: "If only its verses were made clear!" Non-Arabic and Arabic, Say: "For those who believe, it is a guide and healing. As for those who disbelieve, there is a deafness in their ears, and they are blind to it. These will be called from a place far away."

45. And We have given Moses the Scripture, but it was disputed in. And had it not been for your Lord's predetermined decision, they would have been judged immediately. Indeed, they harbour many doubts about it.

46. Whoever does good works does so for his own soul, and whoever works evil shall have the same. Your Lord does not wrong the servants.

47. To Him belongs the knowledge regarding the Hour. And no fruit emerges from its sheath, nor does any female conceive or give birth, except by His knowledge. And on the Day He asks them: "Where are My partners?" They will Say: "By your leave, none of us will testify to that."

48. And they were abandoned by that which they used to call on before, and they realised that there will be no escape.

49. The human being does not tire in imploring for good things. But if adversity touches him, he is disheartened, desperate!

50. And when We let him taste a mercy from Us after adversity had touched him, he will Say: "This was by my actions, and I do not think that the Hour will come to pass. And even if I am returned to my Lord, I will find at Him good things for me." Surely, We will inform the rejecters of all they had done, and We will let them taste the severe retribution.

51. And when We bless the human being, he withdraws and turns away, and when he suffers any adversity, he implores in long prayers!

52. Say: "Do you see if this was from God and then you rejected it? Who is further astray than those who are in opposition?"

53. We will show them Our signs in the horizons, and within themselves, until it becomes clear to them that this is the truth. Is it not enough that your Lord is witness over all things?

54. Indeed, they are in doubt about meeting their Lord; but He is encompassing all things.

Chapter 42

بسم الله الرحمن الرحيم

In the name of God, the Almighty, the Merciful.

1. H.M.
2. A'.S.Q.
3. Similarly, inspiring you and those before you, is God, the Noble, the Wise.
4. To Him belongs all that is in the heavens and all that is in the Earth, and He is the Most High, the Great.
5. The heavens would nearly shatter from above them, and the Angels praise the glory of their Lord, and they ask forgiveness for those on Earth. Surely, God is the Forgiver, the Merciful.
6. And those who take allies besides Him, God is responsible for them; and you are not a guardian over them.
7. And thus We have inspired to you an Arabic compilation, so that you may warn the capital town and all around it, and to warn about the Day of Gathering that is inevitable. A group will be in Paradise, and a group in Hell.
8. And had God willed, He could have made them one nation. But He admits whom He wills into His mercy. And the transgressors will have neither an ally, nor helper.
9. Or have they taken allies besides Him? But God is the ally, and He is the One who resurrects the dead, and He is able to do all things.
10. And anything you dispute in, then its judgment shall be with God. Such is God my Lord. In Him I put my trust, and to Him I repent.
11. Initiator of the heavens and the Earth. He created for you from among yourselves mates, and also mates for the livestock so they may multiply. There is nothing like unto Him. He is the Hearer, the Seer.

12. To Him belongs the possessions of the heavens and the Earth. He spreads out the provision for whomever He wills, and He measures it. He is fully aware of all things.

13. He has decreed for you the same system He ordained for Noah, and what We inspired to you, and what We ordained for Abraham, Moses, and Jesus: "You shall uphold this system, and do not divide in it." Intolerable for those who have set up partners is what you invite them towards. God chooses to Himself whomever He wills; He guides to Himself those who repent.

14. And they only divided after the knowledge had come to them, due to resentment among themselves. And had it not been for a predetermined decision from your Lord, they would have been judged immediately. Indeed, those who inherited the Scripture after them are full of doubts.

15. For that, you shall preach and be upright, as you have been commanded, and do not follow their wishes. And Say: "I believe in all that God has sent down from Scripture, and I was commanded to be with justice between you. God is our Lord and your Lord. We have our deeds and you have your deeds. There is no argument between us and you. God will gather us all together, and to Him is the ultimate destiny."

16. And those who debate about God, after they had been answered, their argument is nullified at their Lord. They have incurred a wrath, and will have a severe retribution.

17. God is the One who sent down the Scripture with truth, and the balance. And for all that you know, the Hour may be very near.

18. Those who do not believe in it seek to hasten it, while those who believe are concerned about it, and they know that it is the truth. Certainly, those who dispute the Hour have gone far astray.

19. God is Gracious to His servants; He gives provisions for whomever He wills, and He is the Powerful, the Noble.

20. Whoever desires the harvest of the Hereafter, We will increase for him his harvest. And whoever seeks the harvest of this world, We will give him therefrom, and he will have no share in the Hereafter.

21. Or do they have partners who decree for them a system which has not been authorized by God? And if it were not for the word already given, they would have been judged immediately. Indeed, the transgressors will have a painful retribution.

22. You see the transgressors worried because of what they had done; and it will come back at them. As for those who believed and do good works, they will

be in the paradises of bliss. They will have what they wish from their Lord. This is the great blessing.

23. Such is the good news from God to His servants who believe and do good works. Say: "I do not ask you for any wage, except that you show compassion to your relatives." And whosoever earns a good deed, We shall increase it for him in goodness. Surely, God is Forgiving, Appreciative.

24. Or do they Say: "He has fabricated lies about God!" If God willed, He could have sealed your heart. And God erases the falsehood and affirms the truth with His words. He is fully aware of what is inside the chests.

25. And He is the One who accepts the repentance from His servants, and He forgives the sins. He is fully aware of what you do.

26. And those that believe and do good works respond to Him, and He increases for them His blessings. As for the rejecters, they have incurred a severe retribution.

27. And if God were to increase the provision for His servants, they would transgress on Earth; but He sends down what He wills in a measure. He is Expert and Seer of His servants.

28. And He is the One who sends down the rain after they had despaired, and spreads His mercy. He is the Supporter, the Praiseworthy.

29. And from among His signs is the creation of the heavens and the Earth, and the creatures He spreads in them. And He is able to gather them, if He wills.

30. And any misfortune that happens to you is a consequence of what your hands have earned. And He overlooks much.

31. And you can never escape, and you have none besides God as an ally or helper.

32. And from His signs are the vessels that sail the sea like flags.

33. If He willed, He could still the winds, leaving them motionless on top of it. In that are signs for every one who is patient, thankful.

34. Or He may drown them, for what they have earned. And He overlooks much.

35. And those who dispute in Our signs may know that they have no place to hide.

36. So whatever you are given is simply an enjoyment of the worldly life, and what is with God is far better and more lasting for those who believe and put their trust in their Lord.

37. And those who avoid gross sins and lewdness, and when they are angered, they forgive.

38. And those who have responded to their Lord, and they honour the oath of allegiance, and their affairs are conducted by mutual consultation among themselves, and from Our provisions to them they give.

39. And those who, when gross injustice befalls them, they seek justice.

40. The recompense for a crime shall be its equivalence, but whoever forgives and makes right, then his reward is upon God. He does not like the wrong-doers.

41. And for any who demand action after being wronged, those are not committing any error.

42. The error is upon those who oppress the people, and they aggress in the land without cause. For these will be a painful retribution.

43. And for he who is patient and forgives, then that is an indication of strength.

44. And whomever God sends astray will not have any ally after Him. And you will see the transgressors, when they see the retribution, saying: "Is there any way we can go back?"

45. And you will see them being displayed to it, in fearful humiliation, and looking, while trying to avoid looking. And those who believed will Say: "The losers are those who lost their souls and their families on the Day of Resurrection. The transgressors will be in a lasting retribution."

46. And they had no allies to help them against God. And whomever God misguides will never find the way.

47. Respond to your Lord before a Day comes from God which cannot be averted. You will have no refuge for you on that Day, nor an advocate.

48. But if they turn away, then We did not send you as their guardian. You are only required to deliver. And when We let the human being taste mercy from Us, he becomes happy with it, and when adversity afflicts them because of what their hands have done, the human being becomes rejecting.

49. To God is the sovereignty of the heavens and the Earth. He creates whatever He wills. He bestows daughters to whomever He wills, and bestows sons to whomever He wills.

50. Or, He may bestow them with both daughters and sons, and He makes whom He wills sterile. He is Knowledgeable, Capable.

51. And it is not for any human being that God would speak to him, except through inspiration, or from behind a barrier, or by sending a messenger to inspire whom He wills by His leave. He is Most High, Wise.

52. And thus, We inspired to you a revelation of Our command. You did not know what was the Scripture, nor what was faith. Yet, We made this a light

to guide whomever We wish from among Our servants. Surely, you guide to a straight path.

53. The path of God, to whom belongs what is in the heavens and what is in the Earth. Ultimately, all matters revert to God.

Chapter 43

بسم الله الرحمن الرحيم

In the name of God, the Almighty, the Merciful.

1. H.M.
2. And the evident Scripture.
3. We have made it into an Arabic compilation, perhaps you may understand.
4. And it is held honourable and wise in the master record with Us.
5. Shall We take away the reminder from you, because you are a transgressing people?
6. And how many a prophet did We send to the previous generations!
7. And every time a prophet went to them, they ridiculed him.
8. We have destroyed those who were even more powerful than these, and the example of the previous generations has already been given.
9. And if you asked them: "Who created the heavens and the Earth?" They will Say: "They were created by the One who is the Noble, the Knowledgeable."
10. He is the One who made the Earth a habitat for you, and He made pathways in it that you may be guided.
11. And He is the One who sends down water from the sky, in exact measure. We then revive with it a dead land. Similarly, you will be brought-out.
12. And He is the One who created all the pairs, and He made for you from the ships and the livestock that which you can ride.
13. So that you may settle on their backs; and then when you have settled on them you may recall your Lord's blessing, by saying: "Glory be to the One who commits this for us, and we could not have done so by ourselves."
14. "And we will ultimately return to our Lord."
15. And they assigned a share to Him from His own servants! The human being is clearly denying.

16. Or has He selected daughters from among His creation, while He has left you with the sons?

17. And when one of them is given news of that which he cites as an example for the Almighty, his face becomes dark, and he is miserable!

18. "What good is an offspring that is brought up to be beautiful, and cannot help in a fight?"

19. And they have claimed the Angels who are with the Almighty are females! Have they been made witness to their creation? We will record their testimony, and they will be asked.

20. And they said: "If the Almighty willed, we would not have worshipped them." They have no knowledge of this; they only conjecture.

21. Or have We given them a scripture before this which they are upholding?

22. The fact is, they have said: "We found our fathers following a certain way, and we are following in their footsteps."

23. And similarly, We did not send a warner to a town, except its carefree ones said: "We found our fathers following a certain way, and we are being guided in their footsteps."

24. He said: "What if I brought to you better guidance than what you found your fathers upon?" They said: "We are disbelievers in that with which you have been sent."

25. Consequently, We took revenge upon them. So see how was the consequences of the deniers.

26. And when Abraham said to his father and his people: "I am innocent of that which you worship."

27. "Except for the One who initiated me, He will guide me."

28. And he made it a word to last in his subsequent generations; perhaps they may turn back.

29. Indeed, I have given these people and their fathers to enjoy, until the truth came to them, and a clarifying messenger.

30. And when the truth came to them, they said: "This is magic, and we reject it."

31. And they said: "If only this Quran was sent down to a great man from the two towns!"

32. Is it they who assign your Lord's mercy? We have assigned their shares in this worldly life, and We raised some of them above others in ranks, so that they would take one another in service. The mercy from your Lord is far better than that which they amass.

33. And if it were not that all the people would become one cluster, We would have provided for those who reject the Almighty silver roofs for their homes, and stairs upon which they could ascend.

34. And for their homes, gates, and furnishings on which they could recline.

35. And many ornaments. All these are the pleasures of this worldly life. And the Hereafter with your Lord is for the righteous.

36. And whosoever turns away from the remembrance of the Almighty, We appoint a devil to be his constant companion.

37. And they hinder from the path, but they think they are guided!

38. Until he comes to Us, he will say, "Oh, I wish that between you and me was the distance of the two easts. What a miserable companion!"

39. It would not benefit you this Day, for you have transgressed; you are partners in the retribution.

40. Can you make the deaf hear, or can you guide the blind and those who are far astray?

41. For when We decease you, We may seek revenge on them.

42. Or We may show you that which We promised for them; for We are able to take them.

43. You shall hold on to that which is inspired to you; you are on a straight path.

44. And this is indeed a reminder for you and your people; and you will all be questioned.

45. And ask those of Our messengers whom We sent before you: "Did We ever appoint gods besides the Almighty to be served?"

46. And We sent Moses with Our signs to Pharaoh and his leaders, saying: "I am a messenger of the Lord of the worlds."

47. But when he came to them with Our signs, they laughed at them.

48. And every sign We showed them was greater than the one before it, and We seized them with the torment, perhaps they would revert.

49. And they said: "O you magician, implore your Lord for us according to what He has agreed with you; we will then be guided."

50. But when We removed the torment from them, they broke their word.

51. And Pharaoh proclaimed among his people: "O my people, do I not possess the kingship of Egypt, and these rivers that flow below me? Do you not see?"

52. "Am I not better than this one who is despised and he can barely be understood?"

53. "Why then are not golden bracelets bestowed on him, or the Angels are accompanying him?"

54. He thus convinced his people, and they obeyed him; they were a wicked people.

55. So when they persisted in opposing Us, We sought revenge from them, and drowned them all.

56. We thus made them a thing of the past, and an example for the others.

57. And when the son of Mary was cited as an example, your people turned away from it.

58. And they said: "Are our gods better or is he?" They only cited this to argue with you. Indeed, they are a quarrelsome people.

59. He was no more than a servant whom We blessed, and We made him an example for the Children of Israel.

60. And if We willed, We could have made some of you Angels to be successors on Earth.

61. And he was a lesson for the Hour. So have no doubt about it. And follow Me; this is a straight path.

62. And let not the devil repel you; he is to you a clear enemy.

63. And when Jesus came with the proofs, he said: "I have come to you with the wisdom, and to clarify some of the matters in which you dispute. So be aware of God and obey me."

64. "God is my Lord and your Lord. So serve Him. This is a straight path."

65. The groups disputed among themselves. Woe to those who have been wicked from the retribution of a painful Day.

66. Do they only wait for the Hour to come to them suddenly, while they do not perceive?

67. Friends on that Day will become enemies of one another, except for the righteous.

68. "O My servants, you will have no fear on this Day, nor will you grieve."

69. They are the ones who believed in Our revelations, and had submitted.

70. "Enter Paradise, together with your spouses, in happiness."

71. They will be served with golden trays and cups, and they will find everything the self desires and the eyes wish for, and you will abide therein forever.

72. And this is the Paradise that you have inherited, in return for your works.

73. In it you will have all kinds of fruits, from which you eat.

74. Surely, the criminals will abide in the retribution of Hell forever.

75. It will not be removed from them; they will be confined therein.

76. And We did not wrong them, but it was they who were the wrongdoers.

77. And they called out: "O Malek, please let your Lord terminate us!" He will Say: "No, you are remaining."

78. We have come to you with the truth, but most of you hate the truth.
79. Or have they devised some scheme? We will also devise.
80. Or do they think that We do not hear their secrets and private counsel? Yes indeed; and Our messengers are with them, recording.
81. Say: "If the Almighty had a son, I would be the first to serve!"
82. Glorified be the Lord of the heavens and the Earth, the Lord of the Throne, from what they describe.
83. So leave them to speak nonsense and play until they meet their Day, which they have been promised.
84. And He is the One who is a god in the heaven and a god on Earth. And He is the Wise, the Knowledgeable.
85. And blessed is the One who possesses the sovereignty of the heavens and the Earth, and everything between them; and with Him is the knowledge of the Hour, and to Him you will be returned.
86. And those whom they call on beside Him do not possess any intercession; except those who bear witness to the truth, and they fully know.
87. And if you asked them who created them, they would say, "God." Why then do they deviate?
88. And it will be said: "O my Lord, these are a people who do not believe."
89. So disregard them and Say: "Peace." For they will come to know.

Chapter 44

بسم الله الرحمن الرحيم

In the name of God, the Almighty, the Merciful.

1. H.M.
2. And the clarifying Scripture.
3. We have sent it down in a blessed night. Surely, We were to warn.
4. In it, is a decree for every matter of wisdom.
5. A decree from Us. Surely, We were to send messengers.
6. A mercy from your Lord. He is the Hearer, the Knowledgeable.
7. The Lord of the heavens and the Earth, and everything between them. If you were certain!
8. There is no god except Him. He gives life and causes death; your Lord and the Lord of your ancestors.
9. No; they are in doubt, playing.
10. Therefore, watch for the day when the sky will bring a visible smoke.
11. It will envelop the people: "This is a painful retribution!"
12. "Our Lord, remove the retribution from us; we are believers."
13. How is it that now they remember, while a clarifying messenger had come to them?
14. But they turned away from him and said: "Clearly educated, but crazy!"
15. We will remove the retribution in a while; you will then revert back.
16. On the Day We strike the great strike, We will avenge.
17. And We had tested before them the people of Pharaoh, and an honourable messenger came to them.
18. "Restore to me the servants of God. I am a trustworthy messenger to you."
19. "And, do not transgress against God. I come to you with clear authority."
20. "And I seek refuge in my Lord and your Lord, should you stone me."

21. "And if you do not wish to believe, then leave me alone."
22. Subsequently, he called on his Lord: "These are a criminal people."
23. You shall travel with My servants during the night; you will be pursued.
24. And cross the sea quickly; their troops will be drowned.
25. How many paradises and springs did they leave behind?
26. And crops and luxurious dwellings?
27. And blessings that they enjoyed?
28. Thus it was; and We caused another people to inherit it.
29. Neither the heaven, nor the Earth wept over them, and they were not respited.
30. And We saved the Children of Israel from the humiliating agony.
31. From Pharaoh; he was a transgressing tyrant.
32. And We have chosen them, out of knowledge, over the worlds.
33. And We granted them signs, which constituted a great test.
34. These people now are saying:
35. "There is nothing but our first death; and we will never be resurrected!"
36. "So bring back our forefathers, if you are truthful!"
37. Are they better or the people of Tubba` and those before them? We destroyed them, they were criminals.
38. And We have not created the heavens and the Earth, and everything between them, for mere play.
39. We did not create them except with the truth, but most of them do not know.
40. Surely, the Day of Separation is the appointment for them all.
41. That is the Day when no friend can help his friend in any way; nor will they be helped.
42. Except him on whom God has mercy. He is the Noble, the Merciful.
43. Surely, the tree of Bitterness,
44. Will be the food for the sinful.
45. Like hot oil, it will boil in the stomachs.
46. Like the boiling of liquid.
47. "Take him and throw him into the midst of Hell."
48. "Then pour upon his head the retribution of boiling liquid."
49. "Taste this; surely you are the noble, the generous!"
50. Surely, this is what you used to doubt!
51. The righteous will be in a place of security.
52. Among paradises and springs.
53. Wearing silk and satin; facing each other.

54. So it is, and We coupled them with wonderful companions.
55. They enjoy in it all kinds of fruits, in perfect peace.
56. They do not taste death therein except for the first death, and He has spared them the retribution of Hell.
57. As a blessing from your Lord. Such is the great triumph.
58. We have thus made it easy in your language, perhaps they may take heed.
59. Therefore, keep watch; for they too will keep watch.

Chapter 45

بسم الله الرحمن الرحيم

In the name of God, the Almighty, the Merciful.

1. H.M.

2. The revelation of the Scripture is from God, the Noble, the Wise.

3. In the heavens and the Earth are signs for the believers.

4. And in your creation, and what creatures He puts forth are signs for people who are certain.

5. And the alternation of the night and the day, and what God sends down from the sky of provisions to revive the land after its death, and the changing of the winds; are signs for a people who understand.

6. These are God's revelations that We recite to you with truth. So, in which narration, after God and His revelations, do they believe?

7. Woe to every sinful fabricator.

8. He hears God's revelations being recited to him, then he persists arrogantly, as if he never heard them. Give him news of a painful retribution.

9. And if he learns anything from Our revelations, he makes fun of them. For these will be a humiliating retribution.

10. Waiting for them is Hell. And that which they earned will not help them, nor those whom they have taken as allies besides God, and for them is a terrible retribution.

11. This is a guidance. And those who reject the revelations of their Lord, for them is an affliction of a painful retribution.

12. God is the One who committed the sea in your service, so that the ships can sail in it by His command, and that you may seek of His provisions, and that you may be appreciative.

13. And He committed in your service all that is in the heavens and in the Earth; all from Him. In that are signs for a people who reflect.

14. Say to those who believed to forgive those who do not look forward to the days of God. He will fully recompense people for whatever they have earned.

15. Whoever works good does so for himself, and whoever works evil will suffer it. Then to your Lord you will be returned.

16. And We had given the Children of Israel the Scripture, and the judgment, and the prophethood, and We provided them with good provisions; and We preferred them over the worlds.

17. And We gave them clarity in the matter, but then they disputed after the knowledge had come to them, out of jealousy amongst themselves. Your Lord will judge them on the Day of Resurrection regarding everything that they have disputed.

18. Then We have established you on the correct path; so follow it and do not follow the desires of those who do not know.

19. They cannot help you against God in the least. And the transgressors are allies to one another, while God is the Protector of the righteous.

20. This is a physical evidence for the people, and a guidance and a mercy for a people who are certain.

21. Or do those who work evil expect that We would treat them the same as those who believe and do good works, in their present life and their death? Miserable is how they judge.

22. And God created the heavens and the Earth with truth, and so that every soul may be recompensed for whatever it earned, and they will not be wronged.

23. Have you seen the one who took his ego as his god, and God led him astray, despite his knowledge, and He sealed his hearing and his heart, and He made a veil on his eyes? Who then can guide him after God? Will you not remember?

24. And they said: "There is nothing but this worldly life; we die and we live and nothing destroys us except the passing of time!" And they have no knowledge about this; they only conjecture.

25. And when Our clear revelations are recited to them, their only argument is to Say: "Then bring back our forefathers, if you are truthful."

26. Say: "God gives you life, then He puts you to death, then He will gather you to the Day of Resurrection, in which there is no doubt. But most people do not know."

27. And to God is the sovereignty of the heavens and the Earth. And on the Day the Hour comes to pass, on that Day the falsifiers will lose.

28. And you will see every nation lined-up together. Every nation will be called to its record. "Today, you be recompensed for everything you have done."

29. "This is Our record; it utters the truth about you. We have been recording everything you did."

30. As for those who believe and did good works, their Lord will admit them into His mercy. Such is the clear triumph.

31. As for those who disbelieve: "Were not My revelations recited to you, but you turned arrogant and were a criminal people?"

32. And when it was said: "Surely God's promise is the truth, and there is no doubt about the coming of the Hour," you said: "We do not know what the Hour is! We are full of conjecture about it; we are not certain."

33. And the evils of their works will become evident to them, and the very thing they ridiculed will be their doom.

34. And it will be said to them: "Today We will forget you, just as you forgot the meeting of this Day. And your abode is the Fire, and you will have no helpers."

35. "This is because you took God's revelations in mockery, and you were deceived by the worldly life." So from this Day, they will never exit therefrom, nor will they be excused.

36. To God belongs all praise; the Lord of the heavens, and the Lord of the Earth; the Lord of the worlds.

37. And to Him belongs all majesty in the heavens and the Earth. He is the Noble, the Wise.

Chapter 46

بسم الله الرحمن الرحيم

In the name of God, the Almighty, the Merciful.

1. H.M.
2. The revelation of the Scripture from God, the Noble, the Wise.
3. We did not create the heavens and the Earth, and everything between them except with truth, and for an appointed time. And those who disbelieve turn away from what they are being warned with.
4. Say: "Do you see those that you call on besides God? Show me what they have created on the Earth, or do they have a share in the heavens? Bring me a scripture before this, or any trace of knowledge, if you are truthful."
5. And who is more astray than one who calls on others besides God that do not respond to him even till the Day of Resurrection? And they are totally unaware of the calls to them!
6. And at the time when the people are gathered, they will be enemies for them, and they will reject their worship.
7. And when Our clear revelations are recited to them, those who rejected said of the truth that came to them: "This is evidently magic!"
8. Or do they Say: "He fabricated this!" Say: "If I fabricated this, then you cannot protect me at all from God. He is fully aware of what you say. He suffices as a witness between me and you. He is the Forgiver, the Merciful."
9. Say: "I am no different from the other messengers, nor do I know what will happen to me or to you. I only follow what is inspired to me. I am no more than a clear warner"
10. Say: "Do you see that if it were from God, and you rejected it, and a witness from the Children of Israel testified to its similarity, and he has believed,

while you have turned arrogant? Surely, God does not guide the wicked people."

11. And those who had rejected said regarding those who had believed: "If it were any good, they would not have beaten us to it." And when they are not able to be guided by it, they will Say: "This is an old fabrication!"

12. And before this was the Scripture of Moses, as a role model and a mercy. And this is an authenticating Scripture, in an Arabic tongue, so that you may warn those who have transgressed, and to give good news to the righteous.

13. Surely, those who said: "Our Lord is God," then they lead a righteous life, there is no fear for them, nor will they grieve.

14. These are the dwellers of Paradise, abiding therein, a reward for what they used to do.

15. And We enjoined the human being to honour his parents. His mother bore him with hardship, gave birth to him in hardship, and his bearing and weaning lasts thirty months. Until he has attained his maturity, and reaches forty years, he says: "My Lord, direct me to appreciate the blessings You have bestowed upon me and upon my parents, and to do righteousness that pleases You. And let my progeny be righteous. I have repented to You; I am of those who have submitted."

16. It is from these that We accept the best of their deeds, and We shall overlook their sins, among the dwellers of Paradise. This is the promise of truth that they had been promised.

17. And the one who says to his parents: "Enough of you! Are you promising me that I will be resurrected, when the generations who died before me never came back?" While they both will implore God: "Woe to you; believe! For God's promise is the truth." He would Say: "This is nothing but tales from the past!"

18. These are the ones against whom the retribution has been deserved in nations who had come before them of humans and Jinn; they are the losers.

19. And to each will be degrees according to what they did, and He will recompense them and they will not be wronged.

20. And on the Day when those who disbelieved will be displayed to the Fire: "You have wasted the good things given to you during your worldly life, and you took pleasure in it. Consequently, today you will be recompensed with a shameful retribution for your arrogance in the land without any right, and for your evil works."

21. And recall that the brother of 'Aad warned his people at the dunes, while numerous warnings were also delivered before him and with him: "You shall not serve except God. For I fear for you the retribution of a great day."

22. They said: "Have you come to us to divert us away from our gods? Then bring us what you are promising us, if you are truthful!"

23. He said: "The knowledge of it is with God; and I only convey to you what I was sent with. However, I see that you are a people who are ignorant."

24. Then when they saw the dense cloud heading towards their valley, they said: "This is a dense cloud that will bring to us much needed rain!" No, this is what you had asked to be hastened; a violent wind wherein there is painful retribution.

25. It destroys everything by the commanded of its Lord. Thus they became such that nothing could be seen except their homes. We thus requite the criminal people.

26. And We had established them in the same way as We established you, and provided them with the hearing, and the eyesight, and the heart. But their hearing, eyesight, and hearts did not help them at all. This is because they used to disregard God's revelations, and they were stricken by that which they used to mock!

27. And We have destroyed the towns around you, after We had explained the proofs, perhaps they would repent.

28. Why then did the idols they set up to bring them closer to God fail to help them? Instead, they abandoned them. Such was their lie, and what they fabricated.

29. And We sent to you a small number of Jinn, in order to let them listen to the Quran. So when they arrived there, they said: "Pay attention." Then, when it was finished, they returned to their people, to warn them.

30. They said: "O our people, we have heard a Scripture that was sent down after Moses, authenticating what is present with him. It guides to the truth; and to a Straight Path."

31. "O our people, respond to God's caller, and believe in Him. He will then forgive your sins, and spare you a painful retribution."

32. And whosoever does not respond to God's caller, then he cannot escape on the Earth, and he will not have besides Him any allies. These are the ones who have gone far astray.

33. Did they not see that God, Who created the heavens and the Earth, and was not tired by their creation, is able to revive the dead? Yes indeed; He is able to do all things.

34. And the Day the disbelievers are displayed to the Fire: "Is this not the truth?" They will answer: "Yes indeed, by our Lord." He will say, "Then taste the retribution for what you had rejected."

35. Therefore, be patient like the messengers of strong-will did before you and do not be in haste regarding them. On the Day they will see what they have been promised, it will be as if they had not remained except for one hour of a single day. A proclamation: "Are any destroyed except for the wicked people?"

Chapter 47

بسم الله الرحمن الرحيم

In the name of God, the Almighty, the Merciful.

1. Those who rejected and repelled from the path of God, He will mislead their works.

2. And those who believe and do good works, and believe in what was sent down to Mohammed, for it is the truth from their Lord, He cancels for them their sins, and relieves their concern.

3. That is because those who disbelieve followed falsehood, while those who believe followed the truth from their Lord. God thus cites for the people their examples.

4. So, if you encounter those who have rejected, then strike their formations until you overcome them, then bind them securely. You may either set them free or ransom them, until the war ends. That, and had God willed, He alone could have beaten them, but He thus tests you by one another. As for those who get killed in the cause of God, He will never let their deeds be put to waste.

5. He will guide them, and relieve their concerns.

6. And He will admit them into Paradise, which He has described to them.

7. O you who believe, if you support God, He will support you, and make your foothold firm.

8. And those who rejected, for them is destruction; and He has misled their works.

9. That is because they hated what God sent down, thus He nullifies their works.

10. Did they not roam the land and note how was the end for those before them? God destroyed them and the rejecters in a similar fate.

11. This is because God is the Master for those who believe, while the disbelievers have no master.

12. God admits those who believe and do good works to paradises with rivers flowing beneath them. As for those who reject, they are enjoying and eating as the cattle eat, and the Fire will be their abode.

13. And many a town was stronger than your own town, which drove you out. We destroyed them, and there was none who could help them.

14. Is one who is based on proof from his Lord, as one for whom his evil works have been adorned for him and they followed their desires?

15. Is the example of Paradise; that the righteous have been promised with rivers of pure water, and rivers of milk whose taste does not change, and rivers of wine that are delicious for the drinkers, and rivers of strained honey, and for them in it are all kinds of fruits, and a forgiveness from their Lord; like that of those who abide in the Fire, and are given to drink boiling water that cuts-up their intestines?

16. And some of them listen to you, until when they go out from you, they say to those who have been given the knowledge: "What did he say?" Those are the ones whom God has sealed upon their hearts, and they followed their desires.

17. And those who are guided, He increases their guidance, and grants them their righteousness.

18. So are they waiting until the Hour comes to them suddenly? For its conditions have already been met. But once it comes to them, how will they benefit from their message?

19. So know that there is no god besides God, and ask forgiveness of your sins and also for the believing men and believing women. And God knows your movements and your place of rest.

20. And those who believe Say: "If only a chapter is sent down!" But when a governing chapter is sent down, and fighting is mentioned in it, you see those who have a disease in their hearts look at you, as if death had already come to them. It thus revealed them.

21. Obedience and to speak righteousness until the matter is decided, then if they trust God it would be better for them.

22. So do you plan that when you turn away, that you will corrupt the land and sever your family ties?

23. These are the ones whom God has cursed and thus He made them deaf and blinded their sight.

24. Do they not reflect on the Quran? Or are there locks on their hearts?

25. Surely, those who reverted back, after the guidance has been made clear to them, the devil has enticed them and led them on.

26. That is because they said to those who hated what God had sent down: "We will obey you in certain matters." And God knows their secrets.

27. So how will it be when the Angels seize them, striking their faces and their backs?

28. That is because they followed that which angered God, and they hated that which pleased Him. Thus, He nullified their works.

29. Or did those who harbour a disease in their hearts think that God would not bring out their evil thoughts?

30. And if We wished, We would show them to you so you would recognize them by their looks. However, you can recognize them by their speech. And God is fully aware of your works.

31. And We will test you for We know those who strive among you and those who are patient. And We will bring out your qualities.

32. Those who have rejected and repelled from the path of God, and stood against the messenger after the guidance has been made clear for them, they will not harm God in the least, and He will nullify their works.

33. O you who believe, obey God, and obey the messenger. And do not render your work in vain.

34. Surely, those who rejected and repelled from the path of God, then they died while still rejecting, God will never forgive them.

35. Therefore, do not be weak and ask for peace, for you are on a higher moral ground, and God is with you. And He will not waste your efforts.

36. This worldly life is no more than play and vanity. But if you believe and lead a righteous life, He will reward you, and He will not ask you for your wealth.

37. If He were to ask you for it, to the extent of creating a hardship for you, you would become stingy, and your hidden evil might be exposed.

38. Here you are being invited to spend in the cause of God, but some among you turn stingy. And whoever is stingy is only being stingy on himself. And God is the Rich, while you are the poor. And if you turn away, He will substitute another people instead of you, then they will not be like you.

Chapter 48

In the name of God, the Almighty, the Merciful.

1. We have given you a clear conquest.
2. So that God may forgive your present sins, as well as those past, and so that He may complete His blessings upon you, and guide you on a straight path.
3. And God will grant you a conquest which is mighty.
4. He is the One who sends down tranquility into the hearts of the believers, so that they may increase in faith along with their present faith. And to God belongs the soldiers of the heavens and the Earth, and God is Knowledge-able, Wise.
5. That He may admit the believing men and believing women into estates with rivers flowing beneath them, abiding eternally therein, and He will remit their sins from them. And with God this is a great triumph.
6. And He will punish the hypocrite men and the hypocrite women, and the idolater men and the idolater women, who think evil thoughts about God. Their evil will come back to them, and God was angry with them, and He has cursed them and prepared for them Hell. What a miserable destiny!
7. And to God belongs the soldiers of the heavens and the Earth. And God is Noble, Wise.
8. We have sent you as a witness, a bearer of good news, and a warner.
9. So that you may believe in God and His messenger, and that you may support Him, honour Him, and glorify Him, morning and evening.
10. Those who pledge allegiance to you, are in-fact pledging allegiance to God; God's hand is above their hands. Those of them who violate such a pledge, are violating it only upon themselves. And whosoever fulfills what he has pledged to God, then He will grant him a great reward.

11. The Nomads who lagged behind will say to you: "We were preoccupied with our money and our family, so ask forgiveness for us." They say with their tongues what is not in their hearts. Say: "Who then would possess any power for you against God if He wanted harm to afflict you or if He wanted benefit for you?" No, God is fully Aware of everything you do.

12. Alas, you thought that the messenger and the believers would not return to their families, and this was deemed pleasant in your hearts, and you thought the worst thoughts; you were a wicked people.

13. Anyone who does not believe in God and His messenger, then We have prepared for the rejecters a Hellfire.

14. And to God is the sovereignty of the heavens and the Earth. He forgives whomever He wills, and punishes whomever He wills. God is Forgiver, Merciful.

15. Those who lagged behind will say, when you venture out to collect the spoils: "Let us follow you!" They want to change God's words. Say: "You will not follow us; this is what God has decreed beforehand." They will then Say: "No, you are envious of us." Alas, they rarely understood anything.

16. Say to those Nomads who lagged behind: "You will be called on to fight a people who are very powerful in warfare, unless they surrender. Then if you obey, God will grant you a good reward, but if you turn away as you turned away before, He will punish you with a painful retribution."

17. There is no burden on the blind, nor is there any burden on the cripple, nor is there on the sick any burden. And whosoever obeys God and His messenger, He will admit them into paradises with rivers flowing beneath; and whosoever turns away, He will punish him with a painful retribution.

18. God is pleased with the believers who pledged allegiance to you under the tree. He thus knew what was in their hearts, so He sent down tranquility upon them, and rewarded them with a near victory.

19. And abundant spoils that they will take. God is Noble, Wise.

20. God has promised you abundant spoils that you will take. Thus He has hastened this for you, and He has withheld the people's hands against you; that it may be a sign for the believers, and that He may guide you to a straight path.

21. And the other group which you could not vanquish, God took care of them. And God was capable of all things.

22. And if the rejecters had fought you, they would have turned and ran, then they would have found neither an ally nor a victor.

23. Such is God's way with those who have passed away before, and you will not find any change in God's way.

24. And He is the One who withheld their hands against you, and your hands against them in the interior of Mecca, after He had made you victorious over them. God is Seer of what you do.

25. They are the ones who rejected and barred you from the Restricted Temple, and barred your donations from reaching their destination. And there had been believing men and women whom you did not know, and you may have hurt them, and on whose account you would have committed a sin unknowingly. God will admit into His mercy whomever He wills. Had they become separated, We would then have punished those of them who rejected with a painful retribution.

26. Those who rejected had put in their hearts the rage of the days of ignorance, then God sent down tranquility upon His messenger and the believers, and directed them to uphold the word of righteousness, and they were well entitled to it and worthy of it. And God is fully aware of all things.

27. God has fulfilled with truth His messenger's vision: "You will enter the Restricted Temple, God willing, secure, with your heads shaven and shortened, having no fear." Thus, He knew what you did not know, and He has coupled with this a near victory.

28. He is the One who sent His messenger with the guidance and the system of truth, so that it would expose all other systems. And God is sufficient as a witness.

29. Mohammed is the messenger of God, and those who are with him are severe against the rejecters, but merciful between themselves. You see them kneeling and prostrating, they seek God's blessings and approval. Their distinction is in their faces, as a result of prostrating. Such is their example in the Torah. And their example in the Injeel is like a plant which shoots out and becomes strong and thick and it stands straight on its trunk, pleasing to the farmers. That He may enrage the rejecters with them. God promises those among them who believe and do good works a forgiveness and a great reward.

Chapter 49

بسم الله الرحمن الرحيم

In the name of God, the Almighty, the Merciful.

1. O you who believe, do not place your opinion above that of God and His messenger. And be aware of God. God is Hearer, Knowledgeable.

2. O you who believe, do not raise your voices above the voice of the prophet, nor shall you speak loudly at him as you would speak loudly to each other, lest your works become nullified while you do not perceive.

3. Surely, those who lower their voices with the messenger of God, they are the ones whose hearts have been tested by God for righteousness. They have deserved forgiveness and a great recompense.

4. Surely, those who call on you from behind the buildings, most of them do not comprehend.

5. And if they had only been patient till you came out to them, it would have been better for them. God is Forgiver, Merciful.

6. O you who believe, if a wicked person comes to you with any news, then you shall investigate it. Lest you harm a people out of ignorance, then you will become regretful over what you have done.

7. And know that among you is the messenger of God. If he were to obey you in many things, you would be in difficulty. But God made you love faith and He adorned it in your hearts, and He made you hate disbelief, wickedness, and disobedience. These are the rightly guided ones.

8. Such is the grace from God and a blessing. God is Knowledgeable, Wise.

9. And if two parties of believers battle with each other, you shall reconcile them; but if one of them aggresses against the other, then you shall fight the one aggressing until it complies with God's command. Once it complies,

then you shall reconcile the two groups with justice, and be equitable; for God loves those who are equitable.

10. The believers are brothers; so reconcile between your brothers, and be aware of God, that you may receive mercy.

11. O you who believe, let not a people ridicule other people, for they may be better than they. Nor shall any women ridicule other women, for they may be better than they. Nor shall you mock one another, or call each other names. Evil indeed is the reversion to wickedness after attaining faith. And anyone who does not repent, then these are the transgressors.

12. O you who believe, you shall avoid much suspicion, for some suspicion is sinful. And do not spy on one another, nor shall you backbite one another. Would one of you enjoy eating the flesh of his dead brother? You certainly would hate this. You shall observe God. God is Redeemer, Merciful.

13. O mankind, We created you from a male and female, and We made you into nations and tribes, that you may know one another. Surely, the most honourable among you in the sight of God is the most righteous. God is Knowledgeable, Expert.

14. The Nomads said: "We believe." Say: "You have not believed; but you should Say: 'We have submitted', for belief has not yet entered into your hearts." If you obey God and His messenger, He will not put any of your works to waste. God is Forgiver, Merciful.

15. Believers are those who believe in God and His messenger, then they became without doubt, and they strive with their money and their lives in the cause of God. These are the truthful ones.

16. Say: "Are you teaching God about your system while God knows everything in the heavens and the Earth? God is knowledgeable of all things."

17. They think they are doing you a favour by having submitted! Say: "Do not think you are doing me any favours by your submission. For it is God who is doing you a favour that He has guided you to the faith, if you are being true."

18. Surely, God knows all the unseen in the heavens and the Earth; God is Seer of everything you do.

Chapter 50

بسم الله الرحمن الرحيم

In the name of God, the Almighty, the Merciful.

1. Q, and the Quran of glory.
2. Are they surprised that a warner has come to them from amongst them, so the rejecters said: "This is something strange!"
3. "Can it be that when we are dead and we become dust, that we come back later?"
4. We know which of them has become consumed with the Earth; and We have with Us a record which keeps track.
5. But they denied the truth when it came to them, so they are in a confused state.
6. Did they not look to the sky above them, how We built it, and adorned it, and how it has no openings?
7. And the land We extended it, and placed in it stabilizers, and We gave growth in it to every kind of healthy pair.
8. Something to see and a reminder for every pious servant.
9. And We sent down from the sky blessed water, and We gave growth with it to gardens and grain that is harvested.
10. And the palm trees, emerging with clustering fruit.
11. A provision for the servants, and We gave life with it to the land which was dead. Such is the resurrection.
12. Before their denial was that of the people of Noah, and the dwellers of Al-Raas, and Thamud.
13. And 'Aad, and Pharaoh, and the brethren of Lot.
14. And the people of the forest, and the people of Tubba`. All of them disbelieved the messengers, so the promise came to pass.

15. Did We have any difficulty in making the first creation? No, they are in confusion about the next creation.

16. And We have created man and We know what his soul whispers to him, and We are closer to him than his jugular vein.

17. When the two receivers meet on the right and on the left.

18. He does not utter a word except with having a constant recorder.

19. And the moment of death came in truth: "This is what you have been trying to avoid!"

20. And the horn is blown on the promised Day.

21. And every soul is brought, being driven, and with a witness.

22. "You were heedless of this, so now We have removed your veil, and your sight today is iron!"

23. And his constant companion said: "Here is one who is a transgressor."

24. Cast in Hell every stubborn rejecter.

25. Denier of good, transgressor, doubter.

26. The one who made with God another god. So cast him into the severe retribution.

27. His constant companion said: "Our Lord, I did not corrupt him, but he was already far astray."

28. He said: "Do not argue with each other before Me, I have already presented you with My promise."

29. "The sentence will not be changed with Me, and I do not wrong the servants."

30. The Day We say to Hell: "Are you full?", and it says: "I can take more."

31. And Paradise is brought near to the righteous, not far off.

32. This is what you have been promised, for every obedient, steadfast

33. The one who feared the Almighty while unseen, and came with a repenting heart

34. Enter it in peace. This is the Day of eternal life.

35. In it they will have what they wish, and We have even more.

36. And how many a generation before them have We destroyed? They were stronger in power, and they had dominated the land. Did they find any sanctity?

37. In that is a reminder for whoever has a heart, or cares to listen while he is heedful.

38. And We have created the heavens and the Earth and what is between them in six days, and no fatigue touched Us.

39. So be patient to what they are saying, and glorify the grace of your Lord before the rising of the sun and before the setting.
40. And from the night glorify Him, and after prostrating.
41. And listen to the Day when the caller will call from a near place.
42. The Day they hear the scream with truth. That is the Day of coming out.
43. We are the Ones who give life and bring death, and to Us is the destiny.
44. The Day when the Earth will rapidly crumble away from them; that will be a gathering which is easy for Us.
45. We are totally aware of what they say, and you are not to be a tyrant over them. So remind with the Quran those who fear My promise.

Chapter 51

بسم الله الرحمن الرحيم

In the name of God, the Almighty, the Merciful.

1. By the winds that blow.
2. Carrying rain.
3. Travelling easily.
4. Distributing as commanded.
5. What you are being promised is true.
6. And the Judgment will come to pass.
7. By the sky that is woven.
8. You are saying what is different.
9. To mislead those who are misled.
10. Woe to the deceitful.
11. Who are in mischief, unaware.
12. They ask: "When is the Day of Judgment?"
13. The Day they ordeal upon the Fire.
14. "Taste this ordeal of yours; this is what you asked to be hastened."
15. The righteous are in paradises and springs.
16. Receiving what their Lord has bestowed to them, for they were before that pious.
17. They used to rarely sleep the whole night.
18. And before dawn, they would seek forgiveness.
19. An in their money was a portion for the beggar and the needy.
20. And in the Earth are signs for those who comprehend.
21. And within yourselves; do you not see?
22. And in the heaven is your provision, and what you are promised.

23. By the Lord of the heaven and the Earth, this is truth just as the fact that you speak.
24. Has the story of Abraham's noble guests come to you?
25. When they entered upon him, they said: "Peace." He said: "Peace to a people unknown!"
26. Then he went to his family and brought a fat roasted calf.
27. He offered it to them, he said: "Do you not eat?"
28. He then became fearful of them. They said: "Do not fear," and they gave him good news of a knowledgeable son.
29. His wife then approached in amazement. She slapped upon her face, and said: "I am a sterile old woman!"
30. They said: "It was such that your Lord has said. He is the Wise, the Knowledgeable."
31. He said: "What is your undertaking, O messengers?"
32. They said: "We have been sent to a criminal people."
33. "To send down upon them rocks of clay."
34. "Prepared by your Lord for the transgressors."
35. We then vacated from it all the believers.
36. But We only found in it one house of those who had submitted.
37. And We have left in it a sign for those who fear the painful retribution.
38. And also Moses, for We sent him to Pharaoh with a clear authority.
39. But he turned away, in arrogance, and he said: "A magician, or crazy."
40. So We took him and his troops; We cast them into the sea, and he was to blame.
41. And also 'Aad, for We sent upon them the hurricane wind.
42. Anything that it came upon was utterly destroyed.
43. And also Thamud, for it was said to them: "Enjoy for a while."
44. But they rebelled against the command of their Lord. So the lightning struck them while they were looking.
45. They were unable to rise up, nor could they win.
46. And the people of Noah before; they were a wicked people.
47. And We constructed the universe using matter, and We will expand it.
48. And the Earth We furnished; glory be to the Makers.
49. And from everything We created a pair, perhaps you may remember.
50. So turn towards God. I am to you from Him a clear warner.
51. And do not make any other god with God. I am to you from Him a clear warner.

52. Likewise, when a messenger went to those before them, they said: "A magician, or crazy."
53. Have they passed down this saying to each other? Indeed, they are a wicked people.
54. So turn away from them; you will not be blamed.
55. And remind, for the reminder benefits the believers.
56. I did not create the Jinn and the humans except to serve Me.
57. I need no provisions from them, nor do I need them to give food.
58. God is the Provider, the One with Power, the Supreme.
59. The transgressors will have the same fate as their previous friends; so let them not be hasty.
60. So woe to those who rejected from the Day that is waiting for them.

Chapter 52

بسم الله الرحمن الرحيم

In the name of God, the Almighty, the Merciful.

1. By the mount.
2. And a recorded Scripture.
3. In parchment unrolled.
4. And the constructed Sanctuary.
5. And the ceiling which is elevated.
6. And the sea that is set aflame.
7. Your Lord's retribution is unavoidable.
8. Nothing can stop it.
9. The Day when the sky will violently thunder.
10. And the mountains will be wiped out.
11. Woe on that Day to the deniers.
12. Who are in their recklessness, playing.
13. The Day they will be called into Hell, forcibly:
14. "This is the Fire which you used to deny!"
15. "Is this magic, or do you not see?"
16. "Enter it, whether you are patient or impatient, it will be the same for you. You are only being requited for what you used to do."
17. The righteous are in paradises and bliss.
18. Delighted by what their Lord has granted them; and their Lord has spared them the retribution of Hell.
19. Eat and drink happily because of what you used to do.
20. They recline on arranged furnishings, and We coupled them with wonderful companions.

21. And those who believed, and their progeny also followed them in belief; We will have their progeny join them. We never fail to reward them for any work. Every person is paid for what he did.
22. We will supply them with fruit and meat such as they desire.
23. They will enjoy drinks in which there is no harm, nor regret.
24. And around them will be children like protected pearls.
25. And they came to one another asking.
26. They said: "We used to be compassionate among our people."
27. "God thus blessed us, and has spared us the agony of the fiery winds."
28. "We used to implore Him before; He is the Kind, the Merciful."
29. Therefore, you shall remind. For by the grace of your Lord, you are neither a soothsayer, nor mad.
30. Or do they Say: "He is a poet; so let us just wait until a disaster befalls him."
31. Say: "Continue waiting; for I will wait along with you."
32. Or do their dreams dictate this to them, or are they a transgressing people?
33. Or do they Say: "He made it all up"? No, they simply do not believe.
34. Let them produce a narration like this, if they are truthful.
35. Or were they created from nothing? Or was it them who created?
36. Or did they create the heavens and the Earth? No, they do not comprehend.
37. Or do they possess the treasures of your Lord? Are they in control?
38. Or do they have a stairway that enables them to listen? Then let their listeners show their proof.
39. Or to Him belong the daughters, and to you belong the sons?
40. Or do you ask them for a wage, thus they are burdened by the fine?
41. Or do they know the future, thus they have it recorded?
42. Or do they intend to scheme? Indeed, it is the rejecters who are schemed against.
43. Or do they have another god besides God? God be glorified above what they set up.
44. And if they see a spectacle from the sky, they will Say: "Piled clouds!"
45. So disregard them until they meet the Day in which they are struck.
46. The Day when their schemes will not protect them, nor will they be helped.
47. And for those who transgressed will be a retribution beyond this, but most of them do not know.
48. You shall be patient for the judgement of your Lord, for you are in Our sights; and glorify the praise of your Lord when you rise.
49. Also from the night glorify Him and after the appearance of the stars.

Chapter 53

بسم الله الرحمن الرحيم

In the name of God, the Almighty, the Merciful.

1. As the star descended.
2. Your friend was not astray, nor was he deceived.
3. Nor does he speak from personal desire.
4. It is a divine inspiration.
5. He has been taught by One mighty in power.
6. Free from any defect, he became stable.
7. While he was at the highest horizon.
8. Then he drew nearer by moving down.
9. Until he became as near as two bow-lengths or nearer.
10. He then conveyed the inspiration to His servant what was to be revealed.
11. The heart did not invent what it saw.
12. Do you doubt him in what he saw?
13. And indeed, he saw him in another descent.
14. At the ultimate point.
15. Near it is the eternal Paradise.
16. The whole place was overwhelmed.
17. The eyes did not waver, nor go blind.
18. He has seen from the great signs of his Lord.
19. Have you considered Allaat and Al-`Uzzah?
20. And Manaat, the third one?
21. Do you have the males, while He has the females?
22. What a strange distribution!

23. These are but names that you made up, you and your forefathers. God never authorized such. They only follow conjecture, and personal desire, while the guidance has come to them from their Lord.
24. Or shall the human being have what he wishes?
25. To God belongs the Hereafter, and the world.
26. And there are many Angels in heaven, who have no power to intercede, except after God gives permission for whom He wishes and is satisfied with him.
27. Those who disbelieve in the Hereafter have given the Angels feminine names.
28. While they had no knowledge about this; they only followed conjecture. And conjecture is no substitute for the truth.
29. So disregard he who turns away from Our reminder, and only desires this worldly life.
30. This is the extent of their knowledge. Your Lord is fully aware of those who strayed away from His path, and He is fully aware of those who are guided.
31. And to God belongs everything in the heavens and everything on Earth. He will requite those who commit evil for their works, and will reward the righteous for their righteousness.
32. They avoid major sins and lewdness, except for minor offences. Your Lord is with vast forgiveness. He has been fully aware of you since He initiated you from the Earth, and while you were embryos in your mothers' wombs. Therefore, do not acclaim yourselves; He is fully aware of the righteous.
33. Have you noted the one who turned away?
34. And he gave very little, then he stopped.
35. Did he possess knowledge of the future? Could he see it?
36. Or was he not informed of the teachings in the Scriptures of Moses?
37. And of Abraham who fulfilled?
38. None can carry the burdens of another.
39. And the human being will have what he sought.
40. And his works will be shown.
41. Then he will be paid fully for such works.
42. And to your Lord is the final destiny.
43. And He is the One who makes laughter and tears.
44. And He is the One who takes life and gives it.
45. And He is the One who created the pair, male and female.
46. From a seed that is put forth.
47. And He will effect the recreation.

48. And He is the One who makes you rich or poor.
49. And He is the Lord of Sirius.
50. And He is the One who destroyed `Aad the first.
51. And from Thamud He left none.
52. And the people of Noah before that; they were evil transgressors.
53. And the evil communities were the lowliest.
54. Consequently, they utterly vanished.
55. So which of your Lord's marvels can you deny?
56. This is a warning like the older ones.
57. The final judgement draws near.
58. None beside God can relieve it.
59. Are you surprised by this narration?
60. And you are laughing, instead of crying?
61. And you are insisting on your ways?
62. You shall prostrate to God, and serve.

Chapter 54

بسم الله الرحمن الرحيم

In the name of God, the Almighty, the Merciful.

1. The Hour draws near, and the moon is breached.
2. And if they see a sign, they turn away and Say: "Continuous magic!"
3. And they disbelieved, and followed their desires, and every old tradition.
4. While the news had come to them in which there was sufficient warning.
5. A perfect wisdom; but the warnings are of no benefit.
6. So turn away from them; the Day will come when the caller will announce a terrible disaster.
7. With their eyes humiliated, they come out of the graves like scattered locusts.
8. Hastening towards the caller, the rejecters will Say: "This is a difficult Day."
9. The people of Noah disbelieved before them. They disbelieved Our servant and said: "He is crazy!" and he was oppressed.
10. So he called on his Lord: "I am beaten, so grant me victory."
11. So We opened the gates of the sky with pouring water.
12. And We caused springs to gush out of the Earth. Thus the waters met to a command which had been measured.
13. We carried him on a craft made of slabs and mortar.
14. It ran under Our watchful eyes; a reward for one who was rejected.
15. And We have left it as a sign. Do any of you wish to learn?
16. So how was My retribution after the warnings!
17. And We made the Quran easy to learn. Do any of you wish to learn?
18. 'Aad disbelieved. So how was My retribution after the warnings!
19. We sent upon them a violent wind, on a day of continuous misery.
20. It uprooted the people as if they were decayed palm tree trunks.

21. So how was My retribution after the warnings!
22. We made the Quran easy to learn. Do any of you wish to learn?
23. Thamud rejected the warnings.
24. They said: "Shall we follow one of us; a human being? We will then go astray, and be in Hell."
25. "Has the message come down to him, instead of us? He is an evil liar."
26. They will find out tomorrow who the evil liar is.
27. We are sending the camel as a test for them. So observe them and be patient.
28. And inform them that the water shall be divided between them; each shall be allowed to drink in the specified time.
29. But they called on their friend, and he was paid to slaughter.
30. So how was My retribution after the warnings!
31. We sent upon them one scream, whereupon they became like harvested hay.
32. We made the Quran easy to learn. Does any of you wish to learn?
33. The people of Lot rejected the warners.
34. We sent upon them projectiles. Except for the family of Lot, We saved them at dawn.
35. A blessing from Us; it is thus that We reward those who are appreciative.
36. And he warned them about Our punishment, but they ridiculed the warnings.
37. And they sought to remove him from his guests; so We diverted their eyes. "Taste My retribution; you have been warned."
38. And in the early morning, a devastating retribution struck them.
39. "Taste My retribution; you have been warned."
40. We made the Quran easy to learn. Do any of you wish to learn?
41. And the warnings had come to the people of Pharaoh.
42. They rejected all Our signs. So We took them, the taking of the Noble, the Able.
43. Are your rejecters better than those? Or have you been absolved by the Scripture?
44. Or do they Say: "We are a large group and we will win."
45. The large group will be defeated; they will turn around and flee.
46. The Hour is their appointed time, and the Hour is far worse and more painful.
47. The criminals are in error and will burn.
48. The Day when they will be dragged upon their faces into the Fire: "Taste the agony of the scorching heat!"
49. Everything We have created in measure.

50. And Our commands are done at once with the blink of an eye.
51. And We have destroyed your counterparts. Do any of you wish to learn?
52. And everything they did is in the records.
53. And everything, small or large, is written down.
54. The righteous will be in paradises and rivers.
55. In a position of honour, at an Omnipotent King.

Chapter 55

In the name of God, the Almighty, the Merciful.
1. The Almighty.
2. He has marked the Quran.
3. He created the human being.
4. He taught him how to distinguish.
5. The sun and the moon are perfectly calculated.
6. And the stars and the trees yield.
7. And He raised the sky and He established the balance.
8. Do not transgress in the balance.
9. And observe the weight with equity, and do not fall short in the balance.
10. And the Earth He has made for all creatures.
11. In it are fruits, and date palms with their hanging fruit.
12. And grains and the spices.
13. So which of your Lord's favours will you deny?
14. He created the human from a clay, like pottery.
15. And the Jinn He created from a smokeless fire.
16. So which of your Lord's favours will you deny?
17. The Lord of the two easts and the two wests.
18. So which of your Lord's favours will you deny?
19. He merges the two seas where they meet.
20. A barrier is placed between them, which they do not cross.
21. So which of your Lord's favours will you deny?
22. Out of both of them comes pearls and coral.
23. So which of your Lord's favours will you deny?
24. And to Him are the ships that roam the sea like flags.

25. So which of your Lord's favours will you deny?
26. Everyone upon it will fade-away.
27. And the presence of your Lord will remain, the One with Majesty and Honour.
28. So which of your Lord's favours will you deny?
29. Those in the heavens and Earth ask Him, everyday He is in some matter.
30. So which of your Lord's favours will you deny?
31. We will call you to account, both of you beings.
32. So which of your Lord's favours will you deny?
33. O tribes of Jinn and humans, if you can penetrate the outer limits of the heavens and the Earth, then go ahead and penetrate. You will not penetrate without might.
34. So which of your Lord's favours will you deny?
35. He sends against both of you projectiles of fire, and of copper; so you will not succeed.
36. So which of your Lord's favours will you deny?
37. Then, when the universe is torn, and turns like a rose coloured paint.
38. So which of your Lord's favours will you deny?
39. On that Day, no more questioning is asked of human or Jinn as to his sins.
40. So which of your Lord's favours will you deny?
41. The guilty will be recognized by their features; they will be taken by the forelocks and the feet.
42. So which of your Lord's favours will you deny?
43. This is Hell that the criminals used to deny.
44. They will move between it and a boiling liquid.
45. So which of your Lord's favours will you deny?
46. And for he who reverenced the majesty of his Lord, will be two paradises.
47. So which of your Lord's favours will you deny?
48. Full of provisions.
49. So which of your Lord's favours will you deny?
50. In them are two springs, flowing.
51. So which of your Lord's favours will you deny?
52. In them will be of every fruit, in pairs.
53. So which of your Lord's favours will you deny?
54. While reclining upon furnishings lined with satin, the fruits of the two paradises are within reach.
55. So which of your Lord's favours will you deny?

56. In them are attendants with a splendid look, unknown before by any human or Jinn.
57. So which of your Lord's favours will you deny?
58. They look like rubies and coral.
59. So which of your Lord's favours will you deny?
60. Is there any reward for goodness except goodness?
61. So which of your Lord's favours will you deny?
62. And besides these will be two other paradises.
63. So which of your Lord's favours will you deny?
64. Dark green in color.
65. So which of your Lord's favours will you deny?
66. In them, two springs which gush forth.
67. So which of your Lord's favours will you deny?
68. In them are fruits, date palms, and pomegranate.
69. So which of your Lord's favours will you deny?
70. In them is what is good and beautiful.
71. So which of your Lord's favours will you deny?
72. Companions, inside grand pavilions.
73. So which of your Lord's favours will you deny?
74. No human has ever touched them, nor Jinn.
75. So which of your Lord's favours will you deny?
76. Reclining on green carpets, in beautiful surroundings.
77. So which of your Lord's favours will you deny?
78. Glorified be the name of your Lord, Possessor of Majesty and Honour.

Chapter 56

In the name of God, the Almighty, the Merciful.

1. When the inevitable comes to pass.
2. Nothing can stop it from happening.
3. It will bring low, and raise up.
4. When the Earth will be shaken a terrible shake.
5. And the mountains will be wiped out.
6. So that they become only scattered dust.
7. And you will be in three groupings.
8. So those on the right, who will be from those on the right?
9. And those on the left, who will be from those on the left?
10. And those foremost, who will be from those foremost?
11. They will be the ones who are brought near.
12. In the paradises of bliss.
13. Many from the first generations.
14. And a few from the later generations.
15. Upon luxurious furnishings.
16. Residing in them, neighbouring each other.
17. Moving amongst them will be immortal children.
18. With cups, pitchers and drinks which are pure.
19. They do not run out, nor do they get bored.
20. And fruits of their choice.
21. And meat of birds that they desire.
22. And wonderful companions.
23. Like pearls which are sheltered.
24. A reward for their works.

25. They never hear any nonsense therein, nor sinful utterances.
26. Only the utterances of: "Peace. Peace."
27. And those on the right, who will be with those on the right?
28. In lush orchards.
29. And fruit-trees which are ripe.
30. And extended shade.
31. And flowing water.
32. And many fruits.
33. Neither ending; nor forbidden.
34. And raised furnishings.
35. We have planted them deeply.
36. And made them never previously touched.
37. Perfect and without spoil.
38. For those on the right side.
39. Many from the early generations.
40. And many from the later generations.
41. And those on the left, who will be from those on the left?
42. In fierce hot winds and boiling water.
43. And a shade that is unpleasant.
44. Neither cool, nor helpful.
45. They used to be indulged in luxury before this.
46. And they persisted in the great blasphemy.
47. And they used to Say: "After we die and turn to dust and bones, we will get resurrected?"
48. "As well as our forefathers?"
49. Say: "The people of old and the later generations,"
50. "Will be summoned to a meeting on a predetermined Day."
51. "Then you, O rejecting strayers,"
52. "Will eat from the tree of Bitterness,"
53. "Filling your bellies therefrom,"
54. "Then drinking on top of it boiling water,"
55. "So you will drink like thirsty camels!"
56. Such is their share on the Day of Judgment.
57. We have created you, if you could only believe!
58. Have you noted the semen that you produce?
59. Did you create it, or were We the Ones who created it?
60. We have predetermined death for you. Nothing can stop Us,

61. From transforming your forms, and establishing you in what you do not know.
62. You have come to know about the first creation. If only you would remember.
63. Have you noted the crops you reap?
64. Did you grow them, or were We the Ones who grew them?
65. If We wished, We can turn them into hay. Then you will be left in wonderment:
66. "We are lost."
67. "No, we are deprived!"
68. Have you noted the water you drink?
69. Did you send it down from the clouds, or was it We who sent it down?
70. If We wished, We can make it salty. If only you would give thanks.
71. Have you noted the fire you kindle?
72. Did you establish its tree, or was it We who established it?
73. We rendered it a reminder, and a useful tool for the users.
74. You shall glorify the name of your Lord, the Great.
75. I do swear by the positions of the stars.
76. This is an oath, if you only knew, that is great.
77. It is an honourable Quran.
78. In a protected record.
79. None can grasp it except those pure.
80. A revelation from the Lord of the worlds.
81. Are you disregarding this narration?
82. And you have your provisions, yet you are denying?
83. So when the time comes and it reaches your throat.
84. And at that moment you look around.
85. We are closer to it than you are, but you do not see.
86. If it is true that you do not owe any account.
87. Then return it, if you are truthful?
88. So, if he is one of those who are made near.
89. Then joy, and rose buds, and paradises of bliss.
90. And if he is one of the people of the right.
91. Then: "Peace" from the people of the right.
92. But if he is one of the deniers, the strayers.
93. Then an abode of boiling water.
94. And a burning in Hell.

95. This is the absolute truth.
96. You shall glorify the name of your Lord, the Great.

Chapter 57

بسم الله الرحمن الرحيم

In the name of God, the Almighty, the Merciful.

1. Glorifying God is everything in the heavens and the Earth. He is the Noble, the Wise.

2. To Him is the kingship of the heavens and the Earth. He brings life and death. And He is capable of all things.

3. He is the First and the Last, the Evident and the Innermost. And He is fully aware of all things.

4. He is the One who created the heavens and the Earth in six days, then He settled over the dominion. He knows everything that enters into the land, and everything that comes out of it, and everything that comes down from the sky, and everything that climbs into it. And He is with you wherever you may be. God is Seer of everything you do.

5. To Him is the kingship of the heavens and the Earth, and to God all matters are returned.

6. He merges the night into the day, and merges the day into the night. He is fully aware of what is inside the chests.

7. Believe in God and His messenger, and spend from what He has made you successors to. Those among you who believe and spend have deserved a great recompense.

8. Why should you not believe in God when the messenger is inviting you to believe in your Lord? And He has already taken a pledge from you, if you are believers.

9. He is the One who sends down to His servant clear revelations, to bring you out of the darkness into the light. God is Compassionate towards you, Merciful.

10. And why do you not spend in the cause of God, when God possesses all wealth in the heavens and the Earth? Not equal among you are those who spent before the victory and fought. They attained a greater rank than those who spent after the victory and fought. And for each, God promises goodness. And God is Expert in everything you do.

11. Who will lend God a loan of goodness, to have it multiplied for him manifold, and he will have a generous recompense?

12. The Day will come when you see the believing men and the believing women with their light radiating around them and to their right. "Good news is yours today, you will have paradises with flowing rivers, abiding therein. This is the great triumph!"

13. On that Day, the hypocrite men and the hypocrite women will say to those who believed: "Wait for us! Let us absorb some of your light." It will be said: "Go back behind you, and seek light." So a barrier will be set up between them, whose gate separates mercy on the inner side, from retribution on the outer side.

14. They will call upon them: "Were we not with you?" They will reply: "Yes, but you led yourselves into temptation, and you hesitated, and doubted, and became misled by wishful thinking, until God's judgment came. You were diverted from God by arrogance."

15. "This Day, no ransom can be taken from you, nor from those who disbelieved. Your abode is the Fire, it is your patron; what a miserable abode."

16. Has not the time come for those who believed to open up their hearts for the remembrance of God, and the truth that is revealed herein? And they should not be like those who were given the Scripture before, and the waiting became long for them, so their hearts became hardened, and many of them were wicked.

17. Know that God revives the land after it had died. We have made clear to you the signs, perhaps you may understand.

18. Surely, the charitable men and charitable women, who have loaned God a loan of goodness, He will multiply their reward, and they will have a generous recompense.

19. And those who believed in God and His messengers are the truthful ones. And the martyrs at their Lord will have their reward and their light. As for those who disbelieved and rejected Our revelations, they are the dwellers of Hell.

20. Know that this worldly life is no more than play and amusement and adornments, and boasting among you, and to increase in wealth and children. It is

like plants that are supplied by an abundant rain, which appear pleasing to the disbelievers. But then they dry-up and turn yellow, and become useless hay. And in the Hereafter there is severe retribution, and forgiveness from God and approval. This worldly life is no more than a deceiving enjoyment.

21. You shall race towards forgiveness from your Lord, and a Paradise whose width is as the width of the heaven and the Earth, prepared for those who believed in God and His messengers. Such is God's grace that He bestows upon whomever He wills. God is the Possessor of Infinite Grace.

22. No misfortune can happen on Earth, or in yourselves, except it is decreed in a record, before We bring it about. This is easy for God to do.

23. In order that you do not despair over anything that has passed you by, nor be happy of anything He has bestowed upon you. God does not like those who are boastful, proud.

24. They are stingy, and order the people to be stingy. And for anyone who turns away, then know that God is the Rich, the Praiseworthy.

25. We have sent Our messengers with clear proofs, and We sent down with them the Scripture and the balance, so that the people may uphold justice. And We sent down the iron, wherein there is great strength, and many benefits for the people. So that God would distinguish those who would support Him and His messengers on faith. God is Powerful, Noble.

26. And We had sent Noah and Abraham, and We placed in their progeny the prophethood and the Scripture. Some of them were guided, while many were wicked.

27. Then We sent in their tracks Our messengers. We sent Jesus the son of Mary, and We gave him the Injeel, and We ordained in the hearts of his followers kindness and mercy. But they invented Monasticism which We never decreed for them. They wanted to please God, but they did not observe it the way it should have been observed. Consequently, We gave those who believed among them their recompense, while many of them were wicked.

28. O you who believe, you shall reverence God and believe in His messenger. He will then grant you double the reward from His mercy, and He will make for you a light by which you shall walk, and He will forgive you. And God is Forgiving, Merciful.

29. So that the followers of the Scripture should know that they have no power over God's grace, and that all grace is in God's hand. He bestows it upon whomever He wills. God is Possessor of Infinite Grace.

Chapter 58

بسم الله الرحمن الرحيم

In the name of God, the Almighty, the Merciful.

1. God has heard the woman who has argued with you regarding her husband, and she complained to God. And God hears the argument between you. God is Hearer, Seer.

2. Those among you who estrange their wives by saying to them: "You are as my mother." They can never be as their mothers, for their mothers are the women who gave birth to them. Indeed, they are uttering what is strange and a falsehood. And God is Pardoner, Forgiver.

3. Those who had estranged their wives in this manner, then they do again repeat it, they shall free a slave before they have sexual contact between them. This is to enlighten you. God is well aware of everything you do.

4. If he cannot find any, then he shall fast two consecutive months before any sexual contact between them. If he cannot, then he shall feed sixty poor people. That is so you would believe in God and His messenger. And these are the limits set by God. The disbelievers have incurred a painful retribution.

5. Those who oppose God and His messenger will be disgraced, like their previous counterparts were disgraced. We have sent down clear proofs, and the rejecters have incurred a shameful retribution.

6. The Day when God resurrects them all, then He informs them of what they had done. God has recorded it, while they have forgotten it. God witnesses all things.

7. Do you not realise that God knows everything in the heavens and everything on Earth? No three people can meet secretly without Him being their fourth, nor five without Him being the sixth, nor less than that, nor more, without Him being there with them wherever they may be. Then, on the

Day of Resurrection, He will inform them of everything they had done. God is fully aware of all things.

8. Have you noted those who were enjoined from holding meetings in secret, but then they insist on it? They meet secretly to commit sin, transgression, and disobedience of the messenger. When they come to you, they greet you with a greeting other than that which God greets you with. They say inside themselves: "Why does God not punish us for our utterances?" Hell will be sufficient for them, wherein they burn; what a miserable destiny.

9. O you who believe, if you must meet secretly, then you shall not meet to commit sin, transgression, and to disobey the messenger. You shall meet to work righteousness and piety. And be aware of God, before whom you will be summoned.

10. Secret meetings are from the devil, to cause grief to those who believed. However, he cannot harm them except if God wills. In God the believers shall put their trust.

11. O you who believe, if you are told to make room in the council, then you shall make room. God will then make room for you. If you are asked to step-down, then step-down. God will raise those among you who believe, and those who acquire knowledge to higher ranks. God is fully aware of everything you do.

12. O you who believe, if you wish to hold a private meeting with the messenger, you shall offer a charity before you do so. This is better for you, and purer. If you cannot do so, then God is Forgiver, Merciful.

13. Are you reluctant to offer a charity before such meeting? If you cannot do such, and God has forgiven you; then you shall honour the oath of allegiance, and contribute towards betterment, and obey God and His messenger. God is fully Aware of everything you do.

14. Have you noted those who befriended people with whom God is angry? They are now neither from you nor from them. And they deliberately swear to lies while they know!

15. God has prepared for them a severe retribution. Miserable indeed is what they used to do.

16. They used their oaths as a means of repelling from the path of God. Consequently, they have incurred a shameful retribution.

17. Neither their money, nor their children will help them against God in the least. They have incurred the Hellfire, in it they will abide.

18. The Day will come when God resurrects them all. Then they will swear to Him, just as they swear to you, thinking that they actually are right! Indeed, they are the liars.

19. The devil has overtaken them, and has caused them to forget the remembrance of God. These are the party of the devil. Absolutely, the party of the devil are the losers.

20. Surely, those who oppose God and His messenger, they will be with the lowliest.

21. God has decreed: "I and My messengers will be the victors." God is Powerful, Noble.

22. You will not find any people who believe in God and the Last Day befriending those who oppose God and His messenger, even if they were their parents, or their children, or their siblings, or their tribe. For these, He decrees faith into their hearts, and supports them with a spirit from Him, and He admits them into paradises with rivers flowing beneath, wherein they will abide. God is pleased with them, and they are pleased with Him. These are the party of God. Most assuredly, the party of God are the winners.

Chapter 59

بسم الله الرحمن الرحيم

In the name of God, the Almighty, the Merciful.

1. Glorifying God is everything in the heavens and the Earth, and He is the Noble, the Wise.

2. He is the One who drove out those who disbelieved among the people of the Scripture from their homes at the very first mobilization. You never thought that they would leave, and they thought that their fortresses would protect them from God. But then God came to them from where they did not expect, and He cast terror into their hearts. They destroyed their homes with their own hands and the hands of the believers. So learn from this, O you who possess vision.

3. And had God not decreed to banish them, He would have punished them in this life. And in the Hereafter they will face the retribution of the Fire.

4. This is because they challenged God and His messenger. And whosoever challenges God, then God is severe in punishment.

5. Whether you cut down a tree or left it standing on its root, it was by God's leave. He will surely humiliate the wicked.

6. And what God provided to His messenger, without you having to battle for it on horses or on foot, was because God sends His emissaries against whomever He wills. And God is capable of all things.

7. And whatever God provided to His messenger from the people of the townships, then it shall be to God and His messenger, and the relatives, and the orphans, and the poor, and the wayfarer. Thus, it will not remain monopolized by the rich among you. And you may take what the messenger gives you, but do not take what he withholds you from taking. And be aware of God, for God is mighty in retribution.

8. For the immigrants who are poor and were driven out of their homes and deprived of their properties, they sought God's grace and pleasure, and they supported God and His messenger. They are the truthful ones.

9. And those who provided them with shelter, and were believers before them; they love those who immigrated to them, and they find no hesitation in their hearts in helping them, and they readily give them priority over themselves, even when they themselves need what they give away. Indeed, those who overcome their desires are the successful ones.

10. And those who came after them saying: "Our Lord, forgive us and our brothers who preceded us to the faith, and do not place in our hearts any animosity towards those who believed. Our Lord, You are Compassionate, Merciful."

11. Have you noted those who are hypocrites, they say to their companions in disbelief among the people of the Scripture: "If you are driven out we will go out with you, and we will never obey anyone who opposes you. And if anyone fights you, we will support you." God bears witness that they are liars.

12. If they were driven out, they would not have gone out with them, and if anyone fought them, they would not have supported them. And even if they supported them, they would have turned around and fled. They could never win.

13. Indeed, you strike more terror in their hearts than their fear of God. This is because they are people who do not comprehend.

14. They will not fight you all unless they are in fortified towns, or from behind walls. Their might appears formidable among themselves. You would think that they are united, but their hearts are divided. This is because they are people who do not understand.

15. Like the example of those who preceded them. They suffered the consequences of their decisions. They have incurred a painful retribution.

16. Like the example of the devil, when he says to the human being: "Disbelieve," then as soon as he disbelieves, he says: "I disown you. I fear God, the Lord of the worlds."

17. So the destiny for both of them is the Fire, abiding therein. And such is the recompense for the wicked.

18. O you who believe, be aware of God, and let every soul examine what it has put forth for tomorrow. And be aware of God; God is fully aware of everything you do.

19. And do not be like those who forgot God, so He made them forget themselves. These are the wicked.

20. Not equal are the dwellers of the Fire and the dwellers of Paradise; the dwellers of Paradise are the winners.

21. Had We sent down this Quran to a mountain, you would have seen it trembling, crumbling, out of reverence for God. And such are the examples We cite for the people, that they may reflect.

22. He is God; there is no other god beside Him. Knower of all secrets and declarations. He is the Almighty, the Merciful.

23. He is God; there is no other god beside Him. The King, the Holy, the Peace, the Faithful, the Supreme, the Noble, the Powerful, the Dignified. God be glorified; far above what they set up.

24. He is God; the Creator, the Initiator, the Designer. To Him belong the most beautiful names. Glorifying Him is everything in the heavens and the Earth. He is the Noble, the Wise.

Chapter 60

بسم الله الرحمن الرحيم

In the name of God, the Almighty, the Merciful.

1. O you who believe, do not take My enemy and your enemy as allies, you extend love to them, even though they have rejected the truth that has come to you. They drive you and the messenger out, simply because you believe in God, your Lord. If you are mobilizing to strive in My cause, seeking My blessings, then how can you secretly love them? I am fully aware of everything you conceal and what you declare. And whosoever of you does this, then he has gone astray from the right path.

2. If they encounter you, they treat you as enemies, and they extend their hands and tongues against you to hurt you. They desire you to disbelieve.

3. Neither your relatives nor your children will benefit you; on the Day of Resurrection He will separate between you. And God is Seer of everything you do.

4. There has been a good example set for you by Abraham and those with him, when they said to their people: "We are innocent from you and what you serve besides God. We have rejected you, and it appears that there shall be animosity and hatred between us and you until you believe in God alone." Except for the saying of Abraham to his father: "I will ask forgiveness for you, but I do not possess any power to protect you from God." "Our Lord, we have put our trust in You, and we turn to You, and to You is the final destiny."

5. "Our Lord, do not let us become a test for those who rejected, and forgive us. Our Lord, You are the Noble, the Wise."

6. Certainly, a good example has been set by them for those who seek God and the Last Day. And whosoever turns away, then God is the Rich, the Praiseworthy.

7. Perhaps God will grant compassion between you and those you consider enemies; and God is Capable. And God is Forgiving, Merciful.

8. God does not forbid you from those who have not fought you because of your system, nor drove you out of your homes, that you deal kindly and equitably with them. For God loves the equitable.

9. But God does forbid you regarding those who fought you because of your system, and drove you out of your homes, and helped to drive you out. You shall not ally with them. Those who ally with them, then such are the transgressors.

10. O you who believe, if the believing women come emigrating to you, then you shall test them. God is fully aware of their belief. Thus, if you establish that they are believers, then you shall not return them to the disbelievers. They are no longer lawful for them, nor are the disbelievers lawful for them. And return the dowries that were paid. And there is no sin upon you to marry them, if you have paid their dowries to them. And do not keep disbelieving wives, and ask back what dowries you paid. And let them ask back what dowries they had paid. Such is God's judgement; He judges between you. God is Knowledgeable, Wise.

11. And if any of your wives have gone-over to the camp of the disbelievers, and you are granted victory over them, then you shall compensate those whose wives have gone-over, to the equivalent of what dowry they spent. And be aware of God, in whom you believe.

12. O you prophet, if the believing women come to make allegiance to you that they will not set up anything beside God, nor steal, nor commit adultery, nor kill their unborn children, nor fabricate any falsehood, nor disobey you in any matter which is righteous, then you shall accept their allegiance, and ask God to forgive them. God is Forgiver, Merciful.

13. O you who believe, do not ally a people with whom God is angry; for they have given-up regarding the Hereafter, just like the rejecters have given-up on the people who are already in the graves.

Chapter 61

In the name of God, the Almighty, the Merciful.

1. Glorifying God is everything in the heavens and everything on the Earth. And He is the Noble, the Wise.
2. O you who believe, why do you say what you do not do?
3. It is most despicable with God that you would say what you do not do.
4. God loves those who fight in His cause as one column; they are like bricks in a wall.
5. And when Moses said to his people: "O my people, why do you harm me, while you know that I am God's messenger to you?" But when they deviated, God diverted their hearts. And God does not guide the wicked people.
6. And when Jesus, son of Mary, said: "O children of Israel, I am God's messenger to you, authenticating what is present with me of the Torah and bringing good news of a messenger to come after me whose name will be 'most acclaimed.'" But when he showed them the clear proofs, they said: 'This is clearly magic'
7. Who is more evil than one who fabricates lies about God, while he is being invited to submission? God does not guide the evil people.
8. They wish to put out God's light with their mouths. But God will continue with His light, even if the rejecters dislike it.
9. He is the One who sent His messenger with the guidance and the system of truth, so that it will expose all other systems, even if those who set up partners dislike it.
10. "O you who believe, shall I lead you to a trade that will save you from painful retribution."

11. "That you believe in God and His messenger and strive in the cause of God with your money and your lives. This is best for you, if only you knew."

12. He will then forgive your sins, and admit you into paradises with rivers flowing beneath, and beautiful mansions in the gardens of Eden. This is the greatest triumph.

13. And also you will receive what you love: a triumph from God and a victory that is close at hand. And give good news to the believers.

14. O you who believe, be God's supporters, as Jesus the son of Mary said to his disciples: "Who are my supporters towards God?" The disciples said: "We are God's supporters." Thus, a group from the Children of Israel believed, and another group rejected. So We supported those who believed against their enemy, and they were successful.

Chapter 62

بسم الله الرحمن الرحيم

In the name of God, the Almighty, the Merciful.

1. Glorifying God is everything in the heavens and everything on the Earth; the King, the Holy, the Noble, the Wise.

2. He is the One who sent to the Gentiles a messenger from among themselves, to recite to them His revelations, and to purify them, and teach them the Scripture and the wisdom. And before this, they were clearly astray.

3. And to other generations subsequent to them. He is the Noble, the Wise.

4. Such is God's grace, which He bestows upon whomever He wills. God is Possessor of Infinite Grace.

5. The example of those who were given the Torah, but then failed to uphold it, is like the donkey that is carrying a cargo of books. Miserable indeed is the example of people who denied God's revelations. And God does not guide the wicked people.

6. Say: "O you who are Jewish, if you claim that you are God's chosen, to the exclusion of all other people, then you should long for death if you are truthful!"

7. But they will never long for it, because of what their hands have brought forth. God is fully aware of the wicked.

8. Say: "The death that you are fleeing from, it will come to find you. Then you will be returned to the Knower of all secrets and declarations, then He will inform you of everything you had done."

9. O you who believe, when the oath of allegiance is called to at the time of gathering, then you shall hasten towards the remembrance of God, and cease all selling. This is better for you, if you only knew.

10. Then, once the oath of allegiance is complete, you shall disperse through the land and seek God's provisions, and remember God frequently, that you may succeed.

11. And if they come across any trade, or some entertainment, they rush to it and leave you standing! Say: "What God possesses is far better than entertainment or trade. And God is the best Provider."

Chapter 63

بسم الله الرحمن الرحيم

In the name of God, the Almighty, the Merciful.

1. When the hypocrites come to you they Say: "We bear witness that you are the messenger of God." And God knows that you are His messenger, and God bears witness that the hypocrites are liars.

2. They have chosen their oath as a deceit, thus they repel from the path of God. Miserable indeed is what they do.

3. That is because they believed, then disbelieved. Hence, their hearts are sealed; they do not understand.

4. And when you see them, you are impressed by their physical stature; and when they speak, you listen to their eloquence. They are like blocks of wood propped-up. They think that every call is intended for them. These are the enemies, so beware of them. May God condemn them; they have deviated.

5. And if they are told: "Come and let the messenger of God ask for your forgiveness," they turn aside their heads, and you see them walking away in pride.

6. It is the same for them, whether you ask for their forgiveness, or do not ask for their forgiveness; God will not forgive them. For God does not guide the wicked people.

7. They are the ones who Say: "Do not spend on those who are with the messenger of God, unless they abandon him!" And to God belongs the treasures of the heavens and the Earth, but the hypocrites do not comprehend.

8. They Say: "When we go back to the city, the noble therein will evict the lowly." But all nobility belongs to God and His messenger, and the believers. However, the hypocrites do not know.

9. O you who believe, do not be distracted by your money and your children from the remembrance of God. And those who do this, then they are the losers.

10. And give from that which We have provided to you, before death comes to one of you, then he says: "My Lord, if only You could delay this for a short while, I would then be charitable and join the righteous!"

11. And God will not delay any soul if its time has come. And God is Expert to all that you do.

Chapter 64

بسم الله الرحمن الرحيم

In the name of God, the Almighty, the Merciful.

1. Glorifying God is everything in the heavens and everything on the Earth. To Him is all kingship, and to Him is all praise, and He is capable of all things.

2. He is the One who created you, then among you there is the rejecter, and among you is the believer. And God is Seer over what you do.

3. He created the heavens and the Earth with truth, and He designed you and perfected your design, and to Him is the final destiny.

4. He knows what is in the heavens and the Earth, and He knows what you conceal and what you declare. And God is aware of what is inside the chests.

5. Did the news not come to you of those who had rejected before? They had tasted the consequences of their decision and they incurred a painful retribution.

6. That was because their messengers came to them with clear proofs, but they said: "Shall mere human beings guide us?" So they rejected and turned away, and God had no need. And God is Rich, Praiseworthy.

7. Those who rejected claim that they will not be resurrected. Say: "Yes, by my Lord, you will be resurrected, then you will be informed of everything you have done, and this is easy for God to do."

8. Therefore, you shall believe in God and His messenger, and the light that We have sent down. And God is Expert over all that you do.

9. The Day when He will gather you, the Day of Gathering. That is the Day of mutual blaming. And whosoever believes in God and does good works, He will remit his sins, and will admit him into paradises with rivers flowing beneath to abide therein forever. Such is the greatest triumph.

10. As for those who reject and deny Our revelations, they are the dwellers of the Fire; they will abide therein. What a miserable destiny!

11. No misfortune strikes except with God's leave. And whosoever believes in God, He will guide his heart. And God is fully aware of all things.

12. Obey God and obey the messenger. And if you turn away, then it is only required of Our messenger to deliver clearly.

13. God, there is no god besides Him. In God the believers shall put their trust.

14. O you who believe, from among your spouses and your children are enemies to you; so beware of them. And if you pardon, and overlook, and forgive, then God is Forgiver, Merciful.

15. Your money and children are a test, and with God is a great recompense.

16. Therefore, be aware of God as much as you can, and listen, and obey, and give for your own good. And whosoever is protected from his own stinginess, then these are the successful ones.

17. If you lend God a loan of righteousness, He will multiply it for you many fold, and forgive you. God is Appreciative, Compassionate.

18. The Knower of all secrets and declarations; the Noble, the Wise.

Chapter 65

بسم الله الرحمن الرحيم

In the name of God, the Almighty, the Merciful.

1. O you prophet, if any of you have divorced the women, then they should be divorced while ensuring that their required interim is fulfilled, and keep count of the interim. You shall reverence God your Lord, and do not evict the women from their homes, nor should they leave, unless they have committed a proven adultery. And these are God's limits. And anyone who transgresses God's limits has wronged his soul. You never know; perhaps God will make something come out of this.

2. Then, once the interim is fulfilled, either you remain together equitably, or part ways equitably and have it witnessed by two just people from among you; and give the testimony for God. This is to enlighten those who believe in God and the Last Day. And whosoever reverences God, He will create a solution for him.

3. And He will provide for him whence he never expected. Anyone who puts his trust in God, then He suffices him. God's commands will be done. God has decreed for everything its fate.

4. As for the women who have reached menopause, if you have any doubts, their interim shall be three months. And as for those whose menstruation has ceased, and those who are already pregnant, their interim is until they give birth. And anyone who reverences God, He makes his matters easy for him.

5. This is God's command that He sends down to you. And anyone who is aware of God, He will remit his sins, and will improve his reward.

6. You shall let them reside in the home you were in when you were together, and do not coerce them to make them leave. And if they are pregnant, you shall spend on them until they give birth. Then, if they nurse the infant, you

shall pay them their due for such. And you shall maintain the amicable relations between you. If you disagree, then another woman may nurse the child.

7. The rich shall provide support in accordance with his means, and the poor shall provide according to the means that God bestowed upon him. God does not burden any soul more than He has given it. God will provide ease after difficulty.

8. Many a community rebelled against the commands of its Lord and His messengers. Thus, We called them to account, and requited them a terrible requital.

9. They tasted the result of their actions, and the consequence of their actions was a total loss.

10. God has prepared for them a severe retribution. Therefore, you shall be aware of God, O you who possess intelligence and believed. God has sent down to you a remembrance.

11. A messenger who recites to you God's revelations, which are clear, to lead those who believe and work righteousness out of the darkness into the light. Anyone who believes in God and does good works, He will admit him into paradises with rivers flowing beneath; they abide therein forever. God has granted for him and excellent reward.

12. God who created seven heavens and the same number of Earths. His command descends between them, that you may know that God is capable of all things, and that God has encompassed all things with His knowledge.

Chapter 66

بسم الله الرحمن الرحيم

In the name of God, the Almighty, the Merciful.

1. O you prophet, why do you prohibit what God has made lawful for you, seeking to please your wives? God is Forgiver, Merciful.

2. God has already given the law, regarding the cancellation of oaths. And God is your Lord, and He is the Knowledgeable, the Wise.

3. And when the prophet disclosed a matter in confidence to some of his wives, then one of them spread it, and God revealed it to him, he recognized part of it and denied part. So when he informed her, she said: "Who informed you of this?" He said: "I was informed by the Knowledgeable, the Expert."

4. If the two of you repent to God, then your hearts have listened. But if you band together against him, then God is his ally, and so are Gabriel and the righteous believers. Also, the Angels are his helpers.

5. It may be that he would divorce you, then his Lord will substitute other wives in your place who are better than you; submitting, believing, obedient, repentant, worshipping, pious, mature and youthful.

6. O you who believe, protect yourselves and your families from a Fire whose fuel is people and rocks. Guarding it are stern and powerful Angels who do not disobey God in what He commanded them; and they carry out what they are commanded to.

7. O you who have rejected, do not apologize today. You are being requited only for what you did.

8. O you who believe, you shall repent to God a sincere repentance. It may be that your Lord will remit your sins and admit you into paradises with rivers flowing beneath. On that Day, God will not disappoint the prophet and those who believed with him. Their light will radiate around them and to

their right. They will Say: "Our Lord, keep perfect our light for us, and forgive us; You are able to do all things."

9. O prophet, strive against the rejecters and the hypocrites and be stern with them. Their abode is Hell, and a miserable destiny.

10. God cites as examples of those who have rejected, the wife of Noah and the wife of Lot. They were married to two of Our righteous servants, but they betrayed them and, consequently, they could not help them at all against God. And it was said: "Enter the Fire, both of you, with those who will enter it."

11. And God cites as an example of those who believed the wife of Pharaoh. She said: "My Lord, build a home for me near You in Paradise, and save me from Pharaoh and his works; and save me from the transgressing people."

12. Also Mary, the daughter of Imran, who maintained her chastity. So We blew into her from Our spirit, and she believed in the words of her Lord and His Scripture; and she was of those who were obedient.

Chapter 67

بسم الله الرحمن الرحيم

In the name of God, the Almighty, the Merciful.

1. Most exalted is the One in whose hands is all sovereignty, and He is capable of all things.

2. The One who created death and life, that He may test you, which of you will do better works? He is the Noble, the Forgiving.

3. He created seven skies in layers. You do not see any imperfection in the creation by the Almighty. Keep looking; do you see any flaw?

4. Then look again twice; your eyes will come back humiliated and tired.

5. And We have adorned this universe with lamps, and We made it with projectiles against the devils; and We prepared for them the retribution of the blazing Fire.

6. And for those who rejected their Lord will be the retribution of Hell. What a miserable destiny.

7. When they are thrown therein, they hear its furor as it boils.

8. It almost explodes from rage. Whenever a group is thrown therein, its keepers would ask them: "Did you not receive a warner?"

9. They said: "Yes indeed; a warner did come to us, but we disbelieved and said: God did not reveal anything, you are being led astray."

10. And they said: "If we had listened or understood, we would not be among the dwellers of the blazing Fire!"

11. Thus, they confessed their sins. So away with the dwellers of the blazing Fire.

12. As for those who reverence their Lord unseen, they have attained forgiveness and a great reward.

13. And whether you keep your utterances secret, or declare them, He is fully aware of what is inside the chests.

14. Should He not know what He created? And He is the Sublime, the Expert.

15. He is the One who made the Earth subservient for you. So roam its paths, and eat from His provisions; and to Him is the final summoning.

16. Are you secure that the One in heaven will not cause the Earth to rupture, thus causing it to shake?

17. Or are you secure that the One in heaven will not send upon you a violent storm? Then you will know the value of the warning.

18. And those before them have disbelieved; so how terrible was My requital!

19. Have they not looked to the birds lined-up together above them, and they launch? The Almighty is the One who holds them in the air. He is Seer of all things.

20. Where is this army of yours to grant you victory without the Almighty? Indeed, the disbelievers are deceived.

21. Where is this who can give you provisions if He holds back His provisions? Indeed, they have plunged deep into transgression and aversion.

22. Is one who walks while his face is slumped better guided, or one who walks straight on the right path?

23. Say: "He is the One who initiated you, and made for you the hearing, the eyes, and the hearts. Little do you give thanks."

24. Say: "He is the One who placed you on Earth, and to Him you will be gathered."

25. And they Say: "When will this promise come to pass, if you are being truthful?"

26. Say: "The knowledge is only with God, and I am but a clear warner."

27. So when they see it near, the faces of those who rejected will turn miserable, and it will be proclaimed: "This is what you had called for!"

28. Say: "Do you see? If God annihilates me and those with me, or He bestows mercy upon us, who is there to protect the disbelievers from a painful retribution?"

29. Say: "He is the Almighty; we believe in Him, and we put our trust in Him. You will come to find out who is clearly astray."

30. Say: "What if your water becomes deep underground, who then can provide you with pure water?"

Chapter 68

بسم الله الرحمن الرحيم

In the name of God, the Almighty, the Merciful.

1. N, the pen, and what they write.
2. You are not, by the blessing of your Lord, a madman.
3. And you will have a reward that is well deserved.
4. And you are of a high moral character.
5. So you will see, and they will see.
6. Which of you are condemned.
7. Your Lord is fully aware of those who strayed off His path, and He is fully aware of those who are guided.
8. So do not obey those who deny.
9. They wish that you compromise, so they too can compromise.
10. And do not obey every lowly swearer.
11. A slanderer, a backbiter.
12. Forbidder of charity, a transgressor, a sinner.
13. Unappreciative, and greedy.
14. Because he possessed money and children.
15. When Our revelations are recited to him, he says: "Tales from the past!"
16. We will mark him on the path.
17. We have tested them like We tested those who owned the farms, when they swore that they will harvest it in the morning.
18. They were without doubt.
19. So a passing sent from your Lord came to it while they all were asleep.
20. Thus, it became barren.
21. They called on one another when they awoke.
22. "Let us go this morning to harvest the crop."

23. So they went, while conversing.
24. That from today, none of them would ever be poor.
25. And they went, ready to harvest.
26. But when they saw it, they said: "We have gone astray!"
27. "Now, we have nothing!"
28. The best among them said: "If only you had glorified!"
29. They said: "Glory be to our Lord. We have transgressed."
30. Then they started to blame each other.
31. They said: "Woe to us. We sinned."
32. "Perhaps our Lord will grant us better than it. We repent to our Lord."
33. Such was the punishment. But the retribution of the Hereafter is far worse, if they only knew.
34. The righteous have deserved, at their Lord, paradises of bliss.
35. Should We treat those who submitted the same as those who are criminals?
36. What is wrong with you, how do you judge?
37. Or do you have another book which you study?
38. In it, you can find what you wish?
39. Or do you have an oath from Us, extending until the Day of Resurrection, that you can judge as you please?
40. Ask them: "Who of them will make such a claim?"
41. Or do they have partners? Then let them bring their partners, if they are truthful.
42. The Day will come when they will be exposed, and they will be required to prostrate, but they will be unable to.
43. With their eyes subdued, humiliation will cover them. They were invited to prostrate when they were whole and able.
44. Therefore, let Me deal with those who reject this narration; We will entice them from where they do not perceive.
45. And I will lead them on; for My scheming is formidable.
46. Or did you ask them for a wage, so they are burdened by the fine?
47. Or do they know the future? So they have it recorded?
48. You shall be patient for the judgement of your Lord. And do not be like the companion of the whale who called out while he was in sorrow.
49. Had it not been for his Lord's grace, he would have remained trapped, while he was to be blamed.
50. But his Lord blessed him, and made him righteous.

51. And those who have rejected almost attack you with their eyes when they hear the reminder, and they Say: "He is crazy!"
52. And it is but a reminder for the worlds.

Chapter 69

بسم الله الرحمن الرحيم

In the name of God, the Almighty, the Merciful.

1. The reality.
2. What is the reality?
3. Absolutely, do you know what is the reality?
4. Thamud and 'Aad disbelieved in the Shocker.
5. As for Thamud, they were annihilated by the devastation.
6. And as for 'Aad, they were annihilated by a furious violent wind.
7. He unleashed it upon them for seven nights and eight days, in succession. You could see the people destroyed in it, as if they are decayed palm trunks.
8. Do you see any legacy for them?
9. And Pharaoh, and those before him, and the sinners, came with wickedness.
10. They disobeyed the messenger of their Lord. So He took them with a devastating requital.
11. And when the water flooded, We carried you on the vessel.
12. That We would make it as a reminder for you, and so that any listening ear may understand.
13. And when the horn is blown once.
14. And the Earth and the mountains will be removed from their place and crushed with a single crush.
15. On that Day the unavoidable event will come to pass.
16. And the heavens will be torn, and on that Day it will be flimsy.
17. And the Angels will be on its borders, and the throne of your Lord will be carried above them by eight.
18. On that Day, you will be exposed, nothing from you can be hidden.

19. As for the one who is given his record in his right, he will Say: "Here, come and read my record!"
20. "I knew that I was going to be held accountable."
21. So he shall be in a life, well-pleasing.
22. In a lofty Paradise.
23. Its fruits are within reach.
24. "Eat and drink merrily in return for your works in days past."
25. As for him who is given his record in his left, he will Say: "Oh, I wish I never received my record,"
26. "And that I never knew my account,"
27. "I wish the end had been final,"
28. "My money cannot help me,"
29. "All my power is gone."
30. Take him and shackle him.
31. Then to Hell cast him.
32. Then, in a chain that is the length of seventy arms, tie him up.
33. For he did not believe in God, the Great.
34. Nor did he advocate the feeding of the poor.
35. Consequently, he has no friend here today.
36. Nor any food, except from pollutants.
37. Food for the sinners.
38. I swear by what you see.
39. And what you do not see.
40. This is the utterance of an honourable messenger.
41. It is not the utterance of a poet; rarely do you believe.
42. Nor the utterance of a soothsayer; rarely do you take heed.
43. A revelation from the Lord of the worlds.
44. And had he attributed anything falsely to Us.
45. We would have seized him by the right.
46. Then, We would have severed his life-line.
47. None of you would be able to prevent it.
48. And this is a reminder for the righteous.
49. And We know that some of you are deniers.
50. And that it is a distress for the rejecters.
51. And it is the absolute truth.
52. Therefore, you shall glorify the name of your Lord, the Great.

Chapter 70

بسم الله الرحمن الرحيم

In the name of God, the Almighty, the Merciful.

1. Someone asked about the inevitable retribution.
2. For the rejecters, there is nothing that will stop it.
3. From God, Possessor of the ascending portals.
4. The Angels and the Spirit ascent to Him in a day which is equivalent to fifty thousand years.
5. So be patient with a good patience.
6. They see it as far away.
7. And We see it as near.
8. On the Day the sky is like molten copper.
9. And the mountains are like wool.
10. And no friend will ask about his friend.
11. When they see it, the criminal will wish he can ransom his children against the retribution.
12. As well as his mate and his brother.
13. As well as his whole clan that protected him.
14. And all who are on Earth, so that he can be saved!
15. No, it is a flame.
16. Eager to roast.
17. It calls on those who turned away.
18. And who hoarded and counted.
19. Indeed, mankind was created anxious.
20. When adversity touches him he is miserable.
21. And when good touches him he is stingy.
22. Except for those who make the oath of allegiance.

23. Who are true to their oath.
24. And those who set aside part of their wealth.
25. For the seeker and the denied.
26. And those who believe in the Day of Judgment.
27. And those who are fearful of their Lord's retribution.
28. The retribution of their Lord is not to be taken for granted.
29. And those who conceal their private parts.
30. Except around their spouses or those committed to by oath, there is no blame.
31. Then, whoever seeks anything beyond this, they are the transgressors.
32. And those who are trustworthy and keep their pledges.
33. And those who uphold their testimonies.
34. And those who are dedicated to their oath.
35. They will be honoured in paradises.
36. So what is wrong with the rejecters staring at you?
37. From the right and the left, in crowds?
38. Does every one of them hope to enter a paradise of bliss?
39. No, We have created them from what they know.
40. So I swear by the Lord of the east and the west that We are able.
41. To replace them with better people, We can never be defeated.
42. So let them talk in vain and play, until they meet their Day which they are promised.
43. When they will come out of the graves in a rush, as if they are racing towards a goal.
44. Their eyes are cast down, with shame covering them. This is the Day which they were promised.

Chapter 71

بسم الله الرحمن الرحيم

In the name of God, the Almighty, the Merciful.

1. We have sent Noah to his people: "Warn your people before a painful retribution comes to them."

2. He said: "My people, I am to you a clear warner."

3. "That you shall serve God and be aware of Him and obey."

4. "He shall forgive your sins and delay you to a predetermined time. When God's time comes, then it cannot be delayed, if you know."

5. He said: "My Lord, I have called on my people night and day."

6. "But my calling only drove them away!"

7. "And every time I called on them so that You may forgive them, they put their fingers in their ears and they covered their heads with their outer garments and they insisted, and they became greatly arrogant."

8. "Then I called to them openly."

9. "Then I announced to them, and I spoke to them in secret."

10. "And I said: Seek forgiveness from your Lord, for He was forgiving."

11. "He sends the clouds upon you constantly."

12. "And He provides you with money and children, and He makes for you gardens, and He makes for you rivers."

13. "Why do you not seek God humbly."

14. "While He created you in stages?"

15. "Did you not see how God created seven skies in layers?"

16. "And He made the moon to illuminate in them, and He made the sun to be a lit flame?"

17. "And God made you grow from the Earth like plants."

18. "Then He returns you to it, and He brings you out totally?"

19. "And God made the land for you as a plain."
20. "So that you may seek in it ways and paths?"
21. Noah said: "My Lord, they have disobeyed me and have followed whose money and children only increased him in loss."
22. And they plotted a great plotting.
23. And they said: "Do not abandon your gods. Do not abandon Destroyer, nor Night Group, nor Helper and Deterrer and Eagle."
24. And they have misguided many, but We only increase the wicked in misguidance.
25. Because of their sins they were drowned, then they were admitted to the Fire, and they could not find beside God any victor.
26. And Noah said: "My Lord, do not leave on the Earth any of the rejecters at all."
27. "If you are to leave them, then they will misguide Your servants and they will only give birth to a wicked rejecter."
28. "My Lord, forgive me and my parents and whoever enters my home as a believer, and to the believing men and believing women, and do not increase the wicked except in destruction."

Chapter 72

بسم الله الرحمن الرحيم

In the name of God, the Almighty, the Merciful.

1. Say: "It has been inspired to me that a group of Jinn were listening." They said: "We have heard a magnificent compilation!"

2. "It guides to what is correct, so we believed in it, and we will not set up anyone with our Lord."

3. "And exalted is the majesty of our Lord, He has not taken a wife nor a son."

4. "And it was the foolish one amongst us who used to say lies about God."

5. "And we had thought that neither mankind nor the Jinn would ever utter a lie against God."

6. "And there were men from among mankind who used to seek help from the men among the Jinn, but they only helped increase them in sin."

7. "And they thought as you thought, that God would not send anyone."

8. "And we touched the heavens, but found it full of powerful guards and projectiles."

9. "And we used to sit in it in places of listening, but anyone who sits now finds a projectile seeking him."

10. "And we do not know, is it bad that is intended for those on Earth, or does their Lord want them to be guided?"

11. "And among us are those who are good doers, and some of us are opposite to that, we are in many paths."

12. "And we acknowledge that we cannot escape God on Earth, nor can we escape Him if we run."

13. "And when we heard the guidance, we believed in it. So whoever believes in his Lord, then he will not fear a decrease in reward, nor a burdensome punishment."

14. "And among us are those who submitted, and among us are the compromisers. As for those who have submitted, they have sought what is correct."
15. And as for the compromisers, they are firewood for Hell.
16. And had they walked on the right path, We would have provided them with abundant water.
17. To test them with it. And whosoever turns away from the remembrance of his Lord, He will enter him a severe retribution.
18. And the temples are for God, so do not call on anyone with God.
19. And when God's servant stood up to call on Him, they nearly banded to oppose him.
20. Say: "I only call on my Lord, and I do not associate anyone with Him."
21. Say: "I have no power to cause you harm nor to show you what is right."
22. Say: "No one can protect me from God, and I will not find any refuge except with Him."
23. It is but an announcement from God, and His messages. And whosoever disobeys God and His messenger, then he will have the fire of Hell to dwell eternally therein.
24. Until they see what they are promised, then they will know who has the weakest ally and is least in number.
25. Say: "I do not know if what you are promised is near, or if my Lord will make it distant."
26. The knower of the unseen, He does not reveal His knowledge to anyone.
27. Except to whom He has accepted as a messenger, then He reveals from the past and the future.
28. So that He knows that they have delivered the messages of their Lord, and He surrounds all that is with them, and He has counted the number of all things.

Chapter 73

بسم الله الرحمن الرحيم

In the name of God, the Almighty, the Merciful.

1. O you who are covered with your garments.
2. Stand the night except for a little.
3. Half of it, or a little less than that.
4. Or a little more, and arrange the Quran in its arrangement.
5. We will place upon you a saying which is heavy.
6. The time of the night is more effective and better for study.
7. For you have many duties during the day.
8. And remember the name of your Lord, and devote to Him completely.
9. The Lord of the east and the west, there is no god but He, so take Him as a protector.
10. And be patient over what they say, and depart from them in a good manner.
11. And leave Me to deal with the deniers who have been given the good things, and give them time for a while.
12. We have with Us chains and a raging fire.
13. And food that chokes, and a painful retribution.
14. The Day the Earth and the mountains shake, and the mountains become a crumbling pile.
15. We have sent to you a messenger as a witness over you, as We have sent to Pharaoh a messenger.
16. But Pharaoh disobeyed the messenger, so We took him in a severe manner.
17. So how can you be righteous if you have rejected, on a Day when the children become grey haired?
18. The heavens will crack with it. His promise is always delivered.
19. This is a reminder, so let he who wishes take a path to his Lord.

20. Your Lord knows that you rise a little less than two thirds of the night, and half of it, and one third of it, as well as a group of those who are with you. And God measures the night and the day. He knows that you will not be able to keep-up, so He pardons you. So read what is made easy of the Quran. He knows that there will be sick among you, and others that venture out in the land seeking from God's bounty, and others who are fighting in the cause of God, so read what you can of it. And honour the oath of allegiance and contribute towards betterment and give God a loan of righteousness. And whatever you put forth yourselves, you will find it with God, for it is better and a greater reward. And seek God's forgiveness, for God is Forgiving, Merciful.

Chapter 74

بســـــــــم الله الرحمن الرحيم

In the name of God, the Almighty, the Merciful.

1. O you who are blanketed.
2. Stand and warn.
3. And your Lord glorify.
4. And purify your garments.
5. And abandon all that is vile.
6. And do not give for a return.
7. And to your Lord be patient.
8. So when the trumpet is sounded.
9. That will be a very difficult Day.
10. Upon the rejecters it will not be easy.
11. So leave Me alone with the one I have created.
12. And I gave him abundant wealth.
13. And children to bear witness.
14. And I made everything comfortable for him.
15. Then he is greedy wanting that I give more.
16. No. He was stubborn to Our revelations.
17. I will exhaust him in climbing.
18. He thought and he analyzed.
19. So woe to him for how he thought.
20. Then woe to him for how he thought.
21. Then he looked.
22. Then he frowned and became bad tempered.
23. Then he turned away and was arrogant.
24. So he said: "This is nothing but the magic of old."

25. "This is nothing but the words of a human being."
26. I will cast him in the Scorching heat.
27. And do you know what is Scorching heat?
28. It does not spare nor leave anything.
29. A scorcher for humans.
30. Upon it is nineteen.
31. And We have made the guardians of the Fire to be Angels; and We did not make their number except as a trial for those who have rejected, so that those who were given the Scripture would understand, and those who have faith would be increased in faith, and so that those who have been given the Scripture and the believers do not have doubt, and so that those who have a sickness in their hearts and the rejecters would Say: "What did God mean with an example such as this?" It is such that God misguides whom He wishes, and He guides whom He wishes. And none know your Lord's soldiers except Him; and it is but a reminder for human beings.
32. No, by the moon.
33. And by the night when it withdraws.
34. And by the morning when it brightens.
35. It is one of the great ones.
36. A warning to humans.
37. For any among you who wishes to advance or regress.
38. Every soul is held by what it earned.
39. Except for the people of the right.
40. In paradises, they will inquire.
41. About the criminals.
42. "What has caused you to be in the scorching heat?"
43. They said: "We were not of those who offered support."
44. "And we did not feed the poor person."
45. "And we used to participate with those who spoke falsehood."
46. "And we used to deny the Day of Judgment."
47. "Until the certainty came to us."
48. So no intercession of intercessors could help them.
49. Why did they turned away from being reminded?
50. They are like fleeing zebras.
51. Running from the lion.
52. Alas, every one of them wants to be given separate scriptures.
53. No, they do not fear the Hereafter.
54. No, it is a reminder.

55. So whosoever wishes will remember it.
56. And none will remember except if God wills. He is the source of righteous-
    ness and the source of forgiveness.

Chapter 75

بسم الله الرحمن الرحيم

In the name of God, the Almighty, the Merciful.

1. I swear by the Day of Judgment.
2. And I swear by the soul which is self blaming.
3. Does man think that We will not gather his bones?
4. Indeed, We were able to make his fingertips.
5. No, man desires that he continue committing sins.
6. He asks: "When is the Day of Resurrection?"
7. So, when the sight is dazzled.
8. And the moon is eclipsed.
9. And the sun and moon are joined together.
10. Man will say on that Day: "Where can I escape!"
11. No. There is no refuge.
12. To your Lord on that Day is the abode.
13. Man will be told on that Day what he has put forward, and what he has done.
14. Indeed, man will testify against himself.
15. Even though he puts forth his excuses.
16. Do not move your tongue with it to make haste.
17. It is for Us to gather it and relate it.
18. So when We relate it, you shall follow its revelation.
19. Then it is for Us to clarify it.
20. Alas, you all like this world.
21. And neglect the Hereafter.
22. Faces on that Day will be shining.
23. Looking at their Lord.

24. And faces on that Day will be gloomy.
25. Thinking that a punishment is coming to them.
26. Alas, when it reaches the throat.
27. And it will be said: "Who can save him?"
28. And he assumes it is the time of passing.
29. And the leg is buckled around the other leg.
30. To your Lord on that Day he will be driven.
31. For he did not believe nor turn towards.
32. But he denied and turned away.
33. Then he went to his family admiring himself.
34. Woe to you and woe to you.
35. Then woe to you and woe to you.
36. Did man think that he will be left neglected?
37. Was he not a seed from sperm put forth?
38. Then he was an embryo, so he was created and developed.
39. Then He made the two pairs, male and female.
40. Is One as such then not able to resurrect the dead?

Chapter 76

بسم الله الرحمن الرحيم

In the name of God, the Almighty, the Merciful.

1. Was there not a time in the past when the human being was nothing to even be mentioned?

2. We have created the human being from a mixed seed; We test him, so We made him hear and see.

3. We have guided him to the path, either to be thankful or to reject.

4. We have prepared for the rejecters chains and collars and a blazing Fire.

5. As for the pious, they will drink from a cup which has the scent of musk.

6. A spring from which the servants of God drink, it gushes forth abundantly.

7. They fulfill their vows, and they fear a Day whose consequences are widespread.

8. And they give food out of love to the poor and the orphan and the captive.

9. "We only feed you for the sake of God; we do not desire from you any reward or thanks."

10. "We fear from our Lord a Day, which will be horrible and difficult."

11. So God shielded them from the evil of that Day, and He cast towards them a look and a smile.

12. And He rewarded them for their patience with paradise and silk.

13. They are reclining in it on raised couches, they do not have in it excessive sun nor bitter cold.

14. And the shade is close upon them, and the fruit is hanging low within reach.

15. And they are served upon with bowls of silver and glasses of crystal.

16. Crystal laced with silver, measured accordingly.

17. And they are given to drink in it from a cup which has the scent of ginger.

18. A spring therein which is called 'Salsabeel'.

19. And they are encircled with eternal children. If you see them you will think they are pearls which have been scattered about.
20. And if you look, then you will see a blessing and a great dominion.
21. They will have garments of fine green silk, and necklaces and bracelets from silver, and their Lord will give them a cleansing drink.
22. "This is the reward for you, and your struggle is appreciated."
23. We have sent down to you the Quran in stages.
24. So be patient to the judgment of your Lord, and do not obey from them any sinner or rejecter.
25. And remember the name of your Lord morning and evening.
26. And from the night you shall prostrate to Him and praise Him throughout.
27. These people like the current life, and they put behind them a heavy Day.
28. We have created them, and established them, and if We wished, We could replace their kind completely.
29. This is a reminder, so let whoever wills take a path to his Lord.
30. And you cannot will, except if God wills. God is Knowledgeable, Wise.
31. He admits whom He wills to His mercy. And as for the wicked, He has prepared for them a painful retribution.

Chapter 77

بسم الله الرحمن الرحيم

In the name of God, the Almighty, the Merciful.

1. By the winds which are sent.
2. Then the gusts that blow.
3. And all that is scattered about.
4. So the separators which divide.
5. Then the remembrance that is found.
6. An excuse or a warning.
7. What you are being promised will come to pass.
8. So when the stars are plunged.
9. And when the sky is opened.
10. And when the mountains are destroyed.
11. And when the messengers are gathered.
12. For what day has it been delayed?
13. For the Day of Separation.
14. And do you know what is the Day of Separation?
15. Woe on that Day to the disbelievers!
16. Did We not destroy the ancient people
17. Then We made others succeed them?
18. It is such that We do to the criminals.
19. Woe on that Day to the disbelievers!
20. Did We not create you from a fragile water,
21. Then We made it in a place of protection,
22. Until a time that is predetermined?
23. So We measured, and We are the best to measure.
24. Woe on that Day to the disbelievers!

25. Did We not make the Earth an abode,
26. Living and dead.
27. And We made massive stabilizers in it, and We gave you to drink fresh water?
28. Woe on that Day to the disbelievers!
29. Away with you towards what you have disbelieved.
30. Away with you to a shadow with three columns.
31. Neither does it shade, nor does it avail from the flames.
32. It throws sparks as huge as logs.
33. As if they were yellow camels.
34. Woe on that Day to the disbelievers!
35. This is a Day when they shall not speak.
36. Nor will it be permitted for them so they can make excuses.
37. Woe on that Day to the disbelievers!
38. This is the Day of Separation where We have gathered you with the ancient people.
39. So if you have a scheme, then make use of it.
40. Woe on that Day to the disbelievers!
41. The righteous are among shades and springs.
42. And fruit from what they desire.
43. "Eat and drink comfortably for what you used to do."
44. It is such that We reward the good doers.
45. Woe on that Day to the disbelievers!
46. "Eat and enjoy for a little while, for you are criminals."
47. Woe on that Day to the disbelievers!
48. And when they are told to kneel, they do not kneel.
49. Woe on that Day to the disbelievers!
50. So in what words after it will they believe?

Chapter 78

بسم الله الرحمن الرحيم

In the name of God, the Almighty, the Merciful.

1. What are they inquiring about?
2. About the weighty news.
3. The one which they are in disagreement about.
4. No, they will come to know.
5. No, then again, they will come to know.
6. Did We not make the Earth a resting ground?
7. And the mountains as pegs?
8. And We created you in pairs?
9. And We made your sleep for resting?
10. And We made the night as a covering?
11. And We made the day to work in?
12. And We constructed above you seven mighty ones?
13. And We made a flaming light?
14. And We sent down abundant water from the rain clouds,
15. To bring out with it seeds and plants,
16. And gardens of thick growth?
17. The Day of Separation is an appointed time.
18. The Day when the horn is blown and you come in crowds.
19. And the universe is opened, so it becomes gates.
20. And the mountains will be moved as if they were a mirage.
21. For Hell is in wait.
22. For the transgressors it is a dwelling place.
23. They will abide in it for eons.
24. They will not taste anything cold in it nor drink.

25. Except for boiling water and filthy discharge.
26. An exact recompense.
27. They did not expect the reckoning.
28. And they denied Our revelations greatly.
29. And everything We have counted in a record.
30. So taste it, for no increase will come to you from Us except in retribution.
31. As for the righteous, they will have success.
32. Gardens and vineyards.
33. And grapes that are ripe.
34. And a cup that is full.
35. They do not hear in it any vile talk or lies.
36. A reward from your Lord, in recognition for what is done.
37. The Lord of heavens and Earth and what is between them, the Almighty. They do not posses any authority beside Him.
38. The Day when the Spirit and the Angels stand in line, none will speak unless the Almighty permits him and he speaks what is true.
39. That is the Day of truth, so let whoever wills seek a way to his Lord.
40. I have warned you of a retribution which is close, the Day when man will look at what he has brought forth and the rejecter will Say: "I wish I were dust!"

Chapter 79

In the name of God, the Almighty, the Merciful.

1. By those that take the person forcibly.
2. And those that take the person gently.
3. And those that swim along.
4. And those that press forward in a race.
5. So as to carry out a command.
6. On the Day the ground shakes.
7. It will be followed by the second blow.
8. Hearts on that Day will be terrified.
9. Their eyes cast down.
10. They will Say: "Shall we be returned to live our lives."
11. "Even after we were crumbled bones?"
12. They said: "This is an impossible recurrence."
13. But all it takes is one blow.
14. Whereupon they will rise-up.
15. Did the story of Moses come to you?
16. His Lord called him at the holy valley of Tuwa.
17. "Go to Pharaoh, for he has transgressed."
18. Tell him: "Would you not be purified?"
19. "And I will guide you to your Lord, that you may turn reverent."
20. He then showed him the great miracle.
21. But he disbelieved and rebelled.
22. Then he turned away in a hurry.
23. So he gathered and proclaimed.
24. He said: "I am your lord, the Most High."

25. So God seized him with retribution in the Hereafter, as well as in the first life.
26. In that is a lesson for those who are aware.
27. Are you a more powerful creation than the sky which He built?
28. He raised its height, and perfected it.
29. And He covered its night and brought out its morning.
30. And the land after that He spread out.
31. He brought forth from it its water and pasture.
32. And the mountains He fixed firmly.
33. All this to be a provision for you and your livestock.
34. Then, when the great blow comes.
35. The Day when the human remembers all that he strove for.
36. And Hell will be apparent to all who can see.
37. As for the one who transgressed.
38. And was preoccupied with the worldly life.
39. Then Hell will be the abode.
40. And as for the one who reverenced the majesty of his Lord, and restrained himself from desire.
41. The Paradise will be the abode.
42. They ask you about the Hour: "When is its appointed time?"
43. You have no knowledge of it.
44. To your Lord is its term.
45. You are simply to warn those who fear it.
46. For the Day they see it, it will be as if they had remained an evening or half a day.

Chapter 80

بسم الله الرحمن الرحيم

In the name of God, the Almighty, the Merciful.

1. He frowned and turned away.
2. When the blind one came to him.
3. And what makes you know, perhaps he is seeking to purify?
4. Or to remember, so the remembrance will benefit him?
5. As for the one who was rich.
6. You were addressing yourself to him.
7. And why does it concern you that he does not want to purify?
8. And as for the one who came to you seeking.
9. While he was fearful.
10. You were too pre-occupied for him.
11. No, this is but a reminder.
12. For whoever wills to remember.
13. In records which are honourable.
14. Raised and pure.
15. By the hands of scribes.
16. Honourable and righteous.
17. Mankind is killed for his rejection.
18. From what did He create him?
19. From a seed He created him and moulded him.
20. Then the path He made easy for him.
21. Then He made him die and buried him.
22. Then if He wishes He resurrects him.
23. Alas, when what has been ordained is complete.
24. Let man look to his provisions.

25. We have poured the water abundantly.
26. Then We cracked the land with cracks.
27. And We made grow in it seeds.
28. And grapes and pasture.
29. And olives and palm trees.
30. And gardens in variety.
31. And fruits and vegetables.
32. An enjoyment for you and your livestock.
33. So when the screaming shout comes.
34. The Day when a person will run from his brother.
35. And his mother and father.
36. And his mate and children.
37. For every person on that Day is a matter that concerns him.
38. Faces on that Day which are openly displayed.
39. Laughing and seeking good news.
40. And faces on that Day with dust on them.
41. Being burdened by remorse.
42. Those are the rejecters, the wicked.

Chapter 81

بسم الله الرحمن الرحيم

In the name of God, the Almighty, the Merciful.

1. When the sun implodes.
2. And when the stars cannot be seen.
3. And when the mountains are made to move.
4. And when the reproduction is ended.
5. And when the beasts are gathered.
6. And when the seas are made to boil.
7. And when the souls are paired.
8. And when the girl killed in infancy is asked,
9. "For what crime was she killed?"
10. And when the records are displayed.
11. And when the sky is removed.
12. And when Hell is ignited.
13. And when Paradise is made near.
14. Every soul will know what it had done!
15. So, I swear by the receding stars.
16. Their orbits swept away.
17. And the night when it passes.
18. And the morning when it breathes.
19. It is the saying of an honourable messenger.
20. With power and influence from the One of the throne.
21. Obeyed, and trustworthy.
22. And your friend is not crazy.
23. And he saw him by the clear horizon.
24. And he has no knowledge of the future.

25. And it is not the saying of an outcast devil.
26. So where will you go?
27. It is but a reminder for the worlds.
28. For whomever of you wishes to be straight.
29. And you cannot will anything except if God also wills, the Lord of the worlds.

Chapter 82

بسم الله الرحمن الرحيم

In the name of God, the Almighty, the Merciful.

1. When the sky is cracked.
2. And when the planets are scattered.
3. And when the seas burst.
4. And when the graves are laid open.
5. Then the soul will know what it has brought forth and what it has left behind.
6. O man, what has turned you arrogant against your Lord, the Generous?
7. The One who created you, then evolved you, then made you upright?
8. In any which picture He chooses, He places you.
9. No, you are but deniers of the system.
10. And over you are those who watch.
11. Honourable scribes.
12. They know what you do.
13. The pious are in Paradise.
14. And the wicked are in Hell.
15. They will enter it on the Day of recompense.
16. And they will not be absent from it.
17. And do you know what is the Day of recompense?
18. Then again, do you know what is the Day of recompense?
19. The Day when no soul possesses anything for any other soul, and the decision on that Day is to God.

Chapter 83

بسم الله الرحمن الرحيم

In the name of God, the Almighty, the Merciful.

1. Woe to those who cheat.
2. Those who when they are receiving any measure from the people, they take it in full.
3. And when they are the ones giving measure or weight, they give less than due.
4. Do these not assume that they will be resurrected
5. To a great Day?
6. The Day the people will stand before the Lord of the worlds.
7. No, the record of the wicked is in Sijjeen.
8. And do you know what is Sijjeen?
9. A numbered record.
10. Woe on that Day to the deniers.
11. Those who denied the Day of recompense.
12. And none will deny it except every transgressor who knows no bounds.
13. When Our verses are recited to him, he says: "Tales of the ancients!"
14. No, a covering has been placed on their hearts for what they have earned.
15. No, they will be blocked from their Lord on that Day.
16. Then they will be entered into the Hell.
17. Then it will be said: "This is what you used to deny!"
18. No, the record of the pious is in Elliyeen.
19. And do you know what is Elliyeen?
20. A numbered record.
21. To be witnessed by those brought near.
22. The pious are in Paradise.

23. Upon luxurious furnishings, observing.
24. You know in their faces the look of Paradise.
25. They are given drink from a pure sealed vial.
26. Its seal will be of musk, so in that let those who are in competition compete.
27. And its taste will be special.
28. A spring from which those who are brought near will drink.
29. Those who were criminals used to laugh at those who had believed.
30. And when they passed by them they used to wink to each other.
31. And when they returned to their people, they would return jesting.
32. And if they see them they Say: "These are indeed misguided!"
33. But they were not sent over them as caretakers.
34. And today, those who had believed are laughing at the rejecters!
35. Upon the luxurious furnishings they are observing.
36. Have the rejecters not been reprised for what they used to do?

Chapter 84

بسم الله الرحمن الرحيم

In the name of God, the Almighty, the Merciful.

1. When the sky is torn.
2. And it permits its Lord, and is ready.
3. And when the earth is stretched.
4. And it spits out what is in it and becomes empty.
5. And it permits its Lord, and is ready.
6. O man, you will be returning to your Lord with your actions and meeting Him.
7. So whoever is given his record in his right.
8. He will then receive an easy reckoning.
9. And he will return to his family in joy!
10. And as for he who is given his record behind his back.
11. He will invoke his destruction.
12. And he will enter a blazing Fire.
13. He used to be joyful amongst his people!
14. He thought he would not be returned.
15. No, He is ever seeing of him.
16. So, I swear by the redness of dusk.
17. And the night and what it is driven on.
18. And the moon when it is full.
19. You will ride a vessel upon a vessel.
20. So what is the matter with them that they do not believe?
21. And when the Quran is being related to them, they do not yield.
22. No, those who have rejected are in denial.
23. And God is more aware of what they gather.

24. So inform them of a painful retribution.
25. Except for those who believe and do good works, they will have a reward that will not end.

Chapter 85

بسم الله الرحمن الرحيم

In the name of God, the Almighty, the Merciful.

1. By the universe laden with towers.
2. And the appointed Day.
3. And a witness and a witnessed.
4. Dead are the people of the canyon.
5. The Fire supplied with fuel.
6. They will be placed in it.
7. And they were witness to what they did to the believers.
8. And all they had asked them was to believe in God, the Noble, the Praise-worthy!
9. The One to whom belongs kingship of heavens and Earth, and God is witness over everything.
10. Those who have put the believing men and women under ordeal, and then did not repent, they will have the retribution of Hell, and they will have the retribution of burning.
11. Those who believe and do good works, they will have estates with rivers flowing beneath. Such is the great reward.
12. The punishment of your Lord is severe.
13. It is He who initiates and then returns.
14. And He is the Forgiver, the Most Kind.
15. Possessor of the throne, the Glorious.
16. Doer of what He wills.
17. Has news come to you of the soldiers?
18. Pharaoh and Thamud?
19. No, those who rejected are in denial.

20. And God after them is encompassing.
21. No, it is a glorious Quran.
22. In a tablet, preserved.

Chapter 86

بسم الله الرحمن الرحيم

In the name of God, the Almighty, the Merciful.
1. By the sky and the herald.
2. And do you know what the herald is?
3. The piercing star.
4. Every soul has a recorder over it.
5. So let man see from what he was created.
6. He was created from water that spurts forth.
7. It comes out from between the spine and the testicles.
8. For He is able to bring him back.
9. The Day when all is revealed.
10. Then he will not have any power or victor.
11. And the sky which gives rain.
12. And the land with small cracks.
13. This is the word that separates matters.
14. And it is not a thing for amusement.
15. They are scheming their schemes.
16. And I scheme a scheme.
17. So respite the rejecters, respite them for a while.

Chapter 87

بسم الله الرحمن الرحيم

In the name of God, the Almighty, the Merciful.

1. Glorify the name of your Lord, the Most High.
2. The One who created and developed.
3. And the One who measured and then guided.
4. And the One who brought out the pasture.
5. So He made it dry-up into hay.
6. We will convey to you, so do not forget.
7. Except for what God wills, He knows what is declared and what is hidden.
8. And We will make easy for you the way.
9. So remind, perhaps the reminder will help.
10. He who is reverent will remember.
11. And he who is wicked will avoid it.
12. He will enter the great Fire.
13. Then he will neither die in it nor live.
14. Whosoever develops will succeed.
15. And remembers the name of his Lord, and turns towards.
16. No, you desire the worldly life.
17. But the Hereafter is better and more lasting.
18. This has been revealed in the previous scripts.
19. The scripts of Abraham and Moses.

Chapter 88

بسم الله الرحمن الرحيم

In the name of God, the Almighty, the Merciful.

1. Has the news come to you of that which will overwhelm?
2. Faces on that Day which will be shamed.
3. Labouring and weary.
4. They will enter a blazing Fire.
5. And be given to drink from a boiling spring.
6. They will have no food except from a thorny plant.
7. It does not nourish nor avail against hunger.
8. And faces on that Day which are soft.
9. For their pursuit they are content.
10. In a high paradise.
11. You will not hear in it any nonsense.
12. In it is a running spring.
13. In it are raised beds.
14. And cups that are set.
15. And cushions arranged in rows.
16. And rich carpets spread out.
17. Will they not look at the camels, how are they created?
18. And to the sky, how is it raised?
19. And to the mountains, how was it set?
20. And to the land, how was it flattened?
21. So remind, for you are but a reminder.
22. You have no power over them.
23. Except for he who turns away and rejects.
24. Then God will punish him with the great retribution.

25. Indeed, to Us is their return.
26. Then to Us is their judgment.

Chapter 89

بسم الله الرحمن الرحيم

In the name of God, the Almighty, the Merciful.

1. By the dawn.
2. And the ten nights.
3. And the even and the odd.
4. And the night when it passes.
5. In this is an oath for the one with intelligence.
6. Did you not see what your Lord did to 'Aad?
7. Irum, with the great columns?
8. The one which was like no other in the land?
9. And Thamud who carved the rocks in the valley?
10. And Pharaoh with the planks?
11. They all transgressed in the land.
12. And made much corruption therein.
13. So your Lord poured upon them a measure of retribution.
14. Your Lord is ever watchful.
15. As for man, if his Lord tests him and grants him much, then he says: "My Lord has blessed me!"
16. And if his Lord tests him and gives him little wealth, then he says: "My Lord has humiliated me!"
17. No, you are not generous to the orphan.
18. And you do not look to feeding the poor.
19. And you consume others inheritance, all with greed.
20. And you love money, a love that is excessive.
21. Alas, when the Earth is pounded into rubble.
22. And your Lord comes with the Angels row after row.

23. And Hell on that Day is brought. On that Day man will remember, but how will the remembrance now help him?
24. He says: "I wish I had worked towards my life!"
25. On that Day, no other will bear his punishment.
26. Nor will anyone be able to free his bonds.
27. "O you soul which is peaceful."
28. "Return to your Lord happy and content."
29. "And enter in amongst My servants."
30. "And enter My Paradise."

Chapter 90

بسـم الله الرحمن الرحيم

In the name of God, the Almighty, the Merciful.

1. I swear by this land.
2. And you remain committed to this land.
3. And a father and what he begets.
4. We have created man to struggle.
5. Does he think that no one is able to best him?
6. He says: "I spent so much money!"
7. Does he think that no one saw him?
8. Did We not make for him two eyes?
9. And a tongue and two lips?
10. And We guided him to both paths?
11. He should choose the better path.
12. Do you know which is the better path?
13. The freeing of slaves.
14. Or the feeding on a day of great hardship.
15. An orphan of relation.
16. Or a poor person in need.
17. Then he has become one of those who have believed, and exhort one another to patience, and exhort one another to kindness.
18. Those are the people of happiness.
19. As for those who rejected Our revelations, they are the people of misery.
20. Upon them is a Fire closed over.

Chapter 91

بســــــــــــــم الله الرحمن الرحيـــــــــــم

In the name of God, the Almighty, the Merciful.

1. By the Sun and its brightness.
2. And the Moon that comes after it.
3. And the day which reveals.
4. And the night which covers.
5. And the sky and what He built.
6. And the Earth and what He sustains.
7. And a soul and what He made.
8. So He gave it its evil and good.
9. Successful is the one who betters it.
10. And failing is the one who hides it.
11. Thamud denied their transgression.
12. They followed the worst amongst them.
13. God's messenger said to them: "This is God's camel, let her drink."
14. They disbelieved him, and they killed her. So their Lord repaid them for their sin and levelled it.
15. Yet, those who came after remain heedless.

Chapter 92

بسم الله الرحمن الرحيم

In the name of God, the Almighty, the Merciful.

1. By the night when it covers.
2. And the day when it appears.
3. And He created the male and female.
4. Your works are various.
5. As for he who gives and is righteous.
6. And trusts in goodness.
7. We will make the easy path for him.
8. And as for he who is stingy and holds back.
9. And denies goodness.
10. We will make the difficult path for him.
11. And his wealth will not avail him when he demises.
12. It is upon Us to guide.
13. And to Us is the end and the beginning.
14. I have warned you of a Fire that blazes.
15. None shall have it but the wicked.
16. The one who denies and turns away.
17. As for the righteous, he will be spared it.
18. The one who gives his money to develop with.
19. Seeking nothing in return.
20. Except the face of His Lord, the Most High.
21. And he will be satisfied.

Chapter 93

بسم الله الرحمن الرحيم

In the name of God, the Almighty, the Merciful.

1. By the late morning.
2. And the night when it falls.
3. Your Lord has not left you, nor did He forget.
4. And the Hereafter is better for you than the first.
5. And your Lord will give you and you will be pleased.
6. Did he not find you an orphan and He sheltered you?
7. And He found you lost, and He guided you?
8. And He found you in need, so He gave you riches?
9. As for the orphan, you shall not make him sad.
10. And as for the beggar, you shall not reprimand.
11. And you shall proclaim the blessings from your Lord.

Chapter 94

بسم الله الرحمن الرحيم

In the name of God, the Almighty, the Merciful.
1. Did We not relieve your chest,
2. And take from you your load,
3. Which had put strain on your back?
4. And We have raised your remembrance,
5. So with hardship comes ease.
6. With hardship comes ease.
7. So when you are done, then stand.
8. And to your Lord you shall seek.

Chapter 95

بســـــــم الله الرحمن الرحيـــــم

In the name of God, the Almighty, the Merciful.

1. By the fig and the olive.
2. And the mount of ages.
3. And this secure land.
4. We have created mankind in the best form.
5. Then We returned him to the lowest of the low.
6. Except those who have believed and done good work, they will have a reward of thanks.
7. So what would make you deny the system after that?
8. Is God not the wisest of the wise?

Chapter 96

بسم الله الرحمن الرحيم

In the name of God, the Almighty, the Merciful.

1. Read in the name of your Lord who has created.
2. He created man from an embryo.
3. Read, and your Lord is the Generous One.
4. The One who taught by the pen.
5. He taught man what he did not know.
6. Alas, man is bound to transgress.
7. When he achieves, he no longer has need!
8. To your Lord is the return.
9. Have you seen the one who deters,
10. A servant from being supportive?
11. Have you seen if he was being guided,
12. Or he ordered righteousness?
13. Have you seen if he lied and turned away?
14. Did he not know that God can see?
15. Alas, if he does not cease, We will strike the frontal lobe.
16. A frontal lobe which lies and errs.
17. So let him call on his supporter.
18. We will call on the guardians.
19. So do not obey him, prostrate and come near.

Chapter 97

بســـــم الله الرحمن الرحيــــم

In the name of God, the Almighty, the Merciful.

1. We have sent it down in the Night of Decree.
2. And do you know what is the Night of Decree?
3. The Night of Decree is better than one thousand months.
4. The Angels and the Spirit come down in it by their Lord's leave to carry out every matter.
5. It is peaceful until the coming of dawn.

Chapter 98

In the name of God, the Almighty, the Merciful.

1. Those who rejected amongst the people of the Scripture and those who set up partners would not leave until proof came to them.

2. A messenger from God reciting purified scripts.

3. In them are valuable books.

4. And those who had previously received the Scripture did not divide except after the proof came to them.

5. And they were not commanded except to serve God and be loyal to His system, monotheists, and honour the oath of allegiance and contribute towards betterment. Such is the valuable system.

6. Those who rejected from the people of the Scripture and those who set up partners are in the fires of Hell abiding therein, those are the worst of creation.

7. As for those who believe and do good works, they are the best of creation.

8. Their reward with their Lord is the gardens of Eden with rivers flowing beneath them, they abide eternally therein. God is satisfied with them, and they are satisfied with Him. That is for whoever feared His Lord.

Chapter 99

بسم الله الرحمن الرحيم

In the name of God, the Almighty, the Merciful.

1. When the Earth rumbles and shakes.
2. And the Earth brings out its mass.
3. And man will Say: "What is wrong with her?"
4. On that Day it will inform its news.
5. That your Lord had inspired her to do so.
6. On that Day, the people will be brought out in throngs to be shown their works.
7. So whoever does an atoms weight of good will see it.
8. And whoever does an atoms weight of evil will see it.

Chapter 100

In the name of God, the Almighty, the Merciful.

1. By the fast gallopers.
2. Striking sparks.
3. Charging in the morning.
4. Forming clouds of dust.
5. Penetrating to the midst together.
6. Surely, the human being is ungrateful to his Lord.
7. He will indeed bear witness to this.
8. He loves wealth tenaciously.
9. Does he not realise that when what is in the graves are scattered.
10. And what is in the chests is gathered.
11. That their Lord has been fully cognizant of them?

Chapter 101

بسم الله الرحمن الرحيم

In the name of God, the Almighty, the Merciful.

1. The Shocker.
2. What is the Shocker?
3. And how would you know what the Shocker is?
4. The Day when people come out like swarms of butterflies.
5. And the mountains will be like fluffed up wool.
6. As for him whose weights are heavy.
7. He will be in a happy life.
8. As for him whose weights are light.
9. His destiny is the lowest.
10. And how would you know what it is?
11. A blazing Fire.

Chapter 102

بسم الله الرحمن الرحيم

In the name of God, the Almighty, the Merciful.

1. Hoarding has distracted you.
2. Until you visit the graves.
3. No, you will find out.
4. Then again, you will find out.
5. No, if only you had the knowledge of certainty.
6. You would then see Hell.
7. Then you will see it with the eye of certainty.
8. Then you will be questioned, on that Day, about the blessings.

Chapter 103

بسم الله الرحمن الرحيم

In the name of God, the Almighty, the Merciful.

1. By time.
2. The human is indeed in loss.
3. Except those who believe, and do good works, and support one another with the truth, and support one another with perseverance.

Chapter 104

بسم الله الرحمن الرحيم

In the name of God, the Almighty, the Merciful.

1. Woe unto every backbiter, slanderer.
2. Who gathered his wealth and counted it.
3. He thinks that his wealth will make him immortal.
4. Never! He will be thrown into the Destroyer.
5. And do you know what is the Destroyer?
6. God's kindled Fire.
7. Which reaches the inside of the hearts.
8. It will confine them therein.
9. In extended columns.

Chapter 105

In the name of God, the Almighty, the Merciful.
1. Have you not seen what your Lord did to the people of the elephant?
2. Did He not cause their schemes to go astray?
3. And He sent upon them formations of birds in flight.
4. Striking them with fiery projectiles.
5. Until He turned them like devoured hay.

Chapter 106

In the name of God, the Almighty, the Merciful.

1. This should be cherished by Quraysh.
2. The way they cherish the journey of the winter and summer.
3. So let them serve the Lord of this Sanctuary.
4. The One who fed them from hunger, and protected them from fear.

Chapter 107

بسم الله الرحمن الرحيم

In the name of God, the Almighty, the Merciful.

1. Have you seen him who is denying the system?
2. It is the one who mistreats the orphan,
3. And does not encourage the feeding of the poor.
4. So woe to those who make the oath of allegiance,
5. But of their oath are heedless.
6. They only want to be seen,
7. And they withhold from far-reaching deeds.

Chapter 108

بسم الله الرحمن الرحيم

In the name of God, the Almighty, the Merciful.

1. We have given you plenty.
2. Therefore, you shall reach out to your Lord, and sacrifice.
3. Indeed your rival will be the loser.

Chapter 109

بسم الله الرحمن الرحيم

In the name of God, the Almighty, the Merciful.

1. Say: "O rejecters,"
2. "I do not serve what you serve,"
3. "Nor do you serve what I serve,"
4. "Nor will I serve what you serve,"
5. "Nor will you serve what I serve,"
6. "To you is your system, and to me is mine."

Chapter 110

بسم الله الرحمن الرحيم

In the name of God, the Almighty, the Merciful.

1. When God's victory and conquest comes.
2. And you see the people entering into God's system in flocks.
3. You shall glorify your Lord's grace, and seek His forgiveness. He is the Redeemer.

Chapter 111

بسم الله الرحمن الرحيم

In the name of God, the Almighty, the Merciful.
1. Condemned is the hand of Abu-Lahab; condemned indeed.
2. His money will not avail him, nor what he has earned.
3. He will be sent to a flaming Fire.
4. And his wife who carries the logs.
5. On her neck will be a rope of thorns.

Chapter 112

بسم الله الرحمن الرحيم

In the name of God, the Almighty, the Merciful.

1. Say: "He is God, the One,"
2. "God, the Absolute,"
3. "He does not beget, nor was He begotten,"
4. "And there is none who are His equal."

Chapter 113

بسم الله الرحمن الرحيم

In the name of God, the Almighty, the Merciful.

1. Say: "I seek refuge with the Lord of the dawn,"
2. "From the evils among His creation,"
3. "And from the evil of darkness as it falls,"
4. "And from the evil of those who practice sorcery,"
5. "And from the evil of the envious when they envy."

Chapter 114

بسم الله الرحمن الرحيم

In the name of God, the Almighty, the Merciful.
1. Say: "I seek refuge with the Lord of the people,"
2. "The King of the people,"
3. "The god of the people,"
4. "From the evil of the sneaking whisperer,"
5. "Who whispers into the chests of the people."
6. "From the Jinn and the people."

Scripture Index—By Topic

Please report any errors or comments to
info@ProgressiveMuslims.Org

978-0-595-29035-2
0-595-29035-3

Printed in the United States
63451LVS00003B/11